κ
BOOK

Stephen Godden

To Liam

My favorite nephew
(more or less)

[signature]

FIREDANCE BOOKS

First published in the UK by Firedance Books in 2013.

ISBN: 978-1-909256-18-7

Firedance Books

firedancebooks.com

For my brother Michael, the best man I've ever known.

Part One

CHAPTER 1

Drustan desainCoid wiped another man's blood from his eyes. Gods, it was hot. Not yet noon and still the sun beat down upon the ragged shieldwall holding the ridge. The grass in front of the Karisae line was churned up, muddy, lubricated by blood and other bodily fluids, despite the baking heat of summer.

He gazed at the broken stub of his sword, which had snapped close to the hilt against the edge of a Vascanar shield. He should have stayed away from this land. *Another summer day, Marisa's body against his...* He snarled and threw the useless hilt over the edge of the ridge.

It tumbled in the air, twisting, falling towards the Vascanar infantry disengaging from the battle line.

They would be back.

He lowered his shield to the ground, released his arm from the straps, and shook out the ache in his shoulder. One more Vascanar attack repelled, so the Karisae defenders would live a little while longer. He should have stayed away, away from... No, no more of that; he had chosen this fight.

The slope of the ridge fell away sharply here, but still the Vascanar had driven their infantry assault up into the line. Thereby, they pinned the bulk of the Karisae army in place, while other units attacked the shieldmen in the valley on the left flank.

Dust caked Drustan's lips. Sweat trickled through the blood and dirt plastered across his face. His breathing calmed and his heartbeat slowed as he recovered his composure after the ferocious fighting. *Her eyes on his in the sunlight. Her body arched. Her—*

'Water,' a wounded Vascanar begged from the pile of dead and dying enemy in front of Drustan.

Prayer scars ripped across the wounded man's face, cut with his own hand in a brutal act of religious devotion. The long-healed scar on

Drustan's face, slashing from above his right eye, across the bridge of his nose and on into his left cheekbone, was an injury received on the field of honour — when he still believed in such things — not a self-inflicted wound to worship rapacious gods. *Marisa weaving her magic with the others, healing his face and weeping as she did so.* Drustan's jaw tightened until his teeth ached.

'Water,' the Vascanar begged again. His bloody hands cradled his stomach, holding his bowels inside a gaping wound.

'Here, Dru,' Cullain said.

Drustan took the offered spear, hefted it, nodded satisfaction at its balance, and drove it down through the Vascanar's throat.

'He should've stayed home.' Cullain looked down at the twitching corpse.

'Vascanar don't have a home.' Drustan jerked the spear free and the corpse slackened into death. The Vascanar never settled, never took a homeland; like locusts they simply arrived, devastated a land, and left. Drustan stretched his neck. 'Damn, it's hot.'

'Rain'd be nice. Best keep hold of that spear.' Cullain rolled his massive shoulders and gestured down the slope. 'It'll take 'em a while to regroup, but they'll be back.'

Lifting a hand to shade his eyes, Drustan studied the Vascanar formations on the coastal plain below the ridge. The enemy's red and black tower shields lay upon the ground in front of the shattered remnants of Barstow town, while the Vascanar infantry knelt and drank from bowls the priests held up to their lips, praying to their foul gods.

Barstow was destroyed, all of its people fled or tortured to death when the Vascanar landed on the Island of the Lake. The shield hall, temple to Vulcas, god of war, caster of the spear *Deathbringer*, burned within the tumbled palisade at the centre of the town.

Beyond the town, Drustan could see the tangled trees of Mornas Marsh. More a wetland forest than a marsh, but still enough to force the Vascanar along this route, along the Shrine Road towards the centre of the Island of the Lake; and so they had to take this ridge.

The Karisae had prayed, too, but their gods had not come. The heroes from the Sunlit Land, who did the gods' bidding, had not come. The kingdom of Symcani stood alone against the predatory Vascanar and their voracious gods. The King and his priests had not succeeded in their prayers.

Ships smouldered on the beach beyond the devastated town. Drustan dropped his hand to his side and balled it into a fist. 'Burning their ships was stupid.'

'Aye, so you said.' Cullain chewed his beard, looked at the ships, and shrugged. 'King wanted vengeance for Barstow. Figured it might call forth Vulcas Deathbringer.'

'It cost him a quarter of his force for bugger-all gain.'

'Burned the ships.'

'Vulcas, god of battle, did not come. Scepteras, king of the gods, did not come. Even Henath, judger of the dead, did not come. So all he did was trap the damn Vascanar here. Now we have to kill every last one of the whoresons.'

Cullain grinned. 'Gotta hold 'em first.' He nodded to the Vascanar cavalry milling around opposite the left flank. There was no point sending horses up against the defended ridgeline, but the men on the flat of the valley were taking a battering.

Drustan returned his old comrade's grin. Could the Karisae defenders hold against the Vascanar? Did it matter? There would always be wars to fight and money to be made. This wasn't his homeland anymore. Marisa had made sure of that. His hands tightened around the spear. Because of her betrayal, they'd broken his sword and cast him out. Now the sword he'd bought to replace it had broken too. An omen? He shivered. 'Why in all the hells did we come back?' he asked.

'For the gold.'

'We're earning every damn piece.' Drustan spat dust-caked saliva onto the ground. They had made him a mercenary, a sell-sword, when they broke his sword on the altar of Vulcas. Marisa's betrayal had torn him from this land and still he returned. What kind of fool was he? He spat again and sneered. 'We should have stayed in that tavern across the Salt.'

'Aye,' Cullain agreed. The old warrior stretched his back, looked along the shieldwall and bellowed, 'Clear out the dead, lads!' His face so battered and scarred that his original features were barely discernible beneath his heavy beard, his powerful body clad in leather and chainmail, and his dark, dangerous eyes, were all the authority he required. 'Throw 'em down the slope.'

The soldiers — who had been farmers, fishermen, labourers, and woodsmen before the call to duty came — grumbled, but did as they were told. Dropping the large round Karisae shields upon the ground, they worked in pairs, throwing the dead down the slope to bounce and tangle upon rocks and bushes, creating an extra obstacle to the next Vascanar attack.

'Water!' a boyish voice yelled. 'Who wants water?'

'Over here, boy!' Drustan drove his spear into the ground, undid his helm, attached it to the hook on his belt, and pushed back the chainmail coif covering his scalp. He wrenched off the padded arming cap and stuffed it into his belt next to the helm. The breeze was cool across his sweat-soaked hair.

Staggering under the weight of waterskins slung across his shoulders, the boy, who looked about twelve, picked his way between the wounded and dead.

'Here, milord,' said the boy, handing him a full waterskin.

'Don't call me that,' Drustan snapped.

'But them boots.' The boy pointed at Drustan's feet. 'Them's noble's boots.'

Damn boots. He should have thrown them out with the rest of his gear, but good boots were so hard to come by — like good women. Drustan poured water over his head and face. He swilled out his mouth. The clean, cold taste of the spring water washed away the stench of battle for a moment. Spitting the cleansing water across a discarded Vascanar shield emblazoned with a red and gold flame upon a black background, he lifted the waterskin again and drank deeply.

'That there's Drustan,' Cullain said. A murmur swept through the men near enough to hear; they hadn't known who fought beside them.

'Drustan the—' The boy caught his words behind his teeth. 'Drustan the Bright Blade.'

Drustan poured the last of the water over his arms, shoulders and neck, washing away the worst of the battle grime from his steel vambraces, leather cuirass, and the chainmail mantle across his shoulders. 'Drustan the Kinless,' he said and threw the empty waterskin into the boy's chest.

The boy caught it. 'I mostly kill for gold these days, but I'll make an exception if you're still here when I open my eyes.' He smiled at the boy and closed his eyes.

When he opened them again, the boy was dodging away between the wounded and the dead.

'Could've done with some water,' Cullain said.

'You gossip like a baker's wife.' Drustan glanced at the men around him, farmers made into soldiers with heirloom weapons and rough-cut shields. Some of the men met his gaze and nodded their respect, but others would not look at him; would not look at the noble who had lost his place and left the isles in disgrace.

'You should've thrown away them boots,' Cullain said.

'Get the men sorted.' Drustan ran a hand through his wet hair. 'Their armsman died in the last assault so they're ours now. I'll send you water.' He picked up his shield, yanked his spear from the ground, and walked away from the line.

He could hear Cullain behind him as he clambered up the rise to where he could see the entire battlefield. 'Right then, lads, stop gawping. Aye, that's Drustan desainCoid all right. The Bright Blade. And I'm Cullain Strongarm. Ah, you've heard of me too, ain't you? Good. Let's see if you can learn to act like soldiers then, instead of like farm boys fresh from tickling your mothers' teats. When those Vascanar whoresons come again, close up the damn line. There's more god-cursed holes than in your mothers' skirts. You … aye, you. On the next attack, don't wave your spear around like your wife's darning needle. Stick it in, twist it, pull it out, keep on doing it 'till the whoreson falls. Don't stab the man in front of you, stab the man to your right. Them damn tower shields of theirs ain't no use if'n you stab 'em in the swordside. Use your shields as sommat more'n sommat to quiver behind. Protect the man on your left, coz them Vascanar know about shieldside and swordside too. And aim low — if'n you can't kill the whoreson, at least stop him bloody breeding.'

Drustan grinned as Cullain's voice faded away into the general noise of an army preparing to defend its line. He spotted a different water-boy and told him where to find Cullain, before climbing the hill to look out over the battlefield.

CHAPTER 2

This high above the battlefield, the wind blew the clean salt smell of the sea into Drustan's nostrils. He breathed in deeply. This was where King Radolf should have set his standard, here where he could see the entire field of battle. Not over on the right flank, where tradition said he should stand. Poor King Radolf: better suited to the drinking hall than the battlefield, but none of his sycophants would ever tell him that.

If the old King, Brantin the Wise, still breathed, if Drustan were still a member of the Hundrin, if King Radolf's military advisors had backbones to match their pretty armour, what then? Drustan shrugged. Not his problem anymore. He was a sell-sword now, a mercenary; all he cared about was getting paid.

She had smiled and taken his hand, led him in the dance, her body against his, her eyes upon his, such a long time ago. *Marisa…* Oh dear gods, Marisa, don't be here. Be far away from here.

He snarled at his weakness, threw his weapons upon the grass and sat beside them.

The music piped around them, but he hardly heard the melody, the beat; the thrust of her heart against his was all he understood as they danced at the turning of the winter. Five long years ago. May Brominii guard you, Marisa, because we cannot stop the Vascanar here upon this ridge.

His jaw tightened, his anger flared, but he did not curse her, not even in his mind; he would never do that. So, he surveyed the battlefield instead. The ridge swooped down into the valley on the left flank of the Karisae line, a flank anchored in the tangled edges of Barstow Wood, which swept around behind the ridge. A flank commanded by Earl Haren desainAbavin of Ramagon Hall, named Duke by the King because this was his demesne; a battle commander whose battles lay decades in the past.

The Vascanar would attack the left flank again. Their cavalry would—

'Resting, warrior?' an avalor asked. Clad in the red robes of his order, the priest of Vulcas smiled down at Drustan.

Drustan looked up at the corpulent priest in his fine silk robes, noting the greasy sweat coating his cheeks and balding scalp, the ceremonial sword of his order in his hand — a sword covered in jewels, with gold wire around the hilt and a blade as blunt as the man's honour.

Drustan touched his fist to his forehead in the salute to Vulcas. 'I wanted to see the battlefield, avalor.'

The avalor nodded, looked Drustan in the eye, and said, 'I am named Maran Willemson, Avalor of Vulcas.'

Drustan looked away, looked at the battlefield, and clenched his jaw. Through gritted teeth he replied, as honour required, 'I'm named Drustan desainCoid.'

Maran sucked air through his teeth. 'You returned to fight for the land that cast you out?'

Drustan grinned. 'I fight for gold. I'm a sell-sword now.' He met Maran's gaze, still grinning. 'Lord Lanier desainGran is paying me. So take it up with him … avalor.'

Maran dropped his gaze first. 'May Vulcas guide your arm, Drustan the Bright Blade. The land needs you this day.'

'If you say so, priest. Is old Pikechucker gonna turn up, do you reckon? Or is he still sleeping off his last drink?'

'You throw away my blessing.'

'One of you broke my sword in front of the King.'

'That could not be helped.'

'I still bear a grudge, though.' Drustan laid his hand upon the spear. 'On your way, priest. Go bless some other fool.'

Maran paused. 'I will go, but since you are the Bright Blade, and must needs fight for this land that cast you aside, I will tell you this. The Korga blessed the ships that brought the Vascanar here.'

'The Korga! Are you sure?'

'Without the blessing of the sea goddess those ships would have foundered, so over-laden, so low to the waterline. They carried horses and far too many men. Yes, the Korga blessed them.'

'Why would she do that?'

'The Korgena sea-witches delight in gold. No doubt the Vascanar paid them to intercede with the goddess Korga on their behalf.'

Drustan rubbed at his forehead. 'So where are our gods, Maran? Where are the gods we sacrifice to at every turn of the seasons?'

Maran's voice dropped to a whisper. 'I don't know.' The fat old priest stumbled away.

Drustan watched him go and returned to surveying the battlefield. The Korga. He shook his head. It did not bode well for the isles if a goddess of the deep sea had taken the Vascanar side.

He looked up into the cloudless summer sky. Cullain was right. A bit of rain would be nice, to limit the effectiveness of the cavalry and the archers, and make the battle more even. He remembered a storm, *caught out in the forest, Marisa's dress stuck to her body, his hand in hers, as they sheltered from the rain.*

He ground his teeth against the memory and looked to the battlefield. The Vascanar cavalry mustered for another charge against the fatigued shieldwall in the dip between the ridge and the forest. How many attacks had the men in that shieldwall withstood since the battle began with the dawn?

Sunlight glinted on the harnesses of the powerful Vascanar warhorses, tall of wither, wide of chest, their flanks spotted with flecks of sweat, snorting and stamping under riders chivvying them into position.

Behind them, the Erisyan archers stepped up to their marks. How had the Vascanar paid for their services? The Erisyan clans were famously fussy about whose gold they took. They could afford to be; they were among the best skirmishers in the known world. Their warbows could throw an armour-piercing shaft nearly five hundred paces, and they could loose three such arrows before the first one struck.

The Vascanar had secured the service of a whole Erisyan clan by the look of it, at least two thousand men. Why would *they* fight for the Vascanar? How much gold did it take to persuade such men to fight for foul cultist scum? More gold than the King held in his treasury. Drustan shook his head again. And the Korgena, the sea-witches — the Vascanar had paid the servants of the Korga too. So much gold spent on this campaign.

But why? What did the Vascanar want upon the isles? What did they seek? They spent years of plunder just to take a land that they would abandon when they were done with it.

It made no sense.

Drustan closed his hands into fists. Why should he care? For long moments he stared at nothing, his eyes unfocused, his mind held by the sound of a blade breaking against an anvil.

The moment passed.

Consciously he loosened his fists, rolled his neck, stretched one leg and then the other. Nothing to do with him. Not his land anymore. All he had to worry about was getting out of this cesspit alive. His fingers brushed across the grass, *Marisa beside him in the tall grass, stroking his face, as…* Let her be safe, let her flee, let her—

The slow, heavy rhythm of Vascanar war drums beat out against the heated summer air. That would be the infantry advancing again. He had to get back to the line, but he still had time to watch the cavalry attack. It took a while for the Vascanar infantry to clamber up the slope before the ridge under the hurled spears and rocks of the Karisae defenders.

The Erisyans loosed the first volley of the next attack. The arrows hissed as they rose, dark against the sky. Another cloud of arrows followed the first as it tipped downwards towards the targets. And yet another before the first arrows struck with devastating speed and accuracy.

The best Karisae archers, with the best Karisae bows, could hit a mark at maybe three hundred and fifty paces and that with a following wind. Damn near useless against the Erisyans. Another cloud of Erisyan arrows rose. And another. And another. A constant stream of death arcing through the sky.

Horns blared amongst the Vascanar cavalry. They started to move. Four waves of brutal men upon the backs of powerful warhorses. From walk to trot, to canter, to gallop, keeping their formation, not allowing any horse to surge ahead of the perfect lines across the battlefield. Building the pace, keeping the cohesion, creating the shocking momentum of man and horse in perfect unity. The Vascanar cavalry was a glorious sight — if you didn't have to stand against it.

Up on the ridgeline it was infantry against infantry, sword against shield, axe against helm, spears stabbing, bodies shoving, blood mingling. But down in the valley…

Sunlight glinted on chainmail and steel. Cloaks the colour of dried blood streamed out behind the charging cavalry. Kite-shaped shields, red and black and gold, held tight to bodies. Spears ready to throw or stab, riders controlling their mounts by knee pressure alone. Hooves thundered. Battle cries screamed from a thousand throats.

And still the Erisyan arrow-storm hissed down upon the shieldwall. The Karisae infantrymen held their shields high to protect against those plunging arrows, waiting for the order to drop the shields to their front, to brace for the impact of the horses.

The Karisae archers loosed their first ragged volley against the charging Vascanar cavalry. Some horsemen fell, but not many.

Drustan spotted Vascanar infantry running behind the cavalry charge. He looked right. The Vascanar general had pulled men from before the shieldwall. Only half the infantry now climbed that slope. Karisae spears fell amongst them, but still they plodded uphill with their tall shields overlapped to protect them.

Good tactics: wear down the defenders in the valley with repeated attacks, then — when the time was right — launch an all-out assault, while still leaving the Karisae forces on the ridgeline pinned by a more limited but still dangerous frontal assault. The Vascanar general knew his business and chose this moment to throw everything against the battered left flank. Against the poor beleaguered fools in the valley.

Drustan glanced back at the men of the Karisae reserve. They were readying their shields, stretching, preparing to rush to bolster the line. Good. They would be needed.

Onward the Vascanar infantry raced. Onward the Vascanar cavalry charged. When horses fell to Karisae arrows, those behind simply leapt over the fallen beast and charged through their fallen comrades, rising in their stirrups, throwing spears at the front of the Karisae lines.

And still the Erisyan arrow-storm slammed into upraised Karisae shields. Those arrows weren't going to stop, Drustan realised. The Vascanar were going to charge into their own arrow-storm. He admired the brutality of the tactic even as he dreaded its effect.

The defenders couldn't drop their shields from overhead to their front. Couldn't set themselves to meet the horses. Perhaps trained troops, professional troops, troops like the Vascanar, could have dropped their shields to defend themselves in the instant before the horses clattered into their lines. But these were not trained troops, these were not professional killers; these were Karisae villagers pressed into service to protect their land. Their training was hurried, inadequate to create the discipline of soldiers and foster the instincts of warriors.

The Vascanar cavalry smashed into the disorganised Karisae shieldwall and the Erisyan archers shifted their arrow-storm away from the point of impact along the line of defenders, softening up that part of the shieldwall for the charging Vascanar infantry.

'Hold,' Drustan whispered. 'Hold.'

Vascanar horses plunged, hooves stamping down upon their enemies. Vascanar swords rose and fell, slashing at the poor fools trapped by the weight of their fellows. Vascanar spears stabbed downwards, skewering the Karisae as they started to panic and break, pushing away from the breach in the shieldwall.

But the line held, the ranks behind surging forward to plug the gaps.

Then the Vascanar infantry threw itself upon the shocked defenders and the line buckled, but the arrow-storm faded away as the Erisyans advanced to bring more of the Karisae line into range.

Now.

This was the moment.

'Use the reserves,' Drustan muttered. 'Use them now.'

But Earl desainAbavin hesitated too long, and the battle was lost.

CHAPTER 3

The Vascanar drove a wedge through the shieldwall, pushing the Karisae away from the forest, losing the left flank its anchor. Once the shield-men were driven away from the tangled trees their cohesion was broken, and nothing could stop the defeat.

Too late did desainAbavin commit his reserves, and to the wrong part of the battle. He sent them to attack the cavalry directly, head-on, rather than bolstering the anchoring force hard up against the forest. Wasted effort. Wasted men.

'Incompetent fool.' Drustan reached for his shield and spear. It was time to disengage, to withdraw, to prepare to fight another day. The troops on the ridgeline could retreat in good order and fade away into the forest. Ambush and raid would slow the Vascanar advance. They would pay in blood for every mile covered until the Karisae were ready to face them again in open battle.

Maybe the King would listen to his soldiers now rather than aging warhorses like desainAbavin.

Drustan stood, stretched his back. He'd look for Cullain in the forest. No point going anywhere near the ridgeline; an old warrior like Cullain wouldn't wait for the order to withdraw. Maybe swing by the House of Falas, make sure the healers were safely out of the line of advance.

Karisae horns blared.

Drustan turned back to the battlefield, barely believing his eyes. 'What's the fool doing?'

Men hastily formed up on the slope of the ridgeline in columns… Columns? They could not be serious. The battle was lost. Any fool could see that. The battle…

Vascanar horses stamped and reared; flashes of light glinted from the upraised swords and spears of the riders. The Vascanar infantrymen pushed forward, butchering any who stood in their path. More enemy infantry streamed across the battlefield to exploit the breach. Erisyan arrows again arced through the air, holding back any possible aid to the battered shieldwall.

DesainAbavin was going to send reinforcements into *that*? He thought he could close the gap by sending disorganised infantry against cavalry through a hail of arrows? He was only weakening the defensive line on the ridge and making any kind of disciplined withdrawal impossible.

'You bloody fool.' Drustan could not believe his eyes. 'You're going to destroy the entire army.'

The Karisae line finally broke under the pressure. The rout started near the breach. Men threw down their weapons and fled towards the forest that curved around behind the ridge. Drustan willed them to make it to the trees, to leave their dead and dying behind; they had no other choices now.

'Run,' he whispered. 'Run.'

A bull-throated voice, a voice he knew well, raised above the clamour of battle, above the clash of steel upon steel and the screams of horses and men. It was the Earl Haren desainAbavin of Ramagon yelling, 'Kill them! Kill those faithless cowards.'

A pause.

The command repeated.

And Karisae archers loosed upon their fleeing comrades. Arrows cut down men running for their lives.

Drustan growled deep in his throat. Enough was enough. He threw aside his spear and shield; too heavy, too unwieldy. He needed to run now and he could always find another shield and spear if he had need of them. There were plenty lying around.

He sprinted down the slope towards the standard of the Earl of Ramagon, towards the battle-leader butchering his own men. Streams of terrified soldiers fleeing for the forest cut across Drustan's path. He dodged, ducked, slammed through some, knocking them sprawling and leaping over their fallen forms.

Still the roaring voice of the Earl: 'Kill them! Kill them all!'

'Stop!' Drustan yelled as he ran. 'Stop, you damn fools!'

He broke clear of the escaping masses; the common soldiers avoided the group of noblemen clustered around the Earl's standard.

A man stepped away from that group, an unsheathed longsword held across his shoulders like a dairy-maid's yoke. He stretched his neck from side to side, his chainmail-covered stomach exposed, inviting a foolhardy attack. He grinned.

Drustan skidded to a halt. The scar on his face burned in memory. The scar this man had given him at a tournament on the turn of a season years before — when Drustan still had his honour, before they broke his sword. A foul blow, dishonourable and sly, the measure of the man who struck it. How Marisa had wept when she looked upon the ruin of his face.

'Always wanted to kill you,' Erik desainAbavin said. 'Drustan the...'

'Let me pass, Erik.'

'...half-breed.'

Drustan sighed, let his right hand fall to the dagger at the back of his belt, and glanced across at the bloody, screaming chaos below. The Vascanar cavalry was rolling up the line along the shallow slope from the valley floor, as Vascanar infantry assaulted the shieldwall from the front. The Karisae defenders were pinned, unable to turn, doomed. The hastily formed columns shattered under the weight of the Vascanar cavalry and the slashing rain of Erisyan arrows.

Those men should have been pulled back into the forest to rearguard the retreat of the rest of the army. It was a rout now, a panicked flight. Men did not easily recover from such a disgrace. The army's spirit had been broken here, along with its shieldwall.

Erik took advantage of Drustan's seeming inattention. His longsword swept around and down in a fast, powerful stroke.

Drustan leapt backwards. The tip of the longsword skidded across his armour, scoring a long, narrow line in the leather. He lunged forward after it passed and knocked aside Erik's returning cut with the vambrace around his left forearm, drawing his dagger with his right. Now he was inside the arc of the sword.

Erik, off balance, tried to step back, but Drustan's left arm snaked around his neck as their bodies slammed together. He bent Erik backwards, drove the needle-pointed dagger through the chainmail into his enemy's back in swift punching strikes, and kept stabbing until he heard the sigh from Erik's lips, the sigh that told him the man was done.

'You forgot who I am,' Drustan snarled into the dying man's ear. He let him fall.

'Murderer,' the Earl screeched, as his son fell to the ground in front of Drustan. 'Mercenary vagabond. Scum. Unclean spawn of an Anthanic bitch.'

Hesitantly, the archers lowered their bows, glancing at each other and at the scene behind them. The Earl's cruel orders had stopped and they didn't really want to kill their own people. A few began to loose at the enemy cavalry cutting a path up the slope towards them, but many more ran away towards the woods.

Drustan cut a strip of cloth from Erik's tabard and used it to clean Erik's blood from the blade of his dagger. The longer he held the Earl's attention, the more men would get away. He kept a careful gaze upon the approaching Vascanar.

'Coward,' the Earl yelled.

'Are you blind, old man?' Drustan studied the dagger carefully. He should have thrown the dagger away, bought another, but he would not be parted from it. A lock of Marisa's hair lay coiled within the hilt. Satisfied that not a speck of blood remained to tarnish the blade, he sheathed it at the back of his belt.

'Kill this man,' the Earl ordered his retainers.

None of them moved.

'Kill him. Kill him now. I command you.' The Earl pushed at the armoured shoulder of one of his men.

The man shrugged his hand away.

'I need a horse.' Drustan picked up Erik's longsword and tested its balance. He jerked his chin at the Earl's grey gelding, held a hundred paces behind the line by a terrified groom. 'Yours will do nicely.'

'Half-breed.' The Earl scrabbled at his sword.

Drustan politely waited for him to set his stance. A good stance for a duel; not so good for uneven ground. Too narrow, too unbalanced, too weak.

'I am Haren desainAbavin, Earl of Ramagon, Duke of the—'

Drustan's new longsword swept upwards and clove desainAbavin's face from chin to brow. 'Nice blade.' He grinned savagely at the Earl's retainers as the Earl's corpse bled at his feet.

'Go on your way, Dru,' one of the men said. 'You have saved the army here today.'

'You mean to stay, Lasac?' Drustan cleaned the tip of the longsword with a piece of cloth cut from the Earl's tunic.

'Tis my duty and my honour.'

'You'll die here and the King will run.'

'My honour is not tied to his.'

Drustan knew that mantra well.

Lasac said, 'They shouldn't have broken your sword.'

'Love is the swordbreaker.' Drustan removed the sword-belt from Erik's corpse.

'You'll be hunted by both sides.'

'Only one side left standing, brother.' Drustan slid the longsword into the scabbard and looped the sword-belt diagonally from his right shoulder to his left hip. He gripped the bottom of the scabbard with his left hand.

Lasac said, 'You still call me brother of the blade.'

'We shed blood together, Lasac desainMortan. I'll leave an offering for you when I pass a shrine.'

'Fare thee well, Drustan desainCoid.' Lasac placed a hand over his heart and bowed.

Drustan returned the gesture, then turned and jogged towards the groom holding the Earl's grey horse.

The groom looked at the scarred face of the warrior running towards him, looked at his master and his master's son lying dead upon the hillside, and looked at the horse he held.

'Wait!' Drustan bellowed and started to sprint. 'I mean you no…'

The groom leapt into the canted saddle and put his heels to the horse's flanks.

'…harm.' Drustan watched the horse gallop away. 'Looks like I'm afoot then.' He loped towards the forest, away from the sounds of a battle lost.

CHAPTER 4

Jerem lay in a pit in the ground with his own sword piercing his body. The pain of the blade tore at his guts but more terrifying was the lack of pain from his legs, the lack of any feeling at all. Done for, dying, here in Barstow Wood, with the merciless enemy hard on his heels.

A ravenous fear rose to his throat. He had seen what the Vascanar did to those they captured: the bodies contorted in agony, the wounds, the blistered skin. And he had laughed then. A soldier about his trade, making dark jokes about the horrors he saw, and then using that repressed rage to tear apart a Vascanar raiding party in the Trassac Mountains across the Salt.

The sound of running feet in the forest to his left. Terror clawed at Jerem, the terror that had ripped his honour apart upon the battlefield. He was Jerem, called Iceblood, a man who never quailed, whatever the odds. He had fought his way into the temple of the Vascanar when the King ordered his stupid raid upon their ships. With his brother beside him he had slaughtered any who stood against him on that bloody night. He had scooped up the gold and jewels from the very altar of the Vascanar and taken it as his due.

He was not some levied farmer called to duty, not knowing one end of his spear from the other. His trade was war and he was a craftsman of death.

And yet, the fear froze his bones, his blood, upon the field below the ridgeline. Iceblood indeed, only now the ice broke his honour. The arrows singing, the horses charging, his brother… Poor Ballun. Jerem's brother *was* a farmer, but not levied to war by royal proclamation; Ballun *chose* to stand in the line beside the brother he admired, stood when the cavalry charged, did not falter, protecting Jerem while Jerem pissed his pants in terror.

Ballun's voice crying out behind Jerem, crying out from the line when Jerem dropped his shield, picked up his pack, and fled. A coward. A false-oathed coward, leaving his brother to die behind him as he fled with the loot they had gathered together from the Vascanar ships.

More feet running in the forest. The Vascanar! They were coming for him. Jerem did not breathe, did not make a sound. Let them run on, let them pass him by; let them take some other fool. Let him die here, alone and untouched.

'Call to him,' a voice sang in his ears. It sounded like his wife Ruth, calling the children in for supper. Torac, Kavin, Jerem the younger — his children would know their father to be a coward. Somebody would tell them before the Vascanar took their souls. *'Call to him.'* The voice pierced his soul as the blade of his sword pierced his body and shattered his spine. *'Call to him.'*

****

Drustan jogged through the trees.

'Help me!' The cry came from his left. 'Help me!' A Karisae voice.

Drustan stopped, sighed, and pushed his way through the undergrowth. A great elm had fallen here, its roots a tangled wall at the end of the round-sided depression. A soldier lay slouched against the crumbled edge of the pit, with blood on his breeches.

He saw Drustan. 'Help me,' he begged.

Drustan looked at the man and then glanced at the edge of the forest not two hundred paces distant. The Vascanar were a bare half-mile away. He should flee through the forest, be gone from this place, but the man needed his help. He was Karisae. But the Vascanar — Drustan snarled. The Vascanar would spend all this night celebrating with wine and torture. There were hours yet until dark fell. He had plenty of time to see to this man and still be away from this place.

'Please,' the man said.

Drustan clambered down into the pit.

'Thank you.'

'Can you walk?' Drustan asked.

'That's not the help I need.'

Drustan pulled aside the man's cloak and wrinkled his nose at the stench of faeces. Two-thirds of a broad-bladed shortsword pierced through the man's brigandine armour and on into his abdomen. The angle of the sword told its own story: this man would never walk again.

'I'm named Jerem,' the man said. 'Jerem of Solglen.' His eyes darted from Drustan's face to the woods, to the edges of the pit, the eyes of a man gripped by terror but trying not to show it.

'I'm named Drustan desainCoid.'

Jerem grinned; there was blood on his teeth. His eyes settled on Drustan's, no longer darting around like a frightened deer's. 'I saw you fight that duel against Arold Holearse and give him his name.'

'He deserved it,' Drustan snapped. Arold desainForas had placed his hands upon Marisa...

Oh dear gods, Marisa, be at home on the StormMarch, don't be at the House of Falas, don't have come here to see to the wounded.

He knew it was a foolish wish.

'I don't doubt it.' Jerem coughed. His eyelids flickered for a moment, but he shook his head — an old soldier fighting off unconsciousness by strength of will. 'I should've known better than to run through a forest with a sword in me hand.'

'Yes,' Drustan said. 'You should.' He reached a hand towards the sword.

'Leave it, it's stuck in bone.' Only Jerem's spine lay in the path of that blade.

Drustan withdrew his hand. 'It plugs the hole anyway.'

'There's wine in me pack.' Jerem gestured weakly at the bag lying under the tangled roots of the fallen tree.

Drustan scrambled under the roots to retrieve the pack. He lifted it with a grunt of effort. 'You ran with this weight? No wonder you fell.' He untied the string and upended the bag. A wineskin fell out, some food wrapped in clean linen from the supply carts — and a rattling deluge of gold, silver, and jewels.

A sound in the forest. Drustan jerked his head around. Vascanar? No, of course not. It was just a bloody fox, or some other poor fool fleeing the battle.

'From the ... the raid ... the raid on the ships.' Jerem coughed up blood. 'Not much ... not much...' He breathed heavily through his nose. The coughing subsided. 'Not much use to me now.'

Drustan lifted the wineskin and drank deeply. Harsh wine, barely given time to mature, a soldier's wine. He shivered as the liquid hit his stomach. Hairs tickled at the back of his neck. Sudden goosebumps on his arms. He tensed, took one step away from Jerem.

'I'd like a taste of that,' Jerem said.

The Vascanar would be coming. They would … What in all the hells was wrong with him? Drustan licked his lips. 'Your … your gut is pierced.' What was that? That noise? His hand dropped to the dagger. Fear tore a hole through his gut. He had to leave. Now.

'Does it matter?'

'What?'

'Does it matter that my … gut … is pierced.' Jerem coughed and sighed, turning his head against the dirt.

A deep breath in. A deep breath out. Honour is an action not a birthright. 'There's a House of Doves at the Falas Bridge.' *Marisa, torn and brutalised, blood pooled around her, her golden hair sticky with it.*

'The sword's severed my spine. No healer can fix that.'

Drustan took another swig of wine to wipe away the image of Marisa lying dead and broken. Blood thudded in his temples. He could barely see for the terror raging through his mind. 'I … I can carry you.' He gritted out the words.

'I'll not survive the journey.'

Drustan blinked. The man was going to die anyway. Leave him here, run … and break his honour as they broke his sword. Prove them right.

No!

He would not leave this man behind to die in agony. Not like this. Let the whoresons come. He was Drustan desainCoid and he would not cast his honour away so cheaply. A single harsh breath. 'No,' he said, his voice calm again, under his control. 'I don't suppose you would.' He knelt beside Jerem, lifted his head, and trickled a little wine between the dying soldier's lips.

Jerem coughed. 'I'll … I'll linger a long time like this.'

'Aye.'

'I went across the Salt with the King.' Jerem spoke of King Radolf's attempt to take some land from the broken remnants of the Maebazray Empire.

'So did I,' Drustan said. He had been Hundrin then. 'A stupid war.'

'I ran.' Tears leaked from Jerem's eyes. 'Today, I ran. The horses. The arrows. I fled. I broke the line.'

Drustan looked away from the man's distress. 'A lot of men fled today.'

'I'm an armsman. I'm a soldier. I fought for coin across the Salt. They named me Iceblood.' A coughing fit overcame Jerem. He clawed at Drustan's arm. 'I ... I ran ... sword still in my hand ... such terror... I pissed myself, I... Men died today ... because I...' Jerem stopped, stared at the ground.

Drustan gripped the man's hand. 'I've heard of you, Jerem Iceblood. You have a name to be proud of.'

Jerem's face calmed. He looked puzzled, embarrassed by his outburst. He spoke quietly. 'I might last 'til morning.'

'You might.'

'You know what these Vascanar animals do to—' Jerem shook his head. 'Not a good way to die.'

'No.' Drustan drew the needle-pointed dagger. 'Close your eyes, Jerem of Solglen.'

'Wait.'

''Tis best it is done quickly, brother.'

'The sword.' Jerem touched the hilt of the blade that pierced him. He coughed. 'It's ... been in ... my family ... generations.'

'I thought the blade too broad for modern steel.'

The coughing fit subsided. 'Made the old way. It'll cleave through the branch of an oak without damage.'

'What is it you want, Jerem?'

'I've sons.'

'I may never meet them.'

'You know your way to Solglen, Drustan desainCoid.'

'I do.' Drustan nodded. 'Very well, Jerem of Solglen, named Iceblood for your honour. I, Drustan desainCoid, will carry this blade that killed you. I swear to give it to one of your blood if ever I meet such. I shall not sell it or give it to any other, but if it breaks, or is lost and cannot be recovered, then this oath is considered satisfied. I swear it true, with heart-blood and breath, with mind and soul, until the dirt claims me.'

'Thank you, Bright Blade.'

'I'm naught but a sell-sword, Jerem. My honour is bought and sold these days.'

'I doubt that.' Jerem smiled through blood-flecked lips. 'But if'n it be so, then take what you like of the baubles I stole.'

Drustan returned the smile. 'I shall, brother. Now turn your head to the side and close your eyes.'

'An old oath.' Jerem closed his eyes. 'The old gods'll hold you to that.' He turned his head to one side.

A single thrust under the ear ended Jerem's pain.

Drustan pulled the shortsword free of the corpse and tossed it to one side before removing Jerem's sword-belt. He sliced a scrap of cloth from the cloak to clean the blade of the shortsword and wrapped the man in what was left, tying it tight with a length of twine from the pack. As gently as he could, Drustan pushed Jerem into the deep shadows beneath the roots of the fallen elm. Stepping back, he bowed his head and recited the death prayer:

'Formed of blood and guts and steel
Made to die but never yield
Born of woman
Born of man
Born upon this shimmering land
Throw the mud and dirt and clay
Freeman born until this day
Dead to woman
Dead to man
Dying for this shimmering land.'

Drustan bowed his head for a moment. 'This will have to do, brother. I have no time to bury you deep.' He swigged at the wine. The deep beat of the Vascanar war-drums echoed through the trees, a wild rhythm, the rhythm of victory. The battle was over, lost; the Vascanar would be here soon, they would—

Deliberately, Drustan closed down the fear. It would not command him.

He adjusted Jerem's sword belt to fit his narrower waist, cleaning the shortsword slowly, carefully, fighting the urge to flee with every stroke of the cloth, before he slipped the sword into its scabbard on the left side of his waist. The food — bread and cheese by the smell and feel of the bundle — he stuffed back into the sack. Finally, he sorted through the looted treasure, choosing the finer, smaller, lighter items.

The fear flared, hot, urgent, making his fingers tremble, his bowels twist, but he focused on the task and pushed the jewellery into his belt pouch. To a sell-sword loot was part of the pay, and he was damned if he was going to leave it behind.

Breathing deeply, calming his mind, he hurled the heavier loot away into the trees; perhaps that would keep two-legged scavengers away from the body.

Drustan saluted Jerem's corpse with the wineskin, poured a libation to the gods, and said, 'May Henath judge you worthy, brother of the shield.' He drank a long, slow swallow of wine.

Terror blazed, hot and bright. With nothing else left to do, no other task to occupy his thoughts, Drustan's courage broke. He fled heedless through the forest, away from the sound of the Vascanar drums and the keening screams of the dead and dying.

CHAPTER 5

The Erisyan archer Jarl Bearclaw fought the urge to vomit at the stench rising from the Vascanar torture pits. The acid taste was part of his penance for another's mistake, a penance that forced him to gaze upon men ripped asunder and to listen to their agonised screams, to smell their flesh burning, to feel the heat upon his skin... Gods above and below, the suffering tore through his soul in a scalding torrent of anguish. His empathic talent was a *dol*, a gift of fate, but here...

Hundreds of heat-stones glowing red-hot beneath the tormented bodies of men and boys, shards of pain burrowing into his soul. No military reason for this slaughter; the Vascanar would gain no information from these men. They simply offered this sacrifice to their gods to call them forth to feast upon this land.

They fed them pain and named it sacrament.

These rituals of agony were the reason why the Vascanar were hated and reviled across the breadth of the world. Jarl's *caedi*, his clan, the Caedi Haroa — the people of the high valleys — were sworn to the Vascanar by a blood-oath harsh and binding.

No amount of gold was worth this. The Erisyans were a diminished people; taking money for such oaths would have been unthinkable only a few decades ago. A blood oath! For money! Jarl held back tears of shame and gazed across the torment before him.

As every life bawled out its pain, the vicious gods of the Vascanar became visible. Dark, pendulous shadows took shape above the glowing heat-stones and screaming victims.

Gluttons at a feast in their honour.

These gods needed a pathway through the salt-forged barriers around the Islands of Symcani, a pathway constructed from the souls of tormented men. The seas protected these lands and to obtain their power the gods first needed their warriors to crush the inhabitants.

Jarl knew his histories; he knew that the Karisae had faced the same problem two and a half centuries earlier. But they hadn't solved it like this, because they weren't a cult of torture and bloody misery.

Why had Gorak, his *hwlman*, the war-leader of the caedi — and Jarl's uncle — signed a pact with these monstrous Vascanar? Screams echoed in the footsteps of these animals. Wherever they trod, the land turned red and the spirit realm darkened.

No payment was worth this. The Caedi Haroa would be reviled amongst the Erisyans. Livia, Jarl's wife, would cast out his bow and leave him divorced and alone. His daughters would find no husbands, for no caedi would allow such tainted bloodlines into their own, and his sons would find no wives, for no caedi would send their daughters to marry those who signed a blood-oath with the Vascanar. The Haroa would become *crydi*, wanderers without a homeland.

Thus, Jarl stood witness to the fall of his dreams.

A swaggering Vascanar horse warrior named Torquesten approached through the shimmering heat. Jarl could taste the vicious brutality of Torquesten's mind. The Vascanar called such as him *Akalac*, knights of the blood, but Torquesten was worse even than that; a creature steeped in darkness and evil, he commanded the hounds, those poor benighted slaves forced by mystical bindings to sniff out magic for the Vascanar.

Torquesten thrust a jug of Arambra brandy into Jarl's hand. 'Drink, bowman Jarl. Drink with victory.' Torquesten's harshly accented Maebaz, the trade-tongue of every place that fallen empire had touched, made his words hard to understand.

'I'm not thirsty,' Jarl said in impeccable Maebaz. Linguistics were easy for an empath; the sense of the word came along with its sound. 'And it is pronounced Yarl'.

'You drink, bowman,' Torquesten demanded. 'Drink.'

Jarl accepted the jug. 'The term is *archer*,' he said, before he let the fiery liquid swill around his mouth, feigned swallowing, and then spat the brandy back into the jug along with his unspoken curse.

'Dead empire, dead tongue, soon all will speak the language of the gods.' Torquesten snatched back the jug and almost overbalanced into a nearby pit filled with glowing heat-stones, where a man was being broiled alive.

Jarl resisted the urge to trip the drunken Vascanar.

Torquesten regained his balance and laughed. 'I like you, bowman. I keep you as pet, yes?' He staggered away.

Jarl closed his eyes. Gorak, what have you done to your people? He spat the sour flavour of the brandy onto the ground and opened his eyes to bear witness.

The dark forms of the Vascanar gods solidified above the sacrifices, dripping secretions that crackled upon the heat-stones, splattered upon the ground, and hissed upon the pathetic flesh of the sacrifices. Slaves rushed forward with delicate pottery bowls to collect this precious fluid, reaching across the heat to save the sacred harvest from exploding on contact with the heat of the stones, taking great care to collect the fluid that etched acid lines of pain upon the skins of men screaming out their last breaths.

Too much; Jarl could bear no more. He turned away from the repulsive sight; but he had stayed too long. Long enough for a Vascanar god to notice him. *'You are mine.'* The rancid, domineering mental voice of the god crawled into his soul. *'You will serve me.'* Such longing in that voice, such hatred.

Jarl took a step back from the thrust of that seductive hate, but only one step; then he cast off the bloody dreams rampant in his mind, cast off the temptation to become a monstrous beast raging upon the surface of the world, and cast the discordance at the centre of his soul back into the gaze of the god.

He was Jarl Bearclaw of the Caedi Haroa. He was archer and warrior, father and lover, man of faith, of truth, of worth. He was Erisyan.

The god screamed.

Jarl drove empathy, truth, clarity, the essential chaotic randomness of humanity into the breach of that glare. They may have noticed him, but he'd suffered with every cry of every soul torn open for their greed; they wouldn't turn him to their ways. He would die before that happened — and he wouldn't die alone.

The scrape of swords on scabbards as the Vascanar readied their blades.

Jarl, with a smile upon his lips, opened his mind fully and thrust out with all that he had, letting his soul slash at every dark form floating above the pain of men. 'Take me, then,' he said, his voice soft in the sudden silence. 'If you have the nerve for it.'

He drew his own sword, the famous *syrthae* blade of the Erisyans, with its distinctive inward-curving cutting-edge, its heavy point to add weight to any cut, and its blade as long as his arm. It shimmered in the light of the glowing heat-stones.

Every god cried out its rage. The screech tore the world open and for a moment, a moment of synchronicity, of information given and received, the gods and Jarl connected in the realm of the spirit.

Jarl staggered. *Demons!* The Vascanar gods were demons. Demons who sought to become gods. Oh, how they coveted that ascension. And these islands, largely untouched by newer faiths, held the power they needed to achieve it.

Demons, not gods — not yet. Just foul creatures loosed upon the world by the tormented cries of dying men. Jarl tried to drag his gaze away from the demon's eyes, tried to pull his soul out of the connection, but this one was tenacious; he thrust deeper into Jarl's soul, into his mind, skewering the very heart of him. Jarl struggled, his fists tight, his face rigid, dragging back his soul, his mind, his heart. In that instant more information flooded through the link.

'We will tear apart your soul,' the demons cried into Jarl's mind — and closed the doors to their own thoughts, freeing him from their hooks.

'Will ain't killed,' Jarl said, and broke the corrosive gaze. He had learned what he needed to know: the Vascanar had sold their souls to demons. Nothing more than that. He almost pitied them, even as he feared for his own people.

Torquesten, at the forefront of the Vascanar, with a longsword above his head, charged towards Jarl.

'Hold!' The bellow came from Gorak, Jarl's hwlman and uncle; the Erisyans had come rushing to Jarl's aid from the shattered stones of the broken town.

With his warbow held at full draw, arrow nocked and pointed at Torquesten, Gorak lifted his chin. 'Spill one drop of Erisyan blood and the pact is broken.' The rest of the caedi stood by Gorak's side, bows drawn, ready to loose upon his command.

The Vascanar skidded to a halt. Jarl flinched at the crackling viciousness of the Demon-tongue, a language that burned across the souls of those who heard it, blazing between the hovering demons and the fools who worshipped them.

Torquesten said, 'The gods say he shall live to suffer. They say you must take him from this place.'

'Your accent's improved,' Jarl commented.

'Quiet now, Jarl,' Gorak said. Like all users of the Erisyan warbow, Gorak was broad across shoulders and back; but even his bull neck bulged at the mounting effort of keeping a powerful bow at full draw. He smiled at Torquesten and said, 'We'll leave now, then.'

'Go,' Torquesten snapped.

Gorak lowered his bow. 'Come along, Jarl. You've seen enough excitement this night.'

As they made their way back to the Erisyan tents, Gorak asked, 'What possessed you to stand there like that?'

'To bear witness,' Jarl said. 'You've no idea what you've done.'

****

'Where is it?' the demon demanded of Bihkat. *'Where is the Xarnac?'* It loomed above the fading heat of the Xantian stone.

A circle of priests crooned their fear while Bihkat, high priest of all the Vascanar existent in the world, lifted his scar-wracked arms in supplication. 'It—'

'You promised us, priest. You promised that it would be recovered at the battle.' The words ripped into Bihkat's soul like the tips of a scourge, scalding and sharp. *'You promised us the recovery of the Xarnac, the amulet, the lodestone of our realisation.'*

'It will be found.' Bihkat threw himself upon the ground in misery. 'The terror it inspires will unman any that bear it. No one can resist its effect.'

'The amulet was at the battle, priest. And now it is gone. Its power brought terror to the enemy and broke their lines. We tasted its perfume upon the souls of the sacrifices. It was there and now it is not. Where is it?'

'The enemy fled. They took it with them.'

'We gave you the ukinak of Pyran, the best of our regiments, to take this island. We made our deals with the sea-ruling Korga to bring your ships

here. *We allowed you to employ mercenaries not of the faith to winnow the enemy. All this we did to secure our fulfilment. This land is the gateway to our godhood.'* The demon struggled to hold itself present in this realm; its agony sang through Bihkat's soul. *'Where is the lodestone of our completion?'*

'It will be found.'

'You allowed it to be taken. You allowed it to be stolen. And you did not tell us of its loss. We had to discover its absence in the scent of the dead souls passing to our realm, the dead who saw the treasure ship burn. And now you fail to recover it as promised?'

'We didn't know!' Bihkat cried out from the ground. 'It must have been taken during the raid. We don't know by whom or how. We thought it safe. We thought it hidden.'

'Fool. Without it all is for naught. The Xarnac guides us through the Tangled Realms to the gate between the worlds, through the gateway into this place, this island of power. The Xarnac burns the souls of men with fear. One has fallen: find his body, rend it clean, bring us the bones that we may taste them. Find the one who holds it now. Already the Xarnac feeds upon his manhood, swallows his courage, burns away all that he is and sanctifies him for our needs. Find him. Find the Xarnac. Unleash the hounds and find it.'

The darkness retreated into the Tangled Realms between worlds, seeping away from Bihkat's soul, freeing him to act once more. He lifted the sharp little dagger on a thong about his neck and cut new lines of supplication through the torn scars of his face.

As the blood flowed, his spirit calmed. He walked away from the place of audience, where the demonic lords spoke and only the priesthood might approach.

Uka Pyran, general and war-leader, knelt upon the freshly stripped skin of a sacrifice. 'What do the lords say, Bihkat, *Ukalac*, priest of the Way?'

Bihkat replied, 'Fetch me Torquesten. Fetch me the Master of the Hounds.'

CHAPTER 6

In the light of the dawn, mist rose from the River Falas and curled over the meadows. Tendrils of moisture pillowed against the bases of the beehives until they looked like mountaintops above clouds.

Marisa desainLegan calmed the bees with a touch of her spirit. The fragment of a haraf stone about her neck pulsed, connecting her soul to her body through the bridge of her mind.

Black and red and white spiralled through the haraf stone; smooth and silky to the touch, it came from the shrine of Redain upon the shores of Lake Kalon, the sacred lake, and was different from the stones of this House of Falas. All the shrines upon the Shrine Road between Falas and Redain had different stones, different mixes of colours and textures. Nobody knew where the monolith stones came from, but they gave power to those who wore the chips of stone around their necks.

Wielding the knife with gloved hands, Marisa cut the combs out of the hive before handing them to Branwen. The Anthanic servant, in her simple, smock-like dress, scraped the honey from the combs into a large basin — honey needed for dressings and poultices when the wounded returned from the battle.

Branwen's crow-black hair was arranged in a simple plait that hung to her waist and contrasted sharply with the shimmering blonde of Marisa's complicated hairstyle, which required constant delicate maintenance by skilled servants such as Branwen.

Neither woman spoke while they worked. Marisa, the haraf stone warm between her breasts, kept her mind focused on the task of calming the bees — their tiny souls pushed against hers as their honey was stolen — and Branwen maintained the vow of silence that all the Anthanic held to in the Houses of the Doves. The Anthanic were a strange people with many strange customs, but this one irritated

Marisa the most. She felt besmirched by their piety, their obeisance to gods not their own; she wondered if she could hold to such a vow if the gods demanded it of her.

The white walls of the House followed the triple-spiral footprint of an ancient Anthanic shrine: tall walls, punctuated by large windows, with dark slate roofs above, curving around a central garden where the spring of the shrine bubbled constantly with pure water containing healing energy.

Powerful healers had travelled from all over the isles to give aid to the soldiers fighting against the Vascanar — as was their duty — but Marisa had another reason to come here to the House of Falas: Drustan.

She had stood and watched as a priest broke Drustan's sword against the edge of an anvil. Drustan's gaze never lifted from the shattered shards of his blade, the blade her father gave him when he reached manhood: his back straight, his shoulders tense, his face a mask.

His eyes — he never looked at her. He did not acknowledge her existence. Turned his back on her, on the life they once shared, and walked away into the world beyond the Salt…

Would he have returned to fight for this land that cast him aside? Would she see him again?

The buzzing of the bees grew louder. Marisa cast Drustan from her mind to focus on the task at hand. Her powers with the creatures were limited; she was a healer, not a witch, and bees were difficult to control.

Branwen clucked her tongue and looked across the meadow towards the grey stones of the bridge spanning the River Falas in seven graceful arches.

Men's voices reached Marisa's ears despite the distance, despite the buzzing of the bees and the thickness of the forest. Anger and fear resonated in the men's cries. Marisa lifted her gaze from the hive. Was he here? Was he dead? Was he…?

The spell broke and the bees began to swarm. Marisa backed away from the hive and dropped the veil across her face, but Branwen simply clucked her tongue again.

A surge of power skated across Marisa's mind.

This Anthanic servant did not calm the bees, she commanded them.

The buzzing quieted; the bees ignored the interlopers in their midst, and the angry cloud of bees disbanded into foraging workers flying out across the meadow to begin the task of replenishing the stolen honey and wax.

Marisa opened her mouth to speak, to ask the question: who was this servant who had such witchly power over the creatures of the fields? But Branwen shook her head and pointed at the forest road.

The thudding beat of horses galloping, kicking up clods of earth. A bubble of sound that should not have reached Marisa's ears at this distance. Powerful magic.

Branwen spoke. 'I must leave. The battle is lost. The shrine will stand, but no blood should be spilled within it. You should leave too, Marisa Gentlehand.'

Gentlehand! A name given to Marisa by the Anthanic of the StormMarch. *Awtyni* in their tongue, *she of the gentle hand,* translated into Karisae by Branwen; who had never spoken in Marisa's presence, but now spoke Karisae in a soft husky voice without a mistake in syntax or pronunciation.

'Who are you?' Marisa asked.

Branwen smiled. 'I am … in your tongue … high priestess of this shrine. In my tongue I am *Amthisraf,* protector of the shrine.'

'But you're a servant.'

'How else could I remain close to the shrine when you Karisae claim it for your own?'

'You break your oath of silence.'

'I am no longer bound by it.' The smile left Branwen's face. 'We flee from this *vinraf,* this shrine-spring. No battle should be fought here. No blood should be spilled at this shrine.' Lifting her chin she whistled, a long low note, which was picked up and repeated by others inside and outside the white walls of the House. A note that echoed through the air and raised goose bumps upon Marisa's flesh.

Branwen placed the bowl of honey upon the ground and ripped the grey servant robes from her body, revealing tight Anthanic undergarments and blue tattoos that swirled across her arms and torso. 'May the Weaver grant that we meet again, Marisa, lady of the Isle of Storms.'

She reached out and touched the haraf stone dangling from Marisa's neck. 'This stone does not come from this shrine and you are not bound here by its resonance.'

Holding Marisa's gaze with calm strong eyes, she repeated, 'You are not bound here, Marisa Gentlehand,' and pointed at the walls of House of Falas and back to Marisa's haraf stone. 'This stone is not your stone.' Her gaze held Marisa's for a moment longer, then she turned and sprinted away into the woods.

Marisa stared after her. Outraged Karisae voices cried out as other Anthanic, men and women both, followed Branwen into the forest in a swirl of blue tattoos and discarded grey clothes.

The mournful whistle died away.

'Slow, sire!' A bellow from the bridge. 'Slow!'

Marisa turned in time to see the King's horse slip upon the stones of the bridge. Other horses plunged, trying to stop, rearing, falling, men leaping clear, at least one man thrown into the river with a splash.

Picking up her skirts, Marisa ran towards the accident.

****

Sunlight on his face woke Drustan. He groaned, opened his eyes, and lifted his right arm to cover them again. His head pounded while his stomach roiled. The empty wineskin lay flaccid on his stomach. He groaned again and wondered what in all the hells he had done last night. Memory smashed into his mind: the Vascanar! The battle. Erik. The Earl. Jerem. Running through the forest, the terror hot and blazing in his gut.

Her eyes upon him as he walked away from the shards of his sword, his honour broken upon a god-blessed anvil. He had fought the urge to look at Marisa, to see her one last time before he left forever; but here he was, back in this accursed land, fighting for a people that despised him.

His mouth twisted and he dropped his arm from his eyes; let the sun burn out the memory of her gaze. He squinted at the sun high in the sky. Gods, it must be nearly noon. Terror flared, her gaze disintegrated in the blood thrusting through his heart. The Vascanar would find him, take him, rend his flesh, pour fire into his eyes. Run. Flee! They were coming for him.

He tried to lunge upward. The sword belt tied around his left arm jerked him back to the branch. He scrabbled at the belt buckle, trying to free himself. Come free, come free damn you. The belt buckle caught at his thumb, pricked it; a slight pain but sudden, yanking him back to the reality of his situation.

What was he doing in a tree? Why had he tied himself to a branch? How in all the worlds had he managed to get so drunk last night that his mouth tasted like tar, and sweat prickled across his temples at the slightest movement? Had he lost his god-cursed mind?

He slumped back to the branch. A sturdy bough, thick and solid beneath his back, high up in the crown of an oak. His arm was tied to a smaller offshoot of the main branch. He blinked, remembered: *running through the dark, frenzied, a stabbing pain under his eye.* His fingers found the scabbed-over wound where a branch had stabbed him. He had clambered up this oak in the darkness, found this branch, tied himself to it, and drunk the wine — all of it — while toasting the dead to keep their ghosts away from him.

What was he doing? Was he trying to get himself killed? Slow, sure, that was the way. Had his mind broken? No. So, why did he feel such dread?

Time enough to find answers later; first he needed to get free of this damn belt.

With steady hands, he unthreaded the belt buckle and freed his arm. Erik's longsword dangled from the scabbard and Drustan grinned savagely. A debt of honour paid. And the Earl, too. A good day's duty done there, but only the gods knew why he had tied himself to this damn tree. If someone had climbed up during the night and found him…

No more. No need to let the fear unman him. Summer heat burned against his skin while he tried to think through the pounding pain of his hangover. This fear was not natural. The Vascanar were said to have dark powers; could they have sent a mist of terror out into the world to infect their enemies? A cowardly trick, cruel enough to delight them, but why hadn't they used it during the battle?

Drustan remembered the panicked pushing and shoving of the Karisae shieldwall when the Vascanar cavalry broke the line.

Maybe they had.

But why did he feel it now?

It had started when he was talking to that poor fool Jerem and drinking his wine. Drustan's gaze flickered over the wineskin. Wine poisoned with fear — was that even possible?

What did he know about magic? He was a warrior not a warlock. But the terror had flared when he drank the wine, had seethed as he toasted the dead, had almost caused him to let go of his honour and leave Jerem to his fate.

Enough!

He had treated Jerem with honour. He had given him the mercy stroke and recited the words. He was still Drustan desainCoid. If the wine was infected then there was none left to infect him anew. He was free of its taint. But what of the food?

Drustan unwrapped the bread and cheese, simple soldier's fare, battle food. He broke a small piece from the cheese, touched it against his tongue. Nothing. Placed it in his mouth. Nothing. Chewed, and terror burst upon his tongue, blazing up into his mind. Spitting out the cheese, he struggled with the thought: food and wine poisoned with fear. Why?

A second, more horrifying, thought: was the oathsworn sword infected with the same fear? To cast away the blade would bring Drustan to the attention of the gods and he did not wish to be their plaything. He touched the sword hilt. Nothing. He drew the blade clear of the scabbard. Nothing. He drew the blade across the back of his left hand, a shallow cut, hardly a scratch but drawing blood. Nothing.

Drustan breathed a sigh of relief; the sword was clean of the foul stinking edge of fear. He rested his forehead upon the cold metal of the blade. *Running, tearing through the forest, casting aside his honour, his courage, until the branch jabbed into his face.*

He touched the jagged wound in his cheek, remembered Marisa's tears when Erik's dishonourable attack had almost cost him his sight. She had loved him then, when she did not know what he was. He looked at his hand. He had raised this to her. He had not hit her, but gods how he had wanted to.

Lowering the hand, he sought distraction from his memories. What else had his fear cost him? He checked his belt. The belt-pouch stuffed full with loot still there with the longsword and the needle-pointed dagger, the arming cap stuffed into his belt; but the helm was gone, lost in the frenzied flight through the dark forest.

Damn it. He liked that helm.

He checked his hidden blades, the throwing daggers in their boot sheaths, the push-dagger tucked into his right vambrace and the thin-bladed stabbing dagger under the left. All there. Good.

Time to move.

He left the food, the empty wineskin, and the sack lying in the branches and clambered down the tree, testing each branch before he trusted his weight to it. Flickers of fear urged him to hurry, but he forced them away. He had to be quiet; the Vascanar would have advanced during the morning. The forest would be full of the rancid whoresons.

No birds sang in the trees. No squirrels or mice rustled in the undergrowth. The creatures of the land were in hiding. Drustan dropped from a low branch onto the soft loam and crouched, waiting, alert to any sound, any movement.

His stomach twisted with sudden nausea. On all fours, he vomited a cascade of dark red wine. Sweat stung his eyes and lay clammy on his skin despite the summer heat. He spat, feeling better without the debris of the night before clogging his stomach. Better find some water, drink his fill. Some *woriwert* would be nice, too.

Time to move. With a bit of luck the Vascanar patrols would have already caught some unfortunates. *Men screaming, feet in the flames, hot coals on their eyes, the sizzle, the stench, skin bleeding from a thousand cuts; men screaming.* Drustan closed his eyes and forced away the vision.

Quiet now, hold the fear inside and release it as anger; a gift learned in his foster father's hall before Earl Pelin desainLegan saved him from the torment. Drustan had never understood why his foster father, the scrub-poor noble Ufas desainSanac, despised him, but the lesson was well learned by the time Drustan had left for StormMarch Hall in his seventh summer: blind rage is less useful than cold anger and fear is no damn use at all.

Pelin had covered up Drustan's crime; murder was murder even if a seven-year-old boy had only wished to make the beatings stop.

Drustan moved through the forest on careful feet. The hangover ached behind his eyes and the memory of Ufas's bulging tongue itched. He had had no choice. *Making the noose, hiding it in the bushes on the edge of the drop, he'd only meant to snag the man's foot, to gain time to run away, but…* No! That was done. He was not that Drustan anymore. Anger was his guide, not fear.

Poor Jerem. The man had died thinking himself a coward, his courage broken by foul magic. May Henath of the dark cloak judge him clean of cowardice. Drustan rested his aching head on the cool earth.

Keep moving forward. All he could do. Gods, how Cullain would laugh to see him like this. Briefly, concern for his old comrade flickered through Drustan's mind, but then he smiled wryly. It would take more than a Vascanar army to kill that old bugger.

Drustan closed his eyes for a moment. Maybe he could find some mystic, some healer or witch, and get them to lift this curse of fear from him. *Marisa?* No, he never wanted to see her again. She had betrayed him. They had broken his sword because of her.

Be safe, Marisa, be far away from here. Drustan snarled in the forest. She was nothing to him, nothing. He needed to find Cullain, find a ship, get away from these damn islands. It had been a mistake to come back.

Voices approached through the woods, speaking the Maebazray trade tongue with thick accents. Drustan licked fear-dried lips.

'Ach, like rabbits they run.' A harsh guttural voice.

An Erisyan-accented voice drawled, 'Yes, they distinctly lack a sense of sport.'

'No sport if not one stand and fight.'

'Aye, so you said.' The Erisyan was very close now. He sounded distracted. Erisyan trackers could spot the traces of men no matter what precautions they took and Drustan had just stumbled through that clearing. He would be discovered, he would die, he would…

Drustan hardened his mind against the heated panic thrusting into his heart and allowed the cold, calculating beat of rage to pour through his veins.

How many were out there? Just these two? Were there others close enough to come to their aid? No matter; he meant to kill these men and he generally did what he intended. Slowly, carefully, without making a sound, he drew the shortsword, rose onto the balls of his feet, and crouched in the undergrowth.

His thigh muscles tightened, bunching for action. He waited, listening for any hint of other voices in the distance, watching for the shadow to fall across his hiding place.

He drew in a breath.

Shadow.

Drustan lunged through the foliage.

The Erisyan was in front of him, his broad back and shoulders hunched as he studied Drustan's tracks. The man only had time to look up and open his mouth to call a warning, but no more than that. The shortsword swung, the blade sliced off the top of his skull, and he fell, twitching.

'Made the old way. It'll cleave through an oak branch without damage.' Jerem's words sang in Drustan's mind.

The Vascanar, dressed in the chainmail hauberk of a horseman — but without the mail leggings since he was afoot — turned at the splatter of Erisyan blood upon the leaves.

'Let's have some sport,' Drustan said in Maebaz.

The Vascanar lifted his spear. It wove through the air, tracking Drustan's swaying movements.

'A Karisae that no flee,' the Vascanar said. 'Funny. Madman are you?'

'You speak the trade-tongue like a man who swallows other men's seed,' Drustan said.

The Vascanar bellowed and attacked. He was good, fast and strong. The spear gave him the advantage of greater reach. Drustan was not stupid enough to try to draw the longsword slung upon his back.

No matter. Drustan gutted him anyway, and watched him die in the dirt of Symcani.

Panting, holding back the fear with anger, Drustan looked at the two corpses. 'Welcome to the Shimmering Isles,' he said. No sound in the forest, nobody close. He pulled the waterskin and a travelling pack full of food from the Erisyan's corpse. The Vascanar were hardly likely to poison their lackeys with fear.

Swinging the pack over his shoulders, he glanced at the Erisyan's cloak. A muddy brown pattern that broke up the outline of the wearer, tightly woven to keep out the rain. Drustan reached around the man's ruined skull to undo the clasp. 'You should have stayed home, sell-bow.'

He scooped up the Vascanar's short spear, a fine weapon, and checked the Vascanar's helm, but it was too small to be worn over Drustan's chainmail coif and arming cap. The Erisyan didn't wear a helm.

Drustan cut a scrap of cloth from the Vascanar's cloak and thrust the shortsword through his belt; no sense in gumming up the scabbard with blood, brains, and hair, and there was no time to clean it now. He moved deeper into the forest before the men attracted by the Vascanar's bellow arrived.

CHAPTER 7

D rustan staggered to a halt and vomited green bile on the bank of a small stream. His throat felt raw, his stomach curdled, and his face was bathed in clammy sweat — but still he grinned. The fear nagged at the back of his mind, but he no longer paid it any attention. He knew it wasn't natural, that his courage hadn't broken, that his cold anger would quench the heated fear and allow him to function.

It was easy to feel anger at the Vascanar. This might no longer be his homeland, its people might have cast him out, but still he raged at its violation. There would be a reckoning. The people of these islands didn't deserve this fate. His bloodline was not their fault.

Drustan swilled the taste of bile out of his mouth with water from the stream and studied the trees around him as he cleaned the blade of the shortsword. He smiled: an alder entwined with a willow, just what the healer ordered. He cocked his head, listening: no sounds of pursuit, no voices in the forest. Not that he expected such, so deep into the woods. He was on the edge of the heart — what the Anthanic called the *Calodrig* — of the Dimas Forest. In these islands there were nine forests, nine Calodrig, nine places where the Karisae did not venture at night.

Dark tales were told of what the original natives of these islands did in the darkness of their forests, but Drustan didn't care about that. Once he passed over the stream and into its gloom, not even Erisyan trackers would be able to follow him. He studied the blade of the shortsword and slipped it back into its sheath.

Anthanic blood ran in his veins alongside that of his Karisae forefathers. He was a half-breed, born to an Anthanic mother by a Karisae father.

This was Marisa's betrayal: she had told a faithless friend what she had discovered in his blood before she even told him. *Lying in a field of wildflowers, her heartbeat close to his, her mouth upon his, her spirit touching his in the gift of a healer. The sunlight warm and soft upon them, laughing… She gasped, pulled away, looked at him, sadness in her gaze.* Drustan snarled and punched the earth.

He squatted there for long moments, fighting the urge to turn towards the House of Falas. She would be there; of course she would be there, she was a healer. But she had betrayed him and he never wanted to set eyes upon her again.

Unclenching his hand, brushing the loam from his knuckles, he drew a dagger from his boot and approached the entwined willow and alder. He dug amongst the roots. It took a little time but he found the woriwert.

Knobbly, wrinkled, dark brown beneath the dirt, the fungi smelled like baking bread. He washed some in the stream and ate it raw. The drunkard's best friend. It had many medicinal uses, but this was one of its finest. He drank his fill of water and refilled his waterskin from the stream. Always drink water from the stream where the woriwert is found — the herbalists said it increased its potency.

It didn't take long for his headache to fade and his stomach to settle. He ate a trail pie from the Erisyan pack: delicious crumbly pastry, solid lumps of pork within, glistening with jelly. The Erisyans knew how to feed themselves on campaign; as professional mercenaries they were always on campaign. Drustan grinned savagely: and now they would learn the folly of taking Vascanar gold.

Still three pies in the pack, wrapped up in muslin. He left them untouched despite his hunger. There would be no time to hunt for food until he entered the tangle of trees across the stream and was free of pursuit.

But there was no way to cross the stream at this point. The flowing water encouraged too much growth on the other bank; a solid wall of tightly packed trees, with brambles and shrubs blocking any spaces in between. He would have to find a break in the trees, an animal trail most likely, and then he would be safe.

At least from the Vascanar.

He slipped through the forest on quiet feet. Despite the summer heat, the Erisyan cloak proved its earth-coloured worth. When the hunting parties came too near, Drustan pulled it tight around himself and hid in the shadows. Still as a statue, he stood and watched scar-faced Vascanar and their broad-backed Erisyan hirelings stalk fleeing Karisae through the trees.

At those times the fear surged through him, but he contained it with anger. Not too much anger, though. The attack on the Erisyan archer and the Vascanar horseman had been reckless, foolhardy. If the Erisyan had been a little quicker, if the Vascanar had had the skill to back up his boasting, then Drustan would be walking the grass sward of the Sunlit Land after screaming his way into the afterlife.

No more reckless assaults. He was a sell-sword, not a Hundrin. Let the invaders do as they would; he just wanted to survive.

After hours of skulking through the trees, he saw a path leading into the Calodrig. He crept towards safety in careful silence. If he were the enemy, he would have stationed men here at an obvious crossroads.

The enemy were not fools.

The scent of burning flesh mixed with wood smoke. He could hear quiet chuckles and burbling moans. Gently, he parted the branches of a blackthorn and peered through the gap.

Nine invaders enjoying their work. Two Vascanar horsemen in chainmail and steel, with longswords at their belts and mugs of *kha* in their hands. Two Erisyan archers in leather and mud-coloured cloaks, with their warbows strung and ready in their hands. Two Vascanar infantrymen in courboille breastplates, with long-axes in their hands and shortswords at their belts. And three other infantrymen, naked to the waist and sweating — torture over a fire was warm work.

Four captives tied to a tree, with gags in their mouths and tears in their eyes, watching their comrade tortured to death in front of them. A man staked out on the ground, spread-eagled, naked, a bloody rag in his mouth, thrashing and moaning as large stones, heated in the fire, were dropped into the torn-open bowl of his stomach. The Vascanar chuckled and the Erisyan archers turned away to scan the forest.

Drustan sneered at the Erisyan hypocrisy; if you don't like the sight of torture then you shouldn't take Vascanar gold.

But nine were too many. There was no point in him dying here too and nobody could take nine armed warriors in open combat, but he would remember the faces of the captives. He would remember them and use the rage if ever he felt pity for a Vascanar or an Erisyan.

Four poor fools tied to a tree. He studied their faces and recognised the water-boy he had scared with talk of murder. Twelve summers old, tied to a tree with a gag in his mouth, watching a man die in agony and shame at his feet.

Drustan closed his eyes for a moment. He should leave, skulk away through the forest, find another path, and leave the prisoners to die.

But the boy?

He couldn't leave a child to face that fate. There really was no choice. Not if he wanted to remain himself. He opened his eyes again and surveyed the terrain.

The spread-eagled man died as one of the horsemen refilled his mug from the kha pot heating upon the fire beside the stones heating for the next victim. The other chainmail-clad horseman pointed at one of the captives as the corpse was cut free and dragged away.

Drustan tensed to attack. Now would be the time, when the Vascanar were busy. But one of the Erisyans turned back to face the fire, guarding the clearing as his comrade guarded the other approaches. Damn Erisyans; too skilled and experienced, may the Weaver blight your dreams.

He would have to do this the hard way, then.

In utter silence, he made his preparations. He drew the shortsword and stabbed it into the earth in front of him. Removed the cloak and laid it to one side. Pulled the cross-belt over his head and stopped, waiting.

He would need a distraction to draw the longsword, and the newly chosen victim provided it. A big man, tall and powerful — even Cullain would have had trouble with him on the sand of a wrestling match — struggled and fought against the Vascanar. He almost broke free, but one of the horsemen drove a mail-gloved fist into his stomach and face until he quieted.

As they struggled, Drustan drew the longsword and thrust it into the earth beside the shortsword. Sliding a throwing dagger from his boot, he laid it on the ground next to the spear. He had to take care of the archers first, if he was to have any chance of saving the boy.

The Vascanar tied the big captive to the ground.

Drustan pulled the arming cap over his head and tied the straps under his chin.

One of the torturers lifted a blade from the fire. Another pulled the gag from the captive's mouth. The prisoner immediately spat into the Vascanar's face, but he could not stop his tongue from being gripped by serrated tongs. The Vascanar laughed.

Drustan slid the coif over his head and pulled the aventail across his mouth, attaching the flap of chainmail to the hook set in the side of the coif.

The big captive jerked as the heated blade sliced through his tongue, but he didn't cry out. Stalwart man, Drustan thought as he picked up the spear and the dagger, rolled his shoulders, stretched his neck, and closed his eyes.

'No need tongue to call lords.' A guttural Vascanar voice. The others laughed. The sizzle of meat thrown into the flames.

Drustan breathed deeply. The stink of iron from the chainmail covering his nose helped him reach into the place where his centre waited. Let the fight dictate the moves. Do not plan, simply act. Do not think, simply be. Let the fight dictate the moves. He opened his eyes, lifted the spear in his right hand and the throwing dagger in his left.

The Erisyan had turned back to scanning the forest with his comrade. The Vascanar were all focused on the spread-eagled man upon the ground, a bloody rag in his mouth.

Drustan stood and launched the spear with a surge of practised muscle. It pierced the back of the more distant Erisyan. Drustan switched the dagger from his left hand to his right and threw it in one smooth motion. The other archer ducked, turned, dropped, and the dagger flew away into the trees.

Gods, he was fast.

No matter. Drustan was committed to the fight. He grabbed up his swords and leapt into the clearing.

The nearest horseman fell to a straight thrust through the bowels with the longsword, which pierced the chainmail with ease. The shortsword deflected an overhead axe-stroke from one of the infantrymen. Drustan ripped the longsword free of the dying horseman's guts and swept it around to hack through the axeman's hamstrings. The man fell screaming.

Then Drustan was moving, spinning, blocking, and parrying. His two swords sweeping, cutting, and stabbing. Trying to keep the Vascanar between him and the archer. Keeping them off-balance, disorganised, ineffective as he worked his way towards the captives.

Sometimes his swords moved as one in sweeping blocks. Other times they flashed in independent cuts and stabs. His wrists knew the work and his feet knew the steps. He took one of the half-naked torturers out of the conflict with a slashing cut that ripped through the man's liver and kidney.

But Drustan took wounds also. Nothing major, nothing debilitating, but all bleeding and weakening him. Unfortunately, the enemy were trained soldiers, too.

'Down,' yelled the Erisyan in Maebaz.

The Vascanar dropped.

Drustan dropped too, taking the opportunity to bury the longsword into a man's back. The Vascanar unexpectedly twisted as he died and tore the sword from Drustan's grasp. Drustan cursed but let it go, hitting the ground and instantly rolling away. An arrow buried itself in the soil less than a handbreadth from his face.

He reared up on his knees. The needle-pointed dagger flowed out from behind his back in a flat spinning throw.

The Erisyan, with another arrow already at full draw, could not dodge the thrown dagger, but he twisted his shoulder in front of his throat. The dagger buried itself into his flesh, but it didn't kill him.

Drustan lunged to his feet. The shortsword swept across to cut a throat. He barely managed to bring it back into line in time to block an axe swinging at his face.

Gasping, backing up for a moment, he came on guard and eyed his three remaining opponents who, like him, were catching their breath after the frenzied first moments of the fight.

The archer had discarded his bow and drawn his syrthae blade. Nasty bloody weapon, that. Cut your hand off at the wrist and barely slow in the cut. The archer hardly seemed to notice the dagger buried in his shoulder.

Tough whoreson.

The remaining Vascanar horseman had let the infantry do the dying, while he had danced around trying to get behind Drustan.

Clever whoreson.

The half-naked torturer, his heated dagger replaced with a long-handled axe, dripped blood from a diagonal sword wound across his chest and stomach. Drustan had been unbalanced and over-extended so the stroke had failed to end the torturer's miserable life.

Lucky whoreson.

Drustan glanced at his longsword quivering upright in a dead man's back.

Now.

He slashed at the torturer, driving him into the horseman, spun, kicked dirt up towards the Erisyan's face, dived into a roll, came to his feet, reached for the longsword—

A tremendous blow to his side. Drustan gasped, somehow managed to block the Erisyan's murderously fast swipe at his head, and fell to his knees.

The syrthae blade rose.

With the last of his strength, Dustan threw the shortsword towards the captives. A weak throw, not quite strong enough to reach their feet.

'No!' the Vascanar horseman yelled. 'No kill!'

The Erisyan stopped the stroke, barely looked at Drustan, and strode across the clearing to the corpse of his clansman.

'You die slow,' the Vascanar said.

Drustan touched the axe buried in his left side. It had cut through the armour under the arm and on into his body. Where had that come from? He looked up, saw the man he had hamstrung in the first moments of the fight, propped against a tree, cursing him in some strange sing-song language.

Oh. Him. He'd forgotten about him in all the excitement.

Drustan's head dropped forward onto his chest but something, some stubbornness deep within his soul, called to him, pushed at him, forced him to raise it again. He could see the boy dangling from the tree, the look of awe in that young face — but he had failed. The boy would die horribly, and there was nothing Drustan could do.

But still, the stubborn need drove him to lift his hand despite the pain, to unclip the chainmail across his face, to push back the coif, to rip away the arming cap, to look the Vascanar in the eye, to sneer.

Let the whoreson see who had almost killed him.

The sound of a boy laughing, and a spider scuttled away into the gloom of the trees.

CHAPTER 8

The Karisae didn't deserve what was about to happen to him, but Jarl found himself disinclined to care. The man had killed Sekem.

Jarl left the dagger in his shoulder and walked across the clearing. Only the bursting pain of his cousin's agony had warned him about the dagger thrown at his back; the second dagger had flown too fast, but at least he'd managed to avoid it lodging in his throat.

Morakis, a Vascanar horseman dressed in chainmail, levelled his blade at the Karisae's face.

Gods, the Karisae had fought well, but what kind of idiot thought he could take on nine armed men in open combat? Still, he'd come pretty close, Jarl had to give him that. Only three men left standing.

The Karisae lifted his head to sneer at Morakis and Jarl recognised him.

The same scar cutting diagonally from above his right eye, across the bridge of his nose and into his left cheek. The same intensity of gaze in those grey eyes, where pain now mollified the arrogance. The same dark hair, but long and unruly, no longer bound up in the complicated braids of a Karisae noble, simply hacked off where it fell into the eyes. The clothing cheaper, simple leather where once he had worn steel chainmail.

But it was him, Drustan desainCoid, and a debt was owed.

They'd met on the mainland. Jarl, a mercenary, employed by a minor lordling competing for land and loot amongst the debris of a fallen empire, in a private contract outside the boundaries of caedi — simple finance. Drustan, a noble, fighting for his king in a battle to take that same land for the throne, in a matter of loyalty to a grasping monarch — simple honour.

Jarl was captured in a skirmish at a place called Forasin Hill, along with thirty other assorted mercenaries and soldiers, and found himself at the mercy of Drustan. Given direct orders to put the prisoners to the sword, Drustan instead freed them in return for their paroles. Was that why he now wore the clothing of a sell-sword? Had that act of decency cost him so much?

Jarl had kept his parole and returned home to his wife and children, but his adherence to his word didn't wipe out the debt. Repaying it, however, was going to take some duplicity and more than a touch of luck.

He sheathed his syrthae blade and sauntered across the clearing. *Don't look at me.* He sent the thought skidding towards the Vascanar. *I'm just a mercenary. Keep your eyes on the man who almost killed you.*

Morakis taunted Drustan. 'I take eyes first, sow, no, I take ears. One ear, one eye, sow. So you see and hear screams that you make, sow.'

'Pig.' Drustan pushed the word through the pain.

Jarl glanced at the crippled Vascanar lying against the tree. The man wept into his hands. It was doubtful that the Vascanar cared for their wounded.

Morakis asked, 'What you say?' and kept his gaze fixed upon the man who had wiped out most of his small command. The other Vascanar soldier, stripped to the waist and glistening with sweat, kept his gaze fixed upon Morakis.

Jarl picked up Drustan's longsword. A good blade.

'Pig.' Drustan gritted out the words. 'Sow means lady pig. You must…' he breathed heavily for a moment, '…you must have noticed. Or are you not … fussy … about … about your bed-mates?'

The boy tied to the tree sneaked a peek at Jarl and smiled past the gag. Jarl grinned and bowed slightly in return. The shortsword Drustan had thrown was mysteriously missing, no doubt hidden behind somebody's back ready to cut the bindings. Jarl could feel the anticipation from here, even through the pain of the tongueless man staked to the ground.

But saving Drustan still fell to him. Only he could get close enough to do something before the Vascanar cut his throat.

Morakis took a little while to translate Drustan's accented Maebaz and then a little while longer to figure out what he meant.

Drustan helped him out. 'Pig-lover.'

Morakis's sword stopped a hairsbreadth from Drustan's neck. 'You no die so easy, pig.'

Drustan spat on Morakis's boots. 'You're not my type.'

Jarl glanced at the spittle. No blood. That was good. He gestured to the half-naked Vascanar torturer. 'Do me a favour, friend. Pull out this accursed dagger.'

The soldier looked to Morakis, who nodded dismissively.

'First cut that.' Morakis pointed at Drustan's crotch with the tip of his sword. 'Make you sow, yes.'

Drustan grinned, cold anger in his eyes. 'Do you intend … intend to … talk me to death, pig-lover?'

Jarl helpfully turned his shoulder towards the torturer so that the man could get a good grip on the dagger with one hand, placing the other on Jarl's bicep. Jarl held Drustan's longsword close into his body. The man pulled sharply. The dagger slid free. Jarl pirouetted and the tip of the longsword cut the man's throat. Morakis started to turn.

Too late.

Jarl stabbed him through the back, pushing the longsword through the chainmail and twisting it in Morakis's heart. Morakis managed to turn his head to stare at Jarl in disbelief. Jarl yanked the sword free. A gout of blood followed the blade from Morakis's body.

The crippled Vascanar lying against the tree screamed for help.

Jarl looked down at the torturer with the cut throat, the man's hands covered in blood as he tried to stem the flow. For a moment, Jarl considered leaving the man to drown in that blood, but he was not Vascanar, he was not a beast who delighted in the suffering of other men, so he plunged the longsword down into the dying man's heart and left it quivering upright in the corpse.

He bent, plucked Drustan's dagger from the ground and walked across the clearing to the crippled Vascanar still screaming for help. Jarl grabbed the man's jaw, forced the head to one side, exposed the back of the skull.

'Traitor,' the man spat through Jarl's controlling hand.

'Define your terms.' Jarl used the mercy thrust to kill the injured man and made the sign of infinity over the corpse, warding the ghost away from his dreams.

Not much time left. Those screams would have alerted any Vascanar within half a mile of this place — even through the trees. Jarl hastened to Drustan's side.

Drustan lifted his head and asked, 'Why?'

'Forasin Hill.'

'Oh, that.' Drustan slumped into unconsciousness.

Jarl checked the pulse in Drustan's neck. Rapid, faint, not good. The boy and the two Karisae soldiers had cut themselves free of their bonds.

'Release him, boy.' Jarl pointed to the spread-eagled man moaning in the dirt. Poor sod, the stub of his tongue would be swollen, blistered, and agonising. He might not survive, because he might not be able to eat for days, maybe even weeks. Jarl shrugged; not his problem. 'You other two watch the path. Sing out if you hear somebody coming. Collect some weapons.'

'Why are you doing this, sell-bow?' the taller of the two men asked in excellent Maebaz.

'When Drustan desainCoid awakes, tell him I consider the debt repaid.'

'I saw him fight a duel once,' the man said. 'Will he live?'

'How should I know? I'm not a healer,' Jarl snapped. 'Go on. We don't have long.'

'I am named Garet Wiseye.'

'And I named Efan,' the other man said in barely comprehensible Maebaz.

Jarl studied the axe embedded in Drustan's side. A fearsome wound and what if it had broken the ribs? The men still stood there. 'Go, take up guard,' Jarl ordered.

'What's your name, stranger?' insisted Garet.

Jarl laughed. 'You think I'll tell you that, so you can scream it from some Vascanar fire? Go, act like soldiers for once. This isn't some city tavern.'

Efan nodded and grabbed Garet's arm. They left Jarl to his doctoring.

If the axe had broken the ribs, Drustan would most likely die, but no blood in his spittle meant his lungs were intact. Jarl reached towards

Drustan's belt-pouch to check for medicinal herbs. A caress of liquid fear stopped his hand.

What was in there?

He didn't have time to investigate that flare of terror. He shivered at the thought of it. No, absolutely no time to go digging into some sort of mystical horror. A shame that.

The newly mute Karisae and the boy approached. The mute held out a handful of fungi. Worthyward.

'Tirac found some woriwert.' The boy gestured to the mute. 'He thinks it might be useful.'

'Worthyward,' Jarl said. 'It's called worthyward.'

'Not here it ain't,' the boy replied.

'Where'd he find it?'

'In the sack beside the cloak.' The boy pointed.

Jarl recognised an Erisyan cloak. So Drustan had killed another of the caedi this day. Jarl closed his eyes. Debts must be paid, whatever the cost in guilt. 'Do you know of daggerbind?' he asked the boy. 'A plant, long leaves, shaped like a crooked dagger.'

'Dagabin.'

'Find as much of it as you can. Go. Not you,' Jarl snapped at Tirac. How was the man even standing? He should be writhing on the ground in agony. These Karisae wouldn't be easy foes to best. 'Find me bandages. Clean bandages. Get me that kha pot from the fire and two beakers. Fetch me some water, use the waterskin beside the pack.' An Erisyan waterskin, woven with brass thread through the weave and magicked to keep the water clean of taint. Who else had Drustan killed out there in the forest? Jarl looked at Sekem's body. *I'm sorry, cousin, I cannot avenge your death.*

Jarl studied Drustan's armour. He undid the straps and pulled the chainmail mantle over the man's head. Mercenary garb; better than a common soldier, but not as good as a noble's. The leather underneath was well made, strong, not as rough as it looked at first glance.

He rapped it with his knuckles; hot wax hardened, double thickness of leather, doubled again over the shoulders. No sleeves, but the chainmail would have draped over the shoulders and leather strips studded with iron swung over the upper arms. Heavy leather vambraces with steel inserts protected the forearms, and similar greaves the shins.

Jarl looked across at Efan and Garet, and spotted Sekem's bow in Efan's hands. He laughed. 'Let's see you draw that,' he challenged.

Efan tried and failed to get the string back far enough for the limbs of the bow to uncoil and relax the pressure on his back and shoulders.

'We train from childhood, Karisae. None can draw an Erisyan warbow but one born to it.' Jarl shook his head and waited for the boy and the mute to return. This was all taking far too long. Why hadn't the Vascanar arrived yet?

It seemed a shame to blunt Drustan's blade on Drustan's armour. Jarl tossed the dagger aside, yanked a broad-bladed knife from Morakis's belt, and set to work cutting away the leather. A shame, too, to ruin such good armour, but it could hardly be pulled over the man's head. The thrown axe had ripped through the rawhide laces up the side and pierced the overlapping layers of leather, so Jarl had to cut around it. It was heavy going.

Where were the Vascanar?

Tirac placed the steaming pot of kha and the two beakers on the ground beside Jarl, then helped him cut through the four-ply thickness of the leather across Drustan's shoulders. The big man ripped the armour away from Drustan's body, nodded to Jarl, and left to find something to use as bandages.

The padded linen arming jacket under the leather was easier to cut. Drustan had an impressive number of scars across his torso.

Mostly in the front.

Jarl tested the axe. A slight tug on the handle. Drustan moaned and shifted. Jarl took his hand away. The axe had moved freely, so it wasn't imbedded in bone. Not a massive surprise; Drustan was built like an ox. His muscle had taken the impact. He might yet live.

Jarl called to Garet. 'Anything?'

Garet shook his head.

Tirac returned with a Vascanar tabard cut into strips.

'I said clean bandages.'

Tirac raised his hands and shrugged.

'Nothing else?'

Tirac shook his head.

'Then they'll have to do. Lay them over that tree.'

The boy arrived with armfuls of daggerbind.

'That's rather a lot,' Jarl said.

'Found me a nice clump. And some of this.' The boy threw some wild garlic at Jarl's feet. 'Saw a wise-woman use that on a cut, once.'

'Good boy,' Jarl said.

'The name's Agus.'

Jarl chuckled. 'Like the god.'

Agus shrugged.

'Very well, godly one, twist the daggerbind in your hands, make sure you crush as many of the stems as you can.' Jarl mashed the worthyward into one of the leather beakers. He used the hilt of his blade as a pestle, but poured some kha over it first. Slicing the garlic roughly, adding it to the mix, grinding it all to a paste, pouring kha over the top and stirring. He tasted the brew, retched, shuddered, and spat it out. 'Just right.' He drank some water to try to clear the taste. 'Now for the hard bit.' He glanced at Tirac. 'Hold him.'

The mute gripped Drustan's shoulders.

Jarl pulled the axe free of the wound. In the moment before the blood obscured his view, he saw the white of unbroken ribs. To the bone but not through the bone: good. He let the blood flow for a while to help cleanse the injury, and then washed away the blood and the shreds of linen and leather with clean water. Before the wound could refill with blood, Jarl poured in the last of the kha. Even unconscious, Drustan jerked at the heat of the cleansing fluid.

'Hold him still,' Jarl grunted as he packed the garlic and worthyward paste into the wound. He rubbed a small portion of the paste over the dagger cut in his own shoulder.

It smarted a bit.

'Come here, Agus,' Jarl hissed through the pain of the healing paste. 'I'll hold Drustan's wound closed. You'll rub the sap of the dagger … dagabin across the edges. Do you understand?'

'I ain't simple.'

'Good to know.'

The daggerbind sap glued the edges of the wound, locking the cleaning goodness of the garlic and worthyward within, clotting the blood almost instantly but taking time to set and bind the flesh. Jarl held the edges together and glanced across at Efan — who had dropped the bow and picked up a Vascanar long-handled axe.

'Anything?' Jarl called.

Efan shook his head.

The Vascanar were taking a long time to investigate what had happened here, thanks be to the gods.

Agus started to collect together Drustan's equipment. Tirac dressed the minor wounds on Drustan's arms and legs with the last of the paste and some of the bandages.

The daggerbind sap became tacky and the flesh held when Jarl released it. Good enough. He placed a large clump of daggerbind leaves over the wound to help it seal and then carefully wrapped the rest of the not-very-clean bandages around Drustan's torso, knotting them together as he did so. Tirac lifted the unconscious man, taking great care not to break the hold of the sap.

Jarl studied the expertly treated minor cuts for a moment and said, 'You know your way around wounds.'

Tirac shrugged.

'He needs a healer,' Jarl said. 'I've done all I can, but without a healer he'll be crippled on that side for life.'

Tirac nodded to show his understanding. A little blood dribbled out of his ruined mouth.

Jarl reached out a hand. 'Let's look at that mou—'

'Someone comes,' Garet hissed.

Tirac grabbed Drustan and hoisted him up over his shoulder.

'Be careful of his wound,' Jarl said.

Tirac gripped Jarl's hand and looked him in the eye. Jarl found himself gazing into dark hazel eyes with flecks of green in the iris; startling eyes, with a depth behind them that spoke of pain immeasurable. *I remember.* The thought absolutely clear in Tirac's mind; Jarl could not doubt its meaning: *I will not forget what you have done here, archer. I owe you a debt, and I will repay it when I can.* The moment passed and Tirac nodded once, firmly, then strode away into the forest with the boy Agus, who carried Drustan's equipment and the sack of food bundled up in the Erisyan cloak.

Efan and Garet clasped hands with Jarl as they passed. 'We remember,' they said and disappeared into the forest.

Jarl had just managed to finish arranging the scene when Torquesten arrived with a full company of men and his spellhounds.

Which were not hounds, but men, scampering around on hands and feet, naked and slimed with filth, bound by magic to think that they were dogs. A magic that gave them the ability to track spell-casters and spells even as it broke their minds.

Why had the Vascanar released the spellhounds?

Jarl remembered the liquid fear in Drustan's belt-pouch and decided not to wonder why the Master of the Hounds was out here in the forest with spellhounds snapping at his heels.

CHAPTER 9

Jarl stood before Torquesten as the spellhounds scampered around the clearing and howled. They'd found some scent. Their broken thoughts yapped away in Jarl's mind, so he closed them out, leaving their shattered memories outside his awareness. How could Gorak have signed on with a people who would do this to another human being?

One of the spellhounds had a shade of skin Jarl had never seen before, almost yellow in its complexion. How far had that poor sod travelled to end up naked and howling?

'Tell again, why they no kill you?' Torquesten demanded.

Jarl sighed. Torquesten had already shown that he could speak perfectly good Maebaz, so why pretend otherwise? Oh let the sod play his games; Jarl would play his own. 'I fell down that slope over there. By the time I'd clambered back up, the fight was over.' Jarl shrugged. 'I didn't feel like dying so I kept my head down.'

'Three, you talk of three.' Torquesten studied the ground. As if this idiot could read sign. 'Three scum kill seven?'

'Eight.' Jarl gestured to Sekem's body.

Torquesten ignored that. 'Blood here.' He picked up the scraps of daggerbind and wild garlic leaves. 'Bad wound?'

'Your men injured one of the attackers. Mortally I'd say, but they took him away anyway.'

'You stink of garlic.'

Jarl pointed at the wound in his shoulder. 'Got to keep it clean. Infections are nasty.'

Gorak arrived, summoned by Torquesten. Now things would get interesting.

'What happened here?' Gorak asked Jarl in Erisyan.

'Nice of you to come, my hwlman,' Jarl replied in the same language.

'Talk trade,' Torquesten snapped.

'What happened here?' Gorak repeated in Maebaz.

'You tell,' Torquesten said. 'No look at him. You read ground, tell truth.'

There was no chance this side of the ice that Gorak would be taken in by Jarl's hasty scene-setting.

Gorak studied the ground. It was said he could read the tracks of fish in the sea. He scanned back and forth across the clearing, absorbed in his task, kicking the spellhounds out of his way, averting his gaze from the brutalised corpse of the Karisae tortured to death before Drustan's intervention.

Jarl had laid Sekem's body out the Erisyan way, using his cousin's bowstring to tie his hands together as if in prayer: fingers entwined except for the two index fingers pointing to the sky. His bow, which lay next to the body, curled into a horseshoe shape as the reflex relaxed without the string to pull it straight. It would be returned to his family, but the string would lead Sekem to the Summerland.

Gorak kissed Sekem's cooling forehead and stood up to address Torquesten. 'Three men. They came through there.' He pointed at the gap in the trees. 'One, a master swordsman; the other two, barely competent. They killed your men and slaughtered the injured man there.' Gorak smiled viciously. 'I don't think they like you very much. The swordmaster was badly injured. They tended to him. Then they took him away into the forest with the freed captives.' Gorak looked Torquesten in the eyes as he lied to his face, then shifted his gaze to Jarl. 'You were lucky.'

'The Weaver kissed me with good fortune.' Jarl bowed to hide the fact that he didn't make the full double circle of infinity; he really didn't need the spider of fate upset at him for lying in her name.

'Indeed,' Gorak said.

'You sure this?' Torquesten asked.

'I'm Gorak,' Gorak said in a tone that brooked no dispute. 'Why have you brought spellhounds into the forest?'

'That is none of your concern.' Torquesten's accent slipped yet again as he spoke.

****

Dread flared across Drustan's soul, burning him, branding him, melting his courage. The pain from the wound in his side, cold, frozen, gave him something to grasp and he clung to it in the blazing terror, using it to keep his soul intact in the flames.

Cool air against his face. In the cavern of his mind he crawled upwards. Not far now. The heated fear tried to haul him back. He pushed higher, into the light, opening his eyes, and became Drustan once more.

For a moment, his physical environment echoed the spiritual plane he had fled. He could not move. His arms held, his legs held. A steady rhythmic movement jerked at his wound in brief flares of pain. He wanted to scratch, but could not move. What was this?

All he could see was ground, muddy ground, tightly bounded by trees. An animal track? He twisted his head. A broad back against his cheek. Somebody carried him. Who? Cullain? No, the legs were too long, the shoulder under his stomach too narrow — still broad, but not the shelf of muscle and bone that defined Cullain's mighty form. Who then? Who carried him?

A big man staked to the ground, fighting his tormenters, losing his tongue… His memory coiled into the fight. He'd won the fight, hadn't he? *Reaching for the sword, standing still for a moment, making himself a target.* Stupid, stupid, almost as stupid as charging into that clearing in the first place. Where was Cullain when you needed him?

The boy? Had he saved the boy? Was it worth it? What—

The water-boy's face smiled up at him. 'You should sleep, Bright Blade,' he said.

'What happened?' Drustan asked.

'You saved us. You were magnificent. Now sleep.'

Drustan slept and terror flooded his dreams.

****

'What happened?' Gorak asked.

Jarl picked a likely branch and drew his syrthae, as much a tool as a weapon. With several solid cuts he severed the hazel branch from the tree and then, taking a firm grip and stance, tugged it free of foliage. He knelt and stripped away the leaves with sweeping slashes, before he measured by eye and cut two sections from the denuded branch.

Handing one piece to Gorak, he wiped the blade of his syrthae, sheathed it, and drew a strong bladed *geithae* dagger from his boot.

'What happened, Jarl?' Gorak repeated as he drew his own geithae blade. The blades of the daggers followed the same pattern as the syrthae swords, but they were kept a great deal sharper, for they had to carve wood.

Jarl trimmed the rough edges away from the piece of hazel. He studied it carefully. A handsbreadth in length and half that in diameter, with the bark still on the wood. No flaws that he could see. He kissed it gently and began to carve out the bowl of the *geidin* cup, pressing down hard and twisting his wrist to gouge out the beginning of the shape.

'Why did you help the man that killed Sekem?' Gorak looked about as he spoke, no doubt to check that none loitered near.

Jarl realised that Gorak no longer trusted his own caedi; the Vascanar were not a people but a cult and even Erisyans could fall victim to it. He remembered the demon's voice in his mind, the feeling of power it had given him until he cast away the offer.

'I told Sekem's mother I'd look after him.' Jarl didn't lift his gaze from his work. 'Told her I'd bring him back if I could. Now all I'll carry back will be a sack of ashes, two lumps of melted gold, and an unstrung bow.'

'Aye,' Gorak said. ''Tis always foolish to make promises to the women. I promised your mother the same fourteen winters ago. I kept my promise: here you stand. But you'll no longer look me in the eye, Jarl Bearclaw.'

Jarl lifted his gaze from the wood as his hands continued the familiar work. 'It'll be dark soon. The fire will be lit and his soul will find its way to the Summerland.'

'What happened, Jarl?'

Jarl sighed, rubbed at his eye with the heel of the hand holding the unfinished carving. 'I told you the tale of Forasin Hill?'

'Aye you did; you were lucky there.' Gorak nodded as he comprehended Jarl's meaning. 'Ah. The debt's repaid.'

'That it is.' Jarl looked his uncle in the eyes and saw the fear and despair in Gorak's soul. He could taste the guilt behind that fear. Gorak still didn't know what he'd done, but he knew he'd made a mistake.

'Why did you make this pact with demon-worshippers?' Jarl asked.

'Our caedi was failing, other caedis taking all the lucrative posts, the garrison posts, the wars upon the lakes. We were out in the cold, nephew. We needed…' Gorak's mind caught up with his ears. 'Demon-worshippers?'

'Aye, Gorak Whitefox,' Jarl said. 'Those things that float above the Vascanar torture pits aren't gods. You've linked our fate to that of demons.'

Gorak dropped the half-finished geidin cup and the geithae blade. He took a step back from the accusation in Jarl's eyes. 'I didn't know.'

'You should've known, uncle.' Jarl turned away. 'You should've had me there at the negotiations, but you chose to send me to meet with the Morfan Caedi instead.'

'I needed to know their intent.'

'More than the intent of our new employers?' Jarl shook his head, looked down at the wood, closed his eyes for a moment, then opened them and began to carve again. 'We're stuck here now. Fighting an oath-sworn war 'til the first snowflake falls. Isn't that the oath?'

'Yes.' Gorak seemed barely able to keep his feet.

'It's high summer, Gorak. It'll be a long time before the snows fall in this place.'

'Oh dear gods above and below.'

'Even the gods will turn their backs on us if the Vascanar have their way.' The blade of the knife slipped and Jarl hissed as it sliced open his thumb.

'Are you sure they're demons?'

Jarl sucked at the cut. 'I looked into the eyes of a demon and threw confusion into its soul. Else it would've eaten mine. I saw what they want here.'

'Here?' Gorak pulled at his hair. 'What do they want here?'

Jarl stepped forward and grabbed Gorak's hand, pulling it away from his hair. His blood smeared across Gorak's face. 'Calm, uncle, calm. You can't throw your mind away now. Your caedi needs you, tracker of fish.'

'I—' Gorak breathed deeply. 'The Vascanar fight in many wars, many places. They conquer, ravage, and move on. They never stay. Blood-mad nomads. All they want is blood.'

'These are the Shimmering Islands, uncle. There's power here. Power enough to make demons into gods.'

'And we're oath-bound to them.' Gorak bent to pick up his dagger and the lump of hazel wood he was carving into a cup to honour his dead kinsman.

'Until the first snowflake falls.'

Gorak straightened. 'We'll be cast out for this.'

'Most likely,' Jarl said. 'We've to burn my cousin's body this night and hope the *Geidiw* allow him passage into the Summerland. He was lucky to die so soon. We may not have that chance when our turn comes. Not after we've fought to make demons into gods.'

CHAPTER 10

D rustan drowns in fear. His spirit gasps inside the wall of sound —
the sound of men screaming, of women, of children, crying
out in agony. He can't live through this. He has nothing to
stand on, nothing to hold him above the phantoms of his past.

A Vascanar begs for water. Drustan stabs him in the throat. The
image changes: Jerem's face, etched with piteous fear; the archer, with
the top of his head sliced off; the Vascanar, his entrails spilling onto
the ground.

They crawl towards Drustan. On they come, so many ghosts. Why
are there women among them? Children?

We are the children unborn, the women unloved, the chains of your
savagery.

Drustan shakes his head. Words will not come, his lips sealed by
flames of hatred and anger. A tripled-eyed creature slathers its way
through the smoke, dragging Drustan's ghosts behind it. *You will die a*
thousand times, the creature intones. *You will die a thousand deaths.*

Drustan looks into those triple eyes and quails. His whole world
crashes in upon him. He sees his birth. Sees his childhood, his first
kill, Marisa weeping, his disgrace, war, death, pestilence, famine. He
breathes in the stench, feels the wounds anew, suffers the fear. Marisa's
hair a fan of gold in a puddle of blood.

But there is a problem. Drustan doesn't deal with fear very well.

His slumbering rage grows ice-cold and sharp. The sneer returns to
suddenly mobile lips. 'You first,' he says to the creature.

Like an axe cutting through wood, the scenery changes. The smoke
dissipates, replaced by cool breezes and the smell of flowers.

'Trickster,' Drustan calls into the flower-scented air.

'I thought you gone.' A woman's voice. 'But you are strong — like
your father.'

Drustan jerks his head away from her touch. 'Who are you?'

'I am your mother. You may call me Eirane.'

'My mother died.'

'No, I simply changed. After they took you from me. After they came in the night and ripped you from my arms. After I had slapped your Karisae father and bade him leave. Yet after his leaving, I was bereft. His love was so strong. Is not that funny? He loved me, a pure-born Anthanic. That is why they took you away from us and broke us apart like—'

'Anthanic witch,' Drustan snaps.

'Not then. Then I was simply a girl. But after I lost all, I went into the forest, into that forest's Calodrig. And I gave myself to it. Body and soul. Then I became Amthisrid, a spirit on the breeze, between the trees. Guardian of that forest. This is our land.'

'You left me,' Drustan says. 'When I found out who I was, I looked for you.'

'I could not come to you with those braids in your hair. With that iron on your back. I could not come to you then.'

'And now?'

'You are in a Calodrig. It is not my forest, nor my Calodrig. Another is steward here, not I. But all forests are connected across the isles. I come because of what you carry.'

'What I carry?'

'It is important. It fell into your hands by the touch of Fate. An amulet that is tied to the demon-gods of the Vascanar. Games are being played here, my son.'

'I'm injured. I am dying.'

'I will bring you aid. She will come.'

Another fear crashes through Drustan's mind. A fear that does not empty his bowels, but simply tears open his heart anew. 'No,' he pleads. 'Not her.'

'I will protect you until she comes. Call her.'

'No.'

'Call out her name.'

'I won't.'

His mind unburdens itself across the field of wild flowers, the meadow of their first caressing touch. She is within him, touching his soul. They are together. She knows all about him, sees all that he is.

As he sees all of her.

Broken children on a field of bladed grass.

Love is the swordbreaker.

She is gone.

'MARISA!' Drustan cries into the scent of flowers.

'She will come,' Eirane says.

There's a presence behind his mother as she fades away into the trees and the wind. A shadow. 'Don't believe everything she said,' the shadow says. 'She means no harm, but she does not know all that is in play — or all the players.'

'Who are you, then?'

'An old friend here to keep you company.'

'I have no friends.'

'You are wrong, Drustan of the Forest. In that world and in this.'

****

Marisa was tending the wounds of her King when the call smashed through her mind like the fall of an axe.

Her haraf stone glowed softly in the gloom. Its striped, spiralling pattern of red, white and black contrasted with the more gaudy, multi-coloured stones from the monoliths of this House upon the river, several of which were arranged on the cardinal points of the King's body. With a simple twist of her soul Marisa had attuned her own stone with those that lay upon the King, until they pulsed with healing power, weaving a tight web of magic around his body.

The King's injuries were catastrophic. His horse had crushed him and at least one other horse had trampled him. Dame Belina, leader of this House, had reached the fallen monarch first, kept him alive long enough for Marisa to arrive at the bridge. With their combined skill, and the bone-setting skills of Halstan, from the House of Ryr on Normache Isle, they stabilised the King's injuries. Porters carried him inside, to a room at the edges of the spirals, where the power of Brominii, goddess of healing, held greatest sway.

The healers gathered at the House were among the most potent in the isles. They worked through the night, winding a shroud of healing magic around the King; lines of energy twisting and coiling, anchored to the shrine by the chips of stone, powered by the souls of the healers, guided by their minds. The spell required constant maintenance, constant supervision, and it tied the healers to the King, to the shrine. They knew that the King's injuries were too severe and that he would die anyway, but he was their King and so they stayed, trapped by honour, in the path of the invading army.

The healers prayed to Brominii, hoping that the goddess would heal the King's injuries so that they could flee, but no answer came. The goddess had forsaken them, it seemed. Marisa recalled Branwen's words: *No blood should be spilled at this shrine. You are not bound here, Marisa Gentlehand. This stone is not your stone.*

Over the next day and night bedraggled soldiers trickled in from the battlefield, many injured or dying, carried on litters by friends and comrades.

Marisa did what she could for the common soldiers, tending their wounds in the dormitories and corridors, working her shifts in this small room, holding the coiling lines of magic tight around the King's injuries. She napped when she could, but there were so many wounded.

In the gloom, Marisa closed her eyes, just for a moment, just to rest them.

And the axe fell and opened her mind and she saw … and she saw … *deep forest, huge, overpowering trees… Scampering figures in the dark, mischievous, treacherous, the smell of sanity leaching away into the dust… Drustan! Oh Drustan, her Drustan, injured, delirious, needing her… A wall of earth magic, forest magic, hiding him from the enemy… Men made to act like dogs, snuffling, searching for something, hunting whatever it was that Drustan carried… A chainmail-clad soldier, tall, blond, with Vascanar scars upon his face… Other Vascanar, ripping at wounded Karisae soldiers, blood flowing under the trees… Drustan crying out her name: 'MARISA!'*

She jerked awake. The King's eyelids fluttered, the healing spells faded; the sound of running feet in the hall.

Dame Belina rushed into the room with Halstan at her heels.

'I'm awake.' Marisa slipped into the healing spell, letting her mind weave the pattern between her soul and her body, praying to Brominii, calling upon the power of the spring, of the stones, of the shrine. Tendrils of magic glowed around the King's shattered body, reweaving the spell, but he still awoke; the spells did not work as well now that Branwen and the other Anthanic had left. Marisa kept that thought hidden away; now was not the time to examine it.

The King's eyes opened. 'Wha … what's happening?' he asked. 'Are they here?'

'Sleep, Majesty, 'tis only a bad dream,' Belina soothed.

'They're coming for me,' the King said, terror in his voice. 'My blood will open the door. It was foreseen.'

'Sleep, sire. All will be well.' Belina and Halstan added their strength to Marisa's and the spellcraft tightened around the King's mind, sending him back into slumber.

'Damn fool,' Halstan snapped. 'Falling asleep here. I wound that magic tight around his broken bones and you let him wake up and move.' He swept his grey hair back from his eyes. 'I'm going to have to reattach the crystals to the streams now. Go suckle a baby, useless wench.'

Marisa's eyes flashed. 'I am Marisa desainLegan of Redain, freeman Halstan of the Ryr House.'

But Halstan was lost in the wounds and injuries of the King.

Belina placed a hand on Marisa's arm. 'We are just bags of flesh to him, Marisa.'

Marisa closed her tired eyes and then blinked them open again. 'I know.'

'We'll take over,' Belina said. 'Illath rises tonight. We will need the whole House to join together to call upon her help to heal our King.'

'As if the blood moon cares,' Halstan muttered.

Marisa said, 'No, I'm fine. I just—'

Halstan lifted his head to look at her. 'You're done in, girl. Don't think I don't know you've been working in the corridors, in the garden, and then coming here.' He smiled wryly. 'I know the touch of your craft, Milady of the House at Redain. Men will live who should have died because of your foolishness. But now you must rest.'

'I—' Marisa admitted defeat. 'You are right.'

'I always am.' Halstan sniffed and returned to his work.

'Go and rest, dear one,' Belina said. 'There's a man at the gate. A soldier. He says he knows you.'

Drustan? 'Did he give a name?'

'Cullain. He looks a rough sort.'

CHAPTER 11

Drustan swam upwards into consciousness from a place where light shattered like glass. The shadowy figure whispered, *'Your injuries festered, so I healed what I could,'* and then Drustan awoke. He didn't open his eyes immediately. Rather, he lay quiet, soaking in the smells of the forest: the damp loam of the earth against the sharper, cleaner scent of the trees. Water close by, running fast — he could hear it tumbling over rocks, and smell the moisture on the air. He badly needed to urinate. Wood smoke, faint but present; a fire.

The torturer's fire!

He listened. No gagged screams, no muffled moans, no hissing heat against flesh, just the sounds of quiet footsteps moving around. The fear receded into his nightmares and he opened his eyes.

A boy's feet close by, standing still. 'He's awake,' the boy said and squatted to look Drustan in the eye. 'Thought you'd sleep the sun to ground.'

'Leave him be, Agus.' A man's voice, strong but no steel, not a soldier's voice; too cultured. The kind of voice that keeps on talking so you don't notice the thumb on the scales.

Drustan tried to sit up; pain flared in his side. He remembered the axe and then the face of the Erisyan when the man spoke of Forasin Hill.

Forasin Hill. The first step of Drustan's downfall. Nineteen summers old. Ordered to kill prisoners by the newly anointed King Radolf, an order he had ignored, taking the prisoners' paroles instead and sending them on their way; honour lies in your actions. Radolf, furious that one of the Hundrin would disobey, had started looking slantwise at Drustan.

But the King had done nothing until Marisa gave him a weapon. Drustan blinked away tears.

'She will come.' A woman's voice in his head, behind his eyes, holding him tight. She claimed to be his mother, this Eirane, this Anthanic

witch. Was she? Drustan let his pain-weighted eyelids flicker closed for a moment, let his mind coil back into the dream, the feelings, the words. *'Yes,'* her voice said, *'I am your mother, Drustan desainCoid. I birthed you and named you for the forest. Then they—'*

Drustan snapped his eyes open.

He didn't want to see Marisa again. Had he really called out her name in the dream world? Her healer's touch had reached inside him, pulled at his blood, teased out his parentage, and discovered what he did not know himself. He didn't want to see her guilt-full face again.

'Why do you weep?' the boy Agus asked.

'You have ambitious parents, boy,' Drustan said. He tried once more to sit upright against the tree behind him.

Agus reached out a hand.

'I need no help, godly one.'

'I can't help me name,' Agus said.

Drustan didn't reply. He needed all his breath just to force his body up through the pain. Sweat ran down his face and his breath hissed between gritted teeth; so much effort for such a simple thing. Finally, he managed to slump back against the tree and look out across the small clearing. His bladder complained about this new posture. He would need to stand soon, find a bush.

Such was the way of the warrior: get wounded and then suffer the recovery. But this wound felt bad. He tried to lean to his left: sharp pain tore at him. To his right: a tearing sensation as the wound stretched. Oh, yes, this was a bad one. This one might just cripple him. Maybe he could get a job making craftworks in some benighted town. Maybe as a weaver, or a potter or, if the wound was really bad, a beggar.

'Wounds will make you maudlin,' the man said. 'I'm Garet, Drustan the Bright Blade. I owe you a debt that can never be repaid.'

'Maybe you can give me a job in your shop then, merchant,' Drustan grunted through the pain.

'I fought in the battle-line just like you, milord.'

'Don't call me that, merchant, and you didn't fight like me, but you stood 'till the end; good enough. I'm named Drustan desainCoid.' Drustan held out a hand.

'I am named Garet Wiseye.'

'You are a man, Garet.'

'As are you…' Garet took the hand '…sell-sword.'

Drustan laughed.

'There're Vascanar not a hundred paces away 'cross the river,' a new voice warned.

With difficulty and pain, Drustan turned to look to his left. This man was stocky, big-shouldered, with strong hands, the look of a farmer about him in his tanned face and open gaze.

'I'm Efan, milord Drustan.'

'Drustan will do fine,' Garet said.

Agus said, 'He don't like being called lord, 'spite them boots.'

'Enough about the damn boots.' Drustan held out a hand to Efan. 'I'm named Drustan desainCoid.'

'I'm named Efan of Trant.' A firm clasp of the hands.

'Are the enemy coming here?' Drustan asked. Would he have to move? *Could* he move? Would one of these conscripts be able to do what was needed if he had to be left behind as they fled? Would dying in a puddle of his own piss be a final humiliation. Would he even care? He thought about it for a moment. Yes, he would care.

'Want a drink?' Agus asked Efan. 'I've some lovely water 'ere.' He poured a little from the waterskin onto the ground.

Drustan's bladder pulsed.

'Don't waste that water, boy,' Efan said.

'There's plenty gurgling in the river,' Agus said. 'Can't you hear it?'

Drustan had been trying to ignore the sound of running water not fifty feet away.

Efan shook his head at the boy and squatted beside Drustan. 'They're out there, mil… Drustan. The Vascanar search for us.'

'In a Calodrig?' Drustan blurted, unable to hide his surprise.

'Aye, I think maybe they're upset with you.' Efan grinned ferociously. 'They'll regret their cheek when the sun falls. The moons rise together tonight, the red chasing the silver. We know the old charms and even we're not truly safe.'

'How do you know?'

'About the moons?' Efan shrugged. 'I can always feel it when Illath returns.'

'Means you're heart-touched,' Agus said. 'Like me ma was.'

Drustan ignored the boy. 'What's the situation?' Would they have to leave him here? He could show them how to perform the thrust, but Garet might botch it. Best to let Efan do it. Mercy-killing a man was not unlike slaughtering livestock, after all.

'We're on an island in the middle of the river. Island's about eighty paces wide, maybe one-fifty long. River's wide and fast. It's shallow on that side, easy enough to cross there, but,' Efan pointed into the trees, 'it's too deep and fast to cross to the other bank.'

'So we're trapped here.' Drustan thought for a moment. 'You said the Vascanar are searching and yet they haven't crossed to the island?'

'Not yet. Tis strange. They come along the bank all right with them man-dogs on chain leash—'

'Man-dogs?'

'Aye, poor sods look like men but act like dogs, snuffling around as if they're searching for a scent. Foul magic there.'

'Spellhounds,' Drustan said. 'They're called spellhounds. Foul magic indeed. What happens then?'

'They comes up to the bank and then they gets some new scent and off they goes. Downstream, towards the falls. Bad place to be at night, them falls.'

'*I will protect you until she comes,*' his mother's voice whispered through Drustan's mind.

'Want some water?' Agus held the waterskin out towards Drustan.

'No.' The last thing Drustan needed was to add more water to his already full bladder, despite his thirst.

'Thank you,' Agus said. 'You're supposed to say no *thank you.*'

'I should've let them gut you, boy.'

'Most likely.' Agus drank from the waterskin. Some water trickled down his face.

Drustan licked his lips. He could swear the sound of the river grew louder. He shook his head to clear it. 'What about the falls?'

Efan chewed his lip. 'I were born round here. Got a farm over that way. A wife and three daughters, plus a couple of sons.'

Drustan didn't care about the man's living arrangements. 'What about the falls, Efan?'

'It's a haunting. We used to dare … when we was children … but … nobody stayed there after dark. Illath rises tonight.' Efan looked away from Drustan. 'And I'm going to fetch my people to safety through the bloodlight.'

'As you should,' Drustan said.

'What else can I do?'

Drustan breathed in against the pressure of his bladder.

'Are you sure you're all right?' Efan asked. 'You're sweating.'

'I'm not an invalid,' Drustan said.

'So get up and run,' Agus said and scampered off behind a bush. The unmistakable sound of pee splattering on the ground followed.

'I need to piss,' Drustan said.

Efan stood. 'You should've said.'

'I'm saying now.'

'That you are.' Efan turned his back.

'What are you doing, man?'

'Might be best if'n you don't move.'

'Give me a hand, damn you.' Drustan almost disgraced himself when Efan pulled him, none too gently, to his feet, but he managed to hold his bladder closed. He sagged against Efan.

'Well, get on with it then,' Efan said.

'A man doesn't piss where he sleeps.'

'Depends what he's been drinking.' Efan wrapped a strong arm around Drustan's waist. 'Or so I've been told. How far?'

'A little way,' Drustan gasped against the pain of his side. 'Why? Do you have anything better to do?' He regretted the words; the man's family was out there with the Vascanar marauders.

'Only to get my shoulder reset. You're no lightweight, Drustan the Bright Blade.' Efan half-carried Drustan into the woods.

'Did the boy tell you my name?' Drustan asked. 'You knew it before I gave it.'

'No,' Efan chuckled. 'No need for that. Everyone knows Drustan desainCoid, the noble butcher who found out he were the same as everybody else. Will this do?'

'Yes.' Drustan leaned against the tree, sweating so hard it washed the dirt from his face into his mouth. Salt and grime, an unlovely taste.

What did the man mean? *The same as everybody else.* He closed his eyes for a moment.

'*I am here.*'

Drustan blinked his eyes open.

'Do you need help?' Efan asked with a dubious and faintly disgusted gesture at the leather thongs holding Drustan's breeches closed.

'I'll call you when I'm finished,' Drustan snapped, gulping back a curse; would the man not just go?

'You're welcome.' Efan left Drustan to do what was needed.

It was a difficult task to untie his breeches. Drustan almost fell once, but that only cost him the pain of grabbing onto a branch to avoid the disgrace of falling flat on his face, so the pain was worth it. He sighed as his bladder emptied.

Somehow he managed to tie up his breeches and stagger back the short distance to the camp, clinging to branches, holding out against the pain.

Efan caught him just before he fell. 'You're a fool, man. Are you trying to rip open that wound?' He laid Drustan back against a tree and gave him the waterskin.

Drustan quenched his thirst, placed the waterskin to one side, and panted. 'Your … your family… May the … may the Weaver watch over them.' He rolled his hands in the twin loops of infinity.

Efan said nothing, simply bowed his head, repeating the loops of infinity, and walked away to stare into the embers of the stealthy fire.

Agus sat on the other side of the fire eating one of the Erisyan pies.

Drustan was suddenly famished. 'Any more of those pies left, boy?'

'Nah, last one, but there's some bread and cheese. Bread's a bit stale, mind.' Agus chewed on the pie. 'Tasty,' he said around a mouthful of pork.

CHAPTER 12

Dame Belina insisted that Marisa take two porters with her to meet Cullain.

The warrior monks pledged to Vulcas, god of war, and set by that god to protect the healers, were dressed in short tunics the colour of milk and carried quarterstaffs. The senior monk, Brother Filas, wore a red sash around his waist, his head shaved but for a tuft of hair above his forehead, the exposed scalp covered in abstract tattoos of many colours. Beneath greying eyebrows, his eyes were calm. When Filas dropped to one knee and bowed his head, Marisa read his rank, and his accomplishments, in those tattoos.

The younger monk dropped to his knee behind and to the left of Filas. Only the sides of the novice's head were shaved, his tattoos small, insignificant. A long tail of hair hung down his back and he wore no sash, just a simple rope to hold his tunic closed.

Filas lifted his head. 'This is Novice Lawen, Milady Marisa.'

Marisa nodded her head to Lawen. 'Novice.'

'Milady.'

The two porter-monks stood.

Lawen's gaze flickered over Marisa's slim form clad in light summer robes of white linen. 'This Cullain is a rough sort, milady,' he said, still looking at her chest.

Filas, who was allowed a wife because of his rank in the order, slapped Lawen across the face. There was no anger or spite in the blow. 'He's young, milady.'

'I know, brother.' Marisa sighed. 'Come along then.' She held Lawen's gaze for a moment. 'Try to keep your eyes on the back of my head.'

She led the two monks along the corridor. The massive stone walls kept out the worst of the morning heat, just as the sweet-smelling incense covered the worst of the inevitable stench. At first, this corridor remained empty because the King's chamber lay beyond and his bodyguards would not allow even the wounded so close to their charge. But even bodyguards to a king knew pity, even the fabled Hundrin.

Between the mighty monoliths of the shrine stones were gaps. In these gaps were doorways into the dormitories that lay between the spirals of the shrine, but the dormitories could not cope with the numbers of the wounded and so the corridors became overflow wards. Even this corridor, at the very entrance of the King's sanctuary.

Men lay on cots against the walls, on blankets upon the floor, or simply slumped down upon naked stone. So many men returned from battle upon the shoulders of their comrades, with missing limbs, gaping stomach wounds, jaws cut away; every example of what sharpened steel could do to a human body. The healers bathed their injuries, bandaged those hideous wounds, struggled to knit broken bodies back together again, but still many would die. There was not enough healing magic in the world to heal so many in so short a time.

This was always the way of it, and good healers had to develop a hard crust upon their hearts to stop pity from overwhelming them. This meant, Marisa supposed, that she was not a good healer.

Lawen leapt forward to unfasten the double doors at the end of the corridor, averting his gaze as Marisa strode through into the garden.

The interlinking spirals of the shrine were most obvious here in the openness of the garden. Gradually the stones stepped down, getting lower and lower as they curved across the ground towards the sacred spring. But the smaller stones were no shorter than the rearing monoliths of the walls; they were simply buried deeper with more of their bulk hidden from view.

It was almost noon and exhaustion weighed upon Marisa in the heat of high summer. She had not slept since the King's horse fell upon the bridge. When was that? She concentrated for a moment, her thoughts sluggish. Two days? No. Dawn yesterday. Yes. Two days since the battle was lost but only a day and a few hours since the fleeing King fell.

The Karisae gods demanded that the monoliths of the Anthanic remained in place. They could be built around, buried in the walls of the House, but they could not be moved. So the huge weathered stones, carved over with runes and symbols, swept across the boundaries of the garden and then inwards. Every colour of rock, even rocks not found anywhere in the islands, stood sentinel to the spring. Widely spaced, dropping in height, they curved through the central area where the spring water flowed into the pool.

Multicoloured minerals glistened beneath that flowing water. As the sun passed across the heavens the colours flared like fire. Refracted and reflected colours bounced from the monoliths, shone through the water, and filled the garden with energetic life. Smaller ponds, connected to the main pool by babbling streams, moistened and cooled the air. There were quiet glades, soft grass swards, and scented rose beds arranged around the standing stones, the streams, the pools, and the elegant paths that curved and spiralled from the edges of the walkways surrounding the garden to the shrine at its centre.

Marisa paused, her eyes closed, her hand cradling the chip of haraf stone about her neck. She remembered the gardens of the House of Redain, her own house. Its interlocking spirals lay upon the shores of Lake Kalon, the outer stones grey sandstone but the inner stones red, and black, and white, a pattern of contrasts, peaceful, inviting contemplation.

Calmed by the touch of the memory, she smiled and opened her eyes again. The walking wounded had colonised the garden with rough laughter and quiet moans. They had erected coarse shelters of cloth and leather against the glare of the sun, but left the covered walkways clear of bodies and debris; a mark of respect to the House and its healers.

By a small drinking fountain, Marisa saw Cullain waiting, a hulking man in leather armour with chainmail across his shoulders. Vorduk and Yaltis, two of the King's Hundrin, stood chatting to him. Even compared to the King's personal bodyguards, Cullain looked impressively martial; his forearms were as big around as Vorduk's biceps.

When she was a child, Marisa had watched Cullain lift a pony upon his back, with the young Drustan sat astride the pony. The effort had burst a blood-vessel in Cullain's forehead and he sweated blood, but he won the bet and paid the healer from his winnings.

'Wait here,' Marisa said to the two monks.

Filas said, 'Milady, we are—'

'Remember your vows, brother.'

'Yes, milady.' Filas bowed.

Marisa wanted to talk to Cullain alone. The porter-monks' vows of obedience wouldn't stop them telling tales to the Dame. Now all Marisa had to do was get rid of Vorduk and Yaltis. She didn't think that would prove to be a problem, not after what she had done to Drustan; warriors do not easily forgive the humiliation of a friend.

Yaltis wore a beard to hide an awful injury to his jaw. Vorduk shaved and bathed in scented soap, but could wield a sword with such skill and speed that very few men could stand against him. He had a broken cheekbone, badly reset, where Drustan had punched him unconscious after trapping his sword.

Men never really grew up; they just grew older. Marisa sighed and nodded her head to the two Hundrin.

'Why, Milady Swordbreaker,' Yaltis said. 'So nice of you to join us.'

'Easy, Yal, 'twas not her fault.' Vorduk bowed to Marisa.

'He were the best of us and she saw him broken and scattered to the winds as a sell-sword,' Yaltis said.

'Have you forgotten I'm here?' Cullain asked, too softly.

'You had to give up your place too, Cully,' Yaltis said.

'I didn't *have* to do anything, brat. Go on. Go see to your pointless bloody defences. If'n the Vascanar come, wave your sword and cry out for honour, King, and land. Go on, get. Milady and I've things to discuss.'

'Come along, Yal.' Vorduk bowed to Marisa again. 'Apologies, milady. Drustan owed him money.'

Cullain chuckled as the two warriors sauntered away, ready to face a battle against overwhelming foes without a trace of fear in their eyes.

'Thank you, armsmaster,' Marisa said.

'I didn't do it for you,' Cullain replied. His bearded face lost all emotion and he looked out across the wounded men. His large fingers tapped an impatient rhythm on his thigh. Armoured soldiers moved amongst the wounded. Soldiers in steel chainmail covered in tabards slashed across with royal purple talked to men in rough leather slashed across with their own blood.

Marisa knew what the royal guardsmen were saying: 'Stand. We stand here and defend His Majesty.'

'You should move the wounded,' Cullain said. 'The enemy'll be here soon.'

'Some cannot be moved.'

'Then leave 'em behind.'

'You know what the Vascanar do to captives.'

Cullain raised a ragged eyebrow. 'There's an easy remedy.'

'We cannot do that.'

'You allow men mercy.'

'Only when their injuries are so severe there is no hope of saving them,' Marisa said.

'No hope left for them that can't flee.'

'The King is here,' Marisa said.

'I know. Injured?'

'Yes, very badly.'

'Can't be moved?'

'I'm afraid not.'

Cullain chewed his beard for a while, then shrugged. 'Least he has heirs. Done that right, anyhow.'

'You are a cynic, armsmaster.'

'I'm a soldier.'

A man with one arm still bound in a splint staggered towards the doors that led to the gate, to the defences, using the spear in his left hand as a crutch. Marisa had healed the worst of his injuries during the past night, but he was in no condition to fight. She leaned back against the cool of the stone. 'Where is he, Cullain?'

Cullain said nothing.

'Where is Drustan?'

Cullain straightened his back. 'Dunno.'

'You set yourself to be at his side. You threw away your whole life. And now you lose him?'

'He left the line of battle afore the last charge.' Cullain sucked air through his teeth. 'I let 'im go.'

'Why?'

'He wanted to be alone.' Cullain's lips twitched into a smile. 'I weren't stupid enough to gainsay that.'

'And then what happened?'

'The line broke.'

'You did not think to look for him?'

'I weren't anxious to die screaming. Figured I might find him here.'

'Why would he come here?'

Cullain blinked. 'Because you're here.'

'He would not come for me.'

'Oh I dunno. He might.' Cullain sniffed. 'Never did have much sense when it came to you.'

Marisa looked away from this hulking brute whose words cut her so deeply. 'I had hoped…' The pool flared in the sun, and Marisa narrowed her eyes against the glare. 'I wanted…'

'To make amends.' Cullain laughed, a harsh bark of sound. Soldiers' heads snapped around, hands fell to sword hilts; there was so much anger in that laugh and they wondered if it was directed at them. When Cullain ignored their paranoid gazes, they settled back into their quiet conversations; but their hands did not move far from their weapons.

Brother Filas and Novice Lawen approached with their quarterstaffs held diagonally across their torsos clad in milk-white tunics.

Cullain rolled his huge shoulders and grinned. 'Best they don't cross me.'

'They come to protect me,' Marisa said.

'Don't care.'

'Is everything all right, milady,' Filas asked. His cool gaze did not move from Cullain's eyes.

'Yes, brother,' Marisa said. 'This man is an old acquaintance.'

'He's a common sell-sword,' Lawen said.

'His common ears work, milky,' Cullain sneered.

The two porters spread out, their quarterstaffs tipped forward towards Cullain, who dropped into a crouch, his big hands curled into loose fists.

'This man is no threat to me,' Marisa said.

'We must ask you to leave,' Filas said to Cullain.

'You can ask,' Cullain replied.

'This is a House of the Doves, a house of healing,' Marisa said. 'Men are dying here right now.'

Even Lawen looked puzzled at her words.

Marisa breathed in and chilled her voice. 'Remember your vows and return to your duties.'

Filas bowed apologetically. 'The Dame Belina set us to protect you.'

'I am Lady Marisa desainLegan of the StormMarch, daughter to an Earl, *and* the foremost healer of the House of Redain, first amongst the Houses of the Doves. Go back to the Dame of this provincial House and ask for her guidance on your vows of obedience.'

Filas shook his head. 'Milady—'

'Go now, brother, or be forsworn.'

'Run along,' Cullain said, adding, after a brief pause, 'milky.' He grinned.

Lawen scowled.

Filas bowed. 'As you wish, milady, but the Dame Belina will not be pleased.'

Cullain opened his mouth to speak.

Marisa snapped, 'Quiet, Armsmaster Cullain.'

Too many years of duty and loyalty to the desainLegan family held Cullain's insults behind his teeth.

'Go now, brother,' Marisa said.

'Milady.' Filas bowed. The two monks backed away from Cullain before turning and going in search of Dame Belina.

Cullain said, 'You spoil me hobby, milady.'

'They are good men. I know what you do to good men.'

'I could say the same.' Cullain looked away from her. 'They're fools that hold vows sacred when all to come is black.' He shook his head. 'I'll be on my way now. Drustan would most likely have headed for the deep forest. Maybe he's gaining wisdom.' An ironic bow. 'Milady.' He turned and then stopped. 'You should leave this place,' he said, without looking at her.

Marisa almost let him go. Almost let it all go. Her path was run. She had betrayed the man she loved. An inadvertent betrayal, the wrong word in the wrong conversation to the wrong friend, but a betrayal none the less. It could all end here. All she had to do was wait and her guilt would be wiped clean by Vascanar blades.

All she had to do... 'Cullain!'

He turned to face her.

'I had a vision,' she said.

'Of Drustan?'

'Yes.'

'Where is he?'

'In the deep forest. He is injured.'

Cullain nodded. 'I'll find 'im.'

'I am coming with you.'

'They'll not let you go. Not with me. Not to him. Don't think for one heartbeat that rank'll work again.'

'Then we will have to be circumspect.'

'Nice word,' Cullain grinned. 'But I prefer sneaky.'

CHAPTER 13

Bihkat gazed at the darkening sky. Twilight would fall soon and then the night. It was an auspicious night when the treacherous moon Illath chose to appear. The Augarin wheel, an artefact stolen from the halls of an island race in the Innas Sea, had, through its connection to the red moon's grace, prophesied that Illath would rise on this night. And again on the night to follow.

Full, strong, bloody light would shine upon this land. Illath was a capricious goddess, leaving the world for months or even years at a time; but when she shone blood-red upon the land, the barriers between worlds grew thin.

In forty days hence Illath would rise with her reliable sister Morgeth and the imperious Sun. In that morning splendour, with the trinity together in the sky, the gate between this world and the Tangled Realms would open and allow his demonic lords to rise, to bring forth the new pantheon of blood. First the Vascanar, the Soldiers of the Gate, must take this land, desecrate its shrines, sacrifice its people to the coming dark. Then the sacred lake at the end of the Shrine Road would become the gateway to his lords' fulfilment.

And he, Bihkat, foremost amongst their priests, would be uplifted into godhood beside them.

So had they promised and he believed. But the Xarnac must be found to guide the lords to the *right* gate in the multitude scattered across this world. Would that fool Torquesten find it? Yes, Bihkat grinned savagely, or he would be stretched backwards and his heart plucked out to feed his hounds.

Two Akalac, blood-knights of the faith, stood guard over the heavy, solid bulk of the treasure wagon. Iron-bound planks of wood, scrawled over with warding sigils against flame and explosion, protected the Ulac, the elixir formed from the secretions of sated demonic godlings.

'Open it,' Bihkat commanded.

The taller of the two Akalac said, 'We have no orders.'

Bihkat looked at the warrior towering over him, who bulked more than three times his weight.

'You're needed,' Bihkat said. 'There are battles yet to come. Your strong arms are needed to wield that mighty sword.' Bihkat pointed to the greatsword hanging from the man's back. 'Your eyes are needed to see where your enemies stand. Your ears are needed to hear their screams. Your tongue is needed to give orders to the faithful. But your nose,' Bihkat smiled, 'you don't need.'

His consciousness, arrow-straight, dagger-sharp, speared into the Akalac's mind. He dug in with taloned thoughts and made the man lift a blade, an eating knife, from his belt, raise it to his own face, saw away his own nose with a blade unsuited for the task.

And he didn't let the man scream, not once, not even a moan.

'Open it,' Bihkat commanded the other guard.

Who leapt to obey.

Bihkat sneered at the Akalac with the gristle of his nose in his hand and blood pouring from the hole in his face. 'Go cauterise the wound.' Bihkat selected two vials of Ulac from the many stored within the wagon. 'Away from here.' Bihkat released the guard's mind.

The man opened his mouth.

'Quietly.'

The injured man swallowed back his scream and staggered away into the lengthening shadows.

'I've counted the vials,' Bihkat said to the remaining Akalac. 'What is my name?'

'Bihkat. Ukalac Bihkat, high priest of the Way.'

'That is correct.' Bihkat handed the Akalac a vial. 'Lock up the wagon and let no other approach unless by my authority or that of Pyran, your Uka.'

'Yes, Ukalac.'

****

Drustan woke from an uneasy sleep. Dreams of the dead held back by the caress of a mother torn from him when he was but a babe. Garet and Agus knelt by the fire talking quietly as a broth steamed into the night. Had the moons risen yet?

'*Not yet.*'

Drustan shook away his mother's love and pulled himself up into a seated position against the tree.

'How're you feeling?' Garet asked.

'Still maudlin?' Agus added with a smirk.

'Hungry,' Drustan said. 'Where's Efan?'

'Gone into the woods to help his people.' Garet ladled a wooden bowl full of broth and carried it across to Drustan.

'He went alone?' With a nod of thanks, Drustan accepted the bowl.

'No, Tirac went with him.'

'Tirac?'

'Aye, you didn't see him, did you?' Garet said 'The one who lost his tongue to the Vascanar blades.'

'Who's on watch then?' Drustan sipped at the hot broth. Not the best he had ever tasted, but he was hungry enough to tear strips from a still-breathing horse.

'No-one,' Garet said.

'No need,' Agus said. 'We're protected. Obvious, innit.'

Drustan raised an eyebrow. 'Obvious will get you killed, boy.'

'Better'n being oblivious,' Agus replied.

****

Marisa changed into travelling clothes of dark colours, with knee-high boots, and a heavy woollen cloak that would serve as a blanket. She unpicked her complicated hairstyle and used a leather thong to tie her hair back from her face. Then, with the hood of her cloak raised to hide her golden hair, she picked up a heavy leather pack, met Cullain at the kitchen gate, and slipped out.

Lawen attacked as they crept along in the shadow of the House. The novice monk managed to get a hit on Cullain's shoulder with his quarterstaff, but he failed to knock the armsmaster down, which was very nearly the last mistake he ever made.

Cullain erupted against Lawen: hit after hit, strike after strike, a kick, and then a twisting throw which ended with his arm like a bar across the younger man's throat. All in total silence; with the arrogance of youth, Lawen did not think to call out for aid until it was too late.

'Let him go, Cullain,' Marisa begged as Lawen's lips turned blue.

Cullain smiled. 'As my lady wishes.' He let the novice monk drop face down upon the dirt.

Sweeping her cloak back, Marisa knelt beside Lawen.

'We don't have time for this,' Cullain murmured.

'Make time,' she whispered back.

'Don't whisper,' Cullain said. 'Too high a note, carries too far. Use a low voice, not a hissed whisper.'

Marisa gently, lest the other healers of the House sense the magic, eased the bruises around Lawen's throat. He would live, but he would be living on soup for a while.

'He's a bright enough lad,' Cullain murmured. 'Knew not to trust you.'

'Which way?' Marisa asked.

'Along the wall, then through the long grass to the river.'

'The bridge is defended.'

'We're not using the bridge. Gimme that pack. We'll have to crawl through the grass.'

'Do not lose it, armsmaster. I know you have a tendency to lose things.'

'Quietly, milady, I'll not play with the next man that crosses our path.' Cullain half-drew his sword. The steel gleamed in the shadows.

'Just do not lose the pack, Cullain.'

'Full of herbs and sundries, is it? For healing Drustan?'

'Yes.'

'I'll not lose it.'

Marisa touched her haraf stone, wrapped in charmed silk to hide its power, the same silk that protected the implements of her craft in the pack. But even through the silk, she could feel the power of the stone about her neck, the power lying at the heart of her craft. It calmed her fear.

'We should wait for full night,' she said.

'Nah,' Cullain said. 'Shadow's better'n night. This way.'

She followed him along the edge of the wall. He moved with speed and silence despite his bulk. They reached the end of the wall and he dropped to his belly with the pack in front of him on the ground.

Slowly, he pushed it through the long grass towards the river's edge.

'Keep your arse down,' he murmured, 'lessen you want to look like a pincushion.'

'I remember your lessons, armsmaster.'

'I were teaching Drustan.'

'So?'

They crawled on, down to the edge of the swift-flowing river. Cullain used the long shadows of dusk to remain hidden from the soldiers digging ditches beside the bridge.

'Fools think a bit of mounded earth'll stop Erisyan arrows,' he muttered. 'Gonna kill me some sell-bows afore this is over.'

'I thought the war was lost,' Marisa said.

'War ain't even begun, missy.'

Cullain waited for something. Clouds, Marisa realised. He waited for clouds to slide across the face of the fading sun making the shadows by the river just a little deeper.

'We'll have to run in a moment,' he murmured. 'They may see us. They may loose arrows. We don't stop. Run to the bend of the river. We don't stop. Understand?'

'Ye—' Marisa's voice squeaked like a mouse. She breathed in deeply. 'Yes,' she said, her mouth dry, her hands trembling. She hardened her gaze, lifted her chin, stiffened her back; she was Lady Marisa desainLegan of the StormMarch.

Cullain glanced across at her. 'Be thankful you changed out of them white robes.'

Marisa moistened her lips before she spoke. 'They did not seem sneaky enough.'

Cullain grinned. 'Use the fear to add speed to your feet, milady. Now … run.'

He charged along the shingle beach, Marisa's heavy pack dangling from one huge hand. Marisa had difficulty keeping up, but she pumped her arms and lifted her knees high under the loose skirt. She drew alongside him.

A shout went up from the men at the bridge.

Cullain did not look around and so neither did Marisa. She wanted to — gods, how she wanted to — but she followed the armsmaster's lead and kept her head down for the sprint.

Arrows fell around them. One thudded into the pack.

Then they were around the bend.

'Hundred and fifty paces and still they missed us.' Cullain yanked the arrow out of the pack. 'The Erisyans will skewer those squint-eyed fools for a Vascanar basting.'

Exhilaration made Marisa whoop for joy, then Cullain's words penetrated and her joy died in guilt. She stifled a sob. 'We are leaving them to die.'

'Aye,' Cullain said. 'Their choice. Keep moving. We better reach the boat afore they send out a patrol.'

'You have a boat?'

'Inherited it.'

CHAPTER 14

Torquesten's mind crawled with hate and greed, but this terrain unnerved him. The long drop of the waterfall, where it spewed into a steep-sided gorge in a roar of sound, called to primal fears and the damp smell of the air made his skin itch. Trees clustered at the edges of the gorge, a wall of wood above the landscape. A group of oaks canted out over the cliffs and a fallen beech tree rested across the narrowest part of the gorge. Beyond that treacherous bridge, willows wept in sprays of green.

A leaf-dappled light, spotty and erratic, illuminated the rim of the falls, and yet the fading daylight shone along the length of the gorge in spears of light. A trick of the terrain, but Torquesten shivered as the light shone bright into his eyes and then flickered away at some random movement of a branch in the wind.

The fast-flowing river cascaded over the edge in a thunderous cacophony, a mist rising as those waters pounded upon the rocks far below. Dark shadows curled through that mist, like sharks prowling through the shallows of a sea.

He didn't like this place. Too damp, too dark, too filled with the smells of decay and life in equal measure, like some place out of time, primordial, untouched by human hands. A moment of fear pressed against Torquesten's heart like a dagger, but he had no choice. If he failed to recover the Xarnac then they would take his soul. But if he succeeded? Ah, if he succeeded they'd grant him rewards beyond measure. So had the priest Bihkat told and Torquesten believed.

The trail of the Xarnac led down this rocky path beside the tumbling waters. Green moss and multicoloured lichen overlaid the rocks. Snagging brambles and twisted ferns tumbled over them in tangled obstacles. Droplets of water hung in the air.

No matter. Torquesten would trail the spell-sensitised souls of the spellhounds. Where they led he would follow. Their naked feet slapped against the rocks as they scampered downwards. No dog could do what they did; like cats they leapt from rock to rock.

Where they could go, so could Torquesten. For they were only men with minds shattered and remade in the semblance of the canine; though more agile than most, their bodies were still human.

Gesturing to his soldiers, Torquesten began the descent, jumping from rock to rock despite the slippery lichen covering the stones, despite the vertiginous drop, the swirls of wind and mist brushing against his eyes. The waterfall's roar bounced back from the sides of the gorge and grew louder with each precipitous leap, such a clamour that he could not hear the sound of his own heartbeat as he leapt ever downwards.

His men tried to match his unnatural agility and failed, for he was Akalac, a blood-knight, his talents and powers honed by decades of intrigue, of assassinations evaded and committed. Born and raised into the Vascanar, Torquesten had trained from birth to fight for his masters.

A soldier slipped and grabbed at Torquesten. Without hesitation, Torquesten knocked the grasping hands away and kicked at the man, causing him to spin and fall, smashing headfirst onto the rocks below. The roar of the falls faded away and the wet splintering echo of bone crunching and brains splattering upon the rocks hung in the air with startling clarity.

A moment only … and then the noise of the falls deafened once again.

'Onward, dogs of spell and hounds of pain,' Torquesten cried out in pure, unaccented Maebaz. The spellhounds couldn't hear him, but the intent in the words pierced their minds. With malicious glee at the archer's contempt, Torquesten had toyed with that empathic fool Jarl. Empathy was nothing compared to the power granted to the Master of the Hounds. 'Find me my prize.'

Again the sound of the waterfall faded for a moment, bounced his words hard back against him. The spellhounds howled, human throats opened to the twilight — raw, agonised shrieks of lost humanity.

Torquesten dropped from the last rock of the path onto the smooth flat ledge at the base of the falls.

His favourite spellhound, a tall man with a shock of red hair straggling from his battered skull, growled and attacked another spellhound. The two men fought naked upon the rocks. Ragged-nailed fingers and toes clawing at skin, blackened teeth tearing at flesh, they rolled around in the gathering gloom until whipped by Torquesten's will.

'Find it,' Torquesten hissed in the language of the faith, a sound that cut through the raging melody of the falls. 'Find me the lodestone of the Way.'

Sunlight faded and the roar of the waterfall rose and fell like the heartbeat of the earth. Torquesten ignored it. His masters required him to find the Xarnac.

Nothing else mattered.

****

Sekem's body was laid out on a pyre, the wood mostly planks and boards scavenged from the shattered remnants of the town that lay behind the Erisyan camp. His hands, still bound with the string of his bow, pointed upwards into the dying light.

Jarl reached into the cadiw pouch around Sekem's neck and drew forth two gold coins. He held them in his hand, weighing them, while he looked down at the face of his young cousin. The denomination of the coins didn't matter so long as they were gold. They called forth the Geidiw, the keepers of the Summerland.

Gorak reached into the cadiw pouch around Sekem's neck and drew forth the wing of a crow, Sekem's totem. It would tell the Geidiw who it was they carried away to rebirth. Gently, Gorak kissed the crow's wing and laid it in the hollow of Sekem's throat, where the breath of home had mixed with his spirit when he was a child.

The cadiw pouch carried the homeland of the Erisyans with them wherever they travelled. Jarl's held the claw of a bear alongside dirt and ash scooped from the hearth of his home.

He could feel the pressure of Illath approaching the sky. An auspicious night to burn the dead.

Gorak stepped back from the pyre and joined the eight other Erisyans here to see off Sekem. In full armour, with their bows and quivers full of arrows, and syrthae blades at their hips, the men stood around the pyre to show honour to their dead kinsman.

Jarl kissed the gold coins and laid them over Sekem's eyes. 'Travel well, cousin,' he whispered.

Around him, in the fields of the destroyed town, other small groups of Erisyans gathered around similar pyres. Families preparing to send their kin onwards. Jarl wondered which one of these pyres held the corpse of the other Erisyan Drustan had killed in the woods.

Was it Tesic, a boy barely older than Sekem, on his first real campaign, stabbed so many times that his face was covered with a cloth and the coins placed where his eyes had been?

Was it Irin, too old really to be on campaign, a man of fine voice and marvellous poetry, killed when he should have been at home watching over his grandchildren — found face down in a stream, held there until he drowned?

Was it Falcan, found with the top of his head cleaved off beside the body of a gutted Vascanar? Jarl had liked Falcan; the man had an infectious laugh.

Or was it one of the other corpses ready to burn this night? Jarl decided he didn't want to know. It didn't matter. He'd repaid his debt to Drustan and he'd bear the cost of that honourable guilt.

He lifted a blazing torch from a small fire and waited for the sun to disappear from the sky. He led the song of the Summerland, his deep baritone buttressing the sweet tenor of Gorak's voice. The words of the song spoke of longing, of the world beyond, of the past and the future melded by the flames of the present.

Other voices across the field harmonised, lifting the words to the twilight skies. The Erisyans carried music and poetry with them wherever they went, for music and poetry weighed nothing but contained the whole world.

The sun cast lines of red across the clouds and dropped below the edge of the land. Jarl plunged the torch into the pyre again and again, kindling the cleansing flames beneath his cousin's body. He stepped back. The smell of burning hair rose into the night. Then the sweet smell of flesh roasting and the harsher scent of Sekem's clothes scorching then catching alight. Intense heat seared Jarl's skin and he took another step away from the fire. He lifted the geidin cup from his belt.

Gorak moved amongst the men standing around Sekem's blazing pyre and filled their geidin cups with strong, rough, soldier's wine. Each man poured a little of the wine upon the earth and together they said: 'We are archers and warriors, fathers and lovers, men of faith, of truth, of worth. We are Erisyan!' — the last word shouted.

They lifted the cups to their lips, drained the wine, and threw the cups upon the pyre to burn with the corpse. The dregs of the wine hissed in the flames.

Around the field other family groups spoke the same words, with the same shout at the end. A shout to draw the Geidiw close, to let them see the flames, to call them forth to reach out and carry the dead away to rebirth.

Flashes of light flared from the pyres across the field: the Geidiw melting the gold of the coins to show that they had come, that the souls of the dead were found worthy, that they had passed on into the Summerland.

Jarl closed his eyes and allowed his empathic talent, his dol, to see the spirits of the keepers, the Geidiw, reach out to Sekem's soul. Jarl smiled; his cousin would be reborn into the Erisyans. He would meet him again.

'Erisyan!' Gorak shouted, for all the world as if he were trying to draw the Geidiw to Sekem's soul. But they were already here. They reached down towards Sekem's burning corpse, reached down with all the history of the Erisyans in their grasp, reached down and…

Sekem refused to come forth to meet them. Jarl could see it through his closed eyelids: the struggle in the flames, the Geidiw trying to bring Sekem into the Summerland, and Sekem refusing to leave.

Jarl opened his eyes.

The coins on Sekem's eyelids flickered brightly, the heat rising for a moment; then the flame guttered, died, and the coins glinted a cold hard yellow again.

'Erisyan!' Gorak shouted again, his shout echoed by the others. But Jarl didn't shout, for he knew.

Sekem had refused the Summerland.

CHAPTER 15

Despite the coldness of the pounding water, Torquesten forced the shivering spellhounds to search behind the waterfall, driving them into the curtain of water with the power of his will. Their filthy skins needed a good wash and they had to search every inch of this doom-laden place.

His red-headed favourite, once more the aggressor, attacked a smaller spellhound with a sallow, yellowish cast to his skin. A rolling frenzy of limbs under the spray. The smaller man stumbled into the full force of the falls, toppling into the foaming river and tumbling away downstream.

As the red-headed spellhound howled his victory, Torquesten sighed and ran a hand through his damp hair.

Not again.

Torquesten lashed out with a mental scourge, forcing the pain into the spellhound's shattered mind. The prize was all and the spellhound had allowed jealous anger to override Torquesten's demands. He should kill the creature now, feed him to the others. Priests could always make more spellhounds. But another dead spellhound meant one less spell-sensitive soul to seek out the Xarnac right now — and the redhead *was* Torquesten's favourite.

Torquesten dragged the man to him by force of will, made him crouch upon the rocky ledge, and beat him with the flat of his sword until the man whined with pain and waggled his naked rump in an attempt to appease his master.

As Torquesten chastised the spellhound, his soldiers worked with flint and tinder to light a fire in the damp air. It was a poor fire, faint and giving out little warmth, but the soldiers only needed it to light their pitch-wrapped torches against the encroaching dusk.

Finally, Torquesten kicked his favourite hound back into the search and sat upon a jagged edge of rock. He gestured to one of the soldiers, who handed over an almost full wineskin. Torquesten took from his belt a flask made of human bone, and poured a little Ulac into the wine, vigorously shaking the skin to mix the two liquids.

He gazed at the lengthening shadows beneath the falls, breathed in the damp scent of earth and rock, and lifted the wineskin to his lips.

The demon-flavoured wine chilled his throat, a lance of freezing energy plunging into his stomach. It touched the centre of him and exploded up along his spine to the back of his skull: fire and ice, the last touches of the world. And the stars bowed down before him.

Only the freshest Ulac, the secretions still seasoned with the screams of the dying, could raise a man to godhood for a while, able to see all, to know all, to understand the whole world as the broken hell the priests described … until the vision faded and he became dull and fearful food for the masters once more. When the Ulac was fresh enough, the spell could last for hours. It made men gods of battle.

The Ulac that Torquesten drank didn't have that potency but, still, the stars bowed down to him.

He giggled.

A soldier gazed at the wineskin with hungry eyes. Torquesten, his mind expanded, punched the greedy soldier in the mouth. The man stumbled and fell, his head hanging over the edge of the rocky ledge. Blood flowed from his broken mouth into the swirling eddies beneath the falls. Torquesten considered stamping on the man's head until the water turned pink. He rose from his seat, delighting in the terror in the man's eyes.

But then the power of the Ulac faded away and Torquesten slumped back upon his rock, flaccid jaws dribbling, dull eyes staring at the swirling water, at the spellhounds searching in the torches' smoky light.

He lived in hell and listened to fools.

And the waterfall roared.

'Where is the prize!' he screeched up at the uncaring falls. He threw the wineskin at the soldier with the bloodied mouth. The man bobbed his head in fearful obeisance and put the wineskin away. He would drink only when Torquesten told him to drink.

The spellhounds began to slow, the water too cold for naked men who thought themselves dogs.

'Feed them. Butcher that and feed them,' Torquesten commanded. Nobody moved. Nobody could hear him. He grabbed a soldier by the arm, pointed at the corpse of the soldier who fell from the path, and then pointed at the spellhounds. The man nodded and drew a butchering-blade.

Torquesten muttered, 'I can still feel the Xarnac.' The last word echoed into the sudden silence. The soldier looked up from his butchery. Torquesten slapped him around the face; the sound of the slap was drowned out by the falls.

The spellhounds gorged on human flesh as Torquesten ate a trail pie.

Between the trees, beyond the smoke rising from the torches, the moon Morgeth rose full and strong, like a ball of silver on a cloth of black velvet.

****

Marisa and Cullain waited for a Vascanar patrol to pass before they made the dash into the safety of the deep woods. A false safety, because this was a dangerous night to travel in a Calodrig.

Morgeth had already risen. The touch of the goddess caressed Marisa through her haraf stone, even though she could not see the silver moon through the canopy of the trees.

Cullain, his hands and feet probing ahead of him, slipped through the dark in near silence, but it was slow going.

Marisa let her magic guide her and followed his indistinct bulk. She didn't need to be a witch to sense the danger around them. She said, 'We need to find some alder.'

'We passed some five hundred paces back,' Cullain replied.

'We need deep-forest alder.'

'It's a tad dark, lass.'

'There is a stream close by, or has your nose been broken one time too many, old man?'

Cullain grabbed her and threw her to the ground, his hand over her mouth. Marisa, outraged, began to fight back.

'Quiet,' Cullain murmured into her ear.

Then she heard it. Vascanar voices talking too loudly in the darkness. Barely thirty paces away. Had they heard them?

Cullain removed his hand from Marisa's mouth. 'Stay here. Be quiet.'

He disappeared into the gloom.

Marisa listened to the night. Her haraf stone increased her awareness of the forest around her. The old ones stirred in their hidden lairs. Skittering sounds, like children's laughter. She cast her net of awareness further afield, deeper into the sniggering night.

The copper-smell of blood flooded the air as Cullain dealt with the Vascanar patrol. Marisa's awareness peaked against the flare of lives ending; Cullain killed two men before the others even recognised the threat.

Wild shouts erupted less than ten paces from where Marisa lay.

A clash of steel, sparks in the night, more blood spilled. Dangerous; they had to be away from here before Illath rose. Cullain killed in silence, slipping between the trees, striking men down, then slipping back into the dark.

There, behind him, Marisa sensed a clump of deep-wood alder: tall, majestic, king of the woods, protector of the living.

Something touched Marisa's hair. She jerked free. A snigger behind her, before her, beside her. She lurched to her feet and dragged the silk cover from the haraf stone. Pearly light blazed out in response to the threat.

Creatures scampered back into the trees, pale, whipcord thin, eyes like saucers of milk with drops of black ink instead of pupils. Marisa, captured by the spiralling threads in those eyes, covered the haraf stone's glare with her hand, took one step, two steps towards them…

Sharp-toothed mouths opening.

The haraf stone pulsed a warning against her flesh and Marisa snapped back to herself, let her hand fall, let the light shine again. The creatures stared at her. She stared at them. With wide-toothed grins they scuttled away into the dark.

Marisa panted, her heart pounding in her chest, sweat trickling down her back. Those creatures, seductive, calling to her, their mouths opening, she had—

A gauntleted hand snaked around her mouth, smelling of leather, of old blood. 'You mine,' a guttural voice hissed into her hair. The flicker of a blade in the dark. 'You die now.'

And then Cullain was there, ripping the man away from her, picking up the tall Vascanar warrior and smashing his head into a tree until his skull cracked open.

'Put out that god-cursed light,' he growled, one eye shut tight against the glare.

Marisa slipped the silken cover back over her haraf stone, feeling its heat against her skin as the brilliance faded. She was blind now, the darkness a physical thing after the light.

Cullain grabbed her hand. 'There's alder close by.'

'How do you know?'

'I saw it when you lit up the night like noon.'

'I cannot see.'

'Should've kept an eye shut.' Cullain dragged her through the woods towards the stream. 'Weren't listening close enough to me lessons.'

'We need to be away from here when Illath rises,' Marisa said.

****

Torquesten and his men stood back to back at the base of the falls. Torches flickered in an unearthly breeze. The fear at the heart of every Vascanar became a blustering cry of hate and retribution. The waterfall hushed in reply.

The spellhounds howled; their human faces stained with human blood, crouching back on their naked haunches, baying at the clear silver light of Morgeth like the dogs they thought they were.

Torquesten realised that the forest had tricked him. He remembered the island in the middle of the river, the island that attracted his gaze, *the perfect hiding place*. Then, in an instant, he'd dismissed the island and followed the spellhounds through the brush to this benighted spot.

The work of spirits. Something had stepped into Torquesten's awareness and into the awareness of the spellhounds, had twisted what they saw, what they smelled, what they sensed, had led them away from the prize.

To this place beside falling water.

It required real power to do such things. This land, this island, was not yet undefended. He must tell the priests or lose his soul to roaring fire.

But first he must survive the night.

****

Jarl lifted the unmelted gold coins and weighed them in his hand. He stood alone beside his cousin's pyre; the others had left rather than be cursed by one refused the Summerland by the Geidiw. But it was Sekem who had refused the Summerland despite the best efforts of the keepers to draw him forth.

'Why did you refuse to go, Sekem? Why did you stay?' He tucked the coins into his belt, lifted the leather bag containing the ashes of his cousin to his forehead, and prayed softly for the man's spirit to be allowed entry into the Summerland, where all flowed onward into the next spinning of the Weaver's threads. He felt Illath rise, but ignored her as he tried to help his fallen cousin into rebirth.

****

Marisa, with a blade of silver, cut away a branch of alder and separated it into two, one piece for her and one for Cullain. She worked carefully, making the correct cuts in the correct sequence. She knew this work, because alder had healing powers.

The silver light of Morgeth was caressed by the pink of a rising Illath. Time grew short.

Cullain shivered and drew his sword.

She said, 'That will be no use against what comes. This is not a place for iron.'

CHAPTER 16

Illath, the red moon, rose high and bright, outshining the silver of her sister Morgeth. Her light shone down upon the Islands of Symcani, islands connected in a web of power along lines untouched since the dawn of time. Illath's bloodlight met the delicate lines and cascaded along them. In the deep places, in the hidden places where humans did not, would not, live, the light became clear, bright, red as rubies, filled with the power of magic. Pure, wild, volatile magic bathed the Islands of Symcani.

And gods dreamed of freedom.

Bihkat drank Ulac diluted in wine and opened his mind to Illath, queen of foretelling. His mind sank into the realms beyond this one and saw such things as crazed the soul.

Torquesten crouched beside the waterfall. The ghosts of the falls, extant in the world, haunted him with memories of times and places he had never known. His training, his abilities, wakened at their touch. The bloodlight of Illath flickered across the water.

****

Drustan hissed, frozen anger flooding into his mind. In the flicker of the firelight, a vortex of wind swirled, twisted, gathering matter from the sticks, the soil, the smoke. The bloodlight caressed it, smoothed it, and the form of a young woman dressed in the greens and browns of a summer forest crouched in the clearing under the trees.

Illath rose and the ancient magics ground down by progress in other parts of the world, ploughed under by priesthoods who saw only part of the whole, renewed themselves upon the shimmering Islands of Symcani.

****

Marisa handed an alder stave, three-foot long and as thick as the armsmaster's thumb, to Cullain. 'Put up your sword, armsmaster. You will only anger them with the bite of iron.'

Cullain slid the sword back into its sheath and hefted the stave. 'I've never been in the deep woods in the bloodlight, but…' His voice died as a keening sound rose amongst the trees.

'You have seen what happens in the barrow fields?' Marisa asked.

'Aye.'

'Most sensible people stay inside when Illath rises.'

Cullain's scarred eyebrow twitched upwards. 'So?' He spun the alder stave around his fingers like a baton and rolled his huge shoulders.

'Martial skill has no power here, armsmaster.'

'We'll see.' He listened to the keening. 'They rise?'

'Their blood is still fresh.'

'This'll get interesting.'

****

Sekem's spirit took shape in front of Jarl, a wisp of smoke from the embers of his own pyre.

Jarl bowed his head, hopeful. 'Goodbye, cousin.'

'I'm not leaving yet,' Sekem's ghost said. *'Why did you not revenge me upon the man who killed me?'*

Jarl glanced up at Illath, baleful above the tree-line and sighed. 'Forasin Hill.'

The smoky spirit considered the answer. *'A debt repaid.'*

'A debt repaid,' Jarl agreed.

'A good choice.' Sekem floated down upon the grass and sat like a man beside his hearth. *'We've much to talk of, cousin, before I leave for the Lands of Summer.'*

'So you'll not haunt me, then?' Jarl sat opposite his cousin and felt the heat of a hearth that wasn't there.

'No.' Sekem smiled. *'You were true to our ways despite the pain it caused you.'* The smile became a grin. *'And I'd rather not be trapped here chasing you across this cold land instead of awaiting my turn in the land of endless sun.'*

'Speak then, cousin,' Jarl said, 'and I'll listen.'

'You can ask questions, too.'

****

Drustan looked at the woman formed from the forest, through tears he did not know he shed. 'Mother?'

'I named you Carad,' she said. 'Beloved of my heart.' She stroked his hair. 'They took that away and named you Drustan for your foster-father's grandfather. A brute of a man, much given to violence, but to me you will always be Carad, beloved and strong.'

Drustan couldn't gaze at her ageless, beautiful face. It hurt too much. He looked away and saw Garet and Agus staring at him, at her, Garet's eyes filled with terror, Agus with a slightly quizzical tilt to his head; youth knows no fear.

'They cannot hear us no matter how hard they try,' she said. 'They can see me here by Illath's light, but it does not give them ears to hear that which passes between us. They should not know of what we speak.'

'Are we safe, then?'

'Three-fold safe, my son, my Carad. This river island is filled with alder and willow, king and queen of the forest. Very few of the shades would brave their dominion. I have raised living palisades of forest magic from my sister forest to hold you safe from those demon-spawned invaders.'

Drustan waited a moment. 'You said three?'

'Another watches over you. What you carry is important to the battle to come.'

'Battle?' Drustan smiled.

****

Torquesten backed away from the waterfall as it flared red, his sword ready to cut or parry. The soldiers at his side lifted their blades and shields as the spirits coalesced in the moonlight. Dark red shapes spun out of the water and swooped around the mortals cowering in their midst. Their hissing voices, undiminished by the roar of the falls, took up a chilling chant: *'They drove us here, with swords of iron. They drove us here and took our land. They drove us here to waters pure. They drove us here when time began. They made these islands whole once more. They held onto the old ways sure. They kept the lines, they kept the shrines, they allowed us to endure.'*

Their words were a whisper in the moonlight, a shifting, atonal song that drove the spellhounds into furious baying madness, spinning around on naked limbs, chasing tails they didn't have.

A spirit darted behind Torquesten. He tried to cut it with his sword, but the sword simply passed through the shadow.

'*You should not have fed them what you did, not here, not tonight, not when we were coming,*' the spirit murmured into Torquesten's ear and then flitted away.

The spellhounds yelped in pain and fell upon their sides, panting, whining, shuddering.

'*Hounds of blood. Hounds of spell,*' the spirits chanted. '*Feel our touch.*' They poured through the bodies of the spellhounds again and again, darting through and beyond, curving back and seeping into the naked, damaged bodies of the men forced to act like dogs. '*Hear our cry.*'

A glissading cacophony raged through the air. Torquesten dropped his sword, clasped his hands over his ears, tried to block the piercing cries of the spirits, but still the bass rhythm of the tumbling water punched into him, forcing his blood to beat in time with the heartbeat of the falls. His hands dropped from his ears, clasped around his chest, tried to block the rumbling beat.

The screeching melody skewered into his mind. '*See with truth within your eye.*'

The spellhounds glowed red in the night and, with the ripping, tearing, splintering sound of flesh and bone transforming, became creatures of nightmare.

****

Bihkat, clasped tight in the power of the Ulac, fell upon the ground, foaming at the mouth, his legs jerking, his arms flailing, his priests seeking to hold him still, to get the stick between his teeth, to stop him biting through his tongue. His was the voice of the gods and they didn't wish to lose that magnificence.

In his splendour, Bihkat didn't feel the hands upon his limbs, didn't feel the spittle spraying across his chest, or the pain of the stick thrust into his mouth. In his journey, he didn't care about the Vascanar, the warriors or his priests. In his revelation, he learned that these islands were not to be conquered so easily.

There were dark forces here, bright forces, old and new, creatures of shadow, creatures already dead. These islands were not undefended. They would fight the approaching pain.

Bihkat's demonic lords hissed their agreement; a weapon must be forged.

Bihkat offered his soul to them.

They refused the offer.

****

On his knees, hands clasped over aching ears, Torquesten lifted his head as the falls pulsed. Deep red light washed over the twitching bodies of the spellhounds. Fumes rose from screaming mouths as the blood of the soldier they had consumed burned away into the night.

Torquesten clambered to his feet, set his men around him, and prepared for battle.

The spellhounds' bodies contorted, stretched, thickened. The air grew cold; ice choked the falls, broke away, shattered like glass on the rocks below. The spellhounds' human skulls widened, lengthened, teeth sharpened into fangs, eyes glowed; pointed ears twitched towards the sound of human heartbeats.

The heartbeats of the Vascanar standing back to back beside the falls.

Hairless still, the spellhounds lurched onto hands become paws and legs bent under their bodies on transformed knees. They had become hounds in truth, hounds without fur, hounds with ridged bone beneath rippling muscle, larger than the men they had been. Amber eyes, filled with intelligence and ferocity, glared at the Vascanar.

The Hounds of the Falls howled. A blast of energy, the last shred of the transformative magic, poured through their bodies. Patches of fur sprouted upon the hounds, like manes, running from their skulls along their spines, outlining the shape of their long, bristled tails. No other fur sprouted on those bulging, muscular forms, just these streaks along their spines, like the hackles of a dog.

The wave of magic spread outwards and slammed into the Vascanar, smashing them into the rocks. The melody of the magic faded away into the rhythm of the falls. Desperately, Torquesten and his men staggered to their feet, retrieved their swords from the wet rocks, and reformed their circle of steel.

The fear that held Torquesten's heart cold and hard within his chest, that made him capable of anything his masters commanded, and corrupted his soul with fire and steel, this fear forged itself into arrogance. What were these things to him? He was an Akalac, a blood-knight, the Master of the Hounds. He ruled their souls.

His will flared into the transformed spellhounds, commanding them to his side, offering them the meat of his men if they would serve him and him alone.

They refused the offer.

Snarling, pacing, haunches low to the ground, the creatures prowled around the circle of Vascanar. Five creatures of the falls against twelve brutal men.

'Hold!' Torquesten yelled above the roar of the water. 'Hold the circle!'

A hound with a band of red fur running from skull-top to tail-tip tilted its head at the sound of Torquesten's yell and licked its lips. It hunkered down, wriggled its haunches; the slits of its pupils locked on Torquesten's throat.

The other hounds sniffed the air, stalked their prey, sensing weak spots within the circle. The stench of urine and faeces rose on the air as brutalised soldiers lost their nerve.

'Hold!' Torquesten twisted the wire-bound grip of his sword between his hands, holding it high above his head, ready to cut down upon the beast. He turned his shoulder towards it, adjusted his stance, found purchase for his feet on the slippery rocks. The amber eyes of the red-furred hound stared into Torquesten's blue and all became still for a moment.

One of the men to Torquesten's left broke from the circle, ran for the cliffs.

'No!' Torquesten screamed without taking his eyes from the beast before him.

Another man turned to follow the first, slipped on the wet rocks; his foot crashed into Torquesten's ankle.

Torquesten stumbled, landed upon one knee.

This was all the creature before him needed. It sprang.

Torquesten's sword clove the air and bit into flesh, but the creature was too fast and powerful to be stopped by a single cut. It slammed into Torquesten, knocking him flat upon the ground.

But he had cut true, his blade slashing through the creature's chest and deep into its torso before exiting at its shoulder. The hound snapped about Torquesten's arm, but the solid metal of the vambrace held out against the pressure. Torquesten stabbed the creature in the side, his blade plunging deep into the flesh again and again.

Around him, the other men smashed with shields, cut with blades, threw the creatures back from the circle. The hounds' battered, bloodied bodies collapsed against the rocks beneath the falls.

Torquesten kicked his kill away, regained his feet, and gave a harsh bark of laughter. 'Is that all?' he cried at the water, at the moon, at the land. 'Is that all you can do?'

'Iron is no defence against these creatures,' the voices whispered into the sudden hush.

Growling, panting, laying upon their sides, glowing ruby red, shuddering, shivering, shimmering in the bloodlight, the Hounds of the Falls healed.

It didn't take them long.

CHAPTER 17

Marisa chanted in the hidden tongue, imbuing the alder staves with magic, calling forth the power of the forest for protection against the walking dead. Illath glistened through the trees, filling the forest with strange half-shadows that crept and darted, glowering malevolence in the dark beneath the trees — held away by the power of the alder.

As she chanted, Cullain set his feet. She shook her head at his rolled shoulders and the stave of alder held in his hand like a club. He had bested swordsmen with such a weapon and not always on the training field, but it would do him no good here. This was old magic, the magic of Illath, goddess of the old ways. You cannot kill the walking dead. Marisa hoped only to keep them away and to survive the night.

The Vascanar warriors Cullain had killed on the path walked out of the forest, their open wounds weeping blood. They stood in a line. No hint of a pupil in their pearlescent eyes, but Marisa's skin crawled at their hungry gaze.

'Do you think I upset 'em?' Cullain asked.

'They cannot come any closer,' Marisa said.

The Vascanar took a step closer and those that still had jaws grinned. The one Cullain had battered against a tree had no face left, but white eyes stared out of the ruin. Then blackness bled across the eyes of the dead Vascanar soldiers until the white disappeared into the darkness.

'Black eyes,' Cullain said. 'That ain't right.'

'No.' Fear crawled along Marisa's spine.

Pupils of fire flared in the eyes of the Vascanar dead as they fixed upon their prey.

Cullain said, 'Ain't never heard of eyes like that.'

Marisa had, but she could not place the knowledge. It stung her with fear, but she could not remember why. Old knowledge, knowledge she did not need as a healer.

The dead took another step forward, keeping their line as clean and precise as soldiers at inspection, grinning through broken faces.

'Something is wrong,' Marisa said.

'You reckon?' Cullain's voice was steady. 'What's happening?'

'I am a healer not a witch.'

Cullain shrugged, nodded, took a step towards the Vascanar. Who did not halt their slow advance. 'Run.'

'I will not lea—'

'Run!' Cullain leapt forward to one side of the line of Vascanar dead. He ducked under a whirling blade, driving inwards, smashing the stave into a face, reaching down with his other hand, picking the creature up, throwing it into its comrades. Three of them stumbled, but the rest surged towards Cullain's flanks.

He jumped backwards, diagonally, placing himself at the edge of the line once more. Smashing aside a sword aimed at his neck, he grabbed the enemy's sword arm in the iron grip of his left hand. The alder stave whirled through the air, striking five times in a blur of motion, hitting at the joints of the Vascanar's arm, wrist, elbow, shoulder, then up across the side of the head before smashing back down into the collar bone.

Cullain stamped hard on the enemy's knee and drove the dead man to the ground. He smashed in the back of the skull with the club.

And leapt backwards again before he was surrounded.

'Run!' he yelled.

The Vascanar shook his shattered head, bits of bloodied bone falling onto the ground, and stood. Joints with white bones sticking out at extreme angles worked as if they were whole.

Marisa gasped; that was not possible, not possible. The dead could not move with broken joints.

'Run!' Cullain drove two dead men into a third; they fell, blocking the others for a brief moment. He grabbed Marisa's arm and dragged her away into the trees. 'Run, milady,' he gasped and smashed through the trees ahead of her, ducking his head as branches whipped at his eyes, forging a path for her to follow through the dark.

A clearing, open ground. They could sprint here. No more blundering through the trees. Cullain still ahead of her, cursing, wiping at his face.

Marisa tried to keep up, looking ahead, Illath's light bloody on the ground. The ground, a dark shadow ahead of them, trees tilting out into the dark as if—

'Cliff!' she screamed and lunged for Cullain's back, only managing to grab the pack bouncing on his shoulder, skidding, pushing her legs forward, tangling them up with his. He grunted as he fell, slamming into the dirt, rolling over, stopping only inches from the edge of an abyss.

Cullain drew back from the edge. 'Thank—'

An arm snaked around Marisa's neck, lifting her to her feet. The foetid stink of a dead man's breath enveloped her face. She scrabbled at her belt, pulled out the silver dagger she had used to cut the alder staves and stabbed back blindly.

With a screech of pain the Vascanar staggered back, hands clutched around the sliver blade embedded in its stomach.

Marisa fell forward onto her knees. Silver! Silver hurt these things. But that meant… Black eyes filled with fire. Bodies that twitched but did not fall whatever the damage. Silver, the untouchable metal of the gods, hurt them.

The Vascanar collapsed. Darkness swirled around it, emptying through its mouth, its eyes, through every opening in its body, streaming past the dagger embedded in its stomach.

Demons.

Here.

On the isles.

'Where'd he come from?' Cullain pulled Marisa to her feet.

From out of the trees, walking slowly, came more Vascanar dead. 'I didn't kill that many,' Cullain said. 'Ain't that against the rules?'

'Demons,' Marisa panted. 'They're inhabited with demon blood.'

'That explains a lot.' Cullain looked at the walking corpses advancing towards them. He looked at the edge of the cliff behind them. He looked right and then left and shook his head. 'We're trapped.'

****

Torquesten ripped the bone flask of Ulac from his belt.

In his terror, he ignored the lesson of the mid-winter sacrifices, when men were forced to drink of the Ulac, of the pure, undiluted elixir. They fell screaming upon the ground, losing their minds, losing their souls, becoming sanctified flesh in the power of the demonic lords as they died. Their consecrated meat sizzled on spits. Their blood became foaming blood-wine, swallowed by the Akalac while still warm, bringing visions to the blood-knights, giving them their name and their power.

Torquesten's fingers scrabbled at the lid of the flask made from a thighbone of one of those mid-winter sacrifices. He backed up against the cliff.

Only three of his men still stood, swords swinging, shields smashing, fighting off yet another attack, but the hounds recovered more quickly, more ferociously with each bout of combat. Blades tore, blood flowed, and the hounds' wounds healed to pink-rimmed scars in less time than it took the exhausted men to lift their blades again.

'Iron is no defence, demon worshipper.' The words hissed into his ear by a shadow of darkened blood.

All would fall in this attack, their bodies meat for the creatures of the falls. The red-furred hound lunged at Torquesten. He kicked it away. The seal on the flask came free. He drained the Ulac in a single swallow…

…to became one with his gods.

His soul squeezed tight, his mind flowing into every crevice of his body. Need, greed, for flesh, power and life surged through him.

Exhaustion fell from his limbs. Clarity rose in his mind. The blood-red shadows were ghosts, ghosts of discarded gods, the gods of a people now gone from the face of the world.

They called themselves Those That Endure and had power beyond imagining, here, at the walls of their prison — but not out there in the forest beyond. Out there the new world breathed and these ghosts could not stand its scent.

He had to escape this place.

Silence, numbing silence; no sound of the falls, just the growls of the hounds and the ragged, gasping breaths of his remaining men.

Without a thought for those three survivors, Torquesten threw aside his useless sword and turned away from the fight. He clambered up the cliff face, closing his ears to the despairing cries of the men he left to die. Power poured through him. He climbed faster than the hounds could tear through his men and snap at his heels.

At the top of the cliff, as the waterfall hollered its heartbeat into the night, he stopped and looked down at the scene below. Most of the hounds ignored him, feeding on the remnants of his men. Only the red-haired hound still growled as it looked up at him.

But it, too, had to leave the blood-knight to his victory and return to the feast, because, despite all that Those That Endure had wrought, dogs cannot climb as men do.

CHAPTER 18

In the forest, on the edge of a cliff, surrounded by the walking dead, Marisa waited to die.

'I count twenty of the rancid little buggers,' Cullain said. He held the alder-wood club in his right hand and the silver dagger in his left.

'Twenty one.' Marisa pointed under an alder tree.

'Didn't think to look there.' Cullain sniffed. 'This is going to be difficult.'

'We can't let them take us alive,' Marisa said.

'There's an easy remedy.' Sadness in Cullain's voice.

'Why do they wait?' she asked.

'Dunno.'

Marisa wanted to live. She wanted to see the sun rise. Not to die here, in Illath's bloody light, her soul torn from her and consumed in the poisoned maw of foul demonic greed. She wanted to live. She wanted to see Drustan one more time.

'I can hold them,' Cullain said. 'You might be able to get away.'

'And leave you to their tenderness.'

'Nobody lives forever.'

'Do you know what they will do to you?'

'Everybody dies.'

'They will take your soul.'

'They'll choke on it.' Cullain took a step towards the Vascanar; they shifted their line to block his escape. 'They ain't as smart as they were alive. There's a gap over by the river. Down the slope'

The river flowed black and turgid in the light of Illath. Marisa spotted movement and looked closer. Her haraf stone showed her what Cullain had missed: 'There are three waiting there.'

Cullain checked and scowled. 'Clever little whoreson corpses, ain't they?' He glanced back at Marisa. 'Lift your head. Close your eyes.'

'I don't want to die.'

'Nobody does.'

'No. I don't want to die like this.' Marisa lifted her chin, but her eyes remained defiantly open. 'I want to fight.'

'Good lass.' Cullain grinned, his teeth black in the bloodlight. 'Any more silver daggers in that pack of yours?'

'No, but I do have this.' Marisa held out a heavy silver chain. 'It is for purifying—'

'Don't care.' Cullain handed her the dagger and took the chain. He flicked his hand, wrapping the silver around his fist. 'Do you remember how to use stick and dagger?'

'Hit with the stick. Stick with the dagger.'

'There's the little lady I taught to kick Drustan in the groin.'

Marisa laughed. 'He was most upset.' Why was she laughing? What was happening to her? Was this how Drustan felt before a battle?

'Women don't understand just how little force is needed.' Cullain gazed at the impromptu knuckle-duster around his left fist. 'No padding. Gonna hurt like a bugger in the morning.' He shook his head ruefully. 'When they come, I'll charge. Stay close behind me. Protect my back. I'll see none get behind you.'

'How?'

'By being taller'n you.' Cullain studied the way she held the dagger and stave. 'Good.' He turned back to the Vascanar dead and roared, 'Let's be having you, then! I ain't got all this bloody night!' He waved the silver-chain-clad fist.

The Vascanar took a single step forward and then stopped.

'I hate it when they do that,' Cullain muttered.

'It is fear. They want us terrified.'

'They'll have a long wait.'

****

Drustan jerked as fear curdled his guts. 'Marisa.'

His mother flickered in the light, her form shifting, ghostlike, aloof. 'They would not dare.'

Gasping with pain, Drustan forced himself to his feet. He swayed, staggered towards his weapons, the torn muscles in his side tightening to protect themselves. Agony surged through him. His legs buckled and he fell to his knees, snarling against the pain. He crawled forward, struggling to make the few feet to where his blades lay.

Garet leapt forward to help him. 'What is it?' Kneeling, he placed his hand on Drustan's shoulder.

Whatever spell Eirane had cast to keep her conversation with Dustan sacrosanct had lost its power.

'Marisa,' Drustan gasped.

'They would not dare,' Eirane repeated. 'This is our land. Our faith.'

'Who's Marisa?' Agus asked, helping to turn Drustan over onto his back.

'The woman who betrayed him,' Garet said. 'Help—'

Drustan closed his hands around Garet's throat. He rolled him, knelt upon his chest. 'You never speak that way of her.'

Garet tried to pull Drustan's hands away, but he was no match for a man who had spent all his life handling swords. He grabbed hold of Drustan's little finger, tried to bend it back; Drustan's hands tightened around the merchant's throat.

Unable to breathe, Garet punched Drustan in his injured side. Drustan jerked at the surge of pain, but did not loosen his grip. Garet punched him again — harder. Drustan grunted, the pain stopping his breath for a moment. His hands relaxed and Garet pulled them away from his throat. The smaller man bucked, throwing aside Drustan's weight, and wriggled free. Blood seeped from the scratches on his neck. He scrambled crabwise away from Drustan.

Both men sucked in vast gulps of air.

Drustan gasped, 'You never … never speak of her. You haven't earned the right.'

Garet massaged his throat as he tried to breathe, his eyes wild, terrified.

Drustan lowered his gaze. The man hadn't deserved that.

Garet coughed. 'Fair point.' He got to his feet and snatched up a waterskin. 'But you're in no shape to fight, milord.'

'Don't call me that.'

'Don't act like one, then.' Garet drank to ease his aching throat. 'Here.' He handed Drustan the waterskin. Drustan drank as Garet checked the bandages wrapped around his chest.

'What are you doing, man?' Drustan asked,

Garet held up a hand slippery with blood. 'You're bleeding.'

Drustan checked the bandages. 'Quite badly.'

'Efan did warn you.' Garet mimicked Efan's accent: 'You're a fool, man, are you trying to rip open that wound?'

Drustan laughed and Garet grinned.

'Will I be crazy when I grow up?' Agus asked.

'We'll have to wait and see.' Drustan grinned, then his eyes became hooded, dangerously cold again. 'You have to save her, mother.' Blood trickled, warm and sticky down his side.

'I know,' Eirane said. 'I must go to my sister. This is her forest, she has the power here.'

'Will she save her?' Drustan asked.

'She must act. Such foulness must not be allowed here. Not in a Calodrig, not in the heart of this forest.' In a swirl of wind, Eirane vanished.

Drustan leaned back against the tree. His eyes stared at the fire. His mind closed down; he could do nothing. Perhaps he would bleed to death. That would solve a lot of problems. But right now, he had to sit here and wait.

****

'Wait,' Cullain said. 'Wait.'

The Vascanar dead took another step forward. A bare eight paces away. A curving line with a radius centred on Marisa and Cullain.

'Why are we waiting?' Marisa asked.

'We need 'em close enough to tangle themselves up, but not so close we've no freedom to choose.'

'Choose what?'

Cullain grinned. 'Our target.'

'They are all the same, demon-infested corpses that feel no pain, have no mercy…' Marisa stopped. 'They are focussing fear upon us.'

'That they are.'

'Are you not scared?'

'Terrified.' Cullain flexed his hand inside the silver chain. 'One more step, me little beauties, one more step.'

The Vascanar took another step.

'Now!' Cullain leapt forward as Marisa stripped the silk from her haraf stone. They had discussed the tactic, though Cullain did not understand why the stone would do anything other than light up the dark and Marisa did not understand why he kept grinning.

Clean white light blazed across the clearing from the stone around her neck. The Vascanar threw their hands across their eyes and cried out, a wailing, whistling sound that should not come from human throats.

Cullain closed with his chosen target. Marisa hurried to catch up, the haraf stone blazing between her breasts, the alder stick in her left hand heavy, solid, strong, the silver of the dagger gleaming in her right.

The alder club in Cullain's hand whirled across the flat of a Vascanar sword, shattering the brittle steel into shards and leaving the path open for Cullain's driving fist. He smashed the chain into a corpse's face, which collapsed around the silver and bled dark fumes.

The Vascanar dead recovered from the initial impact of the haraf stone's light and enfolded the two living humans in their midst.

Marisa parried a sword with her stick and slashed open a dead man's thigh with the dagger. Evil-smelling fumes poured from the wound in a gush of darkness that swirled as if it were alive and then fled the light of the haraf stone. The corpse tottered and fell.

It took only a single strike of silver to end one of these things. But a scratch would not do. It had to be a deep wound.

Cullain drove into the Vascanar, smashing his way through them. Unfortunately, even the mutilated corpses fought as soldiers, working as a squad, taking the damage, folding around their prey, enveloping them, trying to open a gap between them.

A corpse managed to get behind Marisa as she protected Cullain's back. She parried the sword, but could not bring the dagger to bear in time. She screamed.

Cullain glanced back as he clubbed an enemy to the ground. The chain uncoiled from his fist. He whipped it backwards as he parried swords with the alder stave.

The chain snaked around the Vascanar's neck. Cullain jerked savagely and the Vascanar spun through the air, darkness fuming from its shredded throat.

Cullain whirled the chain around his head, lashing at enemies who got too close while he was occupied saving Marisa. A flick of the wrist wrapped the chain back around his fist in time to launch another tremendous, skull-crushing punch into the Vascanar to his front.

More figures appeared out of the dark of the forest.

Marisa knew she sobbed, she could hear the sound, taste the salt of tears on her lips, but she was above the fray. Watching as she cut with the dagger and blocked with the stave. There were too many. Cullain had sent maybe eight of the walking corpses into rest. Marisa had managed to stop only one.

Not enough.

And now more figures ran out of the woods. How many? Did it matter? Cullain could not deal with what lay in front of them. It didn't matter how many more joined the battle.

Wait!

She understood. The figures rushing from the forest ran.

They ran.

They screamed battle-cries.

They were alive, human, Karisae. Silver flashed in the moonlight and living men fell upon the walking dead.

Chapter 19

Eirane, the mother of Drustan, flowed through the spirit realm seeking Wendin.

There were nine Calodrig, nine sacred hearts of nine forests, each one protected by the power of its Amthisrid. Down through the ages in an unbroken line, each Amthisrid cast off their mortality to take up their stewardship of the land. Then when the time came for them to pass on they, through a communion of minds, passed on the spirit lore of the Anthanic people to their successors, before finally giving up their burdens and leaving this world behind. The cycle of death and rebirth was denied them; a price they paid willingly in return for the power to protect their people and their land.

The Karisae called them witches, demons, creatures of the night, but even the magicians of the Karisae had learned to ask favours of the Amthisrid. So the world turned and the invaders became one with the land they invaded.

Amthisrid were always women, and they were always young when they transcended the mortal realm. Few had tasted the pain and delight of birthing a living child, because that link to the mortal world weakened them when the time came to unleash the magic of the land. Eirane was the youngest of the Amthisrid — and she had a living child.

She found Wendin, the Amthisrid of this forest, the oldest of the nine, floating above the River Falas downstream of the Falls of Karcha where Those That Endure were imprisoned.

Older than the Empire of Maebaz, old when the Karisae came to the islands, she would pass great power onto her successor. Eirane did not know if she envied the girl, remembering the pain of her own transcending.

But the threads of fate coiled about Drustan. A deadly fear invaded his soul from the cursed amulet at his belt. Eirane did not know the name of that thing he carried, but she tasted the venom of demons in its stench. How had such a thing come into his hands? Something played games with the threads of her son's life — and so she sought the wisdom of Wendin.

Eirane flowed into the shape of a woman beside Wendin's ancient spirit.

'They are safe, sister,' Wendin said. 'Agusur sent help.'

'I know. I saw,' Eirane said. 'The *muadisri* of your forest attacked Marisa. She had to unveil her haraf amulet to drive them away, drawing the enemy to where she hid in the dark. Why did they attack her?'

'With Illath in the sky the little spirits are difficult to control. They scented her power and wished to feed upon it. You know this, sister.'

'Mine are not so recalcitrant.'

'Yours never had such as Marisa pass through their lands with Illath in the sky.' Wendin laughed. 'You will learn, sister. We guide the muadisri, we advise them, but we do not control them utterly. They are free creatures.'

'If Marisa had died…' Eirane did not finish the sentence.

Wendin cast a hard gaze at Eirane. 'Your son weakens you, sister. You should not have become one of the nine with a living child.'

'Jerizzina did not agree.' Eirane named she who had given her power to Eirane before fading away.

'The living son of an Amthisrid attracts the attention of the Weaver, Riadna herself. She tastes his threads and binds them tight around him. Too many threads for a mortal to bear. There will be a reckoning before all this is finished.'

'He carries something that belongs to the enemy.'

'I know. I hide its stink as best I can, but the powers are moving.'

'I fear for him.'

'As you should. Something, someone, twists the threads. Riadna will not be happy with their meddling.'

'How do you know this?'

'Your Drustan returns, he fights; the amulet of the enemy falls into his hand; a sell-bow is on hand to save his life; the woman he loves is the greatest healer in all the land and she is close enough to aid him; and a brutal protector is provided to get her to him safely. Someone meddles, Eirane. Riadna the Weaver, fate herself, will not leave such twisting of her threads unpunished.'

'Can I protect him?'

'We shall do what we can, but he is a knot in the weave and Riadna will smooth out the threads one way or another. Calm, sister. Not even Riadna can see the future, and so we all, gods and spirits, mortal and immortal, place pieces into play in the hope that they will give us an advantage when the time comes.' Wendin turned away from Eirane and watched a bedraggled figure drag himself from the River Falas.

Eirane knew that she would get nothing further from Wendin, for the ancient Amthisrid had nothing else to say, so she asked, 'Who is that man?'

Naked, shivering, with a strange yellowish tint to his skin, the man crawled away from the water, whimpering like a dog.

'One of the abominations of the Vascanar,' Wendin said.

Eirane smiled. 'Ah, one of the hounds escaped the wrath of Those That Endure. This is good. What the hounds became was never their fault.'

'People are always responsible for what they become.'

'The Vascanar tortured him, twisted his mind with magic, infested him with shards of demon-kind.'

'He did not have to submit. He could have fought. He could have died. He could have travelled onward. He chose this life. In his soul, he chose it.'

'That is a harsh view.'

'But a true one.' Wendin studied the figure sprawled beside the river. 'He did not taste the flesh of men this day, but he has tasted it in the past. Its taint is upon him.'

'Will he change? Will he become a ravening beast like the others?'

'Those that haunt the falls are beyond us, sister. Their origins lie before the line of the Amthisrid existed in this land. They were trapped here by hatred and vengeance. But their power is weak away from the Falls of Karcha. Which is just as well, for they are wild, without discipline or moderation.'

'Is that slight aimed at me?' Eirane asked.

'You are young, sister, arrogant in your youth. Your soul has not yet outlasted the mortality you left behind.' Wendin turned her gaze upon Eirane. 'And you have a living child. I had no child when I transcended the world. I had no ties to what I left behind. It makes you rash, impulsive. You must learn patience.'

'We cannot allow demons to usurp this place.'

'Can we not?' Wendin tilted her head to one side. 'Why is that?'

'They would unleash a pantheon of hate upon the world.'

'And are other gods any better than that?' Wendin shook her head. 'We stand between the gods and the world of mortals, sister. This world, this land, will absorb demons-become-gods as easily as it does any other corruption. There would be wars, there would be deaths, but the world would endure. You fear for your son, which is understandable, but do not fear for the world.'

'Then why do we seek to halt these demons?' Eirane asked.

'These are the Shimmering Isles. There are very few places of power left upon this world where demons can become gods. But we ride the power of these islands, too. If they take that power to facilitate their elevation then we will cease to be.'

'Or be corrupted.'

'Either way, our stewardship of these islands would end. That is why we seek to stop them.' Wendin drew the stuff of the spirit realm into her, became larger, more solid. 'And these are *our* people. Even the Karisae that live on the islands became our people. We must hold to the trust we owe them.'

'There are other places beyond the Salt where such as we exist.'

'Not like us, sister. We are an unbroken line stretching back to the time of the unfettered gods. We exist because this island has never been plundered for its power.'

'I fear for my son, sister, and will do whatever is needed to keep him safe. You fear for yourself.'

'I fear for us all.'

Eirane let the memories of Jerizzina, of all the Amthisrid in her line, flow into her. She tasted the lore and the ghosts of the past, and said, 'I do what I must.'

'As do I,' Wendin said. She extended a hand towards the spellhound lying naked upon the bank.

And the trees whispered into the man's ears, 'You are free.'

****

Marisa sank to her knees, exhausted. Cullain shattered the skull of the last of the Vasacanar with a silver-clad fist. Then stamped the shards of bloody flesh and bones into the ground; dark fumes dissipated into the night. Breathing heavily, the armsmaster hunched over, his hands on his knees.

'Are you hurt?' A man placed his arm around Marisa's shoulders.

'No.'

'Illath fades within the hour,' the man said.

'I know.' Marisa lifted her head. 'Thank you.'

The man smiled down at her; kind eyes, she thought, generous, despite his leather armour. A farmer pressed into service, perhaps.

'What were those things?' he asked. 'We met a couple on the way 'ere, but—'

'Give me your name.' She heard Cullain's harsh demand and lifted her head. The man in front of Cullain was huge, muscular, taller than the armsmaster by nearly a head, naked to the waist. They would be a good match on the sand.

'He can't speak,' the man holding Marisa said. 'The Vascanar took his tongue. His name's Tirac and I'm named Efan of Trant.'

'I'm named Cullain Strongarm,' Cullain said. ''Twas well you arrived when you did.' He gripped Tirac's forearm. 'A good fight.'

Tirac returned the grip and nodded.

Marisa clambered to her feet. People appeared between the trees. Women, children, young folk, old folk. Where had they come from? She let her haraf stone quest between their minds even as she slipped it back into its packet of silk.

'This is my brother, Horol,' Efan said.

'They take his tongue too?' Cullain asked.

'I can speak,' said Horol.

'Then give me your name like a man.'

'I'm named Horol of Trant.'

'I'm named Cullain Strongarm. You fought well.' Cullain leaned over Marisa. 'As did you, lass.'

'I was terrified.' The haraf stone cried Drustan into Marisa's mind.

Some of these people had seen him — recently.

'That's why they call it courage.' Cullain took an alder stick from Efan's hand. 'Look at that.' Silver coins were hammered into the wood, turning it into an effective mace. 'Clever.'

'Yes.' Marisa smiled at one of the women. Not her; she had not seen Drustan slumped injured and sorrowful against a tree.

'Tirac's idea,' Efan said. 'We met one of those things in the forest. It killed old Tam before Tirac killed it.'

'He don't have a club.' Cullain pointed at Tirac.

'Nah.' Efan laughed.

Him. Marisa smiled into the night. Efan had seen Drustan.

Tirac showed his hand to Cullain. He closed it around a piece of leather and then pushed silver coins between his fingers.

Cullain lifted his eyes to Tirac's face. 'Where'd you serve? Because you ain't no farmer-boy from the shieldwall.'

'Farmer-boys fight well enough,' Horol said.

'I know, lad, I were there.' Cullain rolled his shoulders. 'Time we were on our way, milady.'

'I don't think so, Armsmaster Cullain.' Marisa straightened up. 'I am Lady Marisa desainLegan,' she said to Efan. 'Take me to Drustan desainCoid.'

CHAPTER 20

In the damp grass at the side of the river, a man stirred. He shivered, naked, the yellow tint of his skin blotchy and faded. His eyes remained closed as he tried to remember.

That voice, a power beyond him, calling down to him, *'You are free.'* What did that mean? Free? The word tumbled through his mind. Not enslaved, that was what free meant. Free to leave, free to go, free to be whoever he wanted to be. Who was he?

A name. He had a name once. His mother's voice calling him in to eat. *Kihan.* He was Kihan. The name broke chains in his mind. A flash of images: tall buildings, his mother's smile, a game played with sticks and stones. Kihan, he was Kihan.

He smiled into the rain and opened his eyes.

Where was he? What was this place of damp air, gurgling water, rearing trees? Not his homeland. The trees were different, the river sparked no memories, even the grass he lay upon smelled wrong.

Another question slithered into his mind: what had happened to him?

He sat up in the red light of the moon. Did he remember a red moon? Yes. It had a name this moon... Playing in parks by the light of ... *Illath.* That was the name of the red moon. He hugged the word to himself. In the parks, he played by the light of this moon and, if he was very lucky, a shade would waft by and tell him of its death. Such fun; not like this. Here it felt...

...treacherous.

His mind reforming in the damp air, he thought about ghosts, shades, fragments of personality sheared off by the wheel of life as it turned from death to rebirth. Were ghosts dangerous? Not in his childhood, not where he came from, but where had he come from? What was the name of that wondrous place?

The parks with their sculpted trees and glorious patterns of shrubs and flowers — such flowers, such a perfume in the air! The blossoms fell across the stone-built paths and scented the world anew with each season. The buildings taller than the trees, with ten, sometimes fifteen floors of wood and stone. Windows of glass, like eyes looking out upon the world.

Not like this damp place of muddy smells and keening wind, with nature so wild, so dangerously close to where Kihan sat upon the banks of a river and tried to remember what had happened to him.

Memories of childhood lessons: find out what you can because the answer always lies in the compiled facts. He was Kihan, he was naked, and he sat upon grass beside a broad river gurgling over rocks. Trees around him, branches above him, but the shape of the leaves unfamiliar to his gaze.

He was a long way from his homeland.

He sobbed and then sucked in a breath, stopped his tears, tightened his throat. No need for that, no need for self-pity. Consider the situation, but don't consider your predicament. He lifted his chin from his chest and looked.

What wilderness was this? What forest? What river had he dragged his naked body from? Where was he?

'*Symcani,*' the wind whispered.

Where in the teeth of all that's holy was Symcani? The word sparked no memories. No words learned by rote, in classrooms filled with children chanting out their lessons, led him to the word *Symcani*. The word meant nothing. The scent of chalk, of slate, of parchment... He had been taken as a child... Oh dear gods of all that lived, he remembered.

A man in armour grabbed him when he was barely twelve years old *... so proud. He was going to the school for scholars. His father thought he might rise to be a tax collector, raise the family's standing from artisan to bureaucrat.*

An army took down the walls of the city with fire and steel. They were like him, the invaders. What had started the war? He could remember his father telling him, because at twelve he was almost a man. His father talking of ... civil war, but why? An image dashed unbidden against his mind: *his father with a spear through his back, visceral blood bubbling from his mouth. So red. Soldiers... His mother held down and—*

Kihan shook his head to clear it of the memory. He didn't want to remember. He didn't want to see that again. What happened after?

Placed on a plinth, sold to slavers, who'd taken him from his burning home and... *His sisters ... his sisters—*

No!

Those images didn't help. Focus on how he got here.

The grass passing beneath the cage, the mountains cold and biting, the wide rivers crossed, the forests, not like this one, the marshes, the hills, the valleys, the slavers, the sting of the whip... He'd laughed as they died.

Scar-faced warriors attacked the slave caravan... The Vascanar. Kihan shivered and hugged himself close. He had thought himself saved.

The ritual. *Cut in so many places, pain thrust into him; the heat, the lightning, the pain, the pain...* His memories imploded within him. He had lived like a dog, been treated like a dog. *He had eaten the flesh of men.*

Kihan curled around himself and wept for shame as Illath slowly faded from the sky.

****

The Hounds of the Falls ate their fill from the corpses of the dead Vascanar. Growling and snarling, nipping and biting, to the rhythm of the falls. The shadows swirled through them, circled above their heads, ice-cold within their minds.

'*One escaped, washed away, lost to our power, without our say. Find him, break him, take his marrow, feed on his flesh, take him to a barrow.*'

The hound with a strip of red hair slashing down his back pricked up his ears, listened to the voices. The scent of Kihan flooded his mind. He howled.

The last shreds of Illath's light faded from the sky and the shadows retreated into their prison.

The Hounds of the Falls, released from the power of Those That Endure, raced down the river bank, looking for a way out of the gorge. Now they neither howled nor bayed; they were on the hunt, and their prey was Kihan — the hound that escaped.

****

Bihkat rose, groggy, from the ground, his vision drenched in the sanguine imagery of death. His arms ached, his legs ached, his teeth ached from the shattering force that had snapped the twig placed between them. He spat splinters onto the ground.

The future remained unknowable, unwritten, unwoven; only glimpses of what might come to pass could ever be seen, even by the light of Illath, mistress of magic.

Old gods still existed in this old land, these islands untouched by civilisation and steel. Old shrines still held back the surging wave of progress, old ways still held sway in the forests, mountains, and coves.

This was why his demonic overlords had chosen to breach the walls between realms *here*. This place held power in abundance; the skin of the world wore thin here. Here, the bloodlight caused the dead to walk. Not ghosts, not shadows sheared off by the turning of the wheel of life, but the dead, the corpses of those freshly killed.

The gods of the Karisae were weak things, burdened with story, lost to pride and arrogance. They were stretched too thin, their power split between the islands and the mainland beyond the Galla Straits, where competing nations squabbled.

There *were* things here to fear: old creatures, old ghosts and the spirits who defended the forests. But without the might of engaged gods, the barriers would fall before Bihkat's demonic overlords.

His masters had chosen their target well. And they had chosen *someone*, out there in the forest. Not Bihkat; his offer had been refused. But another had been accepted into the exalted state of *Tukalac*, the anointed of the gods.

Bihkat spat a final splinter of wood from his mouth and sneered. The race was not yet run, his promised uplifting not yet lost. Many things could happen before the sacred lake gave up her power and opened the Way between realms.

****

Drustan stared into the embers of the fire and sipped hot kha. The boy Agus made a good mug of kha: not too bitter, sweetened just right. Drustan sat and sipped, staring at the fire.

Some seers used fire to divine the future, examine the past and observe the present. Drustan had never wished for such a skill before. The past was gone, the future took care of itself, and if he wanted to know something of the present then he would go there and look. The scornful words he had once thrown at a fortune-teller across the Salt haunted him now as he sat trapped by a wound that might well kill him. He couldn't walk five paces without collapsing; better he should wield a crutch than a sword.

Garet squatted beside him. 'Here, have some food.'

'The bread is stale.'

'Aye, but the cheese is good.'

Drustan forced himself to eat and washed down the stale bread with kha, not noticing when Agus refilled his leather mug.

Marisa was in danger and he could do nothing. She had betrayed him. But still, but still, oh how he wanted to save her. Cullain had always said he had no sense with her. But the old warhorse had smiled as he said it.

Until they broke Drustan's sword.

Cullain should have turned up by now. Drustan wondered what kept the man. He didn't think for a moment that the Vascanar had managed to kill him.

Marisa, alone in the forest with Illath in the sky.

'The moon will be gone soon,' Agus said as he topped up Drustan's mug again. 'Be dawn soon after.'

'Thank you.'

'You're welcome. Would you like this half of pie I kept back?'

Drustan took the morsel of food. 'I thought you ate it all.'

'You never said thank you before.' Agus looked out into the dark. 'Someone comes.'

Drustan stared into the forest willing it to be Marisa. He didn't care what she had done. He only wanted to see her face again.

Tirac walked into the camp with a young child balanced on his shoulder.

They had saved at least some of Efan's people then, which was good. Drustan lifted a hand in welcome to the mute.

Tirac grinned and nodded.

Other people followed behind, so many people, what in all the hells — had Efan saved his entire damn village?

Cullain, the old bugger. Drustan grinned. 'What kept you, old man?'

'Had to pick something up along the way,' Cullain said and stepped aside.

'Hello, husband.'

Part Two

CHAPTER 21

Marisa.

Standing on the edge of the clearing, looking him in the eye across the embers of the fire. Drustan forced himself to breathe, to meet her gaze.

She looked tired, nervous, even scared. Her hair unkempt, not the hair of a lady primped by the hands of maids. He remembered her hair in just such an unruly mess against the curve of his arm when they lay in a field of wildflowers and laughed at two sparrows squabbling over a perch. Her eyes had changed then as their souls communed, as she learned the truth of his birth, of his lineage, in the coursing of his blood. All had changed, shattered, become dust in that instant.

Drustan looked away from her and spat.

'You are injured,' she said. Her tone brusque with an undertone of misery.

'Aye,' Drustan said. 'Heal me, woman, and then you can go back to your gossiping friends.'

'I will need my pack, Cullain,' she said.

Drustan had forgotten about Cullain, about the villagers still appearing through the trees. Forgotten all except her eyes.

'Did you have trouble on the road, old man?' Drustan asked.

Cullain dropped the pack beside Marisa as she studied the bandages around Drustan's torso. 'Not as much as you,' Cullain said. 'What happened?'

'I stopped moving.' Drustan winced as Marisa cut away the bandages.

'He fought nine for us,' Agus said. 'He were magnificent.' Agus's eyes shone in the dawnlight. 'Like Berasin against the hoard.'

Tirac coughed and squatted by the fire.

'Not that magnificent, boy.' Cullain gestured at the wound Marisa's ministrations revealed in Drustan's side. 'Axe, were it?'

'Aye,' Drustan said. 'Thrown.'

'Lucky it were. Man's weight behind that would've smashed your ribs to kindling.'

'That it would.' Drustan shifted as Marisa probed the wound with ungentle hands.

'This was treated by a buffoon,' she declared. 'Dagabin does not have the strength for such a deep wound.'

'He saved my life,' Drustan snapped. 'Good enough for the place and time of the healing.'

'It'll need stitches.' Marisa sat back. 'Get some water boiling.'

'You heard her, boy,' Cullain said.

'Why me?' Agus asked, his eyes upon the blood seeping from Drustan's side.

'Because you didn't give me water at the line.'

'He threatened to kill me.' Agus pointed at Drustan. 'I gave 'im water and he threatened to kill me.'

'That's no excuse for forgetting your duty.'

A woman approached from the group of villagers huddled together at the other side of the camp. 'I've some knowledge of healing,' she said. 'Not like you, Milady of the Doves, but enough to stitch a wound and see a fever break. My name is Rosana.'

'Thank you, Rosana,' Marisa said. 'There's needle and thread in that pouch on the pack. Set them to boiling. Use the brass bowl.'

Drustan, despite himself, looked across in time to see Marisa's smile. Gods, that smile. 'Get on with it, woman,' he snapped.

'Husband, you called him,' Rosana said as she picked up the bowl and the pouch.

'Not anymore.' Drustan grunted as Marisa pressed upon the wound.

'Dissolved it, did they?' Rosana asked.

'Yes,' Marisa said.

'Lucky you.' Rosana turned away. 'Peggy, Jess, Hirane, get this fire sorted. We'll need a decent flame. Get some porridge cooking. You there, Efan, so proud in your dirty armour, go get us some wood. And some meat might be nice before we move on from this place. Don't be looking at me all slantwise, Horol Woodsmith. Go help your brother with his chores.'

'We need to move,' Drustan complained. 'Not break our fast in peasant splendour.'

'Watch your tongue,' Cullain growled. 'These people walked past death to get 'ere and saved your Marisa from damnation along the way.'

'Not my Marisa,' Drustan said.

Cullain snorted.

'We will be here a while yet,' Marisa said. 'I need to stitch the wound, cover it with a salamin dressing to protect it, and then begin the healing. No infection that I can see, though the gods alone know why.' She turned to look at Cullain. 'He will need a litter. It will be a couple of days before he can walk on his hind legs.'

****

Eirane swooped down into the courtyard of the House of Healing, as invisible as a breath of wind. She drifted across the wounds of dying men, giving them solace, allowing them to pass on, offering them the touch of mercy.

Some of the men, close enough to the gates of death that they saw into the spirit realm, reached out to her, but one man cried out in fear.

A white-robed healer bustled across the gardens to calm his terror. She had iron-grey hair and the flashing eyes of one who commanded. There was no doubting her position as leader of this House. The other healers stopped in their ministrations and bobbed their heads to her as she wove her way through the clots of dying men to the one who had screamed.

'She is here,' the wounded man moaned. He stank of faeces, his stomach torn open and infected. 'Death breathes upon me.'

'Hush now,' the healer said. 'Hush now. Henath will guard your soul on your journey to the other side and no spirit can harm you here.'

Eirane stilled in the air, offended by the words. That this foolish man thought her a demon, a creature of the night, was to be expected. The priests of the Karisae lied to their congregations. But this was a healer and ignorance of the truth was no excuse for such nightmarish tales.

'Cast the spell,' the dying man begged. 'Drive her away. Make the walls shine with light.'

'No such spirit can enter these sacred walls. The gods guard us.'

'She is here. I can see her. Drive her away, I beg of you. She wishes to feed upon my soul. Please. For all that I have given to my King, please.'

The healer lowered her head. 'Very well.' She lifted her hand and drew upon the power of the shrine, of the white-spiralled walls, of the water that bubbled from the spring — a spring fed by the waters of the sacred lake Calovinid, the lake the Karisae called Kalon, the lake at the heart of it all, the lake of Tanaz, the goddess enchained. 'Be gone, foul spirit! I, Dame Belina desainJasi of this House of Falas, command you. Leave this place.'

But the vinraf, the shrine spring, existed long before the Karisae came to this land. The chips of haraf they wore about their necks as amulets were taken from the huge haraf monoliths that encircled each of the shrines. For *haraf* meant *shrine stone* in the language of the Anthanic. And Eirane was as much a part of the chains that bound the goddess as any mere chip of stone or flowing spring.

So, though the amulet around Dame Belina's neck glowed with glorious light, the vinraf, the shrine spring, did not pick up that light, and the haraf of the walls surrounding the vinraf did not glow with magic.

Dame Belina paled, lifted her hand again and called out the same command.

'Is this how you thank me?' Eirane asked the men, though they heard her voice only as a murmur of the wind upon the shrine. Some of them, those sensitive to the spirit realm and those so close to the gates that they were already within its embrace, turned their heads away to hide their faces. *'I come here to help your passing and this is how you thank me, this is how it ends? So be it.'*

Engulfed in sadness, she turned and flowed away from the shrine. And the walls glowed with light.

'There,' Dame Belina said. She smiled down upon the soldier, but he had already died.

****

Jarl struck his tent. The warmth of Sekem's soul wreathed him in clarity as he rolled up the canvas, buckled tight the straps, and tied Sekem's unstrung bow to the outside of the canvas. His cousin's ashes, along with Sekem's blades, were bundled up in Jarl's bedroll, which was already strapped to his travelling pack. But he kept the two gold coins upon his hip, tucked into his belt, placed next to his skin where the heat of reason could suffuse him with understanding.

He slung the canvas roll of the tent over his shoulder and adjusted the straps. 'I'll get you home, cousin,' he whispered. The camp bustled around him, the Erisyans preparing to move out with the rest of the Vascanar forces.

Which ones were tainted?

Sekem had warned him that some of the caedi had drunk of the Vascanar elixir; the ghost could sense it in ways he could not explain. He said that the stench of the demons defiled their souls, but Jarl couldn't rely on his empathic dol to identify their treachery. Not while they still held to the ways of the Erisyan.

'It's a delicate thing,' Sekem had said. *'A delicate thing to rob a man of his destiny.'*

'Destiny?' Jarl had asked.

'The Vascanar take them away from the web of life. Away from their destiny. They become nothing but playthings for demons. All people walk roads untraveled by any other. All paths are new laid upon the wilderness of time. Fate spins out before them, making what she can of the raw threads of life, but she cannot decide their length. My fate wasn't decided until Drustan threw that spear. But that I would be there, beside you, at the moment the spear flew? That was decided when the Weaver wove my thread with yours.'

'So Drustan might have killed me instead of you?'

'Aye, if your thread and his hadn't become entangled at Forasin Hill.' A pause. *'It's strange that you should have been there, though. But then, if you hadn't been there, no other would've survived that dagger, no other would've sensed my death and saved their own life. So he wouldn't have had to deal with an archer, and then,'* Sekem had grinned, a flash of teeth in the smoke, *'he mightn't have been injured at all.'*

'Fate cannot be changed, you said.'

'Aye, but the threads can be twisted.' Sekem's spirit shrugged. *'It's probably nothing. I'm new to this existence.'*

Jarl let the memory of Sekem's words fade, picked up his bow, and went in search of Gorak. He found the hwlman with his *awchti*, his battle commanders, on the mound before the road, drinking wine and planning for a new day. Nobody would speak of Sekem, for the coins hadn't melted and they wouldn't wish to draw his ghost to them.

'I've better things to do than haunt fools like Gorak.'

'Jarl.' Gorak lifted an arm in welcome. He pointed at the Vascanar with his chin. 'They've work for us.' Contempt in his voice, shame in his eyes.

Jarl looked around at the assembled awchti, men of sharp courage, battle commanders for an Erisyan caedi, about their business. Five men, five possible traitors. Jarl let his dol flicker across them, looking for anger at Gorak's new-found disdain for their paymasters. He found nothing.

'That means very little, cousin,' Sekem said. *'They still might be corrupted. The demons might still be burrowing into their souls, making them Vascanar.'*

Uras Swiftarrow shivered and glanced up at the sun. 'It's cold.' Uras could thread an arrow through an iron band thrown into the air, with a speed and accuracy unrivalled amongst the caedi.

'What work?' Jarl asked.

'There's a House of Healing beyond the river. Ten miles along the forest road,' Uras said. 'The idiot Karisae have fortified it.'

'What're they protecting?' Jarl asked.

'The bridge, most likely,' Gorak said. 'Best crossing point on the river.'

Jarl looked over the camp. 'So the hunting is over?'

'For now,' Kerek Liontooth said. 'The Karisae stand to give battle and battle they'll receive.'

'Then, after we have rolled over their little defence, the hunting will begin again,' Uras said.

'Till the first snowflake falls,' Sekem murmured in Jarl's mind.

Gorak clapped his hands. 'Let's get to it then. Uras, take the vanguard. Dump your tents and travelling packs; the main body will carry for you scouts. Battle harness only. Kerek, your men shall hold the rear. We others will fan out beside the roads and protect the flanks. Jarl, I want you to go with Uras. He may have need of your dol. You can sense the thoughts of others; that might be useful out there in the woods.'

'Aye, these woods are filled with foul creatures,' Uras said. 'We lost seven men last night. The Vascanar lost more. Many more.' He grinned.

'Illath raises more than severed spirits on this god-cursed land.' Kerek shuddered.

'Yes, she does,' Sekem murmured.

A cry echoed from the edge of the woods beyond the battlefield. A figure stumbled into view.

'Is that Torquesten?' Gorak asked.

'Looks like he had a rough night,' Jarl said.

'Where are his men?'

'Where are the spellhounds?'

****

Kihan, dressed in clothes pillaged from the dead and equipped with a spear found upon a corpse, ate food scavenged along the way: stale bread and strong cheese from one canvas sack, trail pies from another. He couldn't bring himself to eat meat, not yet. The taste of human flesh still polluted his tongue.

'I w… will e… eat m… meat a… gain,' he said to the bushes he hid within. The first words he had spoken in — how old was he? How long had he been a spellhound? He concentrated on the words, on the way his tongue moved within his mouth, and said, 'W… wh… what they d… did to me w… will not sss… stand. I… I am… I am a man. I… I w… I will… I will eat meat again.'

He pulled one of the trail pies from the sack. Looked at it. Sniffed it. Bile flooded his mouth. He started to place the pie back into his sack, but stopped. 'I am a man.' He lifted the pie, bit into it, chewed the pork with grim determination, swallowed the meat, lifted a waterskin, drowned the taste with water and, in this fashion, finished the pie.

His hands closed into tight fists, his jaw rigid, he fought down the nausea. Sweat dripped into his eyes, clammy across his back and stomach. His legs trembled. He closed his eyes. A flash, an image, *a man being butchered like a pig*. Kihan sucked in air, held it tight within his chest, and fought off the last wave of nausea.

Tentatively, he relaxed his muscles, fearing the return of the bile. He waited a moment, and then a moment longer.

'I'm a man,' he said and placed the half-empty waterskin in the canvas sack.

Lifting the sack and the spear, he stalked through the forest on quiet feet, feet that hurt when he tried to force them into boots, so he discarded all pretence of footwear and walked barefoot through the trees. A minor defeat; his feet were tough enough to walk across broken rock. But he wanted to wear boots like a man.

Was he still human? Something had changed within him, something that he could not ignore. He could hear every creature scurrying in the undergrowth. Differentiate between scents laid by animals to mark their territory and scents laid to attract mates. When he dived to the ground at the sound of approaching feet, he could even smell the scent-trails ants used to create paths to and from their nests. He could smell it all; all of creation passed through his nose. But a deeper smell underlay it all: the scent of life itself.

His ears twitched and he turned his head to listen to the plants growing. Could dogs do that? Could even a spellhound hear shoots and leaves pushing upwards towards the sun? Could anyone hear roots thrusting through the earth in search of moisture and nutrients?

A wind caressed his skin. Softer sounds hummed below the sounds of the forest. He could feel the power of this land. It rose through the soil and into his naked feet.

How much of him remained human?

Vague recollections of other places where he had hunted magic for his masters. He remembered the faces of men, women, and children captured by Vascanar hunting parties and forced to give up their secrets. Their magical artefacts taken, their souls rent open, their screams. *The taste of their flesh.*

Bile flooded his mouth, but he refused to vomit. He was a man. A man forced to think like a hound, to seek the scent of magic to please his brutal owners, but a man none the less. He would gain the dead their vengeance, though he didn't know how, because their vengeance would assuage the guilt lying upon his soul.

The magic tasted cold on his tongue here in the forest. He had never tasted it before. So strong, like the taste of life itself. This land, this Symcani, overflowed with magic. It swirled everywhere, from every tree, every rock, every animal, every bird, from the ground beneath his naked feet and in the air sighing across his questing tongue.

Had this magic freed him?

****

Torquesten stumbled out of the forest, his eyes bruised by the dawnlight. He'd fought his way through the risen dead with the elixir of his gods burning within him, lifting him to greater speed, greater strength, greater power. He had smashed through the trees, casting aside all that he owned to get here, now, on this hillside, above the pavilion of Pyran, his Uka, his general.

He slipped, fell, rolled down the hill, and raved upon the muddy ground, where Vascanar soldiers grabbed him, dragged him past the other Akalac; who laughed, spat upon him, kicked him, beat him with their fists.

Pyran roared, 'Where are my hounds? Where is the Xarnac? You have failed me, blood-knight, hound-master, Torquesten Soulthief.'

Priests cursed him from within ripped-up faces, their eyes bulging, their features ruined by their own hands at the command of their raging overlords. They tore the remaining scraps of cloth from Torquesten's body, leaving him on his knees, blood running down his naked flesh.

'You'll replace what you've cost me,' Pyran said.

The priests raised a keening wail.

A thunderous cry tore through Torquesten's head: *We are one, we are here, you are ours, this is all that there is. We shall forge a weapon of you, Torquesten Soulthief. Have faith in us.* The gods called to him.

'I have faith!' Torquesten screamed up into the sky. 'I am yours!' His mind burned in cleansing passion.

Clouds boiled into the empty sky. Dark clouds rolled across the sun and the threads of his future faded as the sunlight faded into shadowed gloom. A wind, heated and unnatural, whipped across the land.

'Silence him!' Pyran cried into the rising storm. 'Take his tongue, then make him a hound.'

The clamour of Torquesten's mind hushed. Darkness poured itself across his soul, and the Weaver's threads dissolved.

'You shall have silence,' he said. Fire blazed in his eyes, glowering flames casting shadows beyond the cave of his lost soul. The wind raised a cloak of dust about him, spinning tighter, faster, spiralling up into the dark, glowering clouds above. The heat of a furnace roared around Torquesten. He basked in that heat, lifted his arms, curled his fingers, calling forth more power from the clouds.

Soldiers struggled to hold onto his limbs. They screamed at the raging heat blistering their skin, paying a terrible price for their loyalty to Pyran.

The demonic overlords of the Vascanar poured all that they could into that tornado of wind, that pillar of flame, that connection between their world and this. Then, when they could give no more, the spiral of wind collapsed, sucked into Torquesten's body in a thunderclap of implosion.

'He is taken!' one of the priests cried.

'He is blessed,' another voice quavered in exultation.

'It has come.' Bihkat spoke with venomous intent.

'I am here,' Torquesten said. He cast aside the men burned by his anointing as if they were leaves before a wind.

CHAPTER 22

Drustan.

Marisa probed his wound while the touch of his skin sent flame into her heart. She remembered his skin against hers in a field of wildflowers. His calloused hands so gentle and yet so strong, so insistent. They had been married for nearly a year, but he had been away for half that time, fighting across the Salt. His body so covered with scars, so heavy above her, so soft and tender, so truthful. They had lain back in the sun, naked as babes, laughing and talking of nothing. Truth passed between them in the flicker of her talent. She read his blood. She learned his ancestry.

And everything broke on that golden field, leaving her wretched and alone for five long years.

She cast aside memory and returned to the squalid little clearing in the deep forest where the sun rarely glowed with such splendour. No infection deep within the wound. She could smell garlic and woriwert leaking with Drustan's blood. The man who had dealt with this wound had knowledge and skill, but he should have taken the time to stitch it.

Warriors measured time in blows given, enemies killed, and battlefields won or lost. They did what was needed and paid no heed to what was required.

Dagabin could heal a surface cut and barely leave a scar in its wake, but this wound, this bone-deep wound, needed internal stitches and knitted muscle. It needed healing from within to reform the flesh. Too late to reopen the wound now. Too dangerous. She would have to heal it from the outside, sliding into Drustan's flesh with only magic to guide her. Few healers had such skill.

Which was no doubt why she had been called here.

Her needs, her sanity, mattered not in this; her presence was required to heal Drustan the bright-bladed warrior for the land, and so she was called. What did the gods have in store for this man she still loved?

'We can't stay in the deep forest,' Cullain was saying. 'Bad things rise in the bloodlight.'

'What kind of things?' Drustan shifted at her touch.

Marisa's heart ached from the memories of him shifting in another way at the touch of her fingers. 'Demons,' she said harshly. 'The Vascanar are familiars of demons.'

'That explains a lot,' Drustan said.

'Aye,' Cullain agreed.

'I carry something of theirs.'

'Something… What?' Marisa unloosed her haraf stone; unbridled fear crawled across her skin. 'In your pouch. What is that?'

'An amulet,' Drustan said. 'Taken from their ships.'

'We weren't at the attack on the ships,' Cullain said.

'It came into my hand by happenchance.'

'No such thing where such as this is concerned,' Marisa said. 'The Vascanar seek it. They want it back. We must hide it.'

'How do you know?' Drustan asked.

'The same way I knew that you lay here in the forest.' She thought for a moment. Remembered old texts, books copied and recopied, the words always remaining unchanged, for scribes did not tamper with old laws, old rules, old ways. They swore an oath to leave such words untouched by their poetry. But what of demons? Marisa concentrated, allowing her mind to sink lower into a place where the words flowed like pictures upon the soul.

There.

Oh.

Well, that should not be too difficult then, not here in the middle of the deep wood, away from forges and craftsmen. Not difficult at all.

'I'll need an alder branch, about twenty inches long,' Marisa said. 'Formed into a box of green wood, lined with silver, placed within another box of green willow and then sealed within a tight-stitched covering cut from the spell-proof cloth in my pack. That will contain the evil and hide it from them.'

'Don't want much, do you?' Cullain asked.

'Rosana!' Marisa called.

'Yes, milady. The needle and thread are clean now. Just setting up a candle for your other instruments.'

'You called Horol a woodsmith.'

'That he is.'

'Fetch him. I have need of his services.'

'Yes, milady.' Rosana turned and scanned the clearing. 'Tilly, go fetch me your brother. Don't look at me like that, child. I know you scamper through woodland like a squirrel through the branches. Go now. He's needed.'

A girl of thirteen pouted, but ran off into the woods.

'Used to want to be a boy,' Rosana said. 'Now all she wants to be is a woman.'

'Is there a blacksmith here?' Marisa asked.

'No, but most of the men know the way of a forge. Smithing costs money.'

'I need silver crowns beaten and crafted into a single sheet.'

''Tis our village's funds, milady.'

Marisa understood the woman's hesitation. Famine stalked villagers; one bad harvest could leave them destitute and starving. Only hoarded coins could hold against capricious fate.

She lifted her gaze to meet Rosana's. 'I have need of it.'

'Because of those things from the night just passed?' Rosana asked.

'That is part of the need,' Marisa replied.

'Then you'll have it,' Rosana said.

Honesty forced Marisa to say, 'I cannot promise to repay and the silver will be lost forever.'

'Well.' Rosana smiled. 'You don't want all of it, now do you?'

'No, not all.'

'Silver's no use to the dead.' Rosana bustled away to see to all that was needed.

'A good woman,' Cullain said.

'Yes,' Marisa agreed.

'I've carried this thing for a time now,' Drustan said. 'I can carry it a little longer. They have not found it yet. We must move. We cannot take the time to make some box of greenwood and silver.'

'I cannot heal you with that thing uncloaked.'

'Why not?' Drustan asked.

Marisa lifted her eyes to his. A mistake. She couldn't speak, her heart blocking her words, her soul aching for him, knowing that she had forfeited all rights to his love. His eyes, grey as clouds against the sun, so intense and gentle; so filled with hurt.

She broke his gaze and fiddled with her tools.

'Why not, Marisa?' Drustan asked again, his voice soft.

****

Drustan could not bear the grief in her gaze. Her eyes pure hazel, flecked with gold, and filled with pain. His mother had been unkind to bring her here. Another would have done as well. Why did it have to be Marisa?

'Why not?' he asked again.

She lifted a pair of tweezers into the slanting streaks of dawn, turning the instrument as if checking for imperfections. 'Demons are not meant for this place. Their evil would corrupt my arts. That thing you carry might even use them to infest your body with their malign spirits and from there infest your soul. I cannot place such risk upon you.'

'I've carried it for two nights,' Drustan said. 'I'm still intact.'

'I do not understand why,' Marisa said. 'That thing so close to you should have broken you with fear.'

'I learned the futility of fear when I was a lad,' Drustan said. He saw the pain in her eyes, wanted to wipe it away. 'Before your father saved me.' Drustan heard the words before he realised that he had spoken them.

'My father is dead.' Marisa lurched to her feet and left him lying there, bleeding and bereft.

'What happened to him?' Drustan asked Cullain.

'She said he went to see the King on your behalf.'

'On her behalf more like,' Drustan said. 'His sweet little girl tainted by my touch.'

'She'd already entered the Houses by then, Dru.' Cullain squatted and played with a stone. 'Whatever taint you left they washed away with sanctity.' He paused. 'He were a good man.' Cullain stood, tossing the stone away. 'We'll need to set guards if'n we've to stay here long.'

'What happened to him?' Drustan asked.

'Pelin desainLegan was declared traitor and put to the sword by the hand of Erik desainAbavin. She heard,' Cullain pointed at Marisa with his chin, 'that Erik took his time.' Cullain's voice didn't waver. 'I should've been there.' Pelin had been his lord for a long time.

'Would you have gone against your King?' Drustan asked.

'I'd have wrung his scrawny neck and laughed.' Cullain shook his head. 'I still might.'

'I'll be at your back when you do,' Drustan said.

Cullain nodded. 'Least you can do. That secret marriage started all this. You should've gone to her father.' He breathed in deeply. 'I'll set some of these farm boys as pickets out beyond the river.'

'Good idea,' Drustan said, ignoring the memory of his stupidity. 'Fetch my blades, old man.'

'Over by the fire there?'

'Aye, bundled up in that Erisyan cloak.'

Cullain picked up the bundle and carried it back to Drustan. 'So you killed a sell-bow, then?'

'More'n one.'

'Good. I'm going to kill me some afore this war is over.'

'No doubt, but it was an Erisyan that doctored my wound and saved me from dying screaming at a Vascanar fireside.'

'A sell-bow? There's a story there.' Cullain looked across the camp. 'You. Give me your name.'

'I am named Garet Wiseye.'

'I'm named Cullain Strongarm. Tirac, go with him and set up a picket across the river.'

Tirac grabbed Garet's arm and the two men hastened away.

'Good man, that Tirac. Pity he can't speak; make a good armsman.' Cullain turned back to Drustan. 'What's the story of the sell-bow, then?'

Drustan told Cullain of the fight and its aftermath.

'You should've left them to die,' Cullain said when Drustan had finished.

'The boy was there.'

'So? Plenty of boys'll die in this war.'

'I acted as I should.'

'You're a sell-sword now, Dru. Honour's not yours to hold.'

'Honour is an action not a birthright.'

'Wish I'd never taught you that foolishness.'

'I'm glad you did.' Drustan looked across the clearing at Marisa talking to Rosana.

'So why'd this sell-bow deign to help such a lowly sell-sword as yourself?'

'Forasin Hill.'

'He were there?' Cullain whistled.

'Aye.'

'Just as well you didn't let me kill 'em all, then.'

'Just as well.'

'The spider weaves cunning threads around you, Drustan desainCoid. Careful you don't smother in their embrace.'

'Check the blades, old man, and spare me your proverbs about fate.'

Cullain unwrapped the bundle and lifted the shortsword. He drew it from its sheath and studied the blade. 'Made the old way,' he said. 'Good blade. Horse-hair pattern. Don't see many of them around these days. Anthanic steel.'

'Are you sure?'

'Aye, hilt's modern, but the blade's from afore the Karisae came. A rare blade. I envy you its ownership.'

'I hold it for another. Oath-sworn to pass it on to his kin if ever I come across them.'

'You've been busy. I'll hear that story another time.' Cullain picked up the needle-pointed dagger. 'You've pierced chain with this,' he said. 'I'll get it sharpened for you.'

'Try to keep some of the blade.' Drustan grinned. 'Last time you sharpened a sword of mine, I ended up with a knife.'

'Got to get back to good metal.' Cullain sniffed. 'And it were barely a nail's breadth from the point.'

'If you say so. I had to have the hilt reweighted to restore the balance.'

'You always were a fussy swordsman.' Cullain bent down and picked up the longsword. He turned it over in his hand. 'This is the blade of Erik desainAbavin.'

'It is.'

'Where'd you get it?'

'Inherited it.'

Cullain grinned savagely. 'More stories.' His face darkened. 'Too many stories, Dru. Too many fates fight to possess you.' Cullain slid the sword back into its scabbard. 'But I do look forward to hearing that story.' He paused. 'The Earl will seek you across the breadth of the land.'

'No, he won't,' Drustan said.

'The Earl too?'

Drustan shrugged. 'He took an interest.'

'Maybe honour does have some use in these dark days.'

'Maybe it does.'

Marisa returned with Rosana. 'Time to stitch up that wound, milord.'

'Don't call me that, milady.'

'Don't call me that, oh mighty warrior.'

'Just stitch it up, woman, and then we can be gone from this place.'

'This will sting a little,' Marisa said. She poured a clear liquid onto a cloth, smiled at Drustan, and daubed the liquid directly over the livid edges of the wound.

Drustan twitched. His wounded flesh blazed with the touch of the astringent, but by keeping his lips tight, and by neglecting to breathe out, he kept the curses to a minimum.

'Men,' Rosana said. 'Babies every one.'

'I'll check the pickets,' Cullain said. 'Since you've someone to care for you now, Dru.'

Rosana laughed.

Marisa picked the needle from the heated water with tweezers. 'This…'

'…will sting a little,' Drustan said.

Marisa smiled. 'A little.'

CHAPTER 23

A man touched with the strength of demons walked amongst them. Bihkat cut his face to give thanks for the transformation of Torquesten, keeping his envy hidden beneath that tearing blade. Pain opened the gate, created the vacuum, allowed the lords to enter. Pain spurred the soul into places where men walked as gods. The Ulac granted the soul a glimpse of paradise, but married to pain it lifted the soul to awareness.

Torquesten had been chosen as Tukalac and anointed with fire, the compact completed as written in the holy *Uknis* — book of power and map to the realm of blood.

The day had come.

Torquesten stood erect, strong and sure in the centre of Pyran's circling bodyguards — twelve hard-faced men, Akalac knights who had taken the offer of Pyran's preferment and become his bodyguards. Their chainmail stained with rust above grey tunics and under battered breastplates, they had taken the hand of an Uka and given up the blood-wine of the Akalac, which made them less than what they were but placed them closer to the seat of power. Scars ravaged their faces and their minds: killers, butchers, torturers.

They drew their greatswords, tapering spears of steel nearly as long as a man is tall, graceful, sharp — deadly in the hands of the masters these men were — and awaited the command.

Bihkat switched his gaze between the circling pack of bodyguards and Torquesten standing still beneath the darkened sky. Naked Torquesten, feet planted apart, hands curled at his sides, his eyes half-closed against the sunlight, a faint smile upon his lips. Not deigning to notice the men surrounding him with drawn swords and hungry eyes.

Did they not see the flames in Torquesten's eyes? Did they not know their liturgy? Bihkat opened his mouth to warn them.

'Quiet, priest,' Torquesten commanded.

A few of the bodyguards peeked at Bihkat when he allowed the slight to go unanswered. Bihkat watched them switch their gaze from him to Torquesten and then back again.

Yes, look at him. Look at him. Naked, unarmed, and yet he stands in the centre of your wolf pack unconcerned. Look at him. Remember the cloud, the wind, the heat of our demonic overlords pouring through his body.

'Kill him. Burn him. Rend his skin,' Pyran ordered.

'Choose wisely, soldiers of the truth,' Torquesten warned. 'For I am not mercy.' Even his voice had changed, a harsher note to it now, a deeper thrumming resonance indicating other voices beyond his own.

The bodyguard Arnik stepped back from the fight and, after a moment's hesitation, two others followed him. They moved away from the conflict and stood, their swords balanced on their shoulders, beside Bihkat as the Ukalac led the chant and the priests joined in melodious counterpoint. The words heated the air and a shimmering curtain rose above the chanting priests, filling nostrils with the tang of sulphur.

'You're sworn to me,' Pyran said. 'Not to the priests, not to the army, not to the lords.'

The melodious counterpoint halted at the blasphemous words.

Bihkat had to speak now, had to warn, it was required. 'All oaths are under the gaze of the overlords, Pyran, you—'

'Silence, priest,' Torquesten commanded. 'These fools are mine.'

Another bodyguard stepped over to the priests as the rest hesitated. Their oaths bound them to Pyran but they realised that something had changed. They were brave men and strong; they had fought many battles, killed many times in the service of their Uka. But this was wrong.

'Kill him. Kill him now.' The general flung out his hand.

Five bodyguards attacked, driving inwards, their swords cutting downwards. The other three hesitated.

Torquesten moved, avoiding the blades as if his attackers moved through water, the huge swords missing him by moments as he stepped around the steel, his hands blurring, striking, slapping his attackers aside.

He didn't kill.

He didn't cripple.

He ripped aside armour, dented the metal, shattered swords. But he did no damage to the men inside the armour.

Bihkat understood. Torquesten wanted examples, emblems of his rise.

****

'Milady.' Efan bowed his head. 'The silver…' He did not meet her gaze.

'Yes?' Marisa asked.

Beside her, Drustan sipped at some kha, his eyes sardonic. Marisa realised that he knew what Efan was about to say. Cullain squatted beside the tree, using a whetstone to sharpen a dagger that Marisa knew well; she had given it to Drustan on his rise to the Hundrin. A simple little gift, but a lock of her hair lay bound within the hilt.

Efan lifted his hands in apology. 'To heat the metal, to pound it flat, to weld one silver piece to another…'

'Yes?'

'There'll be smoke, noise. It'll take time. We're surrounded by the enemy.' Efan lifted his hands apologetically.

'He's right about that,' Drustan said. 'Shame you've never visited a smithy.'

'I thought silver was easier to work,' Marisa said, forced to defend herself against Drustan's mocking tone.

'Not that much easier,' Cullain said, 'but it were an honest mistake.'

'Aren't they all,' Drustan said.

Efan asked, 'Can't we overlap the coins?'

'No, there must be no gaps.' Marisa had hoped to avoid this. 'In my pack there is a silver box. Use that. It shuts tightly.'

Efan nodded, but did not move.

'What're you waiting for?' Cullain asked.

'I don't want to be poisoned by a healer's curse.'

'She gave you leave,' Cullain said.

Drustan grinned. 'Throw the pack over here. I'll rummage through it.'

Marisa grabbed the pack from the ground and pulled out a small silver box. Fine etchings scrolled across every part of its surface. Stylised leaves and branches coiled across it. Such wonderful workmanship; her jaw tautened and she handed the box to Efan.

Drustan's grin faded. 'I gave you that.'

'Yes.' She lifted her chin.

'You kept it,' Cullain said.

'It's pretty,' she replied.

Drustan scowled.

'Women are such fools for pretty things.' Cullain grinned.

'It's heavy,' Efan said.

'There are stones within it.' They were haraf stones from the shrine at Redain, healing stones imbued with the strength of that shrine. Marisa remembered another text she had read long ago. The power of a haraf stone was not just a healing power. Perhaps… The evil needed to be contained. She made the decision and said, 'Don't remove them.'

Rosana brought Drustan some porridge from the pot. She studied his face for a moment. 'Even the scar's pretty. Here, eat this.'

Drustan handed her the empty mug and took the wooden bowl. 'Thank you.'

'I learned him that,' Agus called from where he hung upside down from a tree-branch above their heads.

'How long?' Drustan asked. 'How long until Horol finishes the carving?'

Efan said, 'The willow box's finished. Only the inside of the alder left to carve. Not long.'

'Then best you get that bit of silver hidden,' Drustan said.

Efan nodded and moved across to where his brother sat cross-legged on the ground, splitting the alder branch in half.

'The stones?' Cullain asked.

Marisa touched the stone around her neck. 'They are haraf. Like this one.'

'There's power there.'

'They are healing stones.' Another memory came unbidden. Haraf stones were connected to the earth, and the river surrounding the small party on this island flowed from the sacred Lake Kalon, and was touched by every shrine along the way: more magic to hold the evil of the Vascanar at bay. 'Find me dark earth, Cullain, from between the roots of alder and willow. And water from the river that feeds them.'

****

Jarl rested his hand on the quiver at his right hip. Thirteen arrows in the quiver, another fifty-two arrows in four bundles on the back of his battle harness. Slide a bundle into the quiver, snip the binding cords, and continue loosing.

'We should be moving out,' Uras said. 'I don't want to be caught on the forest road after dark.'

'That wouldn't be wise,' Jarl agreed. The warmth of Sekem's gold coins heightened his dol. He could taste the words before they left Uras's mouth.

'This is a bad contract,' Uras said.

Jarl glanced at the awchti. 'Gorak did what he had to.' He opened his dol towards Uras, allowing his soul to link into that of the battle commander.

The air chilled.

'Did he?' Uras shivered in the sunlight. Ambition clashed with caution in the depths of his soul. Jarl quested deeper. Uras's ambition sought to rule the Caedi Haroa, not for power's sake, but in the belief that he would rule the caedi more wisely than Gorak.

'He's right.' Sekem's words hung like icicles in the air.

Jarl shrugged. 'If you've a problem take it up with Gorak.'

'You're an honest man, Jarl.' Uras smiled. 'And a loyal one.'

'I take oaths seriously.'

'So do the gods,' Sekem said.

Uras's quiver protruded over his right shoulder. Jarl disliked that arrangement; too easy to snag the arrows when moving through brush and undergrowth. But then, Uras was noted for his speed and it was slightly quicker to draw and loose from such an arrangement. Uras shivered again. 'Gods, it's cold. The sun barely warms me at all.'

'Something comes,' Sekem breathed; panic tinged his frozen words.

Uras blew on his hands. 'The oath to fight for this scum wasn't wise.'

'We should be moving,' Jarl said. 'That'd warm us up.'

Uras laughed. 'Maybe they're too busy killing that animal Torquesten.' He clapped a hand on Jarl's shoulder. 'Spellhounds are expensive things to lose.'

'Spellhounds are men not things,' Jarl said. He thrust another probe into Uras's soul. Was he tainted?

'Not to them,' Uras sneered. No, it was contempt for the Vascanar not the poor fools made into hounds that tainted Uras's thoughts.

'It has begun.' Sekem disappeared, leaving iced air in his wake.

****

No man would have died at Torquesten's hand, but Eogulf, a bodyguard with hair so blond it reminded Bihkat of the mountain peaks in winter, moved faster, used guile, dropped to one knee … and cut Torquesten across the thigh.

Blood flowered on Torquesten's leg, blood that sublimed into a dark mist, a mist that wreathed Torquesten as he bellowed his rage. The sound of that cry echoed across the camp, across the land. Birds scattered into the sky, a vast flock, millions strong, swooping, swirling through the early morning sunlight in an erupting cloud of panic.

****

Uras shivered. 'I feel like—'

A raging scream echoed across the land. Birds swirled into the sky. Jarl staggered, his mind still open from seeking the truth in the heart of Uras.

Unprotected by Sekem's spirit, Jarl fell to his knees. His soul trembled in the heat of that cry; its malevolence poured through him. Flames roared in his ears, fires blazed before his eyes, heat singed his spirit, the stench of men burning, the taste of their agony roiling across his tongue.

He fought back vomit, staring through the spectral flames to the birds screeching above. The pressure waves of the scream slammed against his heart.

He recognised the touch of that hate from the torture pits where he had discovered the truth of the Vascanar 'gods'. But this was not some shadow of the fury to come; this was an echoing scream of demonic rage made real in the world of flesh.

Sekem's whisper, cringing, hidden: *'I should have left when I had the chance.'*

****

Marisa watched Drustan ease his newly bandaged side and struggle to sit up and eat his porridge, without offering to help him. 'Rest,' she said.

'All I do is rest,' Drustan complained.

'Then learn how to dodge,' Cullain said. He looked up at Agus. 'Come down 'ere, boy. I got work for you.'

'The name is—' Agus's eyes suddenly rolled back into his skull.

A roar of anger echoed through the trees. A wind lashed at the branches; birds fled into the sky, and rabbits and foxes scuttled into their burrows and lairs. Marisa recoiled at the pure evil that raged into her body, her mind. What had been unleashed? What *was* that?

Agus's legs lost their grip upon the tree. He fell head-first towards the ground. Cullain cast aside the dagger and surged upward, catching Agus in his two huge hands. Tirac burst into the clearing, eyes wild, his hands like claws.

Fear blazed through the camp.

****

While the birds fled to the sky and the creatures of the forest ran for cover, squealing outrage, Kihan crouched and waited for the spasm to pass, as he somehow knew it would — as he somehow knew that this was a mere prelude of what was to come.

Fear flared across the land, tearing at his self-control, but he forced himself to stay in his crouch. *That* scent he knew, that artefact he'd hunted for the Vascanar. But it was far away to the south-west of where he crouched in the forest. He hoped that whoever held the Xarnac knew what it was they carried. The evil within it stung his soul. It tasted of the ritual that made him spellhound.

And now, almost hidden by the scent of the Xarnac, this new smell upon the air. Kihan twisted his head, listened, heard the panting breaths, the crashing of branches. He realised what hunted him and threw aside the sack and spear. They would only slow him down and he needed all the speed he could muster. As the birds returned from the sky, he began to run.

****

Below the dark fumes, red blood dripped from the wound in Torquesten's thigh, ran down his leg, pooled upon the ground. The blood stopped flowing and the mist swirled away to reveal unbroken skin.

Torquesten, furious, reached out and broke the face of the bodyguard nearest to him with a back-handed slap. He attacked the others, smashing them away from him.

Until only he and Eogulf still stood.

Eogulf looked around at his comrades scattered, groaning, broken upon the ground. He lifted his gaze to the fire in Torquesten's eyes and dropped to his knees.

'Forgive me, Tukalac, I didn't know.'

'I am not mercy.' Torquesten tore Eogulf's head from his shoulders and threw it at the feet of the general. 'Kneel, Pyran.'

Pyran knelt.

'You.' Torquesten pointed at the bodyguard Arnik, the first to step away from this battle. 'Take command of my army.'

The scent of the Xarnac floated out of the forest. Released by the fear, it poured itself into Torquesten — and he knew its location. The island in the river: on that island the spirits of the forest had hidden it from his sight, screened it behind the soul of a man who fought fear with rage, a dangerous man…

But now Torquesten knew where the Xarnac lay.

First, he must make his demonhounds, make his example, show his Vascanar what he had become. Then he would swoop down upon this fearless man and tear his soul apart.

CHAPTER 24

The terrified cries of the villagers echoed the raging scream reverberating across the land. Cullain dropped the unconscious Agus and staggered towards the trees away from Drustan, away from that flaring terror.

Efan stood at the edge of the clearing, bowed forward as if in a high wind, trying to move towards Drustan. His brother Horol, chisel tight in his hand, grimaced but refused to leave Efan's side. Rosana held Tilly tight against the dread.

Fear tore at the heart of Drustan, worse than anything he had felt before. When he itched to leave Jerem to die he had not felt such terror. When he wept in the branches of the oak while toasting the dead he had not felt such terror. Now it ripped at him, wrenched him out of himself. The villagers fled into the trees while he was trapped, unable to move — unable to protect Marisa. Fury at his helplessness surged through him.

He took the rage, chilled it, pushed it into his soul, froze the fear and pushed it away from his courage. His mind steadied, his breathing settled, and he could think again.

The terrified villagers might blunder into Vascanar patrols, which would bring the weight of the enemy down upon this camp. 'Hold!' Drustan yelled. 'Hold!'

Marisa moaned beside him but would not leave him. She clutched at his hand as he roared at the fleeing villagers. The touch of her love, a spark of honesty between them, broke his anger into shards of bitter memories: the fear expanded, flared through him once more, flames of panic racing through his veins. *Marisa's body opened, ruined; crazed edges of blood, death…* Damnation clawed at him; he could not save her, she would die, the fault all his.

'Hold, my love,' Marisa whispered. 'Hold.'

The sound of her voice lightened his mind and he could see again; love conquered fear with a soft word, where rage needed a spur. Drustan could think now, with Marisa's hand in his. Clarity, strategy, tactics.

They had to get away from this place. Before the Vascanar came.

'We have to go,' Drustan said. 'This place is not safe.'

'Tirac.' Marisa pointed with a trembling hand.

Tirac kneeled by the fire, shaking his head, his wild eyes fixed on Drustan, on the pouch where the amulet lay. Murderous rage burned behind those eyes. Drustan knew that look. He had seen it too many times not to recognise a killing rage.

He threw Marisa's hand away as Tirac charged. Marisa would not die here today. He would not allow it.

Even fully fit, Drustan would have had trouble subduing Tirac; the huge man made two of him. Injured, unarmed, unable to move, Drustan did not expect to survive this combat. He drew inward, coldly calculating the odds.

Marisa cried out, screaming for help.

Drustan waited. Timing was everything when your options were few. Tirac almost in range to grab at Drustan's feet, barrelling forward like a bear unable to stop… Drustan rolled towards Marisa. He had to stay between Tirac and her for the first movement of this dance.

Agony as stitches tore in his side.

He rolled again, raised his foot and kicked Tirac in the side of the head, pushing him away, forcing him towards the tree where he himself had lain only a moment before.

The big man slammed shoulder-first into the tree. It shook, leaves fell, and he growled with wordless, tongueless rage.

Drustan rolled away from Marisa now. Take the fight away from her. Gain space.

Cullain had dropped the needle-pointed dagger there. Drustan reached for it. His fingers touched the hilt but, before he could snatch it up, Tirac grabbed his leg and dragged him back towards the tree.

Drustan smashed the back of his hand across Tirac's face. A knuckle-strike, but with no leverage, and little strength from his damaged side, he may as well have been using a feather. Tirac clamped a huge hand around Drustan's throat, his other hand rising like a club. Drustan slammed a knee up into the man's ribs. Tirac grunted. Drustan did it again despite the pain flaring in his side.

Tirac's fist approached with awful speed…

…and stopped inches from Drustan's face as another hand grabbed it.

'Let's be having you, then,' Cullain growled.

His trip-throw sent Tirac sailing through the air and Cullain stood, setting his stance low, wide, and strong. Hands like blades, shoulders hunched forward, waiting.

Tirac shook his head and studied Cullain's stance.

'It's the amulet!' Marisa cried.

'We know, lass,' Cullain replied. 'But our remedies are different.'

Drustan curled around his wounded side, but managed to pick up the dagger. 'I've got your back, old man.'

'See to the boy,' Cullain said.

Agus? What had happened to Agus?

Tirac took three steps towards Cullain. The armsmaster surged forward to meet him. A flurry of blows as each tried to get the right grip, the right leverage, to throw the other. Of course, it ended on the floor, where all such matches ended. In groundwork. Elbows digging, fingers gouging, limbs wrapping around and over, as each man tried to get the hold that would end this contest.

Drustan pulled Marisa towards Agus. 'Help him.'

Tirac managed to lock his legs around Cullain's neck, but he could not straighten out Cullain's arm. Even with the full strength of his back he could not unbend that limb, could not subdue Cullain's struggles.

Cullain bowed his back, got his other arm under Tirac's legs, then rolled up and over, dragging Tirac onto his front, breaking the strangling grip of Tirac's legs around his neck. He dropped his knee into the small of Tirac's back. Grabbed Tirac's arms, tried to bend them back, trying to bow him like a stick until his spine snapped. But Tirac twisted, got a leg free, and kicked Cullain away.

Both men rolled to their feet. Blood trickled from Cullain's nose and Tirac's ear.

The two big men set themselves ready for another flurry of blows, ready to try again for the grip that would let them break the other in two.

Marisa laid her hands on Agus's head and Drustan watched as the boy's eyes flickered, focused, and fixed on Marisa.

'What happened?' Agus said. 'What... Tirac, Tirac, what happened? Tirac!' The boy started to scream and the fear faded away.

Tirac shivered as if suddenly cold. He looked at his hands as if seeing them for the first time. Then he lifted his eyes to Cullain.

Cullain tried to speak, coughed, then tried again. 'How's the back?' He grinned through blood-smeared teeth.

Tirac dropped his hands and stepped away from Cullain who, in his turn, straightened from his wrestler's crouch, his neck raw, red, and bruised. 'What just happened?' Cullain asked, still watching Tirac with careful eyes.

CHAPTER 25

'Who're you?' Jarl asked.

'I Uka Arnik,' the man said. 'I lead the battle on House of Healing.' He sat astride a snorting, restless Vascanar horse that rolled mad eyes at the Erisyans. Jarl could feel the animal's addictions; fed on oats laced with the Vascanar's foul elixir, the poor, agonised creature sought only to share its pain.

'What happened to Pyran?' Gorak asked.

'Pyran no longer Uka here.' Arnik controlled his horse with savage hands upon the reins and vicious spurs upon its sides.

Jarl took a step back and tried to pull Gorak away from the slathering mouth of the beast.

Gorak shook off Jarl's hand, daring the horse to bite him. 'Pyran's no longer general?'

Arnik ignored the question. 'Five hundred horsemen fight. All bowmen fight too.'

'Not hunting today?' Jarl asked.

'No. We smash House today.'

'That's nice.'

'Our contract was with Pyran,' Gorak said.

Hope.

Could it be that simple? A simple change of leadership and they could leave this accursed contract, go home, return to their families and forget what they'd seen here?

'You swear fight until first snowflake fall.' Arnik looked up at the sky. 'I see no snow.'

'I swore my oath to Pyran.'

'Oath no mention Pyran,' Arnik said. 'I there, sell-bow, I hear oath.'

'You were there?' Gorak asked. 'I don't remember you amongst the officers.'

'I bodyguard to Uka,' Arnik said.

'The bodyguard becomes general,' Uras said. 'So how many regiments have you commanded, swordsman?'

'I named Uka by Tukalac Torquesten,' Arnik said.

'Torquesten's now lord of this regiment?' Jarl glanced at Gorak.

'He reborn. Ukinak not regiment.'

'He has the right of it, Gorak,' Kerek said. 'Pyran had the oath phrased without his name.'

'I know.' Gorak tried to look simply irritated, but Jarl could feel his anguish. 'What're your orders, General Arnik?'

'Uka. I Uka Arnik, not general, sell-bow. We attack House of Healing and take for my Tukalac. Then priests join us with rest of the ukinak.'

'The priests don't come with us?' Kerek paused. 'General.'

'Uka. I Uka, not general.'

'Yes, you said. No priests?'

'No, they stay here,' Arnik said. 'Perform ceremonies.'

'Well then, general,' Uras said. 'Let's not disturb their rest.'

'Uka. I Uka, not general. Priests no rest.'

Gorak sighed. 'Take the lead, Uras. Jarl, go with him.'

Jarl bowed. 'As my general commands.'

'Uka. I Uka, not general.'

'I was talking to him.' Jarl pointed at Gorak. 'You don't command me, Arnik.'

****

Drustan leaned back against the tree, clutching a mug of kha. Marisa sat over by the fire stitching Tirac's ear. Too many of the villagers had fled into the forest. Somebody had to fetch them back, but those who had fought the fear, who had remained in the camp, were too dazed and shocked. Drustan sipped at the kha.

Where had the fear gone? No time for thinking about that. Drustan scowled into the half-empty mug. Somebody had to take command. Somebody had to take responsibility. His duty. Easy enough to avoid when injured and helpless, when only three men and a water-boy were with him in the forest. Now there were women and children, the scant remains of a village. Men to command, men who had to trust their commander.

Broken sword or not, wounded or not, the responsibility was his. Cullain was a warrior born, a man to stand alongside, a man to lead men in battle. But he was not a man to lead people to safety.

The way he and Tirac kept glancing at each other made that obvious. Neither of them had won that wrestling match and they were used to finishing what they started. If they ever came to blows again it would be more vicious, more ferocious, and it would not stop until one or the other lay vanquished or, more likely, dead.

Drustan needed both of them alive to have any chance of getting these people away from the Vascanar's pitiless fires and, right now, he needed them here in this camp.

'Efan, Garet,' Drustan called.

'Aye,' Efan said.

'Take five men. Go out, round up as many as you can, bring them back here safe.'

'My family didn't flee,' Efan said. 'They're already safe.'

Garet shook his head. 'There are Vascanar out there.'

'That is not a request.' Drustan forced himself to his feet.

Marisa looked up from tending to Tirac's ear. Drustan bowed his head to her and then winced at the pain.

'Who're you to give us orders?' Efan asked.

'Drustan desainCoid.'

'They broke your sword,' Garet pointed out.

'But not my honour. These people, your people, are my responsibility. I am Drustan the Bright Blade.'

'About bloody time,' Garet said. 'Come along, Efan. We have our orders.' The merchant knuckled his forehead. 'With milord's permission?'

'Don't call me…' Drustan sighed. 'Don't take risks. I need every able-bodied man. Track down the villagers that fled and return with them.'

'And if'n the Vascanar have 'em, milord?' Efan asked.

'Captain.' Cullain walked over from the fire. 'Call him my captain. You go around calling him milord and they'll hang you. Captain's what they call men of ignoble birth who command men in battle.'

'What do we do if'n the Vascanar already have 'em, my captain?' Efan asked.

'You leave 'em be and mark how long it will take 'em to break, then you run back 'ere to tell us how long we have,' Cullain said. 'I should go with 'em, my captain.'

'I need you here,' Drustan said. 'We need to be ready to move when they return.'

'Then send him.' Cullain nodded to Tirac.

Drustan shook his head. 'No.'

'Your command.' Cullain bowed his head briefly. He glared at Garet. 'Get on with it, then. You have your orders.'

'And what should we call you?' Garet asked.

'Armsmaster.' There was no trace of a smile in Cullain's face or voice.

Efan and Garet headed out into the forest with the other men.

'That pouting merchant were right.' Cullain watched them go. 'About bloody time. I'll see to breaking down the camp.'

Marisa left Tirac and strode over to Drustan. 'You're bleeding again, milord captain.'

'Nice of you to notice, milady. How many stitches did Tirac need?'

'Seven, though why that…?' Marisa shook her head. 'You only care because it was your booted foot that tore his ear.'

'Yes.' Drustan grinned.

'Sit down.' Marisa unwrapped the bandages around Drustan's torso and tutted. 'As I suspected. Look here, see this, salamin strips. Torn. I do not have an infinite supply in that pack.'

'Then don't use them.' Drustan hissed as Marisa peeled the strips of cloth away from his livid skin.

'It repels water, allows the wound to breathe, and is pasted on with a dagabin and honey glue that helps to avoid infection.'

'Damn stuff is always tearing.'

'It is fragile, else we would use it for clothing.'

Rosana brought a fresh needle and thread sterilised in the brass bowl. 'Here you are, milady.'

'Thank you, Rosana.' Marisa threaded the needle with the tweezers, a skill made simple by long practice. Drustan shifted. 'Keep still,' Marisa snapped. 'I cannot keep repairing this. The edges of the wound are becoming as ragged as a beggar's beard.'

'Couldn't be helped.' Drustan tried to forget what had passed between them. The touch of her hand against his skin raised ghosts of their past — even when it dragged a needle through his flesh. He hissed a few times, but his mind kept figuring out tactics right through the pain.

'Just try to avoid any more fights until I can bind the wound with spellcraft.' Marisa put away her needle and thread and, after wiping her hands with a lotion, cut long strips of salamin cloth to dress the wound.

'How long before I can walk?'

'A few days.' She pulled out a jar and removed the lid.

The sweet smell of the dagabin paste always reminded Drustan of injuries he had suffered. 'And before I can wield a sword?'

Marisa laughed. 'Weeks maybe.'

'There's a war being fought, Marisa, and we're in the middle of it.'

'I am only a single healer.' Marisa pasted the strips of salamin cloth over the raw edges of the cut. 'I cannot work miracles. A shift of healers, working all day and all night, in the sanctity of a House of Doves, could fix that wound in a day or so.' She picked up a roll of bandages. 'But we need to keep moving. I can only heal you when we stop. We have no sacred site to strengthen the spells and I cannot call on Brominii here in land sacred to the Anthanic.' She leaned across him, her breath on his naked skin, to wrap the bandages around his torso. 'And in any case, I have to moderate my energies to avoid alerting the enemy.' She tied off the bandages and sealed the knot with a daub of dagabin paste.

'That's not good enough, woman.'

'That is the way it is, man.' Marisa packed away the implements of her craft. 'I am going to see to your litter now. You only walk when I say you can.' She lifted the pack as she stood.

Drustan hesitated, then said, 'Thank you for your kindness, Milady Marisa.'

She turned her head away and said nothing more. He wiped at his eye as he watched her walk across the campsite.

'How are you feeling?' Agus asked as he refilled the mug of kha.

'Like I look.' Drustan nodded his thanks. 'So what happened to you?'

Agus shrugged. 'Dunno. Passed out, didn't I? Figured it were the smell of your feet.'

Drustan sipped the kha. 'You fell out of the tree and then the fear was unleashed.'

'Dunno about that,' Agus said. 'I felt something, that scream, then darkness.' He looked up. 'Oh, here they come.'

Horol carried the greenwood box across the camp while Rosana carried the sheath of silk. The box was rough-hewn but showed signs of a craftsman's skill. The round branch, a handsbreadth in diameter and five handsbreadths long, was neatly trimmed and bevelled at both ends, the bark left in place to protect the green wood, the worst of the roughness skimmed away with a sharp blade.

'You didn't need to take the time for all that,' Drustan said.

'Easier to do than not, my captain,' Horol replied. He opened the willow branch to reveal a narrower alder branch within, fitted expertly into the willow. A simple dowel catch opened the alder. The silver box which Drustan had given Marisa at her sixteenth mid-winter feast looked as if it had always lain within the alder.

'You do fine work,' Marisa said. Her voice cool but her eyes red. Had she been crying?

'Best woodsmith in the entire region, milady,' Rosana said proudly. 'Done work for the House of Doves afore now, and worked up at the Earl's Hall, but he always came back to us.'

'Home is home,' Horol said. 'Done the catches with dowels to save time, but best to tie that silk around with leather, too. So I cut this sheet up.' Horol tossed a piece of leather onto the ground. 'It were for making into vellum, but I took it away from the village to make into an arming jacket.'

Drustan rubbed his fingers across the soft leather. 'Aye, split it into two sheets and pad between.'

'That's what I thought.'

'It'd need quilting.'

'Aye, we know,' Rosana said.

'Got anymore of this?' Drustan asked.

'A few sheets,' Horol replied.

'Good. Get Cullain to help you with the design. It'll need some heavier leather over the top, but it would indeed make a fine arming jacket. Use heavy enough leather and it'll be fit for combat.'

'I can make one for you,' Horol said.

'Nah.' Drustan shook his head. 'Best it goes to you and yours. I'll replace my armour another way.'

'As you wish, my captain,' Horol said. He opened the catch on the silver box. Chips of stone glimmered in the dappled sunlight as he placed the opened box of willow, alder and silver in front of Marisa.

'Now we come to it.' Marisa drew the silk from the haraf stone between her breasts. The striped stone glowed when she breathed on it. She poured a small portion of earth over the stones in the box, and then wetted it with river water, before placing her hand over the open box. The haraf stones inside the silver pulsed in time with the stone she wore, a linked heartbeat of magic as the damp soil around the stones in the box steamed and hardened, linking it to the land, the stones and the gods they held quiet.

'There,' Marisa said. 'It is ready.'

Drustan reached into his belt-pouch and pulled out several pieces of fine jewellery. He heard gasps of horror as the fear flowered in all their heads. But these people had stood under the full onslaught of the terror and it was muted now, softened.

'Which one's the amulet?' Cullain asked.

'I don't know,' Drustan replied. 'I got them all from Jerem's pack. I haven't looked at them since.'

'They won't all fit into that little box,' Horol pointed out.

Drustan placed the jewellery on the ground in front of him, separating out the pieces. One caught his eye, a dark triangular piece of some material that seemed to suck light into it and give no shine back in return. All the pieces were corrupted with fear, but this one sent a shock of heated terror through his hand when he touched it.

'This one,' he said.

'Yes,' Marisa agreed.

'What is it?' Horol asked. The triangle was set into a golden cage, but didn't seem to touch any part of the metal, as if it floated there, within the cage but not connected to it or the world.

'Something which is not supposed to exist in this place,' Marisa said. 'Lock it away, Drustan.'

'We could leave it here,' Efan said. 'Abandon it.'

'The Vascanar want it,' Cullain said. 'And I'd not gift them my spit if they were on fire.'

Drustan lifted the amulet, his fingers trembling. Marisa touched his other hand, lightly, as if by accident, and the fear fled from his heart. He pushed the amulet into the box and coiled the chain about it. When he took his hand from the amulet, Marisa did not take her hand from his.

She reached across, closed the lid of the silver box.

Drustan laughed out loud. He relaxed, straightened at the lifting of his spirits, realised that he had been hunched over for three days, tensed against the loaded fear pressing against his heart. He looked at the grinning faces of the others.

'It is gone,' Horol said.

Marisa took her hand from Drustan's. 'Now to hide it.' She closed the wooden boxes around the silver and slipped them into the silken purse made for it. 'You are a fine seamstress, Rosana.'

'I know,' Rosana replied and drew the drawstring tight.

Horol carefully wrapped the calfskin around the whole and tied it tight with rawhide strips, a longer strip tied to create a strap.

Drustan held up the bundle. 'They cannot sense this?'

'No,' Marisa replied. 'And now I can begin to heal your side.'

Horol pointed at the fine jewellery laid out on the ground 'What about them other pieces?'

'You can have them if you want,' Drustan said.

Horol touched one but snatched his hand back. 'There's fear there. Not as strong as that thing in its golden cage, but I wouldn't want to have to try to sell 'em.'

'Ah.' Drustan nodded. 'That explains a lot.' He spoke of the wine and the food tainted with fear.

'Give me that belt-pouch,' Horol said. 'It'll be tainted too.'

'What do you intend?' Drustan asked.

'Those spellhound things track the scent of magic?'

Drustan grinned. 'False trails.'

'Aye.' Horol grinned back.

'Don't take too long.'

'I won't, my captain.'

'Have you finished giving orders, milord?' Marisa asked.

'Call him captain,' Agus said.

'They'll not hang me,' Marisa snapped. 'Now, Captain Drustan desainCoid, late of the Hundrin and leader of our motley band, can I possibly trouble you to shut up for a moment so I can begin your healing.'

'Will it sting a little?' Drustan asked.

CHAPTER 26

Marisa closed her eyes and let her spirit loose. It flowed along her arms, through her fingers, into and under Drustan's skin. Her haraf stone pulsated deeper, brighter, faster with each beat of her heart as she aligned her pulse to Drustan's.

Oh, Drustan.

Could she control her longing for him? Such thoughts were dangerous to a healer. She could be trapped here, deep within him, a presence in his body that would grow malignant and unchecked as her sanity dissolved into her lover's flesh. She must maintain the connection with her own body, keep her mind intact, hold her soul within yet separate from Drustan as she worked.

So hard to do. So hard not to reach out and caress his mind, to awaken the memories of the bladed grass under the sun when all shattered in a moment of revelation, to take him back there, to that moment in time, and remind him of how it used to be.

She cast aside her soul's need for him and focused on the task at hand. Her mind poured into the wound; she winced at the damage. Already beginning to heal, but to heal wrongly. The scar tissue around this wound would weaken the muscles for the rest of his life. If left as they were they would cripple him. Marisa sent tendrils of power to block the nerves leading to the injury, closing off the pain, keeping Drustan calm and quiet as she worked.

A test.

She sent a tendril of energy to scrape a nerve severed by the axe. No pain signals flowed up the nerves and Drustan did not even twitch.

Good.

Carefully, Marisa teased apart the scar tissue already forming along the torn edges of the cut, pulling apart each strand of muscle and connecting it to the other side of the wound in the right place, at the right point, holding the edges together, working deeper into the wound. Blood flowed, but she used it as an agent in the change, as a lubricant and cleanser of the deep tissue.

She itched to work harder, faster, deeper, to flare her talent to the heavens and connect it all in one moment of healing power. But to do this would send a beacon of energy into the world. Anybody with even the slightest talent would sense her presence — and the Vascanar hunted in these woods.

So, with the wound realigned and bound tightly, she withdrew. Her spirit flowed up her arms and back into her body, to rest once more below her heart.

****

Jarl teamed with Obanic as the Erisyans scouted through the forest alongside the road. Obanic was only happy when on campaign; his wife had tossed his bow after one too many bruises appeared on her face. But, for all that the women of the caedi snubbed him at the hearthfire, he was a good man to have by your side in the skirmish line.

The horses of the Vascanar snorted and shied away from the trees. Jarl crouched at the edge of the road and let his mind slip into the forest. Nothing. Just the normal bustling of creatures intent on feeding themselves and avoiding feeding others.

'Do they know something we don't?' he asked Obanic.

'Yes,' said Sekem

'Oh aye,' Obanic said. 'You were seeing to your cousin last night.' He stopped, apologetic for not using Sekem's name. Jarl gestured to continue. 'Aye, well, you didn't see what happened in the bloodlight.'

A hill lay next to the road. Too close. A good place for an ambush. Jarl signalled to a patrol skirting the edge of the forest, ordering them deeper into the trees to scout the hill. The patrol of four Erisyans didn't look happy at the order. Jarl gave the same signal with a more emphatic gesture. The scouts checked their weapons and then circled around behind the hill with nervous stealth.

'No,' Jarl said. 'I didn't see what happened.'

'Too busy talking to me.'

'Be glad you didn't.' Obanic knelt beside a tree. 'They should've cleared that hill by now.'

'It takes longer than five breaths to clear a wooded slope,' Jarl said. 'You're jumpy, Obanic.'

'I saw the dead walk yesterday.' Obanic gazed into the woods, his shoulders hunched.

'Ghosts are normal in the bloodlight,' Jarl said.

Sekem's spectral laugh didn't improve Jarl's mood. *'More than ghosts here, cousin.'*

'Not ghosts, Jarl, bodies. Walking, sneering bodies wielding swords. Even the *dead* natives of this place will try to kill you. There they are.' Obanic sighed with relief when he saw a scout top the hill and wave the all-clear. 'Gods, it's cold under these trees.'

Jarl signalled the scouts on to the next suspect spot: a ditch close by the road and ahead of the column. 'You saw the dead walk?' he asked as they moved forward with the rest of the covering patrol.

'Aye, had to be fresh dead, but they walked all right.' Obanic scanned the woods before moving forward again. Pairs of archers slipped through the forest around them. One pair jogged forward, then stopped. They readied their bows. The other pair trotted beyond the first then covered as the first pair repeated the manoeuvre.

'Just natives?' Jarl asked.

'A dangerous question,' Sekem said. *'Demons stalk this land, cousin.'*

'Go back and hide, then,' Jarl snapped.

'Hide?' Obanic laughed. 'I ran like a child seeking his mother's teat. The Vascanar rise too, but they couldn't be stopped. They just kept on coming. Eyes of fire, grinning at you through shattered faces. I cut the arm from one and the damn hand still grabbed my leg. If—' Obanic gulped. 'I was lucky to get away. The risen native dead of this place fall back down and *stay down* like proper corpses after you smack them around a bit, but the Vascanar…' He shuddered. 'Something else drives them.'

'This is in the deep-forest?' Jarl asked.

'Aye,' Obanic said. 'But it ain't just the dead. There are creatures in these woods that come out at night. Sharp teeth. Very sharp teeth.'

'I wondered why the Vascanar weren't hunting today.' Jarl grinned.

Obanic chuckled. 'I think they've had their fill of this forest for a while.'

'Maybe they chose the wrong land to invade,' Sekem said.

****

'No Vascanar at all?' Drustan asked.

'None,' Efan said. 'We rounded up the people easy enough. Less than two hundred paces away, most of 'em. They couldn't cross the river, too deep to the north, so all of them are along the southern bank.' He frowned. 'But some of 'em we couldn't find.'

'We can't wait for them,' Drustan said.

'If the Vascanar no longer hunt—' Rosana began.

'That won't last,' Drustan said. 'Is Horol back?'

'Here, my captain. Scattered the jewellery on any trail I could find.'

'Cullain, take command of the march. We'll head upriver until we can find a crossing point.'

'That'll take us close to the House of Doves,' Marisa said.

'Not too damn close,' Cullain said. 'There'll be a battle raging there.'

'Are you sure of that?' Drustan asked.

'Aye. That road's the only direct route to the highlands. It's either that or crabwise along the coast. Vorduk and Yaltis were fortifying it when we left. There'll be a battle.'

'There's a ford a few miles downstream of the House,' Efan said. 'We can cross there.'

'The ford it is, Cullain,' Drustan said.

'Right you are, my captain.' Cullain knuckled his forehead and started moving amongst the people, quietly ordering them to pick up their packs. The women and children carried all the food, the bedding, and the other equipment, leaving the men ready to fight.

Drustan knew there was no real need for the quiet words, but Cullain wanted to instil stealth in this group of civilians. Rosana calmed the fears of her people. A good woman that, matriarch of her village by the look of things.

Cullain sent Tirac and Horol to scout ahead and find an easy path for the women and the children.

Efan and three other men were set to act as a rearguard, watching for followers, making sure no stragglers fell behind, and trying to obscure the worst of the tracks they left.

Drustan had only fifteen men at his disposal, including Cullain, and two of those were needed to carry his stretcher. Not nearly enough men to guard over fifty women and children. Some men had hunting bows, some had swords, but most were armed with wooden-tined pitchforks and improvised spears.

'Garet,' Drustan called.

'Yes, my captain.' The merchant carried a Vascanar stabbing-spear.

'Pick two men. I need you to parallel our course, scavenge any weapons, armour or other equipment you can find and bring it back to the main group.'

'Yes, my captain.' Garet grabbed a couple of men and headed across the shallow water and into the forest.

Drustan watched him go. Then, clenching his teeth against the pain, he hauled himself onto the stretcher, lying back on the rough cloth with sweat pouring down his face.

'Easy does it now,' Rosana said to the two men assigned to carry it.

Drustan took a deep breath, wiped the sweat from his face, and said, 'I'm named Drustan desainCoid.'

'I'm named Morac of Trant. That's me wife and kiddies over there.' The big man nodded to a small family group.

The woman at the centre of it shook her head. 'He don't need to know that, you old fool.'

'Captain needs to know why I fight,' Morac said. 'That there's Peg. Cruel tongue she has, but a warm heart. That big lump beside her is my eldest, Yarom. That there is—'

'Quiet your blathering,' Rosana snapped. 'Bright Blade don't need to know all their names.' She shook her head at Peg. 'It's a wonder your ears still work.'

Morac glanced at Drustan and rolled his eyes.

The other man shook his head. 'Now that you have finished, Mor. I'm named Alun Tamson.'

'The walking dead killed his Da in the bloodlight,' Morac added.

Alun's mouth dropped open.

'Morac son of Ceren,' Peg said, 'you flap your lips so hard your brain freezes in the draft.'

'What?' Morac asked. 'The captain needs to know that we'll fight.'

'Pick up the damn stretcher and close your flapping lips,' Alun said.

Morac looked hurt, but took a hold of the stretcher. They lifted Drustan easily.

Dustan nodded to Cullain.

'Quietly now,' Cullain said, 'but step out smartly.'

The villagers strode through the shallow water to the southern bank of the river, before turning west, upriver, towards the ford that would lead them to safety.

CHAPTER 27

Jarl waited to loose arrows at the Karisae defences before the bridge. The white walls of the House of Healing shone in the sunlight, smooth curving walls marred by the ditches and a thicket of stakes thrown up to protect them. A hasty defence — on both sides of the river. The long straight roadway of the bridge piled with stone abutments, which would allow men to stage a fighting retreat to emplaced positions on the other side of the river. Somebody knew their business and had a pragmatic approach to their chances of holding this side of the bridge. But they had no intention of making it easy for the attackers.

The defenders had opened sluices to flood the meadows that stretched downstream of the road. The water stood millpond-smooth and probably a good four feet deep. Upstream, beyond the raised surface of the road, lay wetland forest, a tangle of trees and creepers — and mud deep enough to drown an unwary man.

The road itself was a ribbon of muddy cobbles fifteen paces wide, the only possible approach to the stone bridge. Corpses of horses and men lay scattered across it. The Vascanar had charged along that road four horses abreast, with spears lowered. The charge broke under a hail of arrows and the Vascanar had retreated with the cheers and jeers of their enemies in their ears.

Somebody knew how to marshal a defence even when forced to haste. What Jarl couldn't understand is why they'd bothered. From where he squatted beside the road he could see that no evacuation had taken place, and that nobody was running even now. Surely they didn't think that they could stop the entire Vascanar advance here, with only a few hundred against the ten thousand men of the main Vascanar force?

A holding action made sense. Give their people time to withdraw, to regroup, to set better traps and ambushes along the line of the Vascanar's advance. But to stop them in their tracks, with so few men, with most of the defenders walking wounded by the look of them and the healers scurrying around behind the mounds of earth…

They could at least have got the women out of there.

'*They protect their King,*' Sekem said. '*He lies dying within that House.*'

'Then they're fools,' Jarl muttered.

When the first prideful Vascanar charge failed, Arnik turned to the Erisyans, who crept forward, keeping low, from cover to cover, until they stopped, dropped to one knee, nocked an arrow, and awaited the order to loose.

The road kinked before the bridge, so the Erisyans could not loose from hundreds of paces away. This took away the Erisyan advantage of range. The overhanging trees at the edge of the flooded meadows removed any possibility that arrows shot high into the air would hit their targets, namely the men behind those banks of earth. This took away the Erisyan advantage of accuracy.

Which left only the Erisyan advantage of cunning and skill.

Jarl waited, an arrow nocked, his bow at full draw, his eyes on the mound of earth before the enemy trench. Half the Erisyan force lifted their bows, aimed slightly low — to conserve their arrows from the river — and loosed to a single command.

The arrows thudded into the earthen mound.

Enemy archers, thinking that the Erisyans had to nock new arrows, popped up from behind their defences and raised their longbows. Jarl loosed in that instant, on instinct. His bowstring thrummed, casting the heavy arrow forward to strike the chest of a Karisae archer. The Karisae's arrow plunged harmlessly into the ground only paces before his falling body; he was not the only man to fall victim to the ploy. But this tactic wouldn't work too many times; the Karisae weren't fools.

Jarl nocked another arrow and waited.

****

Torquesten trembled with the power of his demonic overlords and gloried in the bounty of their might. This world of colour and rancid light offended him as it offended them, but still, it was a world within which he could walk. A world he would tear asunder to open the gate to the Tangled Realms. A weak world, filled up with the ghosts of gods long dead, spirits untested, and mortals lost in dreams of comprehension.

Understanding came through pain, not patient investigation; he would show them just what pain could achieve.

Those dead gods, those dark shadows of the falls, Those That Endure in their prison of frozen rock, had shown him something new: how to change men into hounds. Not into men that *acted* like hounds, but men transformed into animals long of tooth and bloody of mind. Delicious anticipation pulsed within him.

He strode in front of the five men stretched out upon the dirt. On their knees, bowed backwards until their heads touched the ground behind them, their arms bound tightly to their bodies, they were a bundle of tortured muscle and sinew.

Off to one side, the priests chanted praises to the gods.

Pyran, who had sought Torquesten's death, bent backwards in the centre of the line. No special privilege given to him here. He would become a demonhound like all the others, a creature bound to Torquesten's will.

Bihkat moved from captive to captive, cutting and scourging in time to the chants of his acolytes. The captives squirmed and moaned when the blade cut into their flesh, but they did not scream. These were soldiers sworn to the gods of the Vascanar. They would bear this ritual, become what Torquesten, the Tukalac, wished, for fear of what would happen to their souls if they did not.

Torquesten watched the cuts with care, for they would open the men to the energy, but Bihkat worked with practised ease. The priest had made these cuts thousands of times. Spellhounds were fragile. They grew ill, got injured, died far too easily; men were not supposed to move like that, on all fours, sniffing the air, searching out magic for the worship of their masters.

The bodyguard whose face Torquesten had smashed moaned through his shattered mouth. Bihkat glanced at Torquesten. Normally such a creature would not be chosen, his chances of survival too slight.

'Continue,' Torquesten commanded.

Bihkat continued, inserting shards of darkness into the cuts — solidified Ulac, cooked in ways known only to the priesthood. Sharp-edged darkness pushed into open wounds. Now the men screamed, for they could do nothing else.

The priests' chants grew wilder.

Once again, dark clouds bubbled out of nothingness above the camp, slipping into this world from someplace else. But these clouds carried no funnel of wind, no raging heat. Instead, they sparkled with points of energy like diamonds in a bed of smoke. Lightning crackled through the air, striking the ground around the naked, bowed-backwards captives, as they screamed and drew the power to them, the power they desired, sanctified by their overlords. Even as their minds were torn apart, they screamed out their adoration.

The dark shards glowed beneath their skin. The snake-like lightning drove the venom of the Ulac into their flesh. They howled in agony and still the lightning struck.

Bihkat cried out, 'Something is wrong. Their minds are already remade.'

'They are unfinished,' said Torquesten. 'Watch the power of the Tukalac, priest. See what I can do with my brethren within me.' He directed the lightning to strike again and again, building up the energy, pulling forth the power. The heated air stung eyes, burned skin.

The chants of the acolytes faltered, and still Torquesten called down the lightning. Bihkat cried out in horrified exultation. 'You change their forms, not just their minds!'

'I am the Tukalac,' Torquesten said. The ghosts of the gods in the falls had shown him this magic, but let the priest think he created it himself. Let the priest feel the same fear Torquesten had felt in the dark red night below the falls!

The captives strained against their bonds, their muscles bulging, their bones bent and twisted into new shapes. Under the pressure of the transformation their bonds snapped and the captives flopped over onto their bellies.

And howled. Their howls changed in pitch and tone as their throats changed, as their faces lengthened, as their fangs grew. And still Torquesten called down the lightning. These would not be foul little creatures with skins almost bereft of fur, only scraps extending along the lines of their spines. These would not be creatures of the falls, hounds of the fallen. These would be his creatures, hounds of the demonkin, demonhounds.

The energy from another place poured into the creatures howling in agonised transformation. Dark bristly fur sprouted across their entire bodies, huge fangs extended beyond the edges of their lips, blood-red eyes glared at all they had left behind.

Their humanity.

A blast of heat. Bihkat and his priests hid their faces behind their upraised arms. Torquesten laughed. The clouds boiled away into nothingness. Sunlight flooded the landscape with hateful light.

The demonhounds howled.

****

'How many hits?' Gorak called.

Jarl lifted his bow and glanced along the line. Only two other bows lifted. Only two other targets hit.

'They're quick learners,' Sekem said.

'Keep it up.' Gorak yelled the order. 'We need to keep their eyes on us, not on their flanks.' He tapped Jarl on the shoulder.

'Aye.' Jarl stepped back out of the line as the Erisyans began loosing again.

'Head out to Uras. He's heading downstream to flank the enemy. See what's holding him up.'

'Any orders for him?'

'Aye, cross the river if he can, get behind them.'

'You realise there are trenches on both sides of this river?'

'Yes.'

'The Karisae will have thought of this, Gorak.'

'The best way to take a river crossing is from both sides at once.'

'We're skirmishers, not heavy infantry,' Jarl said. 'It's unlikely we'll be able to use range to keep us out of trouble.'

'Just give them something to think about, maybe draw some off, give us a chance to cut them down to size.'

'Hit them and fade?'

'Aye.'

'This is their accursed forest,' Jarl said. 'They know it better than we do.'

'We're Erisyan.'

'Maybe that idiot Arnik should've thought to bring some Vascanar infantry along. They could've tortoised up that road and cleared those trenches an hour ago. Karisae bows aren't powerful enough to pierce shields even at point-blank range.'

'I know,' Gorak said. 'I told Arnik to send a rider back.'

'And he said?'

'Nothing, but he didn't send a rider back.'

'The idiot's going to charge again?'

'Soon enough. Drinking more of that demon-wine.'

'What're they going to do about all those bodies in the way?'

'I think they intend to charge across the meadows. They seem to think the water's shallower than it looks.' Gorak grimaced.

Sekem laughed in Jarl's mind, a sound like the whisper of an arrow through trees.

Jarl shook his head. 'Oh, I do hope the Karisae forgot to dig pits and plant spears then. Before they opened the sluices.'

'The Vascanar aren't a patient people, Jarl.'

'At least Pyran knew something about tactics.' Jarl shook his head. 'Exactly how did that fool Arnik come to be in charge?'

'A political appointment.'

Mercenaries knew all about politically appointed war leaders.

A curse from the line and Obanic staggered away with an arrow through his shoulder. Two of his comrades dropped back to see to the injury. One man held Obanic upright as the other snapped off the fletching and pushed the arrow straight through the shoulder; it saved digging around with a blade to cut the arrowhead free. Obanic passed out and his comrades pulled the shaft out of the wound from the back, causing no more damage to Obanic's flesh.

One of the men returned to the line as the other dealt with Obanic's wound. Obanic would live. The arrow had missed all the major blood vessels and Erisyan field medicine would make sure any infection didn't spread.

'A heavy cavalry charge through at least four foot of water.' Jarl shook his head in disbelief. 'Shame about the phrasing of that bloody oath.'

'They had us in a cleft stick,' Gorak said. 'We needed the money or our caedi would've become nothing but a name on the wind.'

'I might've done the same in your place,' Jarl admitted.

'No you wouldn't,' Sekem whispered.

Jarl said firmly, 'They're paying us well enough.'

Gorak bowed his head. 'Thank you, nephew.'

Jarl shrugged. 'Truth is truth. I'll see what Uras is up to. Is Kerek crossing, too?'

'If he can find a crossing point. If not, his orders are to sweep down through that marsh forest and split their attention. I'd hoped we could avoid a crossing.' Gorak gripped Jarl's arm. 'There's supposed to be a ford a couple of miles downstream. Find it and use it.'

'It'll get done.'

Chapter 28

Morac and Alun lowered Drustan to the ground and eased their aching backs. Drustan hauled himself into a sitting position and checked the straggled line. His side felt looser, easier; still painful, but at least he could sit up without having to lean against something.

Marisa knelt beside him. 'How is it?' she asked in a tired voice. She slumped to her knees without grace. Bags were forming under her eyes.

'Healing.' Drustan looked away from her down the line of villagers. 'How are they?'

'Tired,' she said. 'Most have not slept for a day and a night.'

'I know. We need to find some tellis-leaf.'

'That is dangerous, Dru.' She realised what she had said. 'Sorry.' Her voice hardened. 'Milord Drustan.'

He ached for her, wanting her warmth, her love and strength. He banished the memory of her outlined above him against the sun, with harsh words of his own. 'Find us tellis-leaf, milady. We can't stop, not today, maybe not tonight. We have to be clear of the enemy before we can sleep. We have to be clear of this Calodrig, too.'

'Tellis can create a need in the chewer and it will kill any with a weak heart.'

'Any with a weak heart wouldn't have survived last night,' Drustan said. He eased himself back onto the stretcher. 'That's an order, milady. See that it's done.'

'The children, too?'

'Everyone has to walk for another day and another night and maybe a day after that. So yes, the children too old to carry, too.'

'On your soul be it.'

'Do what you need to do now and worry about tomorrow when it comes.'

Cullain walked back from the head of the line. 'Horol sent word back. The ford's clear.'

'Good,' Drustan said. 'We'll take a break here. Get some kha brewing. Then we move. Pull Efan and his rearguard in tight, and send somebody out to fetch in Garet.'

'Best not to leave anybody behind,' Cullain said. He nodded to Marisa. 'Milady.'

'Armsmaster.'

Cullain gestured to the stretcher-bearers. 'Go fetch in Efan and Garet.' He waited a beat as Morac sighed. 'Is there a problem?'

'No, armsmaster,' Alun said. 'Keep some kha warm for us.' He grabbed Morac's arm as the man opened his mouth, and dragged him into the trees.

'Best you do the healing now, milady,' Cullain said. 'We may have to move fast once we're over that ford.'

'The enemy will try to flank the defenders,' Drustan said.

'Aye, best way to take a river crossing.'

'From both sides at once.'

'Can the House be held then?' Marisa placed her hands on Drustan's side.

'No,' Cullain said, 'but I can't see Vorduk and Yaltis making it easy for the whoresons.' He nodded to Drustan and set about sorting out the halt.

Drustan fought the longing for Marisa as she began the healing. He wished he could tell her to wait, to rest, but if they ran into the enemy he had to be able to at least stand. The touch of her hands thrilled him. He tried to think of other things.

'It is done.' Marisa pushed herself to her feet. She swayed and her hands trembled until she shook her head, blinked her eyes, took three deep breaths and stood up straight. 'Rosana will know where to find a tellis bush. That woman is a wonder.'

'So you agree?' Drustan asked.

'You are captain here.'

A commotion in the trees had Drustan reaching for his dagger, but it was only Garet returning laden with arms and armour plundered from the dead.

That was not all he brought back with him. He had brought back more refugees fleeing from the Vascanar advance.

Drustan stared at the dishevelled women and children. 'I sent you to find weapons, Garet.'

'Should I have left them out there, my captain?' Garet asked.

Cullain strode over and ran a hand through his hair. 'That's more civilians to care for.'

Drustan said, 'They're here now, armsmaster.'

'That they are.'

'Place them in the care of Rosana.'

'Aye.'

'Distribute the weapons and armour to the men, Garet. Once we cross the ford, get back out there.'

'We have swords and armour for all, my captain.'

'Find me men, Garet, find me soldiers. Find me enough men to defend the waifs and strays you bring back to us every time you stumble across them.'

'Should I—'

'No, Garet, you shouldn't leave them out there. They're our people. We'll protect them with our lives. But find me warriors!'

Cullain grabbed Garet and took him to one side. 'The more of us there are, the easier we are to track. You've placed them in greater danger with us than if'n you left them out there in the forest.'

'I'll find men.'

'See that you do. Now grab some kha, then you and your men head up to the ford. I want Horol and Tirac to push across to the other side. Check we're not walking into sommat. You hold this side, Horol and Tirac push across. Clear?'

'Yes, armsmaster.'

****

Torquesten raged around the camp, his demonhounds snapping at any that approached their master. The Xarnac had disappeared. They had hidden it behind silver. How had they held such power for so long? It should have broken their puny minds. The Karisae gods were weak here, split into two by the salt water of the straits between the islands and the mainland. Gods not born to these islands, not made to step across even the narrow channels of salt water flowing between the islands themselves.

So how had they known how to hide the Xarnac from him? What trickery was this?

He killed two men with punches that shattered their breastbones and let his demonhounds feed on their corpses. Still the anger tore at his insides.

A path of blood would prepare the breaking of the final shrine, the one they called Redain, which sat on the banks of the sacred lake. After the rupture, the uplifting of his brethren, all would become night; all would become dark. But without the Xarnac, all could be lost.

His demonic brethren had each poured a little of their essence into that gilded cage, all adding something of themselves to the amulet of gold and disconnected darkness, something to guide demons through the Tangled Realms, to lead them here.

Without the Xarnac, the host would scatter, be lost amongst the myriad gates of this world. Chanting and torture would breach the gate, but it would not bring them here — to him. The Xarnac was needed.

And the people of this land had hidden it from him.

****

Jarl found Uras studying a narrow strip of grass, which arced back towards the Karisae trenches. The strip of grass was a dyke holding the river back from the meadows, but the sluices were open and deep water lapped at both sides of the waterlogged grass. No cover out there on the miles-long dyke — a few bushy shrubs didn't constitute cover. It was barely three paces wide and under constant threat of enfilading arrows loosed by archers from the forest on the opposite bank of the river, which was well within the range of even Karisae longbows.

'I'm not sending my men out there,' Uras said.

'*Good man,*' Sekem whispered.

'I don't blame you.' Jarl offered him a waterskin.

'These Karisae know how to defend. We need heavy infantry to punch through those ditch and mound emplacements.' Uras drank some water.

'We may get some after the next charge.'

Uras wiped the back of his hand across his mouth. 'The next charge?'

Jarl pointed at the flooded meadows.

Uras handed back the waterskin. 'That's the stupidest plan I've ever heard.'

'And he has served in the Princeholds of the Tevani plains,' Sekem whispered.

'When it fails, Arnik may send back for infantry.' There was no doubt in Jarl's voice.

'That could take hours.'

'Yes.'

'Illath rises again tonight, the capricious bitch. She'll turn the land to blood for longer this night than the last, according to Risak Raveneye, and he's rarely wrong about Illath's moods,' Uras said.

'I know.'

'Aye, of course, Jarl.' Uras sighed. 'You would feel her presence.'

'Only in the hours before she is about to rise.' Jarl rubbed a hand across the back of his neck. 'No matter. Gorak says there's a ford further downstream. We're to cross and flank up from there.'

'If they aren't holding the ford.'

'I doubt they've enough men for that.'

'But they won't have ignored it, either.'

'No.'

'So a forest full of traps, then.'

'Aye.'

'I'm beginning to hate this land.'

CHAPTER 29

Drustan itched to scout ahead of the column, to be able to survey the terrain before he sent his men into it, but he was trapped on the stretcher, unable to move without pain, forced to listen to men talking incessantly, on the ragged edge of the tellis-leaf.

Morac's sweat stank behind Drustan's head as he babbled at Alun. They had taken off their leather jacks, and the padded jackets underneath, and bundled the armour at Drustan's feet. Sweat slicked their backs, ran down their arms, but they moved steadily, carefully over the rough terrain — unlike Garet.

Garet returned from a scouting mission upstream along the bank towards the bridge. Alun and Morac took the opportunity to lower the stretcher to the ground while Garet hopped from foot to foot in the tellis shuffle, his padded jerkin open to the waist, sweat glistening on his skin.

'It seems clear.' Garet spoke through a mouthful of tellis-leaf, chewing the stimulant before tucking it up between his gum and cheek. 'Saw nothing but birds, and voles, the water looked lovely, sweet, cool, but we didn't bathe, we came straight back, nobody there, all is clear—'

'How far up did you go?' Drustan cut across his chatter.

'Maybe a half a mile. Didn't want to go much further, you can hear the battle from there, sounds as if the defenders are killing a lot of horses, screaming, carries across the water like a charm, men too. Aye, half mile till we heard the screams, lots of screams, horses, sounded—'

'Where did you set your sentry picket?' Drustan snapped.

'Huh … I didn't, came back here to report to you. Didn't set pickets. Only got three men, not enough, we had to get back here, make sure we told—'

'Stop.' Another problem: men did not like to stay in one spot on the tellis. Experienced soldiers knew this and worked around the problem, but Garet had only been a soldier since the Vascanar landed. He couldn't stand still. Eager to move, to charge off on futile missions, just so long as he was moving.

'I was only saying about the—'

'Be quiet, man,' Drustan said. 'It's the tellis talking, not you.' He wondered if the tellis had been a mistake.

Garet shook his head violently. 'No, I'm just saying that—' He stopped, shook his head, and spat out the leaf. 'I may have taken too much.' He still twitched, but at least he seemed aware of his surroundings. 'I should've set a picket.'

'Yes, you should.' Drustan thought for a moment. 'Fetch me Cullain.'

'At once, my captain.' Garet sprinted off.

'How much have you taken?' Drustan asked Alun and Morac.

'Not as much as him,' Alun said. 'We're farmers, my captain. Need it sometimes when there's a lot of work to be done. So we know not to take too much.'

'Aye,' Morac said. 'Garet's a merchant. Babbling's part of who he is. Talks so much his brain falls out of his mouth. We—' Morac breathed suddenly and then smiled. 'It's something you learn to deal with.'

'Takes practice,' Alun said. 'Only take half a leaf and make the damn thing last.'

'I take two,' Morac said.

'You're bigger than me.'

Drustan blew out a breath. 'You can stop chattering now.'

The two men grinned with teeth stained green, but said no more. Their hands twitched as if eager to do some work, any work.

Cullain stalked back along the line of nattering women, shaking his head and ordering them to silence as he passed; their silence lasted less time than it took him to walk ten paces.

'My captain,' he said.

'Armsmaster. Not taken the leaf then?' Drustan grinned.

'Took four,' Cullain said. 'Don't mean I babble like a girl at her wedding feast.' He glared at Alun and Morac. 'That damn Garet's still talking. Told Tirac to knock him out if need be.'

'Tirac is back from the other side of the ford?' Drustan said.

'Aye.'

'Is he twitchy?'

'Nah, he, Efan, and Horol refused the leaf. Good men.'

'So why did you take it?'

'I like it.' Cullain shrugged. 'Send them upstream?' he asked.

'Just Tirac.'

'One man?' Cullain chewed his beard.

'We need Efan and Horol here.' Drustan gestured to Alun and Morac. 'And there is no point sending any babbling fools with Tirac.'

'You ordered us to take the leaf.' Morac's voice rose in accusation.

'Your point being?' Cullain asked, turning towards him.

'Well he called us babbling fools and he ordered us to take the leaf and it don't seem fair that—'

Cullain drove his fist into Morac's stomach. The man folded around the punch and slumped to his knees. 'You refer to your captain as my captain. You refer to me as armsmaster. You do not cast aspersions at either one of us. Is that clear?'

'Yes,' Morac gasped.

'Will that be all, my captain?' Cullain asked.

'That'll be all, armsmaster.'

'Put your armour on,' Cullain growled at the still gasping Morac, before stalking back up to the head of the line.

Drustan hardened his voice as he spoke to Alun and Morac. 'You take the leaf to protect your people. So keep your brains in your heads. Get me to the ford.'

Morac grunted as he got to his feet and lifted the back of the stretcher again. 'Yes, my captain.'

Alun didn't look back from his position in the front. 'Yes, my captain.'

Neither one pulled on their armour.

****

Bihkat envied Torquesten his power to change the shapes of men, to give them greater mass, to change their faces, their jaws, their limbs, and make them into creatures of nightmare. The other priests cowered when Torquesten spoke to them. Bihkat could understand this; he felt the same fear though he hid it behind a sneer. Pyran had been the pre-eminent general of all the Vascanar, as Bihkat was their pre-eminent priest, and yet Pyran had been changed into a demonhound along with his bodyguards.

Even the bodyguards had been Akalac; they might have given up the blood-wine of the winter sacrifice to become the bodyguards of Pyran, but they were still Akalac. Torquesten hadn't cared. He'd changed them anyway, just to show what he could do. An example to all that the demonic gods of the Vascanar worked through him.

Oh yes, Bihkat felt envy.

Torquesten strode about the camp giving orders in a bold voice, to men who would have laughed in his face had he tried to tell them to do anything before the fire poured down from the clouds and made him Tukalac.

Master of the Hounds; a twist of Torquesten's spirit had given him that title. A twist of empathy had made him a good hound-master while he remained a mere mortal. But now he strode around the camp with bull-sized demonhounds bristling with black fur prowling about him. Master of the Hounds indeed.

Such creatures, such power. Bihkat hid his envy and carried out his orders. He would wait, bide his time; his demonic lords had not forsaken him. He was merely being punished for the loss of the Xarnac.

****

The screams of the horses still carried across the water from the bridge.

'They actually did it. They actually charged across ground they couldn't see for the water covering it,' Uras said. 'Fools.'

The Erisyans advanced along the edge of the river. Many of them kept peering nervously into the trees as they scurried from cover to cover. Not the normal watchful suspicion of skirmishers moving through unknown woodland; this nervousness had a deeper cause.

Jarl still didn't quite believe the stories of the walking dead.

'These forests hold more power than even you can imagine, Jarl Bearclaw, hearer of thoughts,' Sekem said.

Jarl shivered in the sudden chill and leaned forward to mutter, 'We're advancing on too narrow a front,' into Uras's ear.

'I know.' Uras gave a resigned shrug. 'But every time I spread 'em out, they bunch up again. I can't keep bellowing orders into the trees.'

'Not very stealthy,' Jarl agreed.

Uras rubbed at the goosebumps on his arms. 'Can't say I blame them. You weren't there last night, Jarl.'

'It's near noon now, not the middle of the accursed night.'

'That matters less than you think in this forest.'

A squad of archers moved in towards the bank of the river rather than out into the forest when faced with a fallen tree.

'Aye. And we'd better take that accursed House before night falls, or we may find ourselves fighting our own dead.'

'We're miles from the heart of the forest here.' Jarl kept his gaze upon the squad. They straightened the line once they were beyond the tree, but they didn't return to their original path. The line of advance narrowed again.

If Jarl commanded the Karisae, he would have placed men in the forest.

Erisyan warbows far outranged the Karisae longbows, but in the close-packed trees range meant nothing. The Erisyans were skirmishers in light armour and without shields. The Karisae heavy infantry were good fighters. Skirmishers did not survive close combat with good solid heavy infantry, not in tight quarters like this forest.

A determined attack by fifty men, backed by maybe forty archers, would decimate the Erisyan advance. Cut their line of travel, split their force, slaughter one group, while archers held back the others, then slaughter the others in their turn.

Uras nodded at the squad. 'I saw it too.' He shuddered. 'We attack a House of Healing, cousin, and they're always built on sites sacred to the gods.'

'You think the gods protect this land?'

'Something does,' Sekem said.

CHAPTER 30

The sharpness of the tellis-leaf jagged across Marisa's senses. Everything cleaner, edged in light, in naked contrast to the normal softness of the forest. She could see the individual pores upon the leaves of the shrubs, hear the insects buzzing, the slither of the snakes. It was all there, just there, she could touch it, feel it, outside of herself, tangible and exciting... Stop.

She tried to control her mind with the help of the haraf stone. She had warned Drustan about the tellis, but he had not listened. Oh no, not to her, not to a mere wo... She stopped the thought. Focus.

The haraf beat a futile pulse against her heart. Focus. They had to cross the ford, the water bubbling, foaming over the pebbles, the rocks, a clean taste to the air, a kingfisher darted, iridescent, diving under the surface, so long, so long under the water, ah! it had caught a fish, it would feast... Focus.

The ford lay in front of them, the river low at the height of summer. It would be possible to cross without getting their feet wet. Jumping from stone to stone, dancing across the water, laughing, shouting for enjoyment, such fun to be had, such—

'Milady.' Rosana grabbed Marisa's arm. 'You have to control it. We have to move quiet as mice now.'

Marisa breathed rapidly and allowed the haraf stone's strength to bolster her self-control. 'How do you do it, Rosana?'

'Control the leaf?'

'Yes.'

Rosana smiled. 'It's part of nature's bounty, but nature always has an edge to it. We live on that edge. In my time, I've delivered five babies in three days. You can't tell women when to go into labour and you can't be twitching like that loon,' she pointed at Garet, 'when they do. It upsets them.'

'Yes, I suppose it would.' Marisa drew the pulse of the haraf stone deep inside her, allowed it to slow her heartbeat, to bring her focus back, to make clarity return. She would have to cross soon. Ethan and Horol scouted ahead, across on the other bank of the river. One final check before the villagers exposed themselves to the open daylight.

'Farmers learn to use it,' Rosana said. 'Learn to control it, otherwise they might cut their foot off with a scythe and not even notice. Cobblers might nail their hand to the shoe. Knew a blacksmith once. Liked the stuff. Used too much of it too often. Reached into his forge to lift out a red-hot bit of steel with his bare hand.' Rosana stopped and breathed and shook her head. 'It does so make you want to talk, though.'

'What happened to the blacksmith?' Marisa had control now; no drug would rule her.

'The shock killed him. He did, after all, burn his own hand off. And tellis makes the blood run faster. His heart broke. Just as well, because he weren't a blacksmith no more. Might have made himself a hook, I suppose, but it were his hammer hand he lost. Not much a blacksmith can do if'n he loses his hammer hand.'

No leaf would rule her, Marisa thought, even as her mouth said, 'I love Drustan. I love him and I betrayed him.'

Rosana gestured to a woman who came too close, shooing her away from the conversation. 'No, you didn't,' she said. 'You were betrayed, too. He just bore the force of it.'

'You know what happened?'

'All know the story of the Bright Blade and his lady,' Rosana said.

'Such dishonour. Anthanic blood flowing through his veins. How can he stand it?'

'The same as the rest of us,' Rosana replied.

Horol led the women with babes in arms across the ford. Slowest first, get them across and the rest could run through the water if need be… What had Rosana said? The words bit through the sharp-edged oblivion of the tellis.

'The same as the rest of you?' Marisa gazed at the older woman.

'My grandmother were Anthanic. My grandfather's father were Anthanic. Little Tilly over there, and Horol, and Efan, their mother were Anthanic. Died of a flux afore we could get a healer for her, poor thing. I look after 'em now, they need a mother, specially a girl-child as pretty and headstrong as Tilly.'

The river was broad here, spread out, its depth lessened by the width, by the stones, by the… 'But the Anthanic are savages!'

Rosana placed a hand on Marisa's arm. 'Only nobles, your people, care about that sort of thing, milady. Anthanic ain't no different from anybody else. Some are lovely and some ain't. You can't tell Anthanic from Karisae if'n they ain't got them tattoos they so love.' Rosana pulled down the shoulder of her dress to reveal a swirl of blue against her skin. Not a large tattoo, but obviously Anthanic. 'They gave me this, came out of the forest and gave me this, when I took on the care of young Tilly. Her brothers have the same. A mark of family. Not Tilly yet; she'll have to choose when she comes of age.'

'But they're savages,' Marisa repeated, aghast, even as she thought of Branwen controlling the creatures of the fields, a priestess in her own right, acting the servant to be near the shrine. The healing magic had not worked as well after the Anthanic ran away into the woods…

'Your man there.' Rosana gestured at Drustan on his litter waiting his turn to cross. 'How many's he killed in single combat?'

'That is honour.'

'Honour.' Rosana laughed. 'Some little slight that breached some little code and some man had to die for it. Men fight, 'tis their nature, but only savages butcher each other for a breach of manners.'

'He fought duels at the behest of his King.' The nursing mothers were almost across now, Horol leaving them to Efan's care and moving back across the river for the rest, for the children, for Drustan on his litter.

'Which means he's naught but a butcher. So who's the savage in this land? The Anthanic or the Karisae who stole it from them?' Rosana glanced upstream suddenly, almost as if she had heard something, something dangerous. 'Don't mistake my meaning, milady. Yon Drustan's a good man, a solid man. He came back to the islands even after they'd thrown him aside. We need such men as him. He's a warrior. Like Cullain. Not a man to cross, Cullain, but…' Rosana smiled slowly '…he's such a big man. Have you ever noticed how big his hands are?'

****

Jarl crouched under a bush and scanned along the line of nervous Erisyans. He studied the ground in front of them. The dense trees and undergrowth didn't invite his smile. Would the enemy have set traps on this side of the river, too? Had they had enough time? He doubted it, but best to take care anyway.

Whatever happened, the Erisyans had to move forward. The only infantry Arnik had at his disposal were their kinsman back at the ford. What was the betting that even now he was trying to get Gorak to attack up that sodding road? Without shields.

'We need to get across and flank,' Uras said. 'Before Arnik throws our people into the arrowstorm.'

'I know,' Jarl said.

Uras gave the command and the Erisyans moved up.

****

Drustan lay on his stretcher and listened to Alun and Morac's babble.

'My father's cousin married a Normache wench,' Alun said. 'Beautiful woman. They left to start afresh in the mountains of that isle.' Water splashed around his ankles. Children chattered around them, youngsters, but old enough to walk on their own. Horol was having difficulty keeping them in line. They wanted to swim. They wanted to dance and play.

They were on the tellis.

'My mother was said to be half-Anthanic. Nobody knows for sure. Her father never spoke of it, but you would see the smile on my grandmother's lips sometimes.'

'Fickle women,' Alun said.

The mothers of the children rushed out into the river. Drustan could hear them calling out, grabbing their youngsters, scolding them. Cullain must have sent them out to take control… What did Morac just say about the Anthanic?

'Hear tell you had a few bastards down in Barstow,' Morac replied. 'Hear tell that's why you disappeared a couple of days back. Getting them out of there, I heard.'

What did he say? Half-Anthanic? His mother? A half-breed? Cullain raced across the ford with a child under each arm. All the men were out on the ford now, any pretence at an orderly crossing forgotten.

'That's different.' Alun stopped in the middle of the river, turned around and glared at Morac.

Garet splashed past, grabbing up a child, carrying her across the ford at speed, until he fell and plunged into the water. If Horol had not grabbed the child, she would have been washed downstream.

'Why so?' Morac asked.

Morac claimed to be half-breed, without shame; Alun hadn't even commented.

'A man must spread his seed. It's our nature.' Alun pushed at the stretcher handles.

Cullain forged his way across the ford, Marisa close beside him.

'Women have a nature too.' Morac pushed back.

'Don't talk to me about women's nature.' Alun twisted the stretcher.

Drustan grabbed onto the poles to stop himself being tipped into the water. 'Get moving, damn you,' he snarled.

'She were right to cut you.' Morac twisted the stretcher back the other way.

'Not there the bitch weren't.' Alun was leaning over Drustan's feet as if trying to close the gap with the other man *through* the stretcher.

'It still works, don't it?'

'Only because I woke up.'

Drustan reached up and grabbed Morac's ear, yanking the man's head down so he could see him eye to eye. 'Get me to the other side of the river, you useless piece of weasel dung.'

'Oh.' Morac realised where they were. 'Sorry, my captain.'

'Why have you stopped?' Cullain raised his hand to Alun but did not finish the blow. 'Get moving, or I swear by the gods I'll gut you and leave you to the crows.'

'Sorry, armsmaster, it's the tellis.'

Marisa dumped cold river water across Morac's head from a leather bucket. Drustan got soaked as well, but Morac puffed out and said, 'Thank you, milady.'

Marisa dipped the bucket back in to the river and threw water into Alun's face. 'Get moving,' she hissed. She grabbed up a child and carried her across the ford.

'Sorry about what I said about your sister.' Alun turned around so he faced the right way.

'I did warn you before you married her.'

They picked their way across the ford.

'That you did, but she's gone now. I had no right to speak of the dead in such a way.'

'Your dreams, your problem,' Morac said. 'You'll have to kill a lot of Vascanar to make up the lack. She never had a merciful bone in her body and I doubt much changed since she died.'

'Bloody tellis,' Alun said.

'What's that?' Morac looked upstream.

'What?' Drustan asked. He was too low to see at any great distance, the bottom of the stretcher wet from the river water.

'I saw something,' Morac said. 'Something flashed.'

'Run!' Cullain bellowed from the other side of the ford.

Arrows slashed into the water, barely leaving a splash. Erisyans!

CHAPTER 31

Jarl couldn't believe that men of his caedi had loosed at the people strung out across the ford. 'They're women and children!' he yelled.

Only some of the archers had taken up their bows, maybe fifty men, giggling with every shaft loosed. The sound of those giggles chilled Jarl's blood.

'They're lost now,' Sekem whispered.

'Shut up.' Jarl ran towards the line of men. He grabbed one by the arm as the man let fly. The arrow thudded into the tree by Jarl's side. A wide barbed head, a hunting arrow used when foraging; an arrow designed to dig into the flesh of an animal, not a war-arrow meant to punch through armour.

He pulled the man around to face him. Gods, it was Iain. Iain, who lived two farms over from Jarl's holding. A neighbour, a friend, kin. 'What are you doing, Iain? By the gods, man, they're women and children.'

'Look at his eyes,' Sekem warned.

Jarl saw the flash of fire behind Iain's rictus stare and took a step back. *'They're lost,'* Sekem repeated.

'No.' Jarl moved forward again.

Iain punched Jarl to the ground. His hand dropped to his syrthae blade.

'No, Iain!' Haukon, Iain's younger brother, yelled from the group of horrified men taking no part in this action. 'No, Iain, don't! He's kin!'

Iain shuddered, turned away from Jarl, nocked another wide-barbed arrow to the string, lifted his bow.

Jarl stared up at him in horror. 'They're women and children.'

'They're the enemy.' Iain giggled and loosed.

Jarl came off the ground in one movement, slammed his fist into Iain's face, wrenched the bow from his hands, threw it away. Iain drew his sword and lunged at Jarl, who parried the thrust with his leather-clad forearm and smelled the stink of demon breath in the air.

'*They're lost,*' Sekem said. '*They're no longer Erisyan.*'

****

Drustan rolled out of the stretcher into the water. Rocks bruised his uninjured side. Alun reached for him.

'No,' Drustan said. 'The children. Save the children.'

For an instant the two men stared into each other's eyes, then Alun nodded, threw aside the stretcher and splashed through the water towards a screaming child, Morac not far behind.

The water closed over Drustan's face but he struggled upwards, struggled to place his feet on the river-bed. The current was stronger than he expected, swirling around him, trying to drag him under. His side ached, but he pushed through the water, dragging himself into the shallows of the ford.

Now he had to crawl. Arrows splashed into the water all around him. He dragged himself forward. Keep going. Don't stop. The only safety is in the trees.

Morac went down under a hail of arrows, but the child in his arms, untouched, squirmed free and ran on, to be picked up by Alun and thrown towards safety. Then Alun himself fell into the water, pierced with arrows. His body entangled with Morac's.

The river carried them away.

'Keep moving,' Drustan muttered to himself.

'Father,' a boy screamed. 'Father!' Weeping, crouched in the stream, his foot trapped between some stones, he looked about eight, maybe nine. Drustan crawled towards him. Pain flared in his side as he grabbed the boy's arm.

'Stop struggling.' Drustan reached down, felt around the boy's foot, found the rock that had slipped. He breathed in sharply, then thrust out the breath as he pulled the stone away. The boy's foot came free.

'Run,' Drustan yelled. 'Run, boy.'

But the child grabbed Drustan's arm.

Drustan swept his other hand up in an almighty slap across the boy's face. 'Run.'

The boy put his hand to his cheek, livid red.

'Run to your mother, afore I gut you myself,' Drustan snarled.

The boy fled across the ford, through the arrows, and Drustan struggled on through the water, pulling himself forward, the water pouring over his head. He gasped, lifted his head up and struggled on.

Then Marisa was there, grabbing him, pulling him upright with a strength he didn't know she possessed.

'Come on,' she said, over and over again.

****

Eirane swept across the river above the ford. Her powers were weak here, far from her own forest, but she could protect the children. Pushing the arrows away from them with gusts of wind was all she could do.

The arrows couldn't be stopped in their flight, some had to taste flesh, but she protected the children. Men died because they held children in their arms, women were injured, but no child was pierced.

Drustan lay in the waters of the ford. Desperate, Eirane turned the arrows away from him, but there were so many in the air. She had to save her son. Drawing along the lines of power, stealing from the force of the sacred lake, even taking some strength from the prison of Those That Endure, she dipped into the waters of the river.

A swirling wind cascaded upwards into the sky, lifting the moisture with it, forming a shimmering curtain across the sight of the archers shooting arrows at her son.

A gentle rain began to fall, but it was imbued with magic, blurring the eyes of the archers. This was beyond her strength.

Who did this? Who aided her child?

'*Protect the children,*' a voice cried upon the wind.

****

With the pommel of his sword, Uras smashed Iain across the back of the head. The line of traitorous Erisyans barely glanced across as they continued to loose at the people pinned down upon the ford.

Jarl drew his syrthae. 'They've drunk of the Vascanar's elixir.'

'They've what?' Uras turned to Jarl. 'You're sure?'

'I can smell the stink of it on their souls.' A gentle rain misted across the river.

'Dear gods, what've we done by bringing our people here? What's Gorak done?'

'What he had to, Uras.'

Some of the corrupted archers began a low guttural chant. Jarl could hear the screams of men in that chant. He could smell seared flesh. The demons were coming to help their new servants.

Jarl gazed in horror at where the arrows fell, then frowned.

Arrows splashed into the water around the people rushing across the ford. At this range, with targets in the open, fifty Erisyans should have cleared that ford in a single volley. And yet they missed. This rain was not enough to obscure their aim. And the rain had not been falling when the archers began loosing at women and children.

These were Erisyan archers, corrupted and lost, but still the finest archers in the known world.

'How are they missing?' murmured Uras.

'Something is blurring their eyes,' Sekem said. *'Why do you think they chant? Why do you think they call their demonic lords?'*

****

Through the misting rain, Marisa saw Horol grab up his sister, Tilly. The woodsmith ran towards the riverbank, to the safety of the trees, where his brother Efan screamed at everybody to hurry, hurry, get to safety.

Cullain carried two small children and dumped them at the feet of Rosana before splashing out into the river for more. He grabbed a young woman, bedraggled as a rat, lifted her over one massive shoulder and surged towards the bank. Almost all the children safe now.

An arrow struck Cullain in the calf. He dropped to the edge of the bank cursing. Rosana and some of the others dragged him and the woman to safety.

So Drustan was her responsibility, then. He could barely walk, but he helped as much as he could. Arrows dropped into the water all around them but none hit. Drustan stumbled over a stone and pulled them both down into the river.

'Go,' he said. 'Get away. Now!'

'We need you,' Marisa said. 'I need you.' She pulled him to his feet.

'You're a fool, Marisa.'

'Come on.' She helped him to skirt a pothole. Drustan pulled her down into the water. A volley of arrows flashed above their heads.

'Stay low and crawl.'

'I'm not leaving you.'

A child cried in the centre of the river.

CHAPTER 32

The mist deepened. Jarl had drawn his sword, but he hesitated. Could he kill his own people? Could he do what was needed? Did it matter that they were trying to kill women and children? They were his people, his caedi, his kin.

'*Not anymore,*' Sekem said.

'Shut up, cousin.' Jarl wiped moisture from his face. 'So it comes to this.' He wished for the skies to open and the snow to fall, for the oath to be breached so he could go upriver and kill as many Vascanar as he could find. He wanted that so fiercely.

He couldn't move, he couldn't kill his own people, but the Vascanar, ah, he could kill them right enough.

'*They're Vascanar now,*' Sekem whispered.

Uras cursed and lifted his sword. 'We can't have this on the honour of our caedi,' he said. 'We must—' His words gurgled to a halt around the arrow that speared through his throat.

Jarl caught the awchti, looked into Uras's eyes, felt the tug of his soul. '*Stop them. Warn Gorak,*' Uras whispered, though his lips didn't move. Jarl looked up at Uras's men, the ones not loosing at the innocents, not lost to the Vascanar elixir. Some stared at their dead commander with horror, some with anger, but none knew what to do. To loose upon their kin; could any man do that? Haukon wept, and he was not the only Erisyan with tears running down his face.

Jarl let the dying Uras fall and turned towards the corrupted Erisyans. They still chanted, still loosed, still... His caedi, his comrades, his kin.

Haukon screamed a warning.

An Erisyan named Menas aimed an arrow at Jarl. No, not Erisyan; this was a Vascanar. Menas might not have the scars on his face, he might've been born to an Erisyan woman, but the madness of the Vascanar blazed in his eyes.

Jarl threw himself forward. His syrthae swept up from a low guard. The heavy point of the blade ripped through Menas's knee, hardly slowing, rising. Jarl reversed the blade at the top of the stroke and cut downward into Menas's neck.

Other corrupted Erisyans swarmed towards him, but not all; most of the others continued loosing at the people on the ford.

Jarl yanked the blade free of Menas's neck and turned. In the looping, swirling fighting style of an Erisyan swordsman he used his off-hand to push away a knife thrust at his stomach, while the heavy blade of the syrthae wove a cutting, slashing circle of steel.

Iain, oh gods, Iain… Why didn't he stay down? Haukon screamed in horror as Iain cut at Jarl's head. Jarl brought his sword up, parrying the cut, then launched a blistering attack of his own. Iain parried and raised his sword above his head.

Had he forgotten every rule of combat?

Jarl kicked low, feinted high, and slashed open Iain's thigh with a rising stroke. Haukon screamed, but Jarl swept the sword out and then back in again, pulling the return cut downwards into Iain's neck, ripping through sinew, muscle and bone, almost decapitating the man.

'Thank you,' Iain's fading spirit whispered.

'Shut up and let him fight,' Sekem snapped.

Would the others help? Would Jarl die here upon the blades of his kin?

A bass growling came from the forest behind Jarl.

Was that a bear?

****

'Run!' Drustan screamed at the child left behind in the middle of the ford. She looked to be around six summers old, a corn dolly clutched to her chest. Wailing at the top of her lungs, she was not moving, not running, but instead stared at the water swirling around the stone she stood upon. Terrified of the water. Not moving from her tiny little island of stone. Maybe she didn't want to get her feet wet. She was only a child.

'Run!' Drustan screamed again. He tried to claw his way towards her, but Marisa fought him back towards the bank.

'Save her,' Drustan yelled at Marisa. 'Save her.'

Marisa ignored his yells and kept pushing him towards the bank.

Horol plunged back into the water with Efan by his side. The two brothers ran across the slippery stones in a frenzied sprint to get to the child, arrows falling all around them.

Efan was hit in the shoulder and stumbled. Horol didn't stop, didn't wait for his brother. Intent on the child, he didn't even look at Drustan and Marisa. He reached the screaming child, grabbed her close to his chest, and began the long run back to the safety of the trees.

Efan snapped the arrow off at the shaft, left the head embedded in his shoulder, and ran towards his brother.

'No,' Horol cried and pointed with his chin to Marisa and Drustan. The mist thickened, but arrows still fell.

Efan didn't hesitate to change direction. 'This is not a healthy place,' he said, grabbing Drustan by the arm, lifting him to his feet, dragging him towards the trees with Marisa's help.

Horol almost in the safety of the trees, throwing the child onto the bank, turning back to help his brother… Three arrows thudded into his chest. He staggered, stared at Efan across the swirling waters. Started to fall.

'NO!' Efan screamed. He dropped Drustan's arm, plunged into the water and caught hold of his brother, pulling him to the bank despite the arrows falling all around. But Efan could not lift his brother's waterlogged weight. Then Rosana was there, and Agus, helping Efan to pull his brother to safety.

Now Drustan and Marisa were the only ones left in the open of the ford.

CHAPTER 33

J arl twisted away from another arrow, forewarned by the thought and the stink of demonic possession that preceded it. He parried a sword thrust to his groin and punched a leering face.

The two hundred uncorrupted Erisyans didn't join the fight. They hesitated, taking a step towards the battle, but then stopped, weeping, crying out warnings to Jarl, but not rushing to his aid. Their awchti killed by one of their own, Jarl fighting for his life — and still the bonds of caedi held them. He couldn't blame them. They didn't know what he fought.

He ducked and rolled. Three arrows flew over him. His empathic sense was the only thing keeping him alive. Too many opponents. He would move the wrong way, soon, avoid one arrow only to step into the path of another.

Up on his feet, parry, try to back up, get away. No longer caring about the people on the ford, about Uras's murder, about the dishonour brought upon his caedi. Just trying to survive, to fight another day, to deal with the ash cloud of this betrayal.

That strange roaring coming closer. The mist thickening, swirling around the blades as they cut through the air.

Two men stood in front of him: stab one through the armpit, push away the other's sword arm. Jarl's sword stuck in the man's ribs. He twisted it free, but now the other attacker swung a savage cut at Jarl's head. He only just managed to raise his sword in time. Edge to edge, couldn't be helped, step to the side, parry, block, parry—

Something charged out of the mist behind Jarl, and the man trying to kill him fell back, gibbering with horror.

Jarl cut open the man's thigh and turned to face the new threat. He saw what came out of the forest.

Oh, the gods were laughing now.

A huge man approached wearing a great bear's skull as a helm. The snout hid his face in shadow. The fur of a bear lay diagonally across his broad torso above a loincloth of leather, and in his hands … in his hands he held a huge club formed from a stave of oak topped with a lump of iron the size of a man's head.

Beran the hero?

Here?

A growling roar came from this eldritch figure's throat. The club swung in an unstoppable arc and shattered the skull of a corrupted Erisyan. The bear-clad figure charged into the fray, roaring. 'I am Berasin! Berasin! BERASIN!'

The corrupted Erisyans loosed arrow after arrow but the shafts shattered against the hero's skin as if hitting stone. Berasin smashed his way through the tainted men. Some tried to fight with swords, but Berasin dodged while his club crushed skulls, splintered chests. To stand against him was to die.

The uncorrupted Erisyans fled. Berasin let them go, but the fifty men who had drunk of the Vascanar's elixir he drove towards the river. Not a single Erisyan who had loosed at women and children survived his onslaught.

Jarl remained crouched on the riverbank, his sword in his hand, bearing witness.

'*We should probably go now,*' Sekem said in the cold, disinterested voice of a ghost.

Berasin smashed a final skull and turned towards Jarl.

****

Marisa could hear the roar of a bear. Was it a bear? Could she hear words?

The arrows stopped falling. The mist thickened about them. She could hardly see the banks of the river.

Cullain, a bloody rag tied around his wounded calf, ran out onto the ford, Garet at his side, racing through the water towards Marisa and Drustan.

From upriver came the screams of terrified men and a sound like a hammer smashing into wet wood. Marisa wanted to see; she didn't care about the water, the arrows, the mist. Cullain would save Drustan and all would be well. She wanted to see what was happening to the archers. She peered into the mist.

Cullain reached them.

'You should've stayed in the forest,' Drustan said.

'I should've stayed in that bloody tavern.' Cullain grabbed Drustan. 'I knew coming back 'ere were a mistake.'

'It was your idea,' Drustan said.

'Don't know why you listened.' Cullain threw Drustan over his shoulder. 'First time you did.' He started running back across the ford.

Garet grabbed Marisa's arm. 'Time to leave, milady.'

'What is happening?' Marisa asked, still peering into the mist as the screams of men slowly faded away to nothing.

'Who cares?'

Marisa tried to shake off his arm.

Garet slapped her across the face. 'You're not safe yet, now move.'

'You hit me!' Marisa said in shock.

'I'm sorry, milady, not my place, just a merchant and all that, but if you don't start running I'll bloody well knock you unconscious and carry you. Horol has need of you.'

Marisa blinked away the tellis. 'Yes, of course.' With Garet by her side, she ran across the ford. The merchant stayed upstream of her, pacing her, shielding her from any arrows with his own body.

The mist ended when they left the water, as if cut with a knife. Drustan lay slumped against a tree, pain in his face, but he seemed well enough.

Efan, weeping, held Horol in his arms.

Horol had trouble breathing. He couldn't speak, but pushed at his brother, urging him to leave.

Efan saw the blade in Marisa's hand. 'No, no, I'll not let you, I'll not.'

'Cullain,' Marisa snapped.

'Aye, milady.' Cullain took three punches from Efan but did not return them, simply lifted the man away from his brother and held his arms.

Marisa knelt beside Horol. 'Help me, Rosana.'

Horol's eyes closed. He slumped into unconsciousness. Marisa cut the leather of his armour, slicing up to where three arrows protruded from his flesh. Rosana joined her with another knife. They cut around the arrows and pulled back the leather.

'Not too deep,' Cullain said. He shook Efan. 'You calm now?'

Efan nodded.

'Say it.'

'I'm calm now.'

'Good.' Cullain let him go.

Marisa threw aside the knife blunted by the leather; she needed a keen edge for the cutting of flesh. She held out her hand and Cullain slapped Drustan's needle-pointed dagger into it.

'Just sharpened that,' he said.

Marisa wondered again if the lock of her hair still lay within the hilt. 'Hold him down,' she said. Cullain reached for Horol. 'Not you, armsmaster. You and my husband see to our safety.' Marisa pointed the dagger at Efan. 'You. Hold your brother still while I cut.'

Efan grabbed Horol's shoulders. Rosana grabbed his legs.

Marisa studied the arrows, trying to judge the plane of the arrowheads. She didn't want to dig around in there to remove the barbs; no need to do any more damage.

'There, milady,' Rosana said. 'The fletching and the heads line up so.'

'Ah, I see.' With brutal speed, Marisa cut into Horol's flesh. No spells of analgesia, nothing to help the man. One arrow released, she threw it aside, and another, and then the last. Her fingers covered in blood, she stripped the silk from around her haraf stone.

She had to keep the healing energy tightly focused, and Horol's wounds were deep. If the Erisyans had used war arrows, then he would already be beyond her help. Why had they used broadheads? The answer was obvious: to kill unarmoured women and children.

Marisa lowered her mind into the worst wound, which had nicked a lung. Gentle as a bird, she healed the wound, but not all the way to the surface. Stitches and cleaning lotion would fix up the skin and stop infection, but the deep wound, the wound that would deny Horol the air he needed, she healed with a brief flash of magic.

The other two wounds were not as dangerous. One lay close to an artery, the source of most of the blood loss, but that was easy to heal.

The last wound needed no real healing, though she forced the blood to clot a little faster.

'He will live.' Marisa sat back on her ankles. 'Rosana, fetch my pack.'

'Yes, milady.'

'Right then, Efan, let's see to that shoulder.'

****

Berasin stalked towards Jarl. The huge man wearing the skin of a bear limped slightly from a bad cut just above his knee, but Jarl had no illusions about his fitness for battle.

Jarl clambered to his feet, took his stance, lifted his sword, and set his shoulders. So here is where he would die.

'I don't think so,' Sekem whispered.

Berasin tilted his head from side to side. The eyes of the bear skull he wore as a helm stared at Jarl as if still filled with life.

'I am Berasin,' the huge warrior said. 'Berasin the God-Eater. Born to these lands before your puny tribe ever trod the world. I fought the Goddess Ursaric and killed her in this very forest before even the Anthanic came to this land. I stood at the gates of the underworld and held back the horde. I fight now upon the Sunlit Plains with your heroes, your men of bow and blade. Only their arrows can pierce this thrice-blessed skin. And there are others, of course. We are what heroes become if they are judged worthy of the honour.'

'Are you going to talk me to death?' Jarl asked.

Berasin laughed. 'Those are not your words, archer, but they are good words. I was there when they were thrown back into the teeth of death.'

Jarl frowned for a moment. Then he remembered: Drustan desainCoid had used those words when on his knees with an axe embedded in his side, facing death.

'I am Berasin.'

'You said.' Jarl moved slightly to the left.

Berasin lifted his mighty iron-tipped club to touch his chest, his helm. 'This is the skin of the Goddess Ursaric, this is her skull. See how she looks at you, archer. She wants your blood to wet her fangs. She wants your soul to keep her warm at night.'

The club swept down, smashing Jarl's sword into shards of steel. Berasin wrapped a huge hand around Jarl's throat and lifted him clear of the ground.

'But I am Berasin.' Jarl found himself gazing into dark hazel eyes with flecks of green in the iris; startling eyes, with a depth behind them that spoke of immeasurable pain. 'And I remember.'

One heave of Berasin's hand sent Jarl flying through the air to slam into the ground ten paces away.

Jarl slipped into unconsciousness wondering why this mighty hero of the old times had let some Vascanar scum cut out his tongue — and how he had grown it back.

CHAPTER 34

Drustan slumped against a tree, with his clothing soaked through and his side driving shards of pain into him at every breath. Two men dead, their bodies lost to the river. It was obvious that the ford would come under attack. He had sent Tirac upstream to protect against it, but Tirac was nowhere to be seen.

Had the enemy killed him? Captured him? Was he at this very moment stretched out over a fire screaming out his last breath? No, the man could not speak, the Vascanar had already taken his tongue. Had he sent him back for them to finish the job?

The tellis had been a mistake. Marisa had warned him. People became disconnected from the world when on the leaf; they forgot where they were, what they were doing, and stopped in the middle of an exposed ford to carry on a family argument.

But without it they would have moved slower, had to rest more often, and his small group of villagers would still be trapped on the other side of that ford trying to figure out a way to cross the river with the enemy already ahead of them — an enemy that loosed barbed arrows at women and children.

Erisyans loosing at civilians? That didn't seem credible. They might be sell-bows, mercenaries, but they were professional soldiers. They didn't kill the weak; it went against their code of honour. And yet they took Vascanar gold... What was going on here?

He needed to know, if he was to save his people from the Vascanar fires. He couldn't lie here slumped against a half-rotted stump of a tree. His people suffered. The mother of the six-year-old girl, who had almost cost Horol his life, cradled the child to her breast and stroked her flaxen hair. Marisa hadn't even looked at the child. She had pushed Drustan ahead of her.

Would she really have left a child to die?

For him?

He closed his eyes, allowed the guilt of command to ebb from him. Do what was needed and worry about the rest as it came. That was his role, his burden. He opened his eyes and surveyed the scene with dispassionate commander's eyes.

Morac's wife Peg wept with her five children ranged around her. The oldest boy — Yarom, was it? — perhaps fourteen summers old, stared at Drustan. Drustan knew he had to get them moving again, but first he had to get back up on his hind legs.

Cullain crouched at the edge of the ford looking upstream, watching for the enemy, waiting for Tirac. The strange mist turned to rain, large droplets splashing into the river. It pattered on the track around Drustan and he lifted his head to feel it fall upon his face. Something had stepped in to save them. One of the gods? But which one? And why?

Drustan shivered.

Marisa dealt with Efan's shoulder wound. Garet constructed a stretcher for the unconscious Horol. Rosana stitched up the wounds in Horol's chest.

Eleven men left fit and able. Nobody to carry a stretcher. Drustan looked around the wretched group. Men with weapons in their hands, bodies taut, shocked at the sudden attack. They were twitchy, refusing to sit, stalking about the track, ready to kill. The women gathered the children to them, held them tight, comforted them as tears streamed down their faces. The children hugged the women back, but some looked around, wide-eyed. The fear didn't really touch them, but they knew that the adults were scared and that was enough to set off wails of distress.

The women hugged them tighter. The men's hands curled into helpless fists. Most of the bedding and food had been lost in that mad rush across the ford.

Drustan looked across at Horol. He would need a stretcher. The women could carry it. Drustan's jaw tightened; they would not carry him. He would walk. No more lying on his back, distanced from what was going on around him. That had gone on long enough.

He pushed back against the tree and straightened his body. The pain from his side tore at him, but he ignored it.

No more the invalid.

No more men dead because they treated him like an invalid.

No more stupid mistakes.

He closed his eyes against the pain and pushed his body the last few inches upright.

A hand closed on his arm. 'I brought you this.' Yarom held out a Vascanar spear. 'My father gave it to me. He said I should use it to defend my mother if he died.'

Drustan looked at the boy, drew in his breath. 'I'm named Drustan desainCoid.'

Yarom was startled; he'd never been asked for his name like a man before. He straightened, and said, 'I ... I ... I'm named Yarom Moracson of Trant.'

'Good man.' Drustan took the spear. 'Then this is just a loan, Yarom. Find me a better crutch and I'll return it to you.'

'Will you teach me how to use it?'

'I can hardly walk.'

'You're Drustan the Bright Blade. I'd learn from you. It were my brother Ceren you saved out there.' Yarom jerked his head at the ford.

Drustan remembered the young boy he had slapped across the face, the boy screaming for his father as his father was washed away with arrows in his chest.

'I'll teach you when I'm able,' Drustan promised. 'Find me a crutch, Yarom.'

'Yes, my captain.' The boy disappeared into the woods.

Had it come to this? A beardless boy now a soldier in Drustan's company. He limped across to where Cullain crouched in the cover of a bush and, breathing out heavily against the pain, squatted beside his armsmaster.

'How's the leg?' Drustan asked.

'It'll heal. The enemy ain't moving up. Something happened. Some sort of attack.'

'Karisae?' Drustan asked.

'Maybe.' Cullain shrugged. 'Didn't sound like a battle. Sounded more like a fight. No orders, just screams. That mist.' He wiped rain from his face. 'That were a strange thing. Came from nowhere and now it's turned to rain.' Cullain touched his lips and heart. 'Thank you, whichever god you were.'

Drustan repeated the gesture and said, 'The tellis may have been a mistake.'

'The tellis got us here.'

'Two men died.'

'They should've worn their armour.' Cullain gestured at Horol. 'He did. We'd be on the wrong side of this ford without the tellis.'

'Do you think she cares?' Drustan nodded to Morac's wife Peg.

'She should,' Cullain said. 'I wouldn't have thought of the tellis. I would've simply left the slow to die.'

'Me included?'

'I'd have carried you until my legs were wore to stumps.' Cullain spat out some green sludge. 'Damn tellis. Makes me talk like a baker's wife.' He pulled Drustan around to stare into his eyes. 'You're captain here. You made a decision. It created other problems. That's the way with decisions. That's why I prefer to just kill the enemy. Much simpler.'

Drustan nodded. He still had Cullain's confidence, which was all he needed to know. 'Erisyans don't miss targets at only a hundred paces.'

'I know.' Cullain scanned the forest. 'And Erisyan bows will punch an arrow straight through leather armour, through the body and out the other side at that range. Even broadheads. And why were they using hunting arrows?'

'The women and children were unarmoured.'

'A war arrow will kill an armoured child as easy as a broadhead. Something else is going on here. That mist came down, but they were missing afore that. Maybe the gods are finally taking an interest in the fight.'

'A bit late.'

'Probably had to sober up.'

'Where's Tirac?' Drustan asked. 'He should've warned us.'

'I'll have his guts when he gets back,' Cullain said. 'Or I'll gut the man that killed him.'

A huge figure clad in the skin of a bear stalked to the edge of the upstream riverbank, raised a mighty iron-tipped club into the rain, and roared.

Cullain squinted. 'That looks like Berasin. A hero come to save us.' He grunted. 'About bloody time someone did.'

'Berasin?' Drustan said. 'Here? Why? He's an Anthanic hero. Why would he help us? The gods abandoned us at the ridge. They sent no aid as half our army died. Why would they send an Anthanic hero to save us now?'

'Older than the Anthanic.' Cullain rolled his massive shoulders. 'The threads thicken, Dru. Who knows the ways of the gods? Or of heroes, but that explains the screams. They say he has the strength of twenty men, the speed of a cat, and skin that no arrow can pierce.' The figure stalked back into the trees and out of sight. 'I'd love a chance at wiping that smile from his face.'

'How do you know that he smiles?'

'I would.'

'We can't wait for Tirac,' Drustan said.

'He'll catch up if'n he can.'

'Aye.' Drustan started to limp away.

'You need that wound fixed, Drustan. You need to be able to fight, or at least run. We were lucky not to lose you.' Cullain looked at where Marisa packed away her medical supplies. 'She stayed with you.'

'I know.'

'She always were an idiot when it came to you.'

****

Torquesten did not stint in his fury when he arrived at the bridge and found Arnik, the man he had made general, still unable to force a crossing. He expected the House taken and everything prepared for his arrival. Instead, he found only the corpses of men and horses floating in the flooded meadows. The casualties were expected, but the House still stood untouched beyond the bridge.

Arnik crouched before him, head bowed. Torquesten scratched one of his demonhounds behind the ear. The rain dripped through the trees above them.

'I'm sorry, Tukalac,' Arnik said. 'The rain—'

Torquesten pointed at him. 'Food.'

The demonhounds leapt forward.

Torquesten turned to another soldier even as Arnik's screams bubbled downward into silence. 'Take me this House.'

'Me, Tukalac?' the man asked.

Torquesten slapped the hound nearest to him across the rump. 'Food.' As the man died, Torquesten pointed at another soldier. 'Take me this House.'

'At once, Tukalac.'

Torquesten glared at Gorak. 'Why have your archers failed to kill this rabble of defenders?'

'The enemy is well-prepared. They knew we were coming,' Gorak said. 'Arnik should've brought infantry along. I've sent men upriver to flank down through that bog and men downriver to cross over and flank up through the woodland.'

'You refused to attack the House directly?'

'We're skirmishers, not heavy infantry. You need men with tower shields to tortoise up that road. We're mercenaries. We came here to fight, not die stupidly.' Gorak jerked his chin at the pinkish waters flooding the meadow.

Torquesten smiled. 'Maybe I should name you food, too.'

'As you wish.' Gorak seemed too eager, sweating with fear despite the rain, but ready to die.

'No, that would break the agreement. Release your tribesmen from fulfilling their oath.'

'There'll be no-one left to hold us to the oath if you keep using up men like this,' Gorak sneered.

'Careful who you taunt, Erisyan,' Torquesten said, but the archer was right. The Vascanar had landed with twelve thousand men, two thousand of them heavy cavalry. Plus the two thousand Erisyan archers. More than two thousand men had died at the battle of the Ridge and over five hundred since. They were only ten miles inland from the battle that should have ended all resistance.

There was time. The Augarin wheel had not prophesied the rise of Illath for over a month — after this night — but still, Torquesten knew he would have to do something about his dwindling forces.

He smiled at Gorak.

CHAPTER 35

M arisa shook her head. 'Impossible.'

'Heal me enough so that I can walk, Marisa,' Drustan said. 'We can't spare the men to carry me. Four women will have to carry Horol's stretcher as it is.'

'The women can carry you too, then,' Marisa said. 'There are enough of us.' Her hair stuck to the back of her neck. She was drenched to the skin, dirty, muddy, she had fought the walking dead, dragged this man across a ford with arrows falling all around her, and now he wanted her to raise a beacon to guide the enemy to them.

Drustan checked that no one was close by. 'I'm captain here, Marisa. I cannot lie on my back while women carry me through the rain.'

'Pride,' she sneered. Such heart-rending pride he had. Always and forever his damnable pride. He had walked ... no, *run* ... he had run away from her because of his pride. He could have taken her with him, they could have... She stopped, closed her eyes for a moment, breathed in, opened her eyes again. The tellis still jagged, tearing her emotions apart.

'Not pride, Marisa, authority,' Drustan said. 'Men died because I couldn't judge their fitness for the fight.' He looked away from her, out over the ford. 'Because I couldn't judge their level of exhaustion. Because I wasn't able to fight alongside them. Because they took off their damn armour to carry me.' His voice hissed its anger into the naked air. 'Heal me enough so I can walk. That's all I ask.'

'Ask? I thought you only gave orders, milord captain.' Marisa knew she was being petty, but he had not even mentioned the role the tellis-leaf played in the debacle of the ford.

The drug stilled buzzed through her system, opening her heart. Every grain of dirt on her skin itched, every runnel of water that dribbled from her soaking hair writhed down under her sopping dress, and, gods help her, she wanted more. She wanted to leave this place behind, to move through it as a butterfly moves through the air, buoyed up on the tellis and immune to all the pain around her.

Drustan said, 'I don't give you orders, milady.'

'You ordered me to give tellis to children.'

'That was a military decision. My decision, my responsibility. No guilt attaches to you. You need to heal me so I can walk.' Remorse carved lines into his face.

She would not have left with him. She would not have left her father heartbroken and alone. She would not have become the camp follower of a sell-sword. She had stood still as he had left, but she had forsaken him as surely as he had abandoned her. She could not refuse him this now, no matter what the cost.

'It will stand as a beacon to the enemy,' she warned.

'One thing at a time, milady. One thing at a time.'

'Take off your shirt.'

With a grunt of pain, Drustan tugged the sopping wet shirt over his head. He sucked air through his teeth, and breathed a sigh of relief as the wet cloth finally cleared his head.

Marisa did not lift a hand to help him. She reached up to uncover her haraf stone.

'One moment,' he said and called, 'Cullain, get them ready to march.'

Cullain and Rosana started sorting out the villagers.

Drustan smiled at Marisa. 'If we are to raise a beacon to the enemy, then it would be best if we are gone when they come to investigate.'

'That would be wise,' Marisa agreed. 'Lie on your uninjured side. This will hurt, but the pain will fade and you will have much freer movement afterwards. But you will not be able to wield a sword, Drustan desainCoid. Remember that.'

'I'm in your hands.'

****

The surge of healing magic smashed against Torquesten's soul. Someone of power had escaped beyond the walls of this House. A healer still free, and of such power that she cast ice into the fire of his blood.

All must die here. No healer would survive this attack on the House.

Oh, some would run, but his cavalry would track them down and slaughter them.

But out there somewhere, a woman — he could taste her scent in her magic — a healer linked to this House, but not of *this* House. She was of the House of Redain! A healer from the other end of the Shrine Road who had wrought her magic here, who had healed many within the walls of the shrine and drunk of the waters of the spring. Out there, somewhere, a healer still lived. A healer of Redain.

She needed to die, or the power of the Shrine Road would still exist within her.

Beyond the House lay mile after mile of open pasture; a good hunting ground for cavalry. But she would not be on that waterlogged grassland pounded by the tears of this land. She would be hidden in the deep forest.

She needed to be found.

Torquesten sniffed the air, lifted his head, opened his nostrils, drew in the scent of the healer. Something else tainted her fragrance…

The Xarnac! Its power had touched her. She knew its location.

What to do?

First, find her. Torquesten focused his soul on the task and left the mortal world behind. Unfettered by his control, the demonhounds lunged into a feeding frenzy. Men scattered into the trees to escape those terrible jaws.

Torquesten did not notice. Deeper into his soul he travelled, until he passed through his mortality and burst forth into the spirit world. He drifted towards the ache of the Xarnac. There! He had her. He could see her, protected by a handful of men wounded and bludgeoned with fear.

Nothing to worry about there.

The Erisyan skirmishers, some would be converted, he could use them. Oh, how her magic froze his very soul. A torn edge of healing energy where all should be dark and polluted. He sent out his corruption to touch the hearts of his new followers amongst the Erisyans.

What's this? Dead? But how?

He quested amongst their trapped spirits. Flickers of memory fading fast; too fast — they would not reanimate. They were killed by a hero out of myth and were lost to the dark lords now.

Send the demonhounds? Let them hunt her down? Yes. They would find her for him. Were they not hounds?

Torquesten returned to his body, opened his eyes, and blinked in puzzlement. He stood alone on the road, his men scattered into the trees, the Erisyans in the branches, bows drawn back. On the road, the demonhounds fought and squabbled over choice pieces of flesh. Torquesten clenched his fists, his jaw, his shoulders. 'Heel!'

The demonhounds' ears pricked up at the sound of his multitudinous voice.

'Heel!'

The demonhounds turned towards him, gobbets of flesh dripping from their mouths.

'Heel!'

Whining, the demonhounds scuttled to his side.

No, he could not send the demonhounds. They were now powers in their own right and he had to maintain his control over them. They would rend their prey, tear her to pieces. He needed her alive to find the Xarnac. Then she would die to free the Shrine Road of her stink.

Torquesten gathered the scent of the healer into his mind, held it there, ready for the hunt. He would deal with this House and then he would deal with her. Once the House was sanctified, he would have all the power he needed to find her again.

Something interfered, a cold anger cutting across his senses. The healer's magic died down to nothingness. Her scent dispersed on the rising wind and he could not find her.

'Who dares to challenge me?' he cried into the spirit realm.

'One of this land, demon-spawn,' came the answer.

He lashed out but the other had already withdrawn.

A wind gusted along the river. The rain poured down, a deluge from clouds stirring into darkness above his head. The hounds howled. He had not asked for this weather, this was not his doing, but he had tasted the woman's magic and he would recognise it again and the Xarnac would return to him.

CHAPTER 36

'*Wake up, cousin!*' Sekem's spectral voice shouted.

Jarl lifted his head. That hurt. His neck tight around a bruised throat. He touched the side of his face and his fingers came away bloody from a deep gash above the temple. Groaning, he rolled over and staggered to his feet.

He slurred out the words, 'Wha… What happened, cousin?'

'*Any nausea?*' Sekem asked.

'No.'

'*You'll probably remember then. You took a bit of a knock to the head. Maybe you should sit down. Before you fall down.*'

Jarl slumped to the ground and leaned back against the tree. Some sort of battle? A fight? He worked his jaw. Something had happened here.

'The forest.' His speech seemed to be improving. 'The river. We were … were … heading up towards a crossing point.'

'*You're doing well,*' Sekem said. '*For a man thrown onto his head.*'

'Thank you, cousin.' Jarl spotted the bodies lying across the river bank. He stared at them, trying to remember what happened. Somebody tried to kill him? Uras? No, he'd died because he stood with Jarl. Then…?

Erisyans, corrupted by the Vascanar elixir, turning on their own people, loosing at women, at children, at him! Uras dying with an arrow through his throat, '*Stop them. Warn Gorak.*' Uras's last words, spoken spirit-wise.

Jarl remembered.

He had to get back to Gorak and tell him, warn him: some of the caedi couldn't be trusted.

Jarl's head throbbed. Perhaps he should sleep, close his eyes—

'*No time for that, cousin.*'

'No.' Jarl blinked his eyes open. 'But I must do one thing before I leave this place.' He crawled across the sodden ground. It was raining.

Not too hard, not enough to force archers to pack away their bows and arrows... When did it start raining? A mist, something roaring out of the mist. He slithered through the mud to where Uras's body lay crumpled.

Where was Uras's bow?

There.

Jarl panted, regained his strength, dragged himself through the muck to Uras's bow. With great difficulty, he unstrung it, pausing twice to alter his grip, placing the shaft between his legs, bending the bow to unhook the string. The limb of the bow snapped back when he released it, but he'd already moved his face out of the way.

He rested, his eyes closed.

'Don't pass out!'

Jarl jerked awake, clambered to his feet, swayed, shook his head — which was a mistake. He waited for the sharp pain to fade and dragged Uras's body into the correct posture, wrapping the bowstring around the awchti's hands, carrying out the rites.

Then he went in search of his own bow, able to stand now, to walk, but still unsteady on his feet. He had no intention of giving the corrupted Erisyans the rites; they could wander for all eternity for all he cared. But he noted the way their bodies, their skulls, their chests were staved in, and remembered the bear eyes staring into his own.

Berasin, a hero out of legend, out of myth, here at this place. No, not Berasin; *Beran* to the Erisyans. Beran the God-Killer. Beran of the iron-headed club. The hero who... Tirac... Gods be, he was Tirac, the man staked out by the fire who'd lost his tongue, the man who'd helped Jarl bandage up Drustan. Tirac was Beran, no, *Berasin*, he called himself Berasin; Berasin the God-Eater, not God-Killer. Was it the same hero? The same man? The same... His club of iron, the bear's-head helm, the... The Erisyans and the people of these islands shared a hero. How?

The boy Agus, named for the Erisyan god Argus. A god the Erisyans cast away with the help of Beran and the other heroes. How was that possible?

The Erisyans shared a hero, shared the name of a god, the boy... Did the boy even know he was named for a god? Did he realise? He hadn't argued the point. Names, heroes, gods ... the same?

And he'd met a hero out of myth and seen that same hero disguised as a man, and—

Why had Berasin not killed him?

Tormented eyes staring into Jarl's: *I remember, I will not forget what you have done here, archer. I owe you a debt, and I will repay it when I can.*

Another debt repaid, but that didn't make the hero out of myth a friend. Had he forsaken the Erisyans now? No. He had let the others go, had only killed the corrupted, had fought against the Vascanar.

Good. The Islands of Symcani would need all the help they could get.

Why had Berasin let the Vascanar cut out his tongue? Why had he allowed that indignity? Was he in hiding? Why had he revealed himself here?

It didn't make any sense.

'You're not thinking clearly,' Sekem said. *'And your bow is over there.'*

Jarl picked up his bow and checked the rest of his equipment. His sword! Berasin's mighty club sweeping down, smashing Jarl's blade to shards. The hero's hand wrapped around Jarl's throat. Berasin's speech. Jarl had always assumed the way heroes spoke was an affectation of the poets.

Obviously not.

What was he going to do about a sword?

'You can have mine,' Sekem said. *'I don't need it anymore.'*

****

The rain lashed at Torquesten, the wind blew the dark cloak away from his shoulders. He watched his new general's tactics with interest.

The man, chosen at the point of a sword, choosing to take command of the army rather than become food for the demonhounds, sent forth his troops.

Torquesten frowned. He needed all to die in that House, none should escape, and this 'general' chose to send infantry instead of horsemen. The infantry moved forward, clearing away the last of the defenders. A withering arrow storm from the Erisyans defended their flanks.

'The House must be surrounded,' Torquesten said. 'None must escape.'

'I know, Tukalac,' the general replied. 'I understand the need. But I cannot send horse across the slippery stone of the bridge, not at the gallop. The infantry shall clear the way and—'

Torquesten frowned. This man chose to lecture him. The demonhounds growled.

The man licked his lips. 'I do this for the glory of our lords, for you, Tukalac. I do this for you.'

'Continue, let us see what it is you do for me … and my brethren.'

The infantry, nearly five thousand men in all, split into two groups after crossing the bridge, sweeping out and around the House of Healing, encircling it.

'None shall escape now, Tukalac.' The man sounded smug, self-satisfied. The demonhounds whined. The man, his voice hesitant, said, 'I shall send out the cavalry to hunt down any that flee, Tukalac.'

Torquesten did not answer. A demonhound surged to its feet, growled at the man, padded towards him, stalked about him, sniffed the air loudly. Torquesten smiled. 'Continue.' He called back the demonhound with a mental command. Interesting; this demonhound had once been the Uka named Pyran. It would be humorous if… No. This new general had done his duty. He had taken the House of Healing.

But he should really learn to guard his tongue.

'What is your name?' Torquesten asked.

'Bradic, Tukalac.'

'I name you Uka, Bradic. Take up the standard, choose your bodyguard, watch your tongue or I shall take it from your mouth and name you food.'

'Yes, Tukalac. Thank you, Tukalac.' Bradic abased himself in the mud of the road.

'Get up, fool, and send out the horsemen.'

This land would fall and the gates would open. Torquesten laughed and his demonhounds howled.

****

Eirane found Wendin above the House of Falas. Vascanar infantry swarmed around the building.

'I could not stop them,' Wendin said, her form tattered, her voice soft upon the wind. 'That creature of demons is too powerful here, too solid, too real; no place for me to strike.'

'I know, sister,' Eirane said.

'The battle is lost here.' Wendin's voice strengthened. 'But the war will continue.'

'At least they fear our forests now.'

'As they should.'

Vascanar cavalry galloped across the open fields beyond the House. Eirane realised that they hunted those that had fled. 'Can you not make the rain fall harder, sister? Raise up a wind? I will aid you. We must turn the ground to slurry beneath the hooves of those demonic horses.'

'Hard rain here will cause drought elsewhere,' Wendin said.

'Drought can be a weapon, too.'

Wendin considered Eirane's words. 'You are harsh, sister.'

'This is war and we are late to join.'

'You speak as the mother of a soldier.' Wendin smiled. 'Which is not such a bad thing to be on this day.'

CHAPTER 37

Drustan pulled the hood of his cloak up against the rain falling through the trees. His side ached from Marisa's healing. He could walk, but he still needed the spear as a walking staff to help him in the mud.

Cullain strode back from the head of the line, his cloak behind his shoulders to leave his weapons within easy reach. The boy Yarom walked beside him with a stave of wood in his hands.

'How goes it?' Drustan asked.

'Boy 'ere has sommat for you,' Cullain said.

'Here, my captain.' Yarom held out a staff of good ash, taller than Drustan, fresh cut, unseasoned, but a good walking staff.

'Thank you, Yarom.' Drustan handed back the spear.

'My first lesson?'

'Hold the spear, there and there,' Drustan said.

'Then what?'

'Just learn to hold it first, then we will see about your stance, your movement, your balance and your gaze.'

'But I want to learn how to fight.'

'I'm not in the habit of breaking my promises, boy,' Drustan snapped. 'Go back to your mother. She has need of you.'

Yarom walked away with the spear held diagonally across his chest.

'The first position,' Cullain said. 'And the first lesson in doing what he's told.'

'He's young.'

'You were younger.'

'My lineage is different.'

'He's good shoulders. He'll do fine.' Cullain studied Drustan's twisted posture with a critical eye. 'But you're bent over like a crone. Stand up straight.'

Dustan straightened his body with a grunt of pain. 'I do when I think about it.'

'Then keep thinking about it.'

'Thanks.' Drustan grinned. 'What's ahead?'

'The forest thins to the west, but we're heading north. May want to bear east for a while.'

'Aye, but that'll place us too far east when we hit the highlands. We need to use the cattle road if we can.'

'We can dogleg.'

'Cost us time. No, we follow the contours. Just be alert where the trees thin down by the Ramagon estates. The Earl was always too fond of the axe and cleared more forest than needed for his farms.'

'For his hall.'

'Much use that'll do him now. Carry on, Cullain.'

'My captain.' Cullain saluted and moved up the line to talk to the scouts.

Drustan held his body vertical despite the discomfort, and waited for Horol's stretcher to catch up. Four women carried the stretcher. They slipped and skidded in the mud, but they didn't drop it.

'How goes it?' Drustan asked.

'He's no babe in arms,' one of the women said.

'He's lovely.' A younger woman smiled down at their burden, her eyes a touch misty.

'And unmarried,' Drustan said with a straight face.

'Is he? I didn't know,' the girl said. She had arrived out of the forest with Garet, one of the many strays he'd picked up on his scouting missions. So many new mouths to feed, bodies to protect, and no increase in the number of warriors.

Horol had a panicked look in his eye. 'You're done, boy,' the older woman said. 'Get used to it. He's a woodsmith they say.'

'A craftsman.' The girl laughed.

'Always be a need for craftsmen.' Drustan grinned at Horol's hurt look at the betrayal. 'Your children won't go hungry.'

The girl blushed, the woman laughed, and Horol said, 'I'm fine. I can walk, my captain. I can take up my duties again.'

'No, Horol, Lady Marisa says you must rest at least a day. You lost a lot of blood.'

'Honest, my captain, I can walk.' Horol sat up on the stretcher, but had to lie back down as his face paled. 'Damn.'

'I need you rested, Horol. Fit and strong, you're one of my best men.' Drustan flicked a look at the pretty girl.

'Do you have to?' Horol asked weakly.

'Of course I do. Carry on, ladies. We'll halt in a little while. He may need to be fed by hand.'

'Can I do that?' the pretty girl asked.

The three older women cackled at Horol's look of horror. Drustan could hear them laughing still as he limped down the line of villagers. Nearly a hundred civilians now. Too many. Garet needed to find some soldiers. The muddy ground left tracks as plain as daylight to any pursuer.

Drustan found Marisa crouched under a bush, dealing with Agus, who had cut his foot on a jagged bit of stone. Efan stood guard with a Karisae longbow in his hands.

'Garet find that?' Drustan asked.

'Aye, my captain. He found some dead archers about three mile back. Looked like they'd been wounded at the Ridge, but managed to get this far. Only three bows, plenty of arrows though.' Efan slapped the quiver at his waist.

'You can use it?'

'Aye, hunt for the pot most weeks.' Efan looked back down the path. 'We're leaving too much of a trail.'

'I know. This damn rain isn't helping.' Drustan looked at Agus. 'Will he need to be carried?'

'I can walk,' Agus said. 'Better'n you.'

'Then get up and walk.'

'I need to finish dressing it first,' Marisa pointed out. 'How is the side?'

'It'll do.' Drustan couldn't look her in the eye. The pain of the healing had blazed along his side, but underneath the pain… Love never leaves you; it just changes. 'Efan.'

'My captain?'

'Take one man back with you and check for followers. Don't engage the enemy, despite that shiny new bow.'

'I'll see it done, my captain.'

'And when you see Garet, tell him to report to me if he finds any more bows. I need to know how my men are armed.'

Efan hesitated. 'Should I keep an eye out for Tirac?'

'Aye, but don't go more'n a mile back. I don't want you heading all the way back to the ford. If he's alive, he'll follow — can't bloody miss us with all the tracks we're leaving.'

Efan nodded. 'I'll see it done.' He jogged away.

'We need to get out of this rain,' Marisa said. 'It'll be dark soon.' She hesitated. 'Illath will rise tonight.'

'Again.' Drustan said. 'Fickle bitch of a goddess.'

Marisa spat to clear the curse. Agus spat to clear the curse. They both looked at Drustan. He spat to clear the curse, made the sign of infinity, and said, 'May Illath's light shine bright upon the world.'

Agus grinned. 'Even the Bright Blade is scared of the gods. Owww.'

'Sorry,' Marisa said. 'Did that hurt? Maybe there is some dirt left in the wound. I should probably probe it again.'

'No,' Agus said. 'It's fine, really.'

Drustan grinned at Agus. 'At least we are not in a Calodrig. Cullain knows what to look for. We'll find a place to camp. No point pushing on tonight in this rain.'

'I know a place,' Agus said.

'What sort of place?' Marisa asked.

'Cave, over in the woods there.'

'How far?'

'Not far.'

'How do you know of this?'

'Raised round here, weren't I? Been my land since we crossed the river.'

CHAPTER 38

Torquesten stalked through the spiralling corridors of the House of Healing with his demonhounds prowling around him. Karisae soldiers threw themselves into a desperate defence against his advance, but his demonhounds killed them all. Bihkat and the priests followed, with sharp knives and buckets of leather to collect the blood.

The Karisae wounded, those too ill to be moved out into the garden for the sacrifices, were bled like animals. Vascanar soldiers held the wounded men upside down while a priest stabbed under the collar bone into the heart and collected the blood in a bucket.

Torquesten strode on. He ignored the Vascanar scurrying around him, carrying the filled buckets of blood out to the spring to await the rise of Illath, and bringing new buckets for the priests to fill.

A long corridor empty of wounded Karisae; four grim men in bloody armour stood with drawn swords before the door at its end.

'Who are you?' Torquesten inquired.

'We're Hundrin,' one of the men answered.

'No,' Torquesten said. 'You are food.'

The demonhounds bounded forward. Torquesten smiled at the warriors fighting with steel blades against things immune to steel. He remembered that dread battle under the falls. Such fear — until he drank the pure Ulac and began the uplift of his spirit.

'Tukalac.' A priest ran panting from a side corridor.

Torquesten turned away from the delightful sight of his demonhounds feeding. 'Yes?'

'We've found the healers, Tukalac. Their protectors vanquished. What should we do with them?'

'How many?'

'Twelve, Tukalac. Seven women and five men.'

'Give them to the troops, but be careful that they do not die. I need their blood tonight.'

'Yes, Tukalac.'

'Let the troops dice for their comforts.' Torquesten laughed. 'And make sure they pay them properly for their favours.'

'Your will be done, Tukalac.' The priest hastened away.

Torquesten snapped his fingers. The demonhounds did not look up from their feeding. 'Heel,' he commanded. They growled at him. He unleashed his power in a blaze of anger. The demonhounds yelped and slunk back to his side. Still he drove the pain of his displeasure into the beasts. They had to know his dominance, his authority. He had made them what they were and they would obey his every gesture.

Finally, he relented — when the demonhounds fawned around his feet.

'Open the door, Bihkat,' he said.

The high priest rushed forward, slipped on the blood, and fell.

'Open it now, priest,' Torquesten said. 'I wish to know what they guarded.'

Bihkat tried to stand, but his leg crumpled under him.

Torquesten waved one of his bodyguards forward. The man opened the door and staggered back with a spear through his chest. A flickering blur of motion from the darkness of the room; a dagger flew out of the dark.

Torquesten grabbed it out of the air by the blade and laughed until the pain burst through his lacerated palm — the piercing, freezing pain of cleansing silver.

'I am Vorduk.' An armoured warrior burst out the room, swinging a silver chain in one hand.

The demonhounds cringed back. The priests threw themselves upon the floor. A warrior moved to intercept Vorduk's charge and fell under the sword the warrior held in his other hand.

But the delay gave Torquesten time to recover, to drop the hated silver blade from his fume-wreathed hand, to move towards the charging Vorduk. He ducked the whirling chain, slapped aside the sword, and crushed Vorduk's skull with one smashing punch.

'Leave,' he commanded the demonhounds sniffing about the corpse.

'You did not earn this flesh.' He glared at Bihkat. 'See that the corpse is thrown into the latrines.'

'Yes, Tukalac,' Bihkat said.

'Your leg seems to have recovered, priest.'

'A cramp, Tukalac.'

'A cramp?' Torquesten grabbed Bihkat by the throat, lifted the scrawny priest clear of the floor. Bihkat's feet kicked fitfully. 'A cramp? Such a painful thing, a cramp. Would you not say so, priest?' Bihkat, his face turning blue, could not answer. 'Well since your "cramp" has passed' — Torquesten shook Bihkat like a terrier shaking a rat — 'let us see what lies behind that door.' He threw the priest into the darkened room.

And waited a moment.

'Well, priest?'

'Yo… you … you may enter, Tukalac,' Bihkat rasped through his damaged throat.

Torquesten strode into the room with the sulking demonhounds at his heels. 'What is this?' he demanded.

'It looks like their King, Tukalac,' Bihkat rasped.

'It was foreseen. My blood will open the door,' the man in the bed moaned. 'It was seen.'

'Your blood is no different to any other,' Torquesten said. 'Bleed him. Add his blood to the rest. We await the moons.'

****

The rain washed the sweat from Jarl's face. He staggered out of the forest chewing fever-bark for his concussion. Only a mild one, thank the gods; no nausea, no ringing in his ears.

A clean bandage covered the fox-leaf pulp slathered across the gash in his forehead and stopped the rain washing the stinging astringent into his eyes. Needs must, but chewing fox-leaf and then plastering the mash across the wound was the most basic of field medicine. Nice to know his taste-buds still worked though; he'd spat the bitter taste onto the ground, but still it lingered.

The silence at the bridge told him the battle was over. No cries and screams of the injured and dying. No clash of steel upon steel. No bellowed orders and yelled assents. No birds singing in the trees. The world held for a moment on the cusp of something new.

In terrified silence.

Rain beat down around him; he turned up the hood of his cloak against the wind.

As he staggered onto the bridge, he stumbled over the corpse of a dead Vascanar. Without thought, Jarl spat in the corpse's face and stumbled on. More corpses. The defenders had put up a good fight, but the power of the tower-shielded infantry had decided the day. Even Erisyan bows had trouble piercing the steel-skinned shields of Vascanar heavy infantry.

Close volleys were the thing. Wait until the enemy were so close you could hear their panting breath and then loose and loose and loose. Break up the formation before leaping in amongst it with whirling syrthaes and war hammers.

Only way for archers to stop a tortoise of heavy infantry. Wait for them to ready their javelins then loose and loose and loose.

Only way—

'Your mind wanders, cousin,' Sekem whispered. *'Best if you focus now.'*

Jarl jerked his gaze up from the rough stones beneath his feet. The Vascanar infantry surrounded the House of Healing, facing inwards, their shields a wall as impassable as any made of stone. No cavalry about; they were no doubt already pursuing any that fled the defeat. Open fields beyond, a long way to the edge of the forest out there, the forest around the House occupied by the Vascanar. Poor sods. Good sport for horsemen, chasing down people on foot. Still, the rain gave them a chance, turning the ground to slurry, allowing them to dodge as the horses stumbled and fell.

Where was the Erisyan camp? Their bows were useless in this deluge. They would've found a place away from the trees, a dip in the land, somewhere out of the rain.

Jarl blinked water out of his eyes and studied the landscape. There, that farm. The sheltered location was perfect for an Erisyan camp — barns, outbuildings, all with the same look about the roof. The Karisae had once been sea-raiders and built their roofs to look like upturned boats. Not a bad design if the rain fell like this all the time; it sluiced over the steep shingles, poured over the broad eaves, cascaded to the ground past windows that shone with lamplight.

There'd be food stored there, dry beds, warm fires, maybe even some wine, beer, or stronger drink. Yes, that's where Gorak would have set the camp.

Foot in front of slipping foot, Jarl staggered towards the farmstead.

****

Bihkat rubbed a healing salve into his bruised throat. The Tukalac went too far, throwing the Ukalac, the priest of priests, through the door like a common soldier — worse, like a slave. Bihkat should be the anointed, not that dog-bred Torquesten.

Hiding his treasonous thoughts behind the mantle of priesthood, lest the Tukalac sniff out the treachery, he directed his priests in the preparations for the ritual. The ritual which began the Path of Blood.

According to the sacred texts of the Vascanar, the Shrine Road must be defiled. Every shrine desecrated between this House of Falas and the House of Redain upon the shores of the sacred lake.

Then would the Shrine Road become the Path of Blood. Then would the gate to the Tangled Realms open and connect one place to another, allowing the lords of the Vascanar to pass from mist into reality.

The bleeding must begin here, on this night, with Illath high in the sky. But the Xarnac had not been recovered. It was out there somewhere, in the forests of this land, in the hands of a man who should have broken with fear but did not.

It had been hidden from them!

To open the gates without the Xarnac, the lodestone of the Way, would scatter the demons. So many gates, in so many places upon the surface of this world, all connected in a single network of shrines and temples and sites holy to many gods. How were the demons to find this single gate without the Xarnac to guide them?

Bihkat shivered in the unnatural rain. The Vascanar would pay for what they had wrought in the service of their demonic lords if those demonic lords did not become gods.

The search for the Xarnac would begin in earnest in the morning, when the pathway began to open at this first desecrated shrine. The lords would still be unable to incarnate in this world, unable to touch the ground of this realm, but dribbles of their powers would leak through the shattered shrine and aid the Vascanar in their search.

CHAPTER 39

Marisa walked alongside the stretcher and checked on Horol's progress. His blood was replenishing itself and his wounds healing. She added a touch of magic to the stitches to hurry that along.

'You are healing well,' she said.

'Will he be all right?' asked the pretty girl helping to carry the stretcher. Like all of them, her hair was bedraggled, her clothing muddy and tattered; but she had found time to wash her face.

'Yes,' Marisa said, wishing that they could find a way to dry out their clothes, but the rain came down, the enemy hunted them, and so they slogged on through the mud.

'Will he be strong?'

'Yes.' Exhaustion pulled at her, as cloying as the mud, and the exuberance of the tellis was a distant memory. How long since she had slept? Two days? No, three days … was it not? Three days since the King fell from his horse, two days since Cullain had come, and this day when she had found Drustan injured, and staggered on through the mud. She could not go on much further.

'How long before he's able to … um … do work?'

'What?' Marisa shook her head. 'Work?' What was the girl babbling about?

The older woman beside the girl snorted. 'Sara means beastly work.'

'Beastly?' Marisa asked.

'Aye, two backs, one rhythm, lots of sweat.'

'Pena!' Sara sounded outraged but there was a giggle in her voice.

'How soon can I walk?' Horol asked.

'What?' Marisa looked down at Horol.

'How long before I can walk?'

'A couple of days. Or perhaps tomorrow.'

'Tomorrow.' Horol nodded. 'Tomorrow is good.'

Marisa looked at him, looked at Sara, thought of a field of wildflowers long ago.

Sara said, 'The captain says Horol is one of his best men.'

Marisa smiled. 'Oh, he is.'

Horol sighed. 'Did you have to?'

Marisa leaned in until her mouth almost brushed Horol's ear. 'Take what you can from this world, Horol,' she whispered. 'Death is stalking us.' She stood up and noted the jealousy in Sara's gaze.

'She's wife to the captain.' Pena shook her head at Marisa. 'Girls don't change.'

Marisa hid the heartache at the casual way Pena referred to her lost love. 'No,' she said, 'they do not.'

She didn't hide her pain well enough; Pena's eyes moistened: 'The man's a fool.'

'They all are,' said a woman at the other end of the stretcher.

'I'm lying right here, you know?' Horol said.

Marisa moved up the line, checking on the villagers. No more tellis-mania to deal with, but some did ask for more leaves. Minor injuries, scrapes and sprains, to be cleaned or bandaged as needed.

This could not go on.

Women carried the younger children on their hips, but the older ones had to walk, stumbling along, querulous, nagging, the women snapping at their questions, at their moaning.

Tilly and Yarom and some other teenagers carried what remained of the villagers' goods — so much lost to the ford. They did not allow their mothers and aunties to bear the loads, but their heads drooped and their hair was flattened to their scalps by sweat as well as rain.

This could not go on.

This frantic pace through such difficult terrain. Nearly fifteen miles since the dawn, including the crossing of the ford. They had to stop soon, to rest, eat, dry their clothes, regroup.

This could not go on.

****

Bihkat wiped the last of the salve upon the hem of his robes and studied the preparations for the ritual.

Slaves carried buckets of blood across the denuded ground, the gardens at the centre of the shrine-spirals cleared of rose bushes and other shrubs to make space for the heat stones. Pits dug into the soft loam would focus the heat of those wondrous artefacts upwards and help slaves to collect the dripping secretions of the lords. Soldiers sweated in the rain, setting up the frames where sacrifices would broil above the blistering heat of the stones.

The heat-stones had been discovered in the kitchens of the land of Xantia far to the east. They had used them to cook their food, a little daub of animal blood all that was needed to awaken the magic. The Vascanar had torn the land of Xantia apart, left it stripped of people, a wasteland, and moved on — as they always did — but every Vascanar regiment carried some of the heat-stones with them. A little daub of human blood all that was needed to awaken the magic. So much more efficient than fires, which this rain would have extinguished anyway.

This rain, this unnatural rain. Bihkat shivered again.

The Vascanar never stayed, it was not their purpose. Empire-building had no meaning for them. They were the Soldiers of the Gate. They only wished to bring their demonic overlords physically present into the world, to make them gods in truth as well as name.

On that glorious day, all the gates would open and the Xarnac would draw the demons to the single gate at the sacred lake in the centre of this island. A gate strong enough and big enough to allow the entire host through in a single day, when Illath and Morgeth shared the sky with the Sun and magic joined with the soul of the world in a blaze of light. Such power would flow then!

There were many gates and they were always protected, but the one here upon this island had lost much of its protection when the Karisae took this land and the Karisae gods drove out the Anthanic gods, who in their turn had driven out the more ancient gods, who in their turn had driven out still more ancient gods, in a line of invasions running back through the millennia to when humans first appeared in the world.

But this invasion would be the last.

Or so Bihkat had believed. This unnatural rain. His soul trembled at the touch of it. There were other stones in this land; he stood amongst spirals of them here in the centre of the shrine. Old, old stones, torn from the earth and set to limit the power of usurper gods. Ancient stones for ancient gods; he could feel it in the tremble of his soul.

The Karisae gods had sought dominion over this place because of the power channelled through these stones, but they were weak here. Spread too thin, on both sides of the Salt, which limited their power. They should have done what other invading gods had done in the past. They should have taken these islands and given up any power they had beyond them. Their greed and stupidity had given the Vascanar their chance at glory.

Yet somehow this land still held so much power. Bihkat glared at the shrine stones, the curving walls of monoliths that shortened in steps across the garden until they disappeared under the arc of the sacred spring.

So much power still here. Attached to humans and nature, bound by laws and customs, that power might be weak compared to Bihkat's mighty lords of flame and blood, but these islands, these stones, had existed for eons and who knew what that power would do if roused?

And this would rouse it. Oh yes, this ritual would rouse it.

Bihkat knew the ways of gods were not the ways of men. Gods would look upon death and destruction with little more than a slight distaste for the smell. Some gods even fed, as his lords did, on anger and despair. But this ritual, this entirely necessary sacrilege would rouse the power that lay dormant in this land. How could it not? That was its purpose.

That power must be roused and channelled along the line of the Path of Blood through the desecrated shrines until it touched the sacred lake. Otherwise the gates would not open and the demonic overlords of the Vascanar would not find their way from the Tangled Realms into this one. That power would be severed from the land in a final flame, a final cut, granting *his* lords their new dominion.

That trail began here, in the ritual of blood beneath the light of Illath, mistress of magic.

But what would be unleashed in response?

****

Agus led them away from the path into the deeper forest beyond, along narrow tracks made by animal rather than human feet. The stretcher-bearers struggled through the trees; at times Drustan had to allow men to take up Horol's weight because the women simply could not make any headway.

'Where's this brat taking us?' Cullain growled.

'He says he knows of a cave. A good campsite, he says.' Drustan wiped the rain from his forehead. Garet paralleled their course, searching for anything that might be of use. Efan and two men hung back, guarding against pursuit, and destroying what sign they could of the villagers' footsteps. Cullain and Drustan followed the scampering Agus at the front of the line.

Men began to stumble in the gloom.

'Pull the men in?' Cullain asked.

'No, leave them out there for a while,' Drustan said. 'I don't like this place. Too closed-in, too tight.'

'Not far now!' Agus shouted.

'Do you wish to wake the dead, boy?' Cullain asked.

'Don't need to.' Agus grinned back at him. 'Illath does that.'

'Drustan should have gutted you back at the ridge.'

'He keeps saying that, too.' Agus stopped in the middle of the trail, looked back, and tilted his head to one side. 'I'm glad he didn't.'

'Just get us to this campsite, Agus,' Drustan said. 'It's getting dark.'

'Not far,' Agus repeated. 'Just over the brow of this hill.' He dashed on ahead.

'Efan didn't know of this place,' Cullain said.

'No, his people rarely crossed the river. The Earl called them poachers and had all sorts of lovely ways to dissuade them from hunting in his forest.'

'*His* forest?' Cullain snorted at the idea that anybody could claim ownership of the forests.

'The Earl was raised across the Salt.'

'Should've left the old whoreson there.'

'Morac and Alun—'

'Were fools who took off their armour for comfort's sake.' Cullain cut across his words.

'I know, but they … they implied … the common folk…'

'Spit it out, Dru.'

'Do the common folk interbreed with the Anthanic?'

Cullain chewed his beard and walked on. 'The tellis made their tongues loose, then. Aye. I've Anthanic blood on both sides.'

'But…' Drustan stopped in the middle of the track and looked back. Plenty of time before the rest of the group caught up. 'You let me call myself half-breed and allow them to break my sword.'

'Nobles are different.' Cullain shrugged. 'Half-breed or peasant, what's the greater insult?'

'You said nothing. Five years across the Salt fighting as a sell-sword and you said nothing.'

'What would you've done?' Cullain asked. 'Come back and faced down that old fool of a King? Demanded your title back?' He shook his shaggy head, and a fine spray of water spattered across Drustan's face. 'Noble houses hide the Anthanic blood in their lineage. We've been in this land for two and half centuries, Dru. Do you think that anybody really knows what blood belongs to 'em anymore? It's not like the Anthanic look any different from us. 'Cepting them tattoos, of course.'

'Don't stop there.'

'I've said enough.'

'The Karisae across the Salt, do they know this?'

'They're no better at keeping their bloodlines pure.'

'Why didn't you tell me?'

Cullain sighed and glanced back down the line to check that nobody could overhear. 'Because you're Drustan the Bright Blade. You use honour as a rod 'gainst your own survival. You'd have come back 'ere and challenged the King's bloodline. They'd have burned you for that.'

'So we're all half-breeds?'

'People love who they love; no bloody law'll stop that.'

'Come on,' Agus called. 'I've found it.'

****

Marisa left the villagers behind and walked to the brow of the hill in search of Drustan. A small valley lay beyond the rise, the trees so high they dwarfed younger trees on the edges of the glade. This ancient place set her haraf stone pulsing. Exhaustion lifted like a veil.

Drustan stood at the edge of the bluff, the furrows of his brow smoothed out with joy. Cullain grinned like a child, not a usual look for his battered features. Only the boy Agus seemed unaffected by the calm emanating from this place. He looked … sad.

'Not far now,' he said.

Marisa heard the mournful quality to his voice and wondered at it.

The boy led the way down into the valley between the massive tree trunks whose roots buttressed out of the earth. The fresh smell of loam dampened by the rain rose into the air. The birds sang a joyful chorus to the villagers walking beneath the mighty branches.

The rain stopped.

There were gaps between the trees where the sky shone golden-red in the sunset, and high crags around the edge of the valley. A river flowed somewhere, potent with soft music.

Marisa stopped for a moment, filled with awe. What was this place?

A stag, with antlers racked above his head, turned to look at them and then bounded away into the gloom. Boars snuffled across their path, the touchy beasts paying no attention to the ragged human band walking through their territory. A wolf stood alone on a crag, staring down upon them before padding off to rejoin his pack, which yelped welcome and then jogged away into the trees. An eagle keened above them, wheeling in the fading light. Sunlight illuminated their steps with shafts of brilliant gold.

'This way,' said Agus.

Marisa laughed as she stepped into the golden light of the sun. Low now, almost at the horizon but, oh, the warmth of that sun upon her chilled blood, lifting her spirits into a calm delight in the fading day!

She stood on a slope, looking out across a valley. On the opposite side of the valley a cave loomed in the hillside. No trees reared into the air around the mouth of that cave; a cleared space lay in front of it, a clearing where a village could stand … no, where a town … where one of the fabled cities from beyond the Salt could stand. A million people could live and love here in this clearing within the trees. But how? When she first looked down upon the valley of the cave it had not seemed so large, barely broad enough to contain the merest fraction of a single farm.

What *was* this place?

People laughed, and danced in the golden light, a procession of delight walking down the slope towards the cave. The clearing shrank once more before the people crossing it, becoming a tiny fragment of the expanse Marisa had just glimpsed.

This was deep magic; magic of the gods and the land. She stopped upon the slope as the people danced forward. Huge jagged rocks, untouched by wind or rain, surrounded the cave entrance, carved with images as fresh as the day the sculptor sat back, his work complete. The bold pictures told of battles, wars, love affairs amongst humans, spirits and gods; of compacts made and kept within this land, this place, this world within the world.

The immense power here set Marisa's haraf stone flickering, its heat burning through the silk, through the cloth of her bodice, into her heart.

'Come along,' said Agus.

And nobody even thought to question him, to wonder why they followed him, or to wonder why they did not wonder.

The boy led them through the rope-carved arch of stone and into the darkness beyond. The cave led down, deep into the earth. No one was afraid.

Inside the cave, Cullain found a torch and lit it with flint and steel. Drustan found another and lit his from Cullain's. There were more torches in brackets upon the walls, which they lit, flame to flame until the whole cave glimmered with light, a shifting, living, yellow-gold light of torches that burned without smoke.

Upon the walls of the cave were painted scenes that came alive in this light. The flanks of beasts no longer seen in this land flexed and bounded forward. Hunters with spears upraised hurtled after them in an unceasing flow of motion.

Marisa touched one of the rocks, one of the paintings, and a shock thrilled through her. These paintings were old, ancient, from the times before, when humanity stood on the cusp of an age of terror.

'*This is my world.*' The voice echoed for a moment in the dark and then faded away. Had she really heard it? Had anybody else heard it? She looked around at the people, who no longer laughed and danced.

Their questions echoed against the darkness pooled beyond the light of the torches.

'What is this place?'

'Where are we?'

'Why do we follow that unknown boy?'

'How does he know this place?'

'How do we not?'

'Come along, not far now,' cried the capering figure of Agus. 'This is a safe place.'

'Armsmaster, take Garet, scout ahead,' Drustan commanded. He looked back. 'Marisa, what do you feel? Is this place safe?'

Marisa looked at the speckled patterns on the walls. The paintings no longer memorialised beasts, hunts, dancing, or joy. The patterns swirled and twisted, calling out to closed places within her mind, within every mind; and the joy returned.

When had the images changed?

Her haraf stone pulsed. The power of this place was stronger, even, than the power of the great spirals of stones from which her haraf stone was chipped. Her eyes focused beyond the images on the stone, beyond the surface, to the incised edges.

Every shrine dotted around the Islands of Symcani was built of haraf, the powerful stone quarried from … somewhere else. This place was that somewhere else, the source of all the haraf in the islands.

Mighty monoliths had been cut from these rocks, then the wounds smoothed over with painted consciousness. Great stones split away from their rocky beds, the monoliths taken out into the land beyond, set up in spirals to build the shrines of the Shrine Road and of other places in the islands.

A trial of strength between man and gods that filled up the Islands of Symcani with spirals of power.

Immense magic lived here. *'You are welcome here,'* the voice said in Marisa's mind. *'You are always welcome here.'*

'We are safe,' Marisa said. 'This is a safe place.'

They followed the boy into the earth, watchful, careful, until they stepped into a cavern that stretched away into darkness.

'We are here,' said Agus.

Marisa stared at the town beneath the mountain.

CHAPTER 40

Jarl approached the outer pickets of the Erisyan camp, where men were huddled up against the rain in mud-coloured cloaks, with spears, not warbows, in their hands. The spearheads followed the same inward-curving pattern of all Erisyan blades, which made the spears a form of halberd. Saplings were cut whenever spears were needed and the blade attached; no point in carrying an eight-foot pole-arm across the land when you could carry a two-foot blade in your pack instead.

The sentries nodded to Jarl as he walked by, but none smiled or greeted him with any kind of joy at his survival. These were his caedi and yet they simply nodded and returned to guarding the camp.

'Something is wrong here,' Sekem whispered.

'I know, cousin.' Jarl made the decision to unleash his empathic dol as he approached the warm glow of the farmhouse door, to probe a little deeper. Two men on guard. He touched their thoughts.

— Killed his own people — Murderer — What would I have done? — Traitor to the caedi — Is it true? Did they loose on women and children? — Murderer —

So that was the way of it. Jarl stepped through the heavy door and into the large room beyond. A fire blazed in the hearth. A chimney of roughcast brick carried the smoke away. Jarl shook out his cloak, and slung it over a hook set close to the door.

Kerek looked up from his place by the fire, a flask of brandy in his hand. Gorak stared into the flames, looking lost amongst the assembled awchti. Some of them followed Kerek's gaze and reacted to Jarl, each in their own way: sneers of disdain; sympathy; nods of welcome.

Kerek kicked Gorak's foot. 'Jarl's here.'

Gorak looked up. 'You've been busy, nephew.'

'In what way?' Jarl knew what Gorak referred to, but it was best not to emphasise his empathic talents. Not when he was about to use them again. He stamped to clear his boots of mud.

'I've been told what happened at the ford.' Gorak gestured and most of the awchti left the fire, leaving only Kerek and Gorak seated upon the benches. 'Sit. Explain.'

'They'll need to call a council,' Sekem said.

'I know,' Jarl agreed.

'You know what?' Gorak asked.

Jarl sat on the bench in front of the fire, stretched out his legs towards the flames, and accepted the brandy flask from Kerek. He shouldn't drink with a concussion, but he did anyway. 'Uras is dead,' Jarl said. 'Killed by an Erisyan arrow through the throat.'

'I know.' Gorak said. 'Tell me what happened. In your own words.'

Jarl sipped some more brandy and handed the flask onto Gorak. 'You'll need this.' He glanced at Kerek. 'You'd best get another.'

Kerek walked over to the corner, picked up a brandy flask and cracked open the ceramic lid. Jarl focused his dol on the awchti as he returned to his seat by the fire. No taint, no stink of demon breath upon him.

Good.

Now for Gorak.

As Jarl told his tale he focused on Gorak's reactions. The hwlman gulped at the brandy with every shocking description, but no scent of demon rose from his soul, only guilt and pain.

'They loosed on women and children?' Gorak asked.

'So you say,' Kerek said in a harsh voice. Not the most eloquent of men, Kerek would stand by whatever decision Gorak made. He didn't want to lead the caedi; he simply wanted to leave a name behind.

Jarl nodded to Kerek but directed his words at Gorak. 'They killed Uras. Put an arrow through his throat. And they would've killed me too if it wasn't for an ancient hero come back to this world.'

'An ancient hero?' Kerek raised a sardonic eyebrow.

'He of the club of iron and skin like stone. He who stands. The God-Killer. We call him Beran and name him amongst those that went before, but he called himself Berasin. He killed any that loosed upon the innocent.'

'Beran the Guardian,' Kerek breathed. 'I would like to have met him.'

'You still might,' Jarl said. 'Well, Gorak, what do you say?'

Gorak stared into the flames. 'They said—'

'He speaks of those that ran away.' Sekem's dead voice filled with contempt. *'They misremember what they saw to heal their own guilt.'*

'They stood by and did nothing.' Jarl leaned forward, watching his uncle gulp at the brandy. 'They stood by and watched traitors kill Uras. They stood by and watched their kin loose upon women and children. Women and children, Gorak. That's not our way. We couldn't do that and remain Erisyan. Our women-folk would walk away from us and they would be right to do so.'

Gorak placed the brandy by his side. 'But—'

Jarl cut across his leader's words. 'They weren't of the caedi anymore, Gorak. They chose their path to damnation.'

'How do you know this?' Kerek asked. 'How can you know that they willingly became Vascanar?'

'How else could they become Vascanar? They were seduced, they gave up their souls for power. I've felt that seduction pouring across my mind, and I cast it off. They did not. The Summerland is closed to them now. They'll wander for all eternity. Go, fetch back their bodies. Carry out the rites. See what happens. See what the Geidiw do to those that worship demons.'

Gorak stirred in his seat. 'You can't know this.'

'I smelled it on them, Gorak. I smelled the breath of the demons on their skin, in their sweat, in their hair, in the very breath that issued from their lungs. I smelled it.'

'They said—'

'Bring me before the caedi, place me upon the mound, let the caedi decide my guilt or innocence, but burn the bodies first.'

'They were taken by the Vascanar gods?' Kerek asked.

'Aye. They attacked me. I merely defended myself.'

'The Vascanar gods are demons? Seducers of men?'

'They are.'

The brandy flask shattered as Kerek closed his strong hand. 'The council will need to know this. We didn't sign on to fight for demons.' He picked a shard of pottery from a cut in his palm.

'It doesn't matter. The oath was to the Vascanar, not to their foul gods,' Gorak said.

Kerek pushed hard at his argument. 'Doesn't subverting our people and turning them into animals constitute harming an Erisyan? Breaking the oath so that we can go home?'

'There'll be no council,' Gorak said.

'There must be,' Kerek said in shock. 'Jarl here killed his own. The rights of that action must be voted upon.'

'The oath isn't broken if those who drank the Vascanar wine did so of their own free-will,' Gorak said.

'We can't know that.'

'Jarl says we can.'

'There'll be others, Gorak,' Jarl warned.

'Others…' Gorak closed his eyes for a moment. His pain shone from his soul like a beacon fire. 'I know, but there's nothing to be done. If we take this to the council then all shall know. If all know, then some will claim our oath broken. If they act on that assumption then…'

'Demons, Gorak,' Kerek said.

'The oath's with the Vascanar,' Gorak repeated. He stared into the fire.

Jarl realised that Gorak had broken. The oath *should* be discarded. The Vascanar had attacked the Erisyans and the Erisyans should pack up their tents and go home. But Gorak couldn't make that decision — the corruption of his kin had broken him. He would make no decision, would do nothing except try to ignore what was in front of his eyes.

'The gods won't be happy if we break the oath,' Gorak said.

'The gods!' Jarl gave a harsh bark of laughter. 'Let them be angry, as if they've ever done anything for the Erisyans. We've been among the Vascanar for barely a month since we embarked on this stupid campaign, and less than a week here in this land, and already members of the caedi have succumbed to their demon-lords. What've our gods done about that? Nothing.' Jarl stabbed his finger at the fire, at the floor, anywhere but at his uncle; Gorak's fragile confidence wouldn't react well to finger-pointing. Jarl's headache came back to bite him for drinking strong alcohol. 'We're going to be here until the snow comes, Gorak. How many more will betray their caedi in that time? How many more Erisyans will we lose?'

'If there's no council, no vote,' Kerek said with careful consideration, 'then some will think Jarl's at fault and that you protect your nephew from the caedi.'

'Kerek really wants to break the oath to the Vascanar,' Sekem said. *'I didn't know he had it in him.'* Admiration tinged the spectral voice.

'That can't be helped,' Gorak said. 'You understand, don't you, Jarl?'

'Careful now, cousin,' Sekem whispered.

'Aye,' Jarl said, though the word soured his mouth. 'I think you're wrong, but I understand. When I drew sword upon my caedi I knew that what I did carried its own cost, but I also knew that if I stood back, did nothing, and allowed women and children to be killed by Erisyan bows, then I'd be nothing but a coward.'

'Do you think I'm a coward, Jarl?' Gorak's voice ran cold with despair.

'No, I think you're a fool.' Jarl stood up. 'I met a hero of the old times today. He didn't kill me, but he did leave me with this.' Jarl pointed at the bandage about his head. 'I must rest now.'

'Are you sure he was Beran?' Kerek asked.

'Arrows shattered on his naked breast as if they hit stone and yet blades cut him as they would any other man. Aye, it was Beran, and he spoke of our heroes in the Summerland. We share a common heritage with the people of this land. Where's my pack?'

'I had it stored here,' Gorak pointed at the back of the room, 'to protect its contents.'

He could say that, acknowledge that Jarl was a marked man amongst the caedi, but he wouldn't call the council to vote upon Jarl's actions. Gorak took another swig of brandy and avoided his nephew's eye.

Jarl lifted his travelling pack, pushed his hand in amongst the blankets and drew out Sekem's sword from beside Sekem's ashes. 'Thank you, cousin,' he murmured.

'You're welcome,' Sekem said. *'Best sharpen it though, and sleep with one eye open.'*

CHAPTER 41

Drustan sat on a bench carved from the rock, staring at the town laid out under the earth. The houses looked awkward, the doors too wide and out of proportion, the shutters on the windows made from sheets of rock cut so thinly that they were translucent. He had never seen anything like this before.

His side ached, his mind refused to forget the feeling of the water closing over his head, the feel of her hands grasping him, pulling him towards safety while arrows fell all around them.

Marisa.

She moved amongst the villagers, checking, always checking if everybody was all right. No cuts, no scrapes that might get infected. No sprains or twisted ankles that might slow up the march. She was a good person, a kind person, his wife... No. Not his wife. They dissolved that.

She was free to marry again and yet she had entered the Houses. To clear the taint on her honour for loving one such as him?

Everybody a half-breed. Everybody. Could it be true?

Aye, Cullain hadn't lied. The armsmaster never bothered with lying about such things. He just didn't speak of them and had kept his counsel for fear of how Drustan might have reacted.

Drustan thought for a moment. Would he have confronted the King? Would he have come back to this land, walked up to the King and demanded his life back? Burst open the petty lies of the Karisae nobility? Fought for his honour, killed any that stood against him until he was beaten down and held as a sacrifice to their lies, burned alive in a place of their choosing so that their little lives of hypocrisy and politics could go on unabated?

Aye, he might. Drustan grinned at the rock floor. He would have stood before the King and made himself a martyr for truth and honour. And a hypocrite. Had he not hated the Anthanic? Had he not killed them? Fought their champions? Had he not left these islands when the truth about his blood was revealed? Had he not hated his own blood?

They would have killed Cullain, too. For the armsmaster would have been there, at his back, fighting a fight he knew was futile. Drustan grimaced.

They might have killed Marisa, too, burned her at the stake, called her witch and worse, just to hold their nasty little world closed against the truth. They had lied to him. They had lied to her. They had... Lies that broke their marriage, tore them apart, five years. Five long years without her.

And all for a lie.

Cullain strode amongst the small group of people, arranging the guard, the watches; the men nodding at his words, the women slumped. The tellis had worn off now. All so very tired.

This place was a wonder. Marisa wandered off into the town. Drustan thought about going after her, but he could not move, not yet.

Five years.

Would she even want him back?

****

Kihan raced through the forest, up the sloping ground onto the moorland, a stark, brutal landscape of moss and tough grass. The chase had lasted for hours and still they followed. They chivvied him, faster on four feet than he was on two, but they lacked his endurance. The Hounds of the Falls were heavier than him, their limbs not designed for long-distance fortitude. But Kihan couldn't keep up this pace forever.

A hound got ahead of him, turned him, forced him to run a different way. The ones chasing simply cut the corner of his turn. Another hundred paces lost to this manoeuvre.

They hunted him. He did not know why, but they hunted him. For some reason he was their prey of choice and after him ... all would fall to their ravenous hunger.

This land ... this gentle land that had saved him, given him back his humanity ... the people of this land didn't deserve to fall to these creatures. But Kihan couldn't keep up this pace.

Could he lure them somewhere? Out to the sea, where the water would drown them, cleanse them, kill them?

On the voyage to this land, the salt air had filled his nose and reminded him that he was human, but the priests had kept a firm grip on the spellhounds, holding the magic inside them even as they squirmed in recognition of their humanity.

Salt water was inimical to this foul magic. It would break the spell on the hounds.

He lifted his head, sucked air into his nostrils. The salt was close. He could smell it on the wind. He would lead them there.

Digging in with his toes, lifting his burning thighs higher with each stride, he broke across the line chosen by the hounds. He lost paces of distance to them by turning again but gasped in air, shook the sweat from his eyes and surged on through the ragged grass and dangerous rocks. If he should trip here, if he should twist an ankle, then it would be over. No matter. He had to try.

This land could not survive with the hounds in it, and he would protect this land because he was human, a man, and he wouldn't let the demons and their spawn destroy another people. *The flames, the anguish…* He choked back the tears for all that he had lost, and ran on.

He was a man, not a hound, and he would protect his kind.

****

Drustan said, 'We lost most of our food at the ford.'

'Aye,' Cullain said, 'looks that way. Some kha left and a bag of fruit, but all the flour's ruined, the oats destroyed, no meat.'

Drustan shifted on the stone bench. 'We'll have to send out a hunting party.'

'Efan's a fair shot by all accounts and can move like a ghost when he wants to. I'll have to go with him. Most of the rest can barely stand.'

'No, I need you here ,' Drustan said. 'If there's an attack—'

'He can't carry that stag back by himself.'

'The stag? You want to kill that beast?'

'Big old thing, done its duty to its descendants. Feed us for a week.'

A voice boomed down from the top of the cave, 'That wouldn't be a good idea.'

Cullain whirled, his sword hissing free of its sheath.

'Tirac?' Efan called, squinting into the dark with an arrow nocked to his bow.

'I AM BERASIN!' The voice echoed through the cave and Drustan could have sworn that he saw the stones of the houses shift under the impact, as if they quailed at the sound.

A huge figure in a bear-skull helm limped down the slope towards the town using a mighty iron-headed club as a walking stick.

'Tirac?' Efan said, his voice a hoarse whisper.

'That is the name you know me by,' Berasin agreed. 'The deceit was required.'

Berasin carried a huge stag over one shoulder, but not the imperious beast that had watched them in the vale beyond. Another beast, equally big, but without the rack of antlers. Three men could not have hoped to carry it and yet Berasin carried it over one shoulder with a large sack in the same hand; he clearly needed the other hand to use his club as a walking stick.

'But they cut out your tongue,' Garet said. 'I saw it. I was there. I saw them throw it into the fire.'

'That was Tirac's tongue,' Berasin said. 'I am not Tirac anymore.' He dropped the sack on the ground, then rolled his shoulder, shrugging off the stag to lie beside it. 'Where are you?' He looked around the cave. 'This is your place, old spirit. Where are you?'

'Berasin,' Garet breathed. 'I've heard… They say… He was seen… We are honoured by the gods this day.'

'Don't get too weak at the knees, Garet,' Drustan said. 'He's only a man the gods smiled on. He isn't a god himself.'

'Warriors.' Rosana sniffed.

'You're late,' Cullain barked. 'Report.'

'I'm not Tirac anymore,' Berasin said. 'I brought you this stag because trying to kill the other would be unwise. Lyrin does not take kindly to being hunted.'

Lyrin, the old forest god of the Anthanic, often took the shape of a stag. He was supposed to be dead, vanquished, his soul locked away somewhere. Drustan looked for Marisa. Where was she?

'Report,' Cullain growled. 'And I mayn't take your guts for a waterskin.'

'I am Berasin!'

'And I'm Cullain Strongarm, your armsmaster. Report, oh hero of the mists. What've you been doing when we could've used your strength?'

'Killing demon-infested archers, repaying a debt, killing this fine beast here, and collecting other food to help it go down. There's wine in that house over there, by the way.'

'That'll make a nice gravy to go with your liver then.' Cullain sheathed his sword. 'Good to see you alive and not smiling.'

Berasin frowned. 'You and I will have a nice chat when you come to the Sunlit Land.'

'We've already had it.'

'That was but an introduction.'

'Let's return to where we were then.'

'No, I will wait for you to meet me in the land beyond death.'

'You'll have a long wait.'

'I can live with that.'

Drustan sighed. 'Have you two quite finished?'

'Yes, Bright Blade.' Berasin bowed.

Cullain grinned.

Rosana and the women clustered around the food. 'We need firewood,' she said.

'In that hut.' Berasin pointed with his club. 'All you need is there, and this hearth will stop the smoke filling up the cave.'

'How?'

'Some magical trickery of the old ones.' Berasin shrugged.

'Take off that damn hat,' Cullain said. 'That bloody bear is leering at me.'

Berasin removed the helm and the man they knew as Tirac stood before them.

'He's smiling, armsmaster,' Drustan said.

'Soon fix that.' Cullain pointed at the mouth of the cave. 'You're on watch, Berasin.'

Berasin laughed.

CHAPTER 42

Marisa wandered through the town beneath the mountain. She strolled alone through the empty streets feeling happier than she had felt for … years.

This town, these houses, these homes, were constructed from rocks quarried from the cavern, the walls of the buildings a marvellous interweaving of colour. Power surged from those walls into the stone Marisa wore about her neck.

Haraf!

Like the shrines, these houses were built of haraf. This place was an abode of the gods — the overthrown gods, those displaced centuries ago by the invading Karisae, who had brought their own pantheon with them.

But gods had not lived in these houses. The energy here was human, and it was filled with harmony and delight. Laughter echoed in her mind, in her heart and soul, whenever she touched one of the houses. Love; they had loved here, these people who built houses from stones of power and threw back the dark edges of the world beyond.

'A king slept there,' Agus said, pointing to a house no different from any of the others. He sat upon a wall, eating an apple, his eyes dark and humorous in the flickering light. 'Next to the bath houses. He liked to be clean.'

'Who *are* you?' Marisa asked.

Agus finished the apple and tossed the core away before he answered. 'A boy, in't I?'

'Are you a god?'

Agus grinned. 'Nah, just a boy. Me parents gave me the wrong name, but they weren't to know. Weren't to know what I were.' His grin faded. 'But I'm just a boy.'

'Then how do you know about the king?'

'Stones told me, didn't they? We can't stay 'ere, milady. Ain't a place for mortals no more. We'd fade away into these stones just like they did — the ones that built it. Can't you feel them? Love and fellowship. They're good people, but we don't want to join 'em in their joy.'

'You have power.'

'So do you.' Agus jumped down from the wall. 'Don't you want to wash your hair?'

Marisa raised a hand to her itchy scalp.

'Bath houses.' Agus pointed. 'Water hot from the earth, only got to open the pipes.'

'But this place is abandoned.'

'I just told you. They're still 'ere, we just can't see 'em.'

Marisa and Agus walked back towards the centre of the town, where the villagers had set up their camp. She heard the shouts and the laughter and glanced at the boy.

He scowled. 'Tirac's returned.'

'I thought he was your friend.'

'Tirac were, but he ain't Tirac no more.'

'I do not understand.'

'He's Berasin now,' Agus said and then grinned. 'Still Tirac to me, though.'

'Berasin the hero?'

'Aye.' Agus pointed with his chin. 'There. See him?'

Tirac stood in the centre of the town square. No, not Tirac; somebody else with the form of Tirac. Was it really Berasin? The big man seemed more real than he ever had when she knew him as Tirac. More powerfully present. The skull of a bear lay on the ground beside him, an iron-tipped club thrown carelessly across it, and he was dressed in the skin of a bear.

She knew the old legends better than most. A delight in reading from a young age had led her to seek out the old stories in her father's library. He had not cared much for scrolls, but they belonged to the family and so he had indulged her inquisitive nature.

Yes, this man was Berasin, there was no doubting that. This man was the Hero of the Gates, He Who Stood Against The Horde. A chill ran down Marisa's spine. Berasin, here, fighting by the side of her love,

Drustan. Men died by Berasin's side; the tales were filled up with his lost comrades.

Marisa looked for her estranged husband, her gaze seeking him out amongst the small crowd. There … there he stood … oh …

Drustan smiled at her and nearly broke her heart. His smile did not turn to a frown. He did not spit out his misery on the ground and turn hard-edged eyes upon her. Instead he gave her a simple smile, open and forgiving; the smile she had fallen in love with.

Love stories crowded her memory from the scrolls of her father's hoarded library. The myth of the young boy abused and beaten who grew to be a great hero, and the woman who stood by his side. Berasin had had such a woman. All the heroes of the past had had such women. And it never ended well.

Love is a dream that breaks the butterfly upon the wheel.

Berasin bowed his head to her as she approached. 'Milady Marisa.' He went down on one knee. 'My arms are yours. My strength is yours. All that I am, I lay at your feet.'

Drustan's soft smile faded as he looked from her to Berasin and back.

'Do not worry, Drustan of the Forest,' Berasin said. 'My time with such things is long past.'

'How's the ear?' Drustan asked.

'Healing nicely.' Berasin stood.

'Seven stitches.'

'A mystical number.' Berasin picked up his club. 'And now only one left to join this gathering.'

Agus asked, 'Do you have to?'

'Yes, boy, I do.'

Agus sighed. 'He'll be cross.'

'Not this time,' Berasin said. 'This time he'll answer the call.' He stalked across the cave floor, loosening his shoulders and hefting his club. The painted images on the rocks flickered madly in the torchlight.

As if they wanted to flee.

'Come forth, old spirit!' Berasin called. 'Come forth.' The club swept around in a fluid arc and smashed into the image of a man made from palm-prints etched in paint.

The palm-prints of children, of women, of men, placed just so on the wall to leave the outline of the strange figure upon the rock. Not quite a man. More robust, stronger, a strange shape around the waist as if the ribs extended further and wider than was normal. The head was misshapen: a low forehead, brow ridges, and a bulge at the back above an almost non-existent neck, the face pinched forward making the skull longer than a human's.

Chips of stone splintered into the air as Berasin's club shattered the solid rock. 'Come forth, old spirit,' he called. 'This is your place. This is where I stood against the horde.' The club swept around again.

A deep sound rang from the rock as if a mighty bell were struck. Stone chips flew from the figure's silhouetted face. 'Come forth. We have need of you!' cried Berasin.

A third time the iron-headed club slammed into the rock and the air shook with the sound of that bell.

And, from out of the shadows, a figure composed itself into light, flowing across the rock, smoothing over the injuries caused by the club. The stone chips floated through the air, returning to their place upon the stone, reforming the palm-painting until no sign remained of the violence of Berasin's club.

'I am here,' the god Agusur said.

CHAPTER 43

Berasin knelt before Agusur and, after the moment of shock had passed, the villagers did likewise. Heads bowed, eyes upon the floor, kneeling before a god. Even Agus knelt.

Until only Marisa remained standing, staring at the god.

Heavy ridges above the eyes, a forehead that sloped back so precipitously that if she had seen it in a child she helped bring into the world she would have wept alongside the mother; such a child would know neither thought nor reason. But this creature's head was larger around than the tiny skulls of such benighted children. A brain larger than a man's lay within that skull.

A large jaw thrust over the bull neck. Huge shoulders and arms, a squat body; he was as large as Cullain and he grinned at her refusal to kneel, revealing teeth like monoliths. His eyes, golden in the torchlight, were filled with intelligence, power — and sadness.

Drustan looked up from where he knelt, tilted his head when he spotted Marisa still standing, and, with a grunt of pain for his injured side, stood beside her.

Cullain was the next, rising beside his captain. Then Rosana stood. Then the other men, then the other women. But they bade their children remain kneeling; they would face the wrath of a god for their captain's sake, for Marisa's, but they would not expose their children to the same danger.

Agus nudged Berasin. The hero frowned and stood alongside the boy. Marisa felt the world hold its breath.

Heroes out of legend stepped forth from the Sunlit Land at the whimsical urgings of honour and delight. They popped up again and again in the old stories to take part in minor disputes between lords, to stand on the battlefield beside and against kings. Sometimes they even appeared to help common people cross swollen rivers... Heroes were always appearing when they were least expected and rarely wanted. But gods…

Gods seldom manifested themselves in this world of toil. They preferred to work through oracles and omens, cryptic clues and frozen lakes, men and women whom they touched and thereby changed forever.

'Good of you to come, old spirit,' Berasin said.

'I am here,' Agusur replied. His voice mellow and soft as a summer breeze, held undertones of earth and sky, sea and flame, humility and arrogance.

Marisa looked upon the god, heard his voice, thought of all that had been lost because the gods had not acted, they had done nothing as the Vascanar took the land. And yet now one stood before her, the oldest of the gods, a being of immense power and wisdom, but still she felt nothing but anger. Should she be awed? Should she let the force of that personality make her quiver with bliss?

No. She should ask questions. It was rare to meet a god.

Pointing to Agus she asked, 'What is he?'

'I told you,' Agus said. 'Don't you want a bath?'

'He is just a boy,' Agusur said.

'He is human then?' Marisa asked. 'Not some creation of your imagination?'

'You care for him,' Agusur said.

'I do.'

'We do,' Drustan said. 'We all do.'

'Don't let your head swell, boy,' Cullain warned.

'I shouldn't be listening to this, should I?' Agus asked.

'You should hear it,' Berasin said.

'The boy is just a boy.' Agusur walked towards Marisa, his smile twisted with sardonic respect. 'But one born to such power should not be given the name of a god.'

Fear clutched at Marisa's heart. 'What is he?'

Agus scowled. 'Tell her.'

Agusur bowed his head to Agus. 'It is time for such things to be known.' He lifted his golden eyes to Marisa. 'He breaks the oaths.'

'A warlock?' she asked, knowing that it was true, and fearing the road that Agus would walk. A child who could bend fate to his will;

something that not even the gods could do.

Agusur nodded. 'That is your name for them, yes.'

'What do you call them?'

'A nuisance.'

Berasin laughed. 'He's that already.'

Cullain chuckled. 'Sharp-witted as a tax collector.' He ruffled Agus's hair.

'An irritant.' Drustan grinned. 'Or was that you?' He turned his gaze full upon the god and did not look away.

Marisa's heart almost burst from pride. She could look upon a god because she dealt with magic every day and even she had felt the force of that personality pushing at her. Drustan did not have her advantage and yet he did not look away.

'He took the information and used it as he would,' Agusur said.

'You had to get up to pee anyway.' Agus dodged away from Cullain's clip around the ear.

'Snotty little…' Drustan shook his head and laughed. Then he winced at the pain from his injured side. He looked at Agusur. 'You were there, with my mother, calling to Marisa.'

Marisa started. 'But I heard you call me.'

'Not without help, and I recognise his voice.' Drustan's tone hardened. 'Warning me against my mother.'

'Eirane is young for an Amthisrid and you are her son. There is danger there,' Agusur said. 'She could not drive the call through to Marisa without my help.'

'Why did you help?' Drustan asked.

'You carry the Xarnac, that amulet. It must be taken to the sacred Lake Kalon and thrown into the waters. Then Tanaz will deal with these demons.'

'Tanaz sleeps,' Marisa said. The House of Redain was consecrated to Tanaz, a goddess of the Anthanic as well as the Karisae. As was Agusur. 'She is the Sleeping Goddess. It is rare for her to answer a prayer.'

'Tanaz does not like to be disturbed,' Berasin agreed. 'But she likes demons even less.'

Drustan again lifted his gaze to the god. 'You protected us at the ford.' It was not a question.

'I did what I could,' Agusur said. 'That river is sacred to Tanaz and the heart of that forest is in the care of the Amthisrid Wendin. My powers are limited there.'

'Is that why you unleashed Berasin?'

Berasin pointed at the bear's skull. 'She unleashed me. I called her and she came.'

'Ursaric feels the battle to come like a quickening in her blood,' Agusur agreed.

'She's dead,' Efan pointed out.

'She is a goddess. We do not fade so easily.'

'You wear a goddess on your head?' Garet asked.

'Where else?' Berasin shrugged.

'Did someone mention a bath?' asked Rosana.

****

The screams of the sacrifices arched upwards into the darkening sky and Torquesten drank in their pain. He strode through the gardens of the House. The pristine white of the circular walls glistened with the vaporised fat of delicious deaths.

The air above the garden thickened and darkened — his brethren coming for the feast. Torquesten laughed as, bunched together by the sacred walls, the gods of the Vascanar closed out the sky in a demonic ceiling dark and roiling. The rain hissed into steam a full ten paces above the darkness of his brethren. Torquesten lifted his arms in joy. The rain, the detestable rain, no longer washed his body clean.

A flash of light flickered across the stones, a desperate last attempt by the shrine to defend itself. But the shrine was weakened by the pain of the dying, and the flash of light from the luminous water of the spring stuttered and faded.

Illath would rise soon and add her power to the ritual and all would balance on the edge of the blade. Without the Xarnac, and that errant healer, the ritual would be incomplete, but still, the defilement of this spring would begin the Path of Blood.

It had to happen this night and then he would seek out the Xarnac and guide his brethren to their rightful pantheon.

Torquesten strode across the garden. He paused at a sacrifice screaming as his eyes were burned out, and slashed open the man's stomach with a flick of his sword.

'Heat up his insides with stones,' he commanded and moved on, pausing from time to time to add delicate new ingredients into the stew of pain. His men removed their armour in the heat, worked feverishly, and tried to outdo each other in the infliction of agony. The suffering must reach new heights to aid his brethren in their journey. Anguish would have to serve for a while. Until the Xarnac was recovered.

Torquesten paused beneath the arches of the walkways where the demonhounds sprawled in a corner, gnawing on bones and resting.

There would be work for them in the morning.

CHAPTER 44

D rustan slipped into the hot water with a gasp. Gods, that felt good. Horol floated off to one side, the livid wounds on his chest hidden under patches of salamin cloth. An obviously Anthanic tattoo of interlaced knots formed a triangle below his collarbone. Drustan wondered what it meant.

Garet lounged at the other end of the bath, up to his chest in water, his eyes closed as he luxuriated in the warmth.

Marisa's laugh pealed through the dividing wall. How could he walk away from her again?

Cullain stumped into the room with a towel around his waist, his arms bloody to the elbows from butchering the stag. 'Now here's a place,' he said.

The bath house was divided into male and female sections by intricately carved walls that obscured sight but not sound or light. The coiling, lace-like patterns repeated across the solid walls surrounding the bath, but as a bas relief cut into the multicoloured stones. Drustan had never seen anything like this in all his travels as a wandering sell-sword. The iridescent stone bounced the light of the torches into sparkling radiance, like the scales of the *Oragnig* — a mythical sea-beast.

'It is a delight, armsmaster,' Garet said, floating in the buoyant water, arms outstretched.

Cullain sniffed. 'Should've known you'd be here.' He slid into the water and sighed. 'A man could get used to this.'

'Like the passion baths of Maebaz.' Drustan grinned.

'Have you seen them?' Horol asked.

'Nah,' Drustan admitted. 'I've never been to the Unchanging City. Not much call for sell-swords there.'

'There's house-guarding, joining the city watch, killing the city watch, or fighting in the pits,' Cullain said.

'Like I said, not much need for sell-swords, but plenty of need for scum of the earth.'

'I'd like to see the city,' Horol said. 'One day.'

'Gotta kill the Vascanar first, lad.' Cullain scrubbed the deer blood from his arms. It stained the water for a moment and then dissipated. A laugh from the women's side, husky, low, incredibly sensual. Cullain grinned. 'Rosana spitted that deer,' he said.

Drustan raised an eyebrow and Cullain looked away.

'Efan watching it cook?' Horol asked.

'No,' Efan said from the door to the changing room.

'Didn't think so,' Horol said. 'You always burn the damn things.'

'I like the meat crispy.'

'Burned.'

'Crispy.' Efan whipped away his towel, sprinted forward and leapt into the pool. The splash washed over the lounging men.

Cullain cursed.

'Gods,' Efan spluttered as he resurfaced. 'That's damned hot water.'

'Aye,' Horol said. 'Armsmaster wants a word with you.'

'Splash me again and I'll rip your guts out and hang you from that damn ceiling,' Cullain growled.

'He would too,' Drustan said. 'Seen him do it. Nasty way to go.'

Efan laughed, and then stopped when neither Drustan nor Cullain so much as cracked a smile. 'Really?'

Cullain laughed first. 'Nah.'

Efan laughed again.

'I'd just break your legs.'

Drustan chuckled. 'Only a toe, armsmaster, take one of his toes. I've need of warriors.'

'Right you are, my captain. Which foot?'

'You choose.'

Cullain nodded. 'Thank you for the kindness.'

Agus sprinted through the door of the changing room, closely followed by Yarom.

Cullain yelled, 'Don't you dare!'

Too late; the boys were already leaping into the air.

Drustan wiped the splashed water from his face. 'The brats you can hang from the ceiling, armsmaster.'

****

Morgeth's light shone down in slivers of silver, turning the landscape monochrome, but Kihan could see the edge of the cliff cutting across the moonlit landscape in front of him.

He could make the final jump there. The hounds would follow and fall into the sea, dying in that briny water but at least returning to the form of men before they drowned. He could do no more for them. This land had made them into beasts. He did not know how. Neither did he care.

He pushed his exhausted legs into a final sprint, the hounds snapping at his heels. If one managed to get a single bite on him he would die here within taste of the sea.

What was that rearing out of the shadow? A pinnacle of rock, a stack broken away from the cliff-face by the action of the sea crashing below. A sanctuary. Could he reach it? Could he make that leap and survive, while the hounds plunged to their deaths?

Kihan changed the angle of his run. The hounds gained a few paces; one almost caught his heel, but it was tired now — the salt in the air limiting its powers of recuperation — and Kihan let terror add speed to his feet.

One last effort. One last push. Only paces now.

The edge of the cliff.

He leapt out over the crashing sea, out over his inevitable death. He started to fall, the rock of the pinnacle rushing towards him in the dark, but further away than he had thought. He slammed into the rock. His fingers scrabbled for holds as he started to slip downwards. His left hand scraped a cleft. He clutched at it as his fall started to gather pace. A tearing pain in his shoulder. He clung on, his full weight hanging from one torn arm. He clung on, shaking his head to clear it of the blood flowing into his eyes from a gash across his forehead.

The sea crashed hungrily into the rocks three hundred paces below him.

A mighty effort needed, his willpower almost exhausted. He threw up his other arm, found a hold for his right hand, found toeholds for his feet, took the pressure from his damaged shoulder and looked back.

The hounds paced back and forth along the edge of the cliff, snarling at him, but not attempting the leap.

A pity.

He started to climb.

****

Cullain stormed out of the bathhouse. 'Where's my armour?'

Drustan limped after him, still tying the drawstring of his breeches, made of the same wonderfully soft material as the loose shirt. All the clothing any of them could find after taking their bath. Simple leather sandals in the place of muddy boots.

'Being cleaned,' Agusur said.

'Cleaned?' Cullain said. 'Who by?'

'Those that live here.'

'I told him that,' Agus said.

Cullain checked his blades were where he had left them.

Agusur spoke in a sonorous voice. 'Your armour will be returned to you, Cullain Strongarm, son of Alain Irongrip, son of Ravenna Ravenhair, born upon the StormMarch when the Widder wind howled in the depths of winter.'

Cullain suddenly remembered who he was speaking to. He chewed his beard. 'My armour will be returned to me before we leave?'

'It will. Better than before it was taken.' Agusur smiled. 'Sit, armsmaster, I must tell you of the Vascanar and what they seek upon these isles.'

Cullain picked up his blades and carried them with him to sit beside the god. Drustan grinned, but then he caught sight of Marisa, dressed in a smock-like dress made of the same soft material as his shirt, with a rope belt tied about her slim waist, and wet hair hanging free and golden across her shoulders. His smile faded.

She looked away from his gaze and sat beside the god. Drustan limped across to join them and lowered himself to the ground, careful not to disturb the newly wrapped bandages around his torso. She had stood before the god when all gave obeisance. Drustan had never been prouder in his life than at that moment. But now, in this moment, his heart broke again at the sight of her.

Agusur smiled sadly at Drustan and explained what it was the Vascanar sought.

'The Vascanar worship demons that wish to become gods. They will transform the shrine road into a path of blood. Every shrine from Falas to Redain will be corrupted, desecrated with blood and suffering. This will weaken the bonds upon the gates between this world and the Tangled Realms of the demons. Such a place.' Agusur shook his great head. 'A place where nothing is fixed, nothing remains the same, nothing has form or shape or purpose. To fall into the Tangled Realms is to lose all that makes you real. To escape it is an all-consuming need.'

'All the shrines?' Marisa asked.

'All of them.'

'They will kill hundreds of people.'

'Thousands. It takes a lot of pain and suffering to corrupt a shrine.'

'And this will open the gate?' Drustan asked.

'There are many gates in this world. Many places where the old ways are kept pure.' Agusur bowed his head. 'But few are as powerful as the one here in the Islands of Symcani. Few have a sleeping goddess at their heart.'

'This is why they need the Xarnac?' Rosana called across from the fire pit. 'They call it the lodestone, you said as I were preparing this stag.' She ladled fat over the meat and it sizzled into the flames.

'Yes.' Agusur bowed his head to her. 'The Xarnac is a lodestone. It is not of this world but neither is it of theirs. It is outside the realms as we understand them.'

'As gods understand them,' Agus said and grinned.

Agusur ignored him. 'Without that amulet the demons will be lost amongst the many paths out of the Tangled Realms. They will not be able to find their way to the gate of Tanaz, the enchained goddess.'

'All the gates will open?' Drustan glanced at Marisa.

'Yes.'

'Everywhere in this world?'

'Not just in this world.' Agusur lifted his hands. 'If the Xarnac is not recovered then the demons will remain demons, scattered, isolated, weak. But if they recover the Xarnac then they will come through in one spot, in one mighty rush, and then they will shake this world to its core. A new pantheon of gods shall arise.'

'But they will not destroy the world,' Cullain said. 'They'll just be gods, like any other gods.' His eyes strayed towards the fire, where Rosana fussed over the roasting stag. 'Like you.'

'No, armsmaster, not like me, or those of my ilk.' Agusur stared into the shadows. 'I am one of the oldest of all the gods. This form comes from those that gave me homage before men like you came to this land. These houses were built here in the centre of my power by hands like these.' He turned his large, stubby-fingered hands over in the torchlight and closed them into fists. 'I was a spirit, a thought, an emanation of the world. In truth, I don't know what I was before I became what I am. They painted my form on the Wall-that-Rings.' He pointed at the hand-printed figure. 'I was only a spirit of the rocks then. But time wears on and everything grows — even gods. Other spirits did battle for their tribes and I did battle for mine. Every victory made me stronger and I became a god of war. No, not war; not as you know war. A god of raids and ambushes, of battles that left few dead but joined peoples together.'

'These people that came before,' Garet said. 'Where are they now?'

Agusur smiled. 'You carry their blood within you still.' He glanced at Cullain. 'Some more than others.'

Garet laughed at Cullain's discomfited frown.

'They became us?' Marisa asked.

'No. They bred with you. Love knows no boundaries between peoples. But gods, ah now, gods are jealous creatures. The first gods of these new folk, your folk, drove my pantheon into a waterfall and bound them there. They would have destroyed them utterly but I would not allow it.'

'You would not allow it?'

'I had become a god of the land by that point. The first peoples from beyond the sea, those that became you with time, had other gods more suited to your ways of war.'

'People from beyond the sea,' Efan said. 'The Karisae?'

Berasin laughed. 'Karisae. This all happened before the Karisae became a people, before the Anthanic invaded these islands. This happened before I was born, before my people invaded these islands, before the last time the demons tried to break through from the Tangled Realms and I stood right here,' Berasin stabbed his finger at the rock beneath his feet, 'and stopped them.'

'Still can't hold a choke-hold though.' Cullain rolled his shoulders.

Agusur laughed. 'You are a man, Cullain Strongarm.'

'I know.'

'The stories say you came full-grown from the body of a troll,' Garet said. 'The stories call you god of wisdom and the dawn.'

'The stories are just stories,' Agusur answered. The rocks around them growled as if in anger. 'Oh growl away, whippersnapper, you think I tell them something they do not already know?' Agusur looked at Garet. 'I know the pain you carry. I know the pains you all carry. That is my curse for surviving so long, for slipping from pantheon to pantheon, for shifting my shape and my story to match that which is needed. But I do not believe the stories. Remember this: a god that believes its own story is dangerous.'

'Who is the whippersnapper?' Cullain asked.

'You call him Henath, god of the underworld. He is another interloper into your Karisae pantheon. Have you never wondered why you need a god of the underworld when you expect to go to the Sunlit Land?'

'He judges the dead,' Garet said.

'He does now.' Agusur laughed, then his voice softened. 'Do not worry. He that fell was judged worthy.'

Garet got up and walked into the shadows without another word.

Drustan watched him go as the silence stretched around the small group eating fruit and drinking wine. 'Why me?' he asked harshly into that silence. 'Why did Agus approach me on the battlefield? Why did that Vascanar amulet fall into my hands?'

'I placed Agus in your path and in the path of others' — Agusur raised his eyes towards Garet sitting in the shadows — 'because I saw the line of your fate glowing golden in Riadna's web. I saw so many other lines connecting to yours, entangled with yours, golden and strong, from both sides of the battle.' The god's voice dropped. 'But I saw darkness around you all. The darkness of threads broken from the web by the malice of the Vascanar's worship. You were important and so I placed Agus in your path.'

'Then why did you let me be almost crippled?'

Agusur said, 'You should not have stopped moving.'

Cullain harrumphed agreement.

'No,' Drustan said. 'Not enough.'

Agusur looked at the boy Agus. 'Gods cannot twist the threads of fate, Bright Blade. Not even Riadna herself knows where they lead. She simply weaves the cloth from what she is given.'

'If you'd survived the fight uninjured,' Agus said, 'what would you have done?'

Drustan looked at the boy warlock.

'You wouldn't have stayed with us. You would've freed us and then left us behind. I saw your fate, Drustan. I saw the fates of all connected to you.' Agus glanced at Marisa. 'I twisted them to make them better.'

Marisa put her hand to her mouth. 'To twist fate is to change the balance of the world.'

'It were worth it,' Agus said, defiant.

CHAPTER 45

Marisa watched a god eat good venison and burp his satisfaction. He sat on the floor with squat legs crossed beneath him and the stone bowl held in his lap. Rosana accepted the burp as a compliment and nodded her satisfaction in return. Marisa could hear the words the woman would say to her grandchildren: *'I once fed a god and he was satisfied.'*

'Come,' Agusur said.

When had he stood and walked across to her? She looked back and saw him still sitting there, eating and burping.

'I am a god,' Agusur pointed out. 'Come.'

'Where?'

'It is time we completed the healing of the Bright Blade.'

'You are not a god of healing.'

'I am many things,' Agusur said.

Drustan limped towards her with Agusur by his side. Marisa glanced from one Agusur to another.

'I am a god,' Agusur said. 'And this is the place I knew first.'

Then there was only one Agusur, the one standing beside Marisa. She had not seen the others disappear or merge; one moment three parts of the god sat, walked, and stood, and the next there was only one, holding out his hand and helping her to her feet.

The touch of his skin thrilled into her very soul, a chord of ecstatic joy that made her cry out. Nobody looked up. Nobody even seemed to notice that they stood there on the edge of the firelight.

Except Drustan.

'His touch is … interesting,' Drustan said with a grin. 'But at least I didn't yelp.'

'That was not a yelp.' Marisa smiled back at him.

'It sounded like a yelp to me.' Drustan nodded to the god. 'Where is this place of healing that you mentioned and where have the other two gone?'

Agusur gazed at Drustan for a moment and Marisa realised that he had not expected Drustan to see though the glamour of three. 'They were never really there.'

'Tricksy beggar, aren't you?' Drustan's grey eyes did not waver as he stared into the god's golden irises.

'That is one of my aspects,' Agusur agreed. 'Shall we?'

The god led them away from the lounging villagers. Nobody looked up to watch them go. Tricksy indeed.

****

Only Agus watched Agusur lead Drustan and Marisa away down the cavern.

He had saved her. Was that wrong? He had held the fear away by shunting it into the spirit realm, where the Amthisrid could quench its fire. Was that wrong? He had helped Drustan.

It wasn't his fault about the other healers. He couldn't save them all. By causing Drustan's injury, by making him stay, he had saved all the villagers too. He had saved Marisa. He was helping. He had got Tirac to remain Tirac long enough for Drustan to make the right choice, the choice that made him the Bright Blade again.

Was that wrong?

But, here in the Vale, the threads of fate shone bright. And he could see the shadows against that brightness. Something had changed; something hunted them, dangerous powers that needed to be stopped. No thread was as darkened with death as Drustan's.

What to do? How to help Drustan survive?

Agus grinned.

Drustan had left his swords behind.

****

Agusur led them through the town, but Drustan stopped at the edge of the slope leading downwards. He sucked in his breath. 'How much further?'

'You had better help him,' Agusur said. 'There is a way to go yet. And I would not like to hear such a proud warrior yelp. It would be a disconcerting sound.'

So Marisa found herself with her arm around Drustan, helping him limp down the slope. The darkness ebbed and flowed around them as they walked in the light of a god towards a sound that roared like thunder.

Marisa was very aware of Drustan's weight upon her, of the firmness of his muscles under her hand. The heat of his body touched hers through the softness of her dress. She licked suddenly dry lips.

He was so close to her.

'Are you sure we don't need to place guards at the entrance to the caves?' Drustan asked, his voice hoarse and strained.

'The Vascanar cannot find this place and those in the Vale protect it. You are safe here.'

'But we cannot stay here?' Marisa was surprised at the high pitch of her voice.

'This is not a place for mortals.'

The growling thunder grew louder.

'What's that noise?' Drustan asked. He was breathing heavily now. Marisa could feel his heart beating against her hand.

'The River Storac.'

'The River of Life?' Marisa had to keep talking, keep asking questions, Drustan so close, his arm around her shoulder, his skin touching hers, only the thin barrier of cloth between them. Gods, how she had to talk, or else she might stop and shame herself by asking for what she knew was no longer hers to have. Why hadn't he brought his walking stick?

'I should've brought my walking stick,' Drustan said. 'I didn't realise it was so far.'

'It is not a problem,' Marisa lied.

'I might be able to walk by myself now,' Drustan said when the cave floor levelled out.

'No!' Marisa sucked in air. 'No,' she said in a voice that almost sounded calm. 'It is best that I help you rather than you get tired.'

'Not far now,' Agusur said. The sound of the river swelled until Marisa couldn't hear her own voice. Her world became the roar of the river, the thumping of Drustan's heart, the heat pulsing into her body from his, the smell of him, oh, gods, the smell of him.

'Jerem,' Drustan said suddenly. She could hear his voice despite the roar of the water. She could hear it and the desperation within it. Agusur must be allowing them to hear each other despite the roar of the river.

What game was this god playing?

Drustan said, 'You arranged Jerem's death. Placed him in my path. So I would carry the amulet.'

Agusur said, 'I arranged the raid on the ships, or rather, Berasin did. Tirac had some uses as a disguise.'

'Why?' Drustan asked. 'That took away the Vascanar's line of retreat.'

Marisa realised that he was trying to keep his mind on other things. Tactics and war had always been his distraction of choice as a boy. She remembered him desperately talking of old battles when she first set her eyes at him, and struggled not to giggle at the memory of a young Drustan stammering about shieldwalls versus cavalry as she'd plaited daisies into his hair.

'The Vascanar were never going to retreat,' Agusur said.

'So the raid was simply to steal the amulet?' Marisa asked in a voice that squeaked.

Agusur smiled at her before continuing on his way. 'That was something unexpected. The Xarnac was hidden from the spirit realm in the Vascanar's shrine to their foul overlords, but Jerem's greed and swordsmanship were all too mortal. Once the amulet was free in the world, I could see it and hide it from the Vascanar, but I could not stop the fear eating away at Jerem. I have not the power to destroy the Xarnac; only Tanaz can deal with that small piece of hell. But the raid was meant to do what it did. To burn the ships.'

'Why burn the ships?' Drustan asked and then answered his own question. 'They were sea-witch blessed.'

'Yes.' Now Agusur smiled at Drustan before continuing on his way. 'It will be a while before the Korgena sea-witches can do that again. The sea goddess Korga is fickle and will not so easily give up such a blessing for mere gold.'

'You expect reinforcements?'

'Don't you?'

'I do not understand,' Marisa said.

'The ships were blessed by the Korgena not to founder or sink,' Drustan said. 'They could have brought reinforcements across the Galla Straits in their thousands, repeatedly. We would have been swamped by Vascanar regiments. So you burn the ships, and force the Vascanar to cross the sea in unblessed ships. Some of those ships will be damaged, some will sink, and every crossing from the mainland will diminish their fleet. Korga is a sea goddess, she has no need of gold, but the Korgena were human once, like the Amthisrid, and love the stuff. It is unlikely that the Vascanar can buy such a blessing again, because the Korgena had to give something to the Korga to receive the blessing and such a blessing would cost more than they could pay twice.'

'Part of their souls,' Agusur said. 'If they give any more they will cease to exist.' He walked up a slight rise in the cave floor. 'We are here.' He pointed downward and light blazed up around him from below.

****

Agus walked across the floor of the cavern, playing with fate, playing with the odds, twisting the world — ever so slightly — so that he remained overlooked. Unnoticed, he reached for Drustan's blades.

Which sword? The longsword: big, heavy, obvious, hard to hide if he carried that. He reached down and drew the shortsword from its scabbard. That he could carry. He slipped it into his belt and wandered over to the big earthenware jar where the villagers hid their money.

It wasn't stealing. They'd want to help Drustan. And he was only taking a little bit.

Rosana smiled at Cullain. Efan and Horol chatted. The other villagers sat around in family groups. Garet lay back with his hands behind his head staring at the paintings on the rock. Old paintings. Agus could feel their age.

He shivered, reached into the jar and pulled out a handful of coins. Gold, silver, and bronze; he'd need them all for the spell. He shifted the world around a bit so that the villagers wouldn't miss the money and then — still unnoticed — wandered away down the cavern.

****

Marisa and Drustan topped the final edge of the cave floor.

She gasped: a small cave split away from the main tunnel and blazed with light. The river roared, so close now, a tumult of noise behind the walls of the cave. Walls of crystal, bright, shimmering crystals, their jagged facets casting their light across the soft carpet of moss upon the floor of the cave. Colours swirled, spun, twisted through that crystal light, spirals of energy flickering through the darkness obscuring Agusur's face.

'This is the cave of a goddess lost to the mists of time,' Agusur said. 'Only I remember her name now and I will not speak it here. She was a goddess of healing. The first goddess of healing to guard these lands. The crystals will focus your power, healer. Make him whole again.'

Then Agusur was gone.

Marisa led Drustan into the cave. 'Take off your shirt,' she said.

****

A small cave jutted off from the main path, more of a tunnel, really, so low that Agus had to wriggle through on his tummy, the handful of coins in one hand and the shortsword in the other. He knew he wouldn't need a candle.

The cave beyond the tunnel glowed with light. Water dripped down the rocks. Agus could hear it splashing in the shadows beyond the shrine. Where water flowed in this cavern, the rocks glowed with multicoloured light, because this was the water of the River Storac, the River of Life.

Agus didn't know how he knew all this. He didn't know how he knew about fate, how he knew the spell he needed to cast upon Drustan's sword, how he knew that this shrine would be here. He'd always known such things, ever since he was little. He couldn't read, but he knew things.

It were fun being a warlock.

Agus walked into the triple-spiral of haraf stones — the original spirals, the spirals that stood at the centre of the world.

CHAPTER 46

Torquesten, naked beneath the glowering ceiling of his brethren, stepped into the pool of the sacred spring. Secretions dripped from the demonic forms above him, splattering into the bowls held by slaves, flashing into flame on contact with the hot surface of the glowing heat-stones.

The secretions hissed when they touched the flesh of the screaming sacrifices, acid etching its way into their skins, increasing their torment, increasing the homage paid to the demons. The lines of pain drawn across the tissue of humanity made an Ulac highly prized for its potency and slaves reached out with their bowls to catch every drop, even as the acid burned into their own skins.

Torquesten stood in the swirling water of the spring. His feet were numbed by a cold force that tried to drive him from the shrine, but he revelled in the sting of this land losing its battle with his brethren. The touch of the pure shrine water held no fear for Torquesten. Not when he stood in the acerbic shower of his brethrens' gift to their people.

He would stand tall amongst their pantheon, for he was the Tukalac, the anointed, the one who would open the gates.

All would be as it should be.

The acidic heat of the secretions dripped across Torquesten's face, trickled into his flesh, dripped downwards, hissed into the chilled water at his feet. He screamed in joyous agony. Dark fumes writhed around his upraised arms, his tilted-back head, his widespread legs.

His scream bounced from the ceiling of demons above him and reverberated through the gardens. Slaves died in that scream, sacrifices died, even soldiers died. The death of so many in one moment excited the demons. They shuddered, a coiling, rhythmic movement curling across their tightly packed forms, crying out in his mind: *We are here!*

****

Eirane soared into the rain clouds above the House of Healing, above the demons packed into that small space feeding upon the suffering below. The gods of the Karisae had not protected the House and the demons' rancid energy coiled and flowed in the darkness.

The ragged edge of Wendin glistened in the moonlit clouds.

'You must stop, sister,' Eirane cried out into the storm. 'You have done enough. Night has fallen. Morgeth is in the sky. You must stop now.'

'I must soak the land, spurn the heat of the demons, I must soak the land,' came Wendin's voice, as ragged as her form.

'You must stop, sister.'

Wendin's voice faded away to the lightest breath upon the wind as she broke free of her chant, but the constricting obsession remained: 'I must create a quagmire.' She was stretched so thin that Eirane could hardly see her translucent form. This was Wendin, the oldest of the Amthisrid, the most powerful of the nine. Her voice strengthened like a gust of wind, and then faded to almost nothing: 'I must ... hinder those demonic fools ... give time to those that need it...'

'Sister, you give too much.' Eirane tried to grasp the edge of Wendin, to pull her away from the storm and bring her back to sanity. But Wendin was lost in the magic, in the horror of the feeding demons below her and the battle already ended. 'You must return to your Calodrig!' urged Eirane, but Wendin's spirit curled away from her grasp. 'You must replenish yourself, sister. I beg of you, give up this magic, you are not a god.'

Eirane wept bitter tears. This was her idea, she had helped Wendin to start this storm, but she had not thought that Wendin, of all the Amthisrid, would fall victim to the lure of spell-craft. 'Please, sister, stop this.'

'... the pain ... burning me ... are there ... feeding ... blood ... blood ... blood ... the vinraf ... the spring ... under attack ... they pollute...' Wendin's voice strengthened into a gale of anguish. 'Flee, sister, flee! Do not get sucked down into this abyss of agony. Flee. The shrine is lost, the forest is corrupted. Flee, sister.'

Eirane looked down upon the House of Healing. She remembered its beauty, the brightness of its stone, the multicoloured haraf glistening in the moonlight. She could see that stone shot through with darkness now, webbed with hatred and bile. The House failing, the shrine failing, the pure spring waters carrying the pollution away to smash against the purity of this land, into the River Storac, the river that engirdled the world.

'Why don't the gods act?' she yelled into the storm. 'Why don't they act?'

'… they cannot … ringed … the cave … the vale … the shrine … the stones taken … boundaries … holding them … I am lost, sister, hold me always in your memory.'

Eirane fled.

****

Agus walked through the spirals of huge stones, which towered over him as he slipped between them to the centre of the spirals, to the altar that the shrines, out in the world beyond the Vale, did not possess. The altar was low and broad, lit by the glinting light of the Storac's waters shining through the stones. It had been set there long, long ago. For a moment, Agus could see the ceremonies performed here, see priests shaped like Agusur lifting bowls of food up to the light, calling out in an ancient tongue, drawing forth their gods from the walls of the cave.

Old gods, dangerous gods, gods demanding more than food, whose time was ended. Yet Agus saw them as they were, when their people offered them prayers and food, prime cuts of meat from the hunt, in return for protection and help.

The image flickered, faded; flames blazed high for a moment, dancing shadows on the walls. Agus turned his gaze away before he saw the plunge into blood and flame, Agusur's form at the centre of it all. Agusur had lived a long time as a god. A clever god. Slippery. And he had seen what gods could do when they believed their own stories.

Agus sat cross-legged on the altar stone and weighed the coins in his hands. The spell was obvious to him, the words just a way of setting it into the metal of the sword, just like his da used to set the edges of a blade before plunging it back into the fire to allow the heat to bind edge to core, making the whole blade strong and sharp.

CHAPTER 47

Bihkat's acolytes, their ears firmly stuffed with wax, lifted the first of the buckets of blood.

Illath rose.

In the cave of crystals sanctified to an unnamed goddess, Marisa gasped as the power of healing coursed through her and into Drustan. So much power. The energy crackled from crystal to crystal in a wave of light. She was filled with light, overburdened with light; a golden blaze between her and Drustan, joining them more closely than mortals should ever be joined: one heart, one mind, one soul.

The bloodlight scintillated across the web-strung islands.

In the despoiled garden of the House of Healing, Torquesten lifted his arms to his brethren.

You are our favoured son, Torquesten Soulthief.

In the Erisyan camp a careful footstep near Jarl's bed, harsh breathing muffled by a scarf tied around a face. Sekem screamed a warning into his cousin's mind, but the stench of fear sweeping through the spirit realm washed all such warnings into nothingness. Jarl moaned in his sleep and Haukon hesitated.

Kihan stood atop his pinnacle above a raging sea. The hounds paced back and forth on the cliff-top opposite him, but they could not cross and he could not escape. What could he do to rid the world of them?

The blood hissed on contact with Torquesten's naked skin. Heating in an instant. Steaming into the air, the stench terrible as it ran down his body and into the waters of the spring. Swirling waters that turned pink, then red, then black as night as bucket after bucket of human blood poured across Torquesten's body, transmuted by his power into a corruption that polluted the spring and, through that connection, the River of Life itself.

Feed us. Hear us. Obey us.

The web of power glowed ruby red across the ancient lands of Symcani and then out into the world beyond the salt sea. In far-flung temples, and shrines, and sacred places, the eyes of priests and priestesses widened in horror. What was beginning this night?

Marisa cast off her clothes and threw herself upon Drustan. He, healed and whole once more, caught her into his embrace. Her skin so soft, so sweet — ah, the smell of her. They rolled on the soft moss that covered the floor of the cave. Her lips met his.

'*Wake up, cousin!*' Jarl was yanked from his dreams of blood and flame. A shadow loomed above him in the dark. The sound of weeping. A glint of light from the blade plunging towards his throat.

The River Storac, the River of Life, roared through the spirit realm, through the Lands of Summer, through all the realms of creation. It linked the worlds together and protected them from the Tangled Realms. The blackened blood seeped into the river from the defiled shrine, but then, in response, from the cave of crystal in the vale of forgotten gods, a golden light blazed from the entwined souls of lovers.

Wendin faded to almost nothing above the boiling darkness engulfing the House of Healing. The pain rose to meet her and blew away her sanity. Only one thought remained: soak the land.

In the side cave, amongst the mighty monoliths of the original spiralled shrine, Agus, slowly, gently, began to rub a handful of coins along every inch of the blade of the shortsword. 'You are Drustan's sword,' he said. 'You will always return to his hand. You will never break, never chip, never fail him. You will cut what cannot be cut. You will always return to his hand. You are Drustan's sword…' He repeated the words over and over.

Jarl grabbed his attacker's wrist with desperate hands. The descending blade drew blood as it skated across his forearm. He shifted his head away from the dagger thrust, but the point of the blade cut into the side of his neck.

The flux of agony poured through his soul. The whole world was screaming.

At the Falls of Karcha, the prison of Those That Endure, the golden light smashed into the darkness flooding outwards from the corrupted spring. The rocks of the falls shuddered under the impact and shifted slightly.

In the nine Calodrig, the Muadisri, creatures with eyes of swirling ink, huddled away from the rampaging violence of that impact under the bloodlight of Illath.

With his brethren crawling through his mind, Torquesten called forth the last desecration, the final insult to all that this land held pure: the twelve healers were brought to the shrine, naked, raped, each rape paid for with another scar upon their bodies, a nose slit, an ear sliced, an eye put out. Their bodies were a gaping mass of wounds. So many soldiers. So many payments. They could not stand, or walk, but the beating hands and feet of the Vascanar drove them forwards, crawling towards the shrine.

Where Torquesten stood, laughing.

Drustan and Marisa, skin on skin, soul held within soul. She arched her back and dug her fingers into his flesh. And the golden light swirled about them.

Jarl grunted and slowly pushed the blade away from his throat. No skill in this combat, not yet, just one man pushing against another in a fight for life. Blood ran down Jarl's neck. The blade had missed the arteries, not by much, but by enough.

Then the blade no longer touched his flesh.

Agus smoothed the metal of the coins into the metal of the sword: copper, tin, silver, and gold mixed with the iron and the carbon and the tiniest traces of other minerals. The coins disappeared into the blade. Metals bonded to metals, leaving the blade looking just as it did before, but now with magic bound into the steel.

A hiss of outrage in the darkness beyond the monoliths. 'Stop. Mortal. Creature of this world. Forbidden rites. Forbidden place. Binding steel to the fate of man. Stop. Stop. Stop.'

Agus looked up and grinned. 'Hello, Riadna.'

One of the healers managed to speak through a mouth without lips when she fell at Torquesten's feet. 'I am Dame Belin—' He struck off her head with a single blow of his sword. Her blood gushed into the spring water. Her healing power, her magic, sucked into the swirling vortex around Torquesten's feet.

Ah, the power builds! So opens the Path of Blood.

The golden light flowed out of the cave of crystal and flooded through the cavern. Berasin's wounds healed in an instant. Horol opened his eyes, the pain gone, his needs reawakened. He grabbed Sara's hand and pulled her down into his bed. Rosana and Cullain met in a clash of passion. Men loved their wives, women loved their husbands. New loves and old loves rekindled in the golden light. Berasin found Peg beside him in his furs.

Only Garet wept in the darkness for a love he would never see again.

Jarl shifted his grip on his attacker's wrist. Applied leverage. Forced the man to his knees. Snapped his elbow into the man's face.

The man jerked back.

Jarl rolled away from his attacker and dropped to the floor on the other side of the bed.

Riadna, goddess of fate, hissed at Agus. 'You bend my threads. Make a binding that cannot be undone. Old rites. Forbidden rites. Broken rites. Stop. Stop. Stop.'

'Nah,' said Agus. 'Fun, innit.'

Above the defiled House of Healing, a column of darkness reared upwards into the air. Wendin tumbled away from its rise, flowed upwards into the clouds, unleashed more rain to try to wash away the stain.

The golden light bathed the bear-skull helm left neglected upon the floor of the cavern. It swirled around the skull, rebuilding all that had been lost to Berasin's ancient butchery. Bone, sinew, veins, muscles, skin, fur, eyes — ah, the eyes that gleamed within that skull! The reborn goddess Ursaric tipped back her head and roared.

Berasin lifted his head from Peg's embrace and smiled. 'Good hunting, my goddess,' he breathed and then once more allowed himself to be embraced, pulled down, engulfed in mortality.

Jarl crouched in the dark.

'You killed him,' a voice wept in the darkness. 'I saw you kill him.'

'Haukon?'

The scrape of steel on leather. Haukon was drawing his sword. Jarl backed away from the sound.

Riadna advanced out of the shadows. She'd taken the form of a huge spider. The venom that dripped from her fangs hissed as it struck the floor. Behind this form, Agus could see the shape of an old woman, a blind woman, a young woman, and he heard the clattering sound of a spinning wheel, of a loom, of the shuttle smashing back and forth, of needles clacking. The weaver, the seamstress, fate herself — all upset with him.

'You breach an oath upon that sword,' Riadna said. 'An oath given to a dying man. An oath given freely. An old oath, made the old way, with the old words. You shift fate, bend threads.'

'Warlock, in't I?'

In the waters of the River Storac, the River of Life, the battle raged between the golden light and the creeping darkness. Torquesten felt this battle thrumming through his soul, but he did not care. Drunk with the power of the ritual, he cast out his command and it flashed across the world.

'Come! Come! Come to me!'

Sieges were abandoned that day, nations released from the terror, as a million Vascanar, spread across the whole surface of the globe, began their march towards the Islands of Symcani. Some of these troops would take years to reach this place, some would take days. All obeyed the command of Torquesten, their Tukalac.

Ursaric lumbered up the slope into the vale where her sister goddess Izia, goddess of the air, swooped down in the guise of an eagle. The air of the Vale shimmered in the light of a goddess reborn. The bindings that held them here, these gods of the Anthanic, faded away into the bloodlight.

Izia felt the call of battle and swooped away from the Vale towards the column of blackness rising above the house of healing.

'My sword is behind you, cousin. Beside the bed,' Sekem whispered.

Jarl ignored the spectral voice.

'He means to kill you, cousin.'

A floorboard creaked under Jarl's foot.

Izia, still in the form of an eagle, flew to where Wendin languished in a drifting current above the polluted shrine. The goddess touched the mind of the Amthisrid and sanity returned to Wendin.

'You have returned! You have returned!' she cried with all that was left of her failing strength.

'I have returned,' Izia said. She clasped Wendin's fading spirit to her. 'I will lift up your burden, Wendin, eldest of the Amthisrid. Go now. There is something you must do.'

Wendin thrilled to the touch of the goddess and without thought slipped away through the night.

Izia kissed the clouds.

Ah, the pain, like needles of ice upon our souls. A goddess kisses this rain.

'No!' Torquesten bellowed. 'No!' The ritual unfinished, the battle unwon: the tide of darkness had not yet vanquished the blaze of golden light. He thrust his arms upwards, tried to hold the ceiling of his brethren intact by force of his will alone.

Haukon rushed out of the darkness. Instinct screamed and Jarl ducked. The sword-blade hissed over his head. Close the distance. He threw himself forward, slammed his shoulder into Haukon's midriff, picked up the younger man and drove him backwards. The weight of him. Jarl pumped his legs, gained momentum, smashed Haukon into a wall. He jerked his head upwards. The back of his skull crashed into the man's face as Haukon gasped for air.

In the House of Healing the chant faltered. Bihkat looked up, saw the roiling darkness bulging downwards, heard the screech of the demons. He turned, fled the garden, raced along the corridors of the House. Terror added speed to his aged legs. His lungs burned, his heart thudded painfully hard within his chest, but still he ran. The screech of Torquesten's agony melted the plugs of wax in Bihkat's ears. The wax ran down his cheeks, splattered on the ground about his pounding feet. The walls about him trembled,

Ahhhh! The pain, the pain, it drives us from this place.

For a moment, the descent of Torquesten's brethren halted, for a moment their screech of agony modulated down to a mere screech of rage, for a moment he held them in place with the power of his will.

For a moment.

Jarl grabbed Haukon's arm, dragged it down to reach his rising knee. A sharp crack in the darkness as bones snapped. Haukon's sword clattered onto the wooden floorboards.

The moment passed. Pure white stones untouched by the malice of the demons toppled onto the ground and rolled towards the shrine spring. Torquesten had to leap backwards, out of the way. He watched with furious eyes as the white stones blocked up the spring, protecting it from what was to come.

A blast of power from the shrine drove him to his knees.

You have failed us.

The demons collapsed under the weight of their bile and hate. The walls of the House of Healing splintered and shattered around Bihkat as he staggered the final few steps into the safety of the goddess-kissed rain.

Haukon screamed as Jarl punched him in the groin, kicked his legs away, dropped him to the floor and then knelt on the side of his head to keep him down. Footsteps pounded up the stairs. With a lantern held high, Kerek burst through the door.

Wendin found Kihan upon his pillar in the midst of a raging sea. *'Have all that is left of me,'* she whispered and gave up her power to him.

Kihan fell to his knees as the life-force of the Amthisrid poured into him. The forests, the land itself, cried out a welcome to him. The blood light of Illath washed over him and helped him accept the energy of Wendin into his soul.

On the cliffs opposite, the Hounds of the Falls lay down and panted, looking back at Kihan, their tails wagging furiously.

Drustan's face above Marisa's. They lay tangled in the golden light of the crystals. It passed through them and into them.

But it only stayed within Marisa.

CHAPTER 48

Jarl clutched a pad to his throat while Gorak threaded the needle. Kerek splinted Haukon's arm in the corner of the room, after resetting it with a distinct lack of interest in reducing Haukon's pain.

Haukon had gone out with the others to return the Erisyan dead to their caedi. And found his brother Iain with his head almost severed by Jarl's syrthae, an act Haukon had seen before he ran away with others. Grief-driven anger, when mixed with guilt, knew no logic or moderation or patience; Haukon sneaked into the farmhouse intent on taking Jarl's life.

'We'll have to call a council now,' Kerek said. 'Haukon must be judged.'

'He's still trying,' said Sekem. *'Good for him.'*

'No,' Gorak said. He leaned in towards Jarl's throat. 'Let's see the wound, then.'

'To judge Haukon, you must judge me.' Jarl lifted the pad away from his neck. The slash on his arm had already stopped bleeding on its own, but this cut was deeper; another inch and Jarl would be dead.

'Gorak,' Kerek said. 'We can't let this go on. Others will want Jarl's blood. He must be judged.'

'No.' Gorak lifted the lamp to see the wound more clearly. 'You were lucky, nephew.'

'I know,' Jarl said. 'Don't waste your breath, Kerek. There'll be no council.'

Gorak began to stitch the wound closed.

'I'll set three of my best to defend you,' Kerek said. 'All will know that I stand by your actions.'

'Thank you.' Jarl winced. 'Careful with that needle, uncle. That's my neck, not some broken bit of leather.'

'Stop your whining.' Gorak didn't look up.

Jarl and Kerek glanced at Haukon weeping on the floor.

'He'll try again,' Kerek warned.

'That's his right,' Jarl said.

'There.' Gorak leaned back and studied his needlework. 'All fixed now.'

You wish.

****

Kihan squatted on his pillar of rock, his torn shoulder swollen and useless after his desperate leap. The sea crashed below, Illath faded behind him, and ten paces of open air lay between him and the Hounds of the Falls. The hounds wagged their tails and yelped for him.

His brothers of the spell. They were men once, just like him. They weren't to blame for what they had become. He felt Wendin's ebbing soul become restive at that assertion, but he didn't care about her judgements. She didn't know what it felt like to have your soul torn open and embedded with shards of demonic hatred. He understood the survival instinct that could clog the throat of a man who wished to remain a man.

Death wasn't a triumph. Death was just death. Survival — survival was a triumph.

Whatever the Vascanar had done to him, he had survived, and now he squatted here, on a pillar of stone in the rain, with a ruined shoulder and no way to get back to his brothers.

Could he climb down, swim across that fearsome sea and then, exhausted, climb that towering cliff? He looked over the edge. Wave after wave crashed against the rocks at the base of the cliff. That stretch of water, maybe fifteen paces wide, would kill him as surely as any hunter's arrow. He couldn't swim that.

Kihan had learned to swim in his lost youth, but only in the canals that criss-crossed the city of his birth. This heaving maelstrom was another thing entirely.

And the climb down. Even fully fit, it would test a man born to rocks and gulls' eggs. Kihan had been born in a great city; the only things he had ever climbed were stairs, and the ladders beneath shelves of scrolls. He was trapped and he wouldn't throw his life away needlessly.

He wanted to go home.

Not much chance of that if he couldn't get off this rock. Something buried beyond his own mind nagged at him. Thoughts, memories that did not belong to him. Were these Wendin's thoughts?

No.

These thoughts were of places beyond this land. Memories of mountains that towered into the sky miles above the earth, of rivers that cascaded down rocky slopes and cut through fertile plains, of rolling grasslands as wide as an ocean, of swamps, and deserts, and the sea; love for the sea poured through him. These memories weren't his.

He looked at the hounds. These were their memories, disjointed, disorientated, without a consciousness to put them into order. Kihan had absorbed the memories of men scrambled within the minds of beasts. Tears burned behind his eyes. He remembered his own mind howling and scratching at memories without meaning.

He lowered his head and wept.

The hounds yapped at him, whined, wanting to make him feel better, wanting to take away this hurt.

Something else. His tears dried at the touch of ice-cold souls; behind the minds trapped in the bodies of the hounds lay ancient memories that did not belong to the hound-men, but to something that had touched them, touched their souls: memories from a time before this land knew the rule of iron ... the memories of gods. The ghosts of the gods trapped in the falls had left something behind when they transformed the spellhounds into the Hounds of the Falls. Memories of this land.

Kihan, on his knees, could *see* this pillar of rock as it had looked when it was still connected to the land, before the sea cut it away from the cliff.

Illath raised ghosts, opened doorways, and through one of these doorways, without really knowing what he did, Kihan raised the ghost of this land. A mist flowed into the gap between the pillar and the cliff, a mist of spirit, of the rocks that had once connected the two. He gazed at that mist, at the darkness of the rocks within it. There was a hush, a stillness on the air. He couldn't hear the sea, or the wind.

A voice, sharp and clear, rang in his mind. Not the ragged voice of Wendin as she faded. This voice spoke from high above the plain of the world, from a place where everything was possible and nothing was forgotten: *'Walk, Kihan, walk upon the ghosts of this land.'*

Without thought, fear, or hesitation, Kihan walked out onto the mist. It supported his weight, felt like cold stone beneath his naked feet. Step after step, his mind blank of everything except the movement, Kihan walked across the spirit of the rocks.

To safety.

The hounds bounded around him, wagging their tails, licking his face. Their breath stank, but their affection raised delight in Kihan. He laughed into the last light of the red moon and the voice of Illath rang out again in his mind: *'Welcome, Ghostwalker.'*

CHAPTER 49

Torquesten crawled out of the wreckage of the House into the pouring rain. The god-kissed rain itched across his skin like the bite of insects.

He scratched at his face.

The broken stones of the House of Healing lay scattered before him, threads of darkness squirming though the rock. The torrent of water falling from the sky plastered his hair to his head, hissing as it touched his skin, worming its way into his armour — pure, clean water washing over him. His brethren had fled, the ritual disrupted. The spring bubbled black but had not succeeded in forcing that darkness into the river encircling the spiritual heart of this realm.

A goddess had kissed the rain. The sacred spring was now blocked, protected, with stones pearl white, no dark threads there, despite the blackened waters beneath, closing the darkness away from its source, weakening it.

Would that matter?

'This is my land now!' Torquesten screamed into the dawn. 'Mine!'

A gust of wind threw him backwards into the devastated walls of the House of Healing. He bounced back to his feet and sneered at the sky, 'Blow some more. Is that all you can do?'

He waited. No answer, no crackling lightning, no strengthening of the rain, no gale to lift him and cast him away from this land.

'You are trapped here by the salt seas that protect you!' he shouted into the storm. 'I shall vanquish you yet and make this world a fit place for my brethren.'

The words spoken in haste spun up into the clouds, tugged by the wind, spun faster, faster, and then exploded outwards into the world. Torquesten waited nervously for the response.

None came.

Torquesten smiled. They feared him. He stood when they hid. He walked where they dared not.

He slicked back his hair and whistled his demonhounds to heel. They had been trapped in the fall of the House of Falas, but they — like him — had nothing to fear from tumbled stone and broken wood. Bloated on the flesh of the dead, they cringed from his voice, but moved slowly, their bellies full, hardly bothering to growl at Bihkat.

'Tukalac,' Bihkat said.

Torquesten considered the high priest. Should he kill him? The man had been in charge of the ritual, after all. He should have understood the danger of the storm.

'You survived the fall, priest.' Torquesten pondered the problem. Did he want to take on the mantle of Ukalac? So much work, all that cutting and scourging, the picking of acolytes, the doling out of Ulac.

Let Bihkat do it.

'I'd left the House to fetch more captives for the sacrifice, Tukalac.' Bihkat lowered his gaze.

'A fortunate occurrence.' Torquesten slapped away a hound creeping close to him for warmth.

'Yes, Tukalac. Many of my acolytes died, but enough survived for what is needed.' Bihkat paused. 'The Ulac is gone. All we have is what we gleaned at the end of the battle. It will not last beyond another few days.'

'Not all gone.' Torquesten walked into the rubble and brought forth five filled vials. 'These survive.'

'Shall we keep it for ourselves, Tukalac?' Bihkat asked. His eyes locked on the vials while saliva dribbled from his mouth.

'We, priest? Who is this *we*?'

'I'm sorry, Tukalac. It's just… The fresher the elixir, the greater the effect.'

'I know and I have plans for this.' Torquesten smiled. 'The Erisyan will burn their dead this day. Fifty Vascanar converts killed out there in the forest.'

'A minor inconvenience, Tukalac,' Bihkat began. 'Fifty men are—'

'They were Erisyan archers, priest. And now I wish more to join our ranks to replace their dead fellows.'

'We have some that are seeking to con—'

'That will take too long, priest. Take these four vials and sanctify their wineskins. The ones they will drink from in libation to their dead.'

'But they'll not be drinking the Ulac willing—'

'I wish it done, priest.'

'Yes, Tukalac.'

'And, Bihkat, make sure all the Ulac is used in this way. The more they drink, the stronger the effect.'

'Of course, Tukalac.'

'This rain makes me itch. Find me shelter, and send my general.' Torquesten searched for the name. 'Send Uka Bradic to me.'

'He died in there, Tukalac. It seems he enjoyed the comfort of the healers and wanted to see their sacrifice as a final mark of his contempt.'

'Who is his second in command?'

'You didn't appoint one, Tukalac.'

Torquesten and the hounds bared their teeth at the priest, but without any real menace. 'Must I do everything myself?'

'You're the Tukalac.'

'Pick me eleven men. Ten shall have charge of a thousand. One shall have charge over all. Pick them wisely, priest. Horseman to command horsemen, foot soldier to command foot soldiers. Bring them to me and I will anoint them.'

'Yes, Tukalac.'

'Send the cavalry out again to continue the hunt for those that flee.'

'Before or after the anointing of their commander, Tukalac?'

'Do it now. They are escaping.'

'But then how should I bring the one to be anointed by you, Tukalac?'

'Pick your chosen men and send the rest to hunt. Must I think for you as well?'

'Yes, Tukalac. All shall be done as you say.'

'And dig out the heat-stones from within this rubble. They will be needed to replenish the Ulac we lost last night.'

'Yes, Tukalac.'

CHAPTER 50

Marisa awoke smiling. Drustan's strong arms encircled her, holding her warm in the flickering light of the crystals. She breathed out into the roar of the river beyond the walls. The tumult of energies ebbed away from her, but he was there, her head pillowed on his arm, her skin pressed against his, their scents intermingled. Their heated passion spent.

Her smile faded.

Would he awaken and pull away from her?

Let it all be gone. Let all that went before be mended along with his broken side. Let them be one again, as they once were, as they were in the ecstatic flare of the crystals, the rushing force of the river, the soft comfort of the moss upon which they lay. Let it all be gone and she would give all that she had to this moment.

The unspoken prayer smoothed away her doubts — but only for a moment.

She had done him so much harm. He had lost so much to her inadvertent betrayal. She would take back those words shared in whispers, but such words can never be unsaid. They lay between them like a broken sword in the marriage bed.

How could he ever forgive her?

What had happened in this cave could not remove his dishonour. She had healed him complete, his wound gone as if it had never existed, except for the pink line of the new scar upon his skin. But wounded honour is not so easily mended. They broke his sword, cast him out. She had turned her back on him from shame and guilt, not loathing and distaste, but he did not know that.

He stirred beside her, flexing his arm. He would awaken soon and recoil from what they had done; this night of passion would disgust him.

Her Drustan belonged to her no more. She had given up that sanctuary. Her work here was done. He was whole again, a warrior fit to serve a king, but his honour still lay melted in the ashes of her words.

No. It had all changed. The native people of this land had welcomed the invading Karisae into their beds, into their hearts, into their genealogies. The peoples of this island had always done so, the god Agusur evidence of that; his people still lived in the blood of her people.

Blood, honour, race: such useless words.

But would Drustan forgive her? Would all be as it was once more?

He lifted his head. She did not turn to see his eyes; she did not want to see his shame, his rejection.

She felt his muscles tense. He had awoken without memory of what they had done and now the images, the pure, glorious images of their passion returned to him. She wanted to turn, to look at him, to see him in that moment before the revulsion, but she knew it was already too late.

Drustan pulled his arm out from beneath her head and moved away from her, but gently, quietly, as if he did not wish to disturb her sleep.

She should turn, speak to him, apologise for what had happened. For what she had let happen. Oh, how the needs of her heart had betrayed her — betrayed them both.

Again.

He leaned back against the wall. The crystal's glistening light cast his shadow beside him on the wall of the cave.

'Do I disgust you so much, Marisa?' he asked, his voice dead in the air.

She turned towards him now, her eyes seeking his, and saw the pain deep within them.

'I love you,' she said.

'I love you,' he replied.

She could feel it now; a sense of peace.

He reached out, touched her face, his hand hesitant, his gaze holding hers.

She placed her hand over his, saw the dampness in his eyes. She breathed out softly releasing the tension in her belly.

'The past...'

'...is the past.'

**End of Kinless Book One of Two.
The story concludes in Kinless, Book Two of Two.**

ABOUT THE AUTHOR

STEPHEN GODDEN writes speculative fiction. He reads pretty much anything. He uses the second to fuel the first. (And writes this stuff in the third, because somebody told him once that he should and he didn't like to argue.) Other than that, Steve's just a bloke of independent penury and incidental personality. He also writes under the name T F Grant. Well, gotta have some variety in your life.

ACKNOWLEDGEMENTS

To Ren Warom and the Firedance team who worked on this story with me, and kept chipping away at all the problems and mistakes until scene by scene it all came into focus: thank you. The entire editorial process was an absolute joy for me and that is down to your professionalism, passion, skill, and merciless respect for the work.

To my Beta-readers, from henceforth to be known as the 'Bear Pit': you all helped to shape this story through its initial draft. It wouldn't be what it is without your keen eyes and honest appraisals of what worked and what didn't. Cheers all, I hope you like what we did.

Also Available!

Available from Firedance Books...

TALES OF THE SHONRI: CITY OF LIGHTS by Stephen Godden.
Darkness never falls in the City of Lights. The last hope of a broken world, the remaining Shonri warriors brave the ever-vigilant city to fight their war against the vicious Magi — or meet their deaths. For the last witch, Medina, powerful, seductive, and untrustworthy, has sold her art to their enemies.

Can the handful of Shonri end the battle before Medina's magic reveals them? Can Medina survive her attempts to use the Magi for her own means? And can any of them live with the results of the battle they are about to face...

For while they scheme and fight, something stirs beneath the City of Lights... something more perilous than death itself...

Available from Firedance Books...

STILLNESS DANCING by Jae Erwin.
Lilliane has always been drawn by the desert — its emptiness, its eerie beauty and its people. When she takes the trip of a lifetime to a Bedu camp, she finds herself ensnared in a complex web of politics, blood feuds, terrorism and ancient spirits.

Karim is trying to find his path in the material world and to marry the girl of his dreams. But his soul cries out for the spiritual path of his fathers.

Lilliane's and Karim's stories collide in a forgotten, blood-soaked corner of Sinai. Brutalised, captive and bereft, they must find their own ways to survive.

A taut, unusual thriller set in the fascinating world of the modern Bedouin, *Stillness Dancing* shows us that the hardest paths can lead to the deepest wells.

ALSO AVAILABLE!

Available from Firedance Books...

EXPECT CIVILIAN CASUALTIES by Gary Bonn.
Jason has spent the last six years living wild on beaches. Now he's seventeen and a feral girl walks into his life.

A girl with no name.

He calls her Anna. She's fun, she's kind — and she's the most dangerous person in the world.

The most unusual love story, and a truly strange war story... Expect Civilian Casualties turns how we see the world upside down.

Available from Firedance Books...

THE EVIL AND THE FEAR by Gary Bonn.
An ancient magic released. A world of pain and fear hurtling towards catastrophe. A collision that will bring death and destruction to mankind.

Only two young women stand between the fury of the magic and the apathy of the world. Unfortunately one of them is dead and the other one is psychotic.

While her dead friend holds the fury of the magic at bay, Beatha must journey into the half-world to discover the secret at the heart of all things...

But a journey like this requires allies and, in Beatha's case, a truck-load of medication. Is the world ready for heroes like these?

The Evil And The Fear is a wildly inspirational story about being more than people expect, and learning to expect more than you ever believed was possible.

Also Available!

Available from Firedance Books...

THE WALKER'S DAUGHTER by Janet Allison Brown.
When her mother dies at the hands of a silver-haired figure in black, six-year-old spirit-walker Cora Bloux hides out in her own body. Twenty years later she's still there, fiercely maintaining an outwardly stable, conventional life.

But when her own daughter is hit by a car, Cora is forced to spirit-walk again — and discovers that the spirit world has been waiting for her.

In the extraordinary, fast-paced world of spirit-walkers, body-swappers, rock bands and second chances, Cora must discover her true self and learn the ordinary lessons of courage, trust and love.

To see the world as it really is, sometimes you have to close your eyes and... walk.

Available from Firedance Books...

OUT OF NOWHERE by Patrick LeClerc.
An urban fantasy, pacy, funny and compelling to the last page...

Healer Sean Danet is immortal — a fact he has cloaked for centuries, behind army lines and now a paramedic's uniform. Having forgotten most of his distant past, he has finally found peace — and love.

But there are some things you cannot escape, however much distance you put behind you. When Sean heals the wrong man, he uncovers a lethal enemy who holds all the cards. And this time he can't run.

It's time to stand and fight, for himself, for his friends, for the woman he loves. It's time, finally, for Sean to face his past — and choose a future.

A story of love, of battle — and of facing your true self when there's nowhere left to hide.

ALSO AVAILABLE!

Anthologies Available from Firedance Books…

THE FIREDANCE ANTHOLOGY – Words That Burn.
A searing selection of short stories from the circle of Firedance authors on the theme of "Firedance". A collection to paint pictures in your mind, tug on your heartstrings and whisper in your ear.

BROKEN WORLDS Volume One.
What do we do when God becomes an unwanted houseguest, you're in love with the wrong girl and aliens decide to eat California? Take a wild ride with 15 writers from around the globe to discover their version of a broken world… and the humour, compassion and love which saves us. From murder to manga, heartbreak to horror, *Broken Worlds* dances us through times, genres and worlds. Prepare to be thrilled, tickled, scared and enchanted… it's one hell of a ride.

THE BEST OF WRITERLOT Volume One.
Wild women, warriors, the first moments of love… Muses, metafiction and murder. Find new voices, new series and cracking stories in this dizzying collection from the WriterLot team. WriterLot.net produces great new fiction for its followers every day. This collection celebrates some of the best, filled with unforgettable characters, heart-stopping action, and the trembling uncertainty of personal relationships. It captures the essence of what it is to be human (or, in one case, what it is to be a dog).